The Game of War

of War

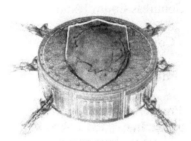

THE CHRONICLES OF CHAOS

STANDALONE PREQUEL

0

GLEN DAHLGREN

ISBN: 978-1-0879-0258-6
Library of Congress Control Number: 2021916381

Cover Design by: Miblart

Edited by: Samantha Cook

Proofread and formatted by:
Partners in Crime Book Services

Published by Mysterium Storyworks
5243 Crystyl Ranch Drive
Concord, CA 94521
www.mysterium.blog

First Edition: August 2021
10 9 8 7 6 5 4 3 2 1

DEDICATION

WHILE MANY PEOPLE are necessary to create a book like this, nothing would have been possible without my family: Sabrina, Amanda, and Emmett. Their love and support is the heart of my every creation.

If anything moves you emotionally within these pages, it's due to them.

PROLOGUE

A STAR DROPPED from the sky, trailing golden fire in its wake. The misshapen rock tore through a mountaintop with explosive fury, leaving the mountain shorter, but also home to a fragment of the fiery projectile.

The star finally came to rest many miles away, where the gods of Order dared not touch it, but instead encased it in a vault to protect against the Child of Chaos. The fragment, on the other hand, lay undiscovered for thousands of years nestled in the jagged mountaintop.

One day, a boy who lived in the village at the mountain's base found himself drawn to the fragment's hiding place. He took the strange rock home with him.

It wasn't long before that boy climbed back up that mountain, deathly ill, trying to undo everything that happened to him and his family—indeed, his entire village.

He perished there, wishing he had never laid eyes on that cursed rock.

4

PART I

THE TEST

CHAPTER ONE

THE BRANCH WHISTLED over Dantess' head with enough force to blow his short brown hair back, but thanks to his quick reflexes, he avoided the impact. "Whew, close!" said Dantess. "But I'm too fast—"

Jyn wasn't done. Instead of stopping her swing, she pivoted the branch using her grip in the center. The other end slammed into Dantess' unsuspecting head with a thud.

"Ow!" Dantess took a step back and held the side of his head. "What was *that*? These are supposed to be swords, not staves! You can't wield a sword that way!"

With a wicked smile, Jyn relented. She let the branch's tip drop as she whipped her long brown bangs away from her eyes. "Oh! Was that not fair?"

Dantess loved the way her large blue eyes looked when she was truly happy, but hated that he saw the smile mostly when he was losing. "Well, that's not what they teach at War's temple."

"Does *this* look like War's temple?" Jyn waved her branch at the dirt ground—the grass had been stomped away by years of training—and the trees surrounding the clearing. "Besides, how would you know? You've never even been inside. I hate to tell you, but as much as you'd like to be one, you are *not* a priest like your grandfather." Still ready to fight, she stepped back and forth, her lithe frame moving easily in her loose shirt and brown, high-waisted pants. She was like a spring, ready to explode into action.

"Maybe I haven't been there, but I've seen priests fight. It's perfect, like a dance. And from the way they describe my grandfather, he was the best of them. I would have loved to see Varyon in action."

"Why do you worship the man so? You never even met him."

"I feel like I did. The stories—his *legends*—are amazing. And he's my grandfather."

"Whatever. Are we here to talk about your hero or train? Fantasizing about being your grandpa won't help you. Unless you somehow discover the Longing, *this* is the only way you'll get better." She chuckled. "And you need to!"

It was a little funny being dressed down by someone more than a year younger than him, but even at fourteen, Jyn was at least his equal in combat. Dantess may have had more strength—the last few years had added pounds of muscle to his limbs—but Jyn was fast and cunning. They had trained together almost their whole lives, and Dantess knew better than to ever underestimate her.

Dantess hefted his branch. "So, let's train, then. Swords or staves?"

Jyn shrugged and, with no warning, leapt off the ground in a new attack.

The two friends lay on the hard-packed dirt, panting. It had been a taxing session. Even though Dantess was tired, he also felt invigorated. Inspired.

"We've both gotten a lot better," he said. "I think we're ready."

"Ready for what?" asked Jyn.

"To guard my father's supply run to War's temple. He's going on one today."

"Guard a supply run? From what? No one would dare try anything so close to the temple."

"That's what I thought, but I heard a rumor some bandits were spotted along the road from Freethorn Creek to War's temple." Dantess' eyes lit up. The idea of guarding a shipment was exciting, but he was more interested in the destination. "If he heard the rumor, my da will want protection but can't afford to hire real guards. You and I are better than nothing!"

Jyn's mouth dropped open. "You're not serious. We don't even have weapons. Who is going to be scared of a tree branch?"

"We can scrounge up something better. Regardless, I'm sure it's just a rumor. We'll be perfectly safe. Besides, Da won't take me otherwise. He hates the place. And he hates the idea of *me* there even more."

"Why?" Jyn propped herself up on her elbow.

"Something happened between Grandfather and him. Da won't talk about it. He doesn't like to talk about the temple either, even though they are his store's biggest customer." Out of habit, Dantess twisted a silver ring on his finger, delicately inscribed with the shape of a shield. "I'm surprised Da let me have this ring. It was Varyon's. He left it to me when he died."

"It must be tough for your da, having to take supplies to the temple every week if he hates it so much."

"Yeah, I guess so." Dantess wanted to go to the temple so badly, it was hard not to think of his father as lucky. "He only has the job because he's Varyon's son. It pays well enough to keep us ahead of the tithe, but he'd stay far away if he could. I doubt we'd even live in Freethorn Creek."

"Well, you aren't your father. You could join the temple if you wanted. Even without a Longing, faithless can still join up as soldiers."

"If I did that, it would kill him. Da can't argue with a Longing—that's the *god of War* saying I need to go—but if I volunteered to become a bound faithless?" Dantess shook his head. "I couldn't do that to him, not after everything he's done for me. He kept us alive on his own, doing a job he hates, ever since I was born."

Jyn stared up into the clouds and sighed. "Do you really think there aren't any bandits?"

"No way. It's just a rumor."

"Well, my mother could use some help paying the tithe. She works herself to the bone and still has trouble scraping enough together. He may not need protection, but do you think Tolliver would pay us if we helped load and unload?"

Dantess sprung to his feet. "Sure he would! Maybe. A little, probably. So, you'll do it?"

"If your da agrees, I guess."

"We should get back to the store, then. We'll start by helping him pack up, and then slip the idea of guarding the shipment into the conversation."

Jyn climbed to her feet and glanced around. "Wait. I need to collect Warren." She scanned the tree line, but her younger brother was nowhere to be seen. "Warren? Warren, where are you?"

"Aren't you supposed to be watching him?" asked Dantess, smirking.

"I can't watch him and fight you at the same time. He's supposed to stay close." She cupped her hands around her mouth and yelled, "Warren!"

Dantess grabbed the sack with his few belongings and slung it over his shoulder. "I wouldn't worry. He's a smart kid. Where do you think he might have gone?"

"If he's not here and he didn't go home, my guess is he went to Mother Nettle's camp." Jyn began to gather up her gear as well.

"Mother Nettle?" Dantess raised an eyebrow. "The crazy lady who turns strays into thieves?"

"She's not crazy. Just a bit eccentric."

"She steals orphans away from Charity's sanctuary to add to her army of pickpockets. Even if she's not crazy, are you sure you want your little brother playing there?"

"Charity's sanctuary isn't for everyone. Some kids would do anything to get away from there. Besides, you don't know anything about Mother Nettle's camp. It's fun. We visit sometimes." The girl turned her head back and forth. "When I know where it is. She moves a lot."

"To keep ahead of Law, right?"

"Maybe. But she's also easily bored." Jyn pointed down one of the paths leading from the clearing and started walking. "I think it's this way. At least it was last week."

They'd only walked about a mile when they encountered a young, skinny boy wandering on the path heading the opposite direction. He was so distracted by the book he held in front of him, he was about to walk right into a tree.

"Warren, watch out!" yelled Jyn.

Warren snapped his head up, saw the tree, and stopped in his tracks. He scratched his short, dark hair in the shape of a bowl, smiled sheepishly, and said, "Thanks. That would have been the third tree I hit."

"Why did you leave?" asked Jyn, hugging him. "I was worried."

He huffed. "I was *bored.* I've watched you two hit each other before. Mother Nettle's is way more fun. And I traded my shiny rock for this!" He held up his tattered book, its pages almost falling out of the ragged binding. "It's a book of War stories! Dantess, I think your grandpa is in here."

Dantess grinned and winked. "Wouldn't surprise me."

Jyn looked at the book's worn cover. It had a faint shield emblem, the symbol of War. "You got this for a rock? That's a great trade. You love new books."

"Well, it was my *shiny* rock. She said it was *perfect* for her Gift. It might be the last thing she needs to finish making it."

"A Gift?" asked Dantess. "Like a temple's Gift?"

Jyn rolled her eyes. "Kind of. It's a game they play. The kids pretend her camp is a temple and Mother Nettle is the high priestess." She turned back to Warren. "I don't care if you get bored, you *always* check with me before you go anywhere. I have to know where you are. Agreed?"

As Warren nodded, Dantess looked up at the sun. "We have to get back. My da might already be loading by now, and I need him in a good mood."

The three headed straight back to Freethorn Creek. Somewhere between a sprawling village and a small town, it was the only settlement anywhere close to War's temple and often served as a waypoint for travelers headed there. In fact, Dantess noticed a few faces on the road he didn't recognize—likely planning to head to the temple tomorrow for its monthly testing.

Dantess led Jyn and Warren along a road of hard-packed dirt into a market street. It wasn't Freethorn Creek's main market—that was in the more upscale section of town—but it was reputable enough. The wooden buildings along the street stood on their own and, while old and worn, many were painted and in reasonable repair. What's more, every week, vendors filled this street with colorful booths that offered goods of all sorts. Dantess enjoyed market day; it felt like a celebration.

A sturdy wagon was parked just outside of his father's store. A sign proclaimed the establishment as 'Tolliver and Son General Supplies' in green and blue letters. Dantess' heart sank when he noticed that the wagon already had a number of crates inside. Hopefully, Da wasn't too upset if he had to load those himself.

"Da!" Dantess yelled. "I'm here to help. Sorry if I'm a bit late."

"Dantess?" a faint voice called from inside the store.

The boy stepped through the open door into a single, large room filled with well-organized shelves, barrels, and crates. Tolliver's had a little bit of everything: food, tools, seeds, and more. People came from all over the town to shop here—not just for the quality goods, but also to chat with the cheery proprietor.

"Down here!" The mat on the floor had been pulled back from an open trapdoor. A staircase led down into a storage room below ground level. "I'm glad you're here. It was going to be tough getting these up myself."

From below, Tolliver held a box up to Dantess. The boy grabbed it, set it aside, and asked, "Are we clearing out the cold storage? How much did War order this time?"

"About double." The pudgy, balding man in his signature festive vest wiped sweat from his brow and turned back to grab another box. "They're really loading up for the testing-day welcome festivities this month. Should be a good trip, and not just for us. A few other shop owners gave me their goods, too. If all goes well, we'll *all* make enough gold to keep the tithe away." As he handed up an open box filled with straw and eggs, his wide face showed his famous smile.

Dantess grinned as well. His da was in a good mood.

"That's great, Da. With so much stuff, maybe you could use some help unloading it at all at the temple. You know..." Dantess cleared his throat. "I could help. And Jyn's here. She'd be happy to help, too."

Tolliver stopped, his hands on a small barrel, his back to Dantess. "That's not a good idea."

"Da, you're not a young man. Your back has been bothering you. I'm worried about you hurting yourself with all these heavy boxes. I'm old enough now to really help. Don't you want me to learn the business?"

Tolliver stood and turned to look up the stairs, eyebrows raised. "You're interested in the business? That's new."

"Of course I am! And I'm not just worried about your back. The road between here and the temple is getting more dangerous.

You shouldn't be alone out there. Jyn and I could, you know, help protect the shipment."

Tolliver dusted his hands together and grunted. "You're not wrong about the road. War says they keep it safe, but they don't care if a faithless or two get robbed—which happened to a coach last month. When they stopped to move a tree that blocked the road, they were robbed. Maybe I *should* hire a guard or two."

Dantess was a little taken aback—he thought the bandits were just rumors—but he refused to give up. In fact, he was more determined now that he knew his father might actually need protection. "How much would that cost? Anyone good would eat all the profits from the trip. Come on, Da. Give me and Jyn a try. We've been training." When Dantess noticed Tolliver's glare, he added, "And remember, we're both strong and ready to move the load. Wouldn't you rather relax, rest your back, and watch us do it?"

Tolliver walked up the stairs and looked Dantess in the eye with a narrowed gaze. "You just want to visit the temple, don't you?" But his smile didn't leave his face. That's when Dantess knew his da already decided to let him go.

"Would that be so bad? And it's not like they'd let us inside anyway. We'd only get as far as the gatehouse."

"I don't like it," said Tolliver. "You shouldn't have anything to do with War."

"But if I'm truly going to take over the business someday—like you've said you wanted—that means I'd have to deal with War. They're your biggest customer. I'd have to go there sometime. Wouldn't you rather be there when I do?"

"You really want to do this? Run this shop?" asked Tolliver. "I thought you'd end up on the water. You always had a fascination for sailing. Maybe you could start your own shipping business?"

Dantess refused to be distracted, even though he did enjoy the thought of sailing. "Pirates are worse than bandits, Da. You can't defend against a frigate's cannons with a sword. Speaking of which, can I borrow a couple of those?" Dantess pointed out two metal fireplace pokers in the corner. "They're better than tree branches if we have to fight. Just in case."

Tolliver stood for a moment with a sober expression, but couldn't help but break out into his contagious grin. He hugged his son and said, "I know you and every kid your age would love to become a priest, but without a Longing, you have to be practical. If

13

you're finally coming to understand this, I'm proud of you. Shows you're growing up. This shop has given us both a good living. Even if we have to deal with priests to stay afloat, there are far worse fates for faithless."

"You're letting me go with you?" asked Dantess, eyes wide.

"Don't make me regret it!" Tolliver chuckled. "Tell Jyn she can come, too. I'll even pay her a bit, if she helps."

"She will!" Dantess hugged his father and ran outside to tell Jyn.

Dantess couldn't believe it. After so many years, he was going to the temple of War! This was one of the happiest days of his life.

CHAPTER TWO

WHILE SETTLING A barrel into the back of the tightly packed wagon, Dantess accidentally dislodged its stopper. An overwhelming smell of hard cider blasted him in the face. "Oh, wow. I don't remember the cider being that strong."

"Special order," said Tolliver with a chuckle. "The temple wants to celebrate, so I asked Jolli to keep a few barrels until they had a bit more kick."

Before Dantess replaced the stopper, he asked, "Can I try some?"

Rolling his eyes, his da pointed at the barrel. Dantess shrugged and shoved the cork back in.

Jyn emerged from the store front, avoided running into a couple of children running by, and announced, "I think that's all of it."

"Good work," said Tolliver. "We should go. It'll take half the day to get there, maybe longer with a load this heavy."

Warren, sitting cross-legged on the store's porch, glanced up from reading his book. He was almost at the last page. He looked at the packed wagon bed and then to the long, empty driver's seat. "Yay! Do I get to sit in the front? There's no room in the back."

Jyn and Dantess shared a look. Jyn said, "Sorry, Warren. You can't come. Go back home to Mama. And go straight there!"

"What? That's not fair! I want to see the temple of War, too! I've read all about it. Please let me come!"

"Not this trip," said Dantess. "Jyn and I are only going because we're working. And it's too dangerous for little kids."

"I'm not that little. If Jyn's going, I should, too!" Warren's lip began to quiver.

Dantess could see where this was headed. Before Warren broke into a crying fit, Dantess reached into a sack on the cart and pulled out an apple. "Listen, if you stay here, this is yours. Does that sound good?"

Warren's face scrunched in a grimace, but he reached out to take the apple. "All mine? Do I have to share with Mama?"

Dantess gave an exaggerated sigh, pulled out another apple, and handed it over. "And one for your mother as well."

Tolliver finished hooking the horse up to the wagon and saw the exchange. His eyebrow rose.

His eyes wide, Warren held up both apples and showed them to Jyn. "Look. I bet they're so sweet."

Jyn smiled and said, "Get these to Mama, quick. She'll be so happy with you, you might not have to do chores tonight."

The young boy clutched the apples, nodded, and ran off down the road. "Thank you," he yelled over his shoulder.

"Sorry about that, Da," said Dantess. "You can take the cost from my pay."

Tolliver chuckled. "The look on his face was payment enough. But I wasn't exaggerating." He looked up at the midday sun. "We need to get going. It's a long trip and it'll be night by the time we return. I'd rather not travel in that forest too long after dark."

The driver's seat was just big enough for all of them to fit, so they climbed up and nestled there. Dantess tried to give the other passengers as much room as possible, but his broad shoulders kept brushing against the others. Given the choice, he leaned slightly toward Jyn. He didn't mind their shoulders touching as much, and she didn't seem to either.

Tolliver flicked the reins and the wagon lurched into motion.

The road wasn't special. The dirt was packed by years of travelers—both on horseback and on foot—and rutted by countless wagons. The leafy trees that provided some shade from the day's hot sun were no different from those that surrounded Freethorn Creek on all sides.

But, to Dantess, it was like no other road. Despite this being one of the main routes from Freethorn Creek, Dantess had never traveled it. Tolliver forbade him from ever visiting the temple, and there wasn't any other reason to use it.

Dantess was excited, even though he tried to hide how much. He *knew* the temple was ahead. He could even point to it with his eyes closed. For a moment, he thought this certainty may have been the Longing finally making itself known. But no. The way to the temple was obvious—that's where the road led—but he didn't feel *pulled* there. Everyone said that if you had it, you *knew*. And you had no choice. The god's call would bring you to the temple, and nothing could keep you away.

It was just wishful thinking.

But knowing that didn't decrease his excitement. He examined every bush, every tree, even every rock on the road. He wanted to remember *all* the details of his first visit to the temple of War.

Every time the wind rustled a nearby bush, Dantess reached for his fireplace poker. He knew he was being jumpy, but after Da confirmed the robbery last month, he couldn't help it. He took his role as protector seriously. The fifth time Dantess did this, Tolliver laughed, slapped his back, and told him to relax.

His da was probably right. Watching for an attack didn't mean it was coming. He was just winding himself up.

Eventually, after hours of travel, excitement and wariness turned into impatience. Rocks and trees could only provide so much fascination. "How much longer?" asked Dantess. "Shouldn't we be getting close?"

Tolliver chuckled. "Can't you see it?"

Dantess whipped his head around. "See what? Where?"

"Up there." Tolliver pointed up and ahead. "The view will become clearer soon."

A mountain peeked through the trees. Dantess squinted. "The temple is near to that mountain?"

"The temple *is* the mountain. We're closer than you think."

That's the temple? thought Dantess, craning his neck and trying to see as much as he could through the leaves. *We're almost there! I can't believe I'm about to visit the temple of War.*

The abrupt end of the forest fast approached. One moment, they were surrounded by trees; the next, the wagon rolled onto a huge stretch of empty ground. The tree line, a green curtain of leaves, stretched for miles on either side, straight as an arrow. In contrast, the dark, rocky field ahead contained no life at all—not even a bush or clump of grass.

It was like rolling into a different world. The gentle wind dancing in the trees and buzz of insects fell away. The fresh forest smells were replaced by hot, still air baking above barren dirt—as if even the wind didn't dare disturb the solemnity of approaching the temple. Tolliver gestured to the empty field. "If the thought of becoming one of War's bound faithless ever flits through your head, remember this."

"Why?" asked Dantess.

"Most of the faithless here aren't soldiers. Inside the temple, they clean the latrines, care for the livestock, and cook the food, but out here, they maintain this field. Can you imagine being responsible for keeping all of this land clear? The land is salted, but if even a clump of grass grows, a faithless is severely punished. War allows a visitor no place to hide for the last mile of approach to the temple."

Dantess stared out at the acres of cleared land that surrounded the mountain. He whispered to himself, "No one sneaks up on War. Impressive."

Finally, he swung his gaze back to the field's only distinguishing feature: the hard-packed, dirt road that led directly to the mountain.

But as Tolliver said, it wasn't just a mountain.

The road ended at an elaborate stone-built structure at the mountain's base. "Look," said Jyn. "It's a castle."

Dantess elbowed Jyn. "That's just the gatehouse. The temple is up there!"

The mountain was a plateau, but where the rock flattened out, War's fortress took over the task of reaching the sky. Thick walls and ramparts protected countless looming towers. Layers upon layers culminated in a peak far in the distance.

Dantess whistled.

As the small group approached the gatehouse, Dantess noticed that a wall, starting on either side of the structure, surrounded the mountain. Even a mile away, if he squinted, he could make out the reflective armor of watchmen stationed every fifty feet atop that wall.

"Is this what you imagined it would be like, Dantess?" asked Tolliver.

Dantess couldn't keep the look of awe from his face. "I've heard descriptions, but I wasn't prepared. It's everything I hoped it would be. Thank you for bringing me, Da."

"Remember, we're only going to enter the gatehouse. Faithless like us aren't allowed inside the temple proper."

"Unless that faithless is testing," said Jyn.

"True. This place will be packed tomorrow." Tolliver sighed. "All those kids giving up their freedom for the prospect of fighting at War."

"There are worse things," said Dantess. Immediately, he regretted saying that aloud.

"What? Don't even joke about that." Scowling, Tolliver pulled at the reins and the horse stopped. "You don't know what happens here. Outside the temple, we have some measure of freedom. Inside there?" Anger quickened his words as he gestured to the mountain fortress reaching up to the sky. "Faithless might as well be slaves. I know better than most."

Dantess wanted to argue, but he nodded to avoid a fight. After a moment, Tolliver started the wagon moving again, but the scowl didn't leave his face. "Maybe this was a mistake," he mumbled to himself.

The huge wooden gates of the gatehouse stood open. Jyn and Dantess ogled the impressive architecture as the wagon rolled through into a vast open courtyard. Armored guards holding longspears watched them pass with mild interest. Other people milled about the yard, most wearing simple brown tunics.

Jyn elbowed Dantess and pointed at one of the faithless workers. "You see his mask?" Indeed, a black tattooed mask surrounded the man's eyes. "They've all got them."

Tolliver grunted. "These poor folks are property of War, marked so everyone will know." He guided the wagon close to another set of doors on the courtyard's far side. "Unload here. War's workers will take it further in." Tolliver, with a hint of a smile, slapped Dantess on the shoulder. "I'll wait here resting my back as my thoughtful son promised."

Dantess nodded and jumped out of the wagon. "Come on, Jyn. Let's deliver these goods to War!"

The pile of crates, casks, and boxes next to the wagon grew larger as they unloaded their stock. Dantess was placing a corn-filled woven basket onto the pile when a young, hulking, clean-shaven priest of War lumbered out from a doorway along the courtyard's walls. He knew the man was a priest because, unlike the fully-armored guards, this man wore only a shining breastplate as protection—and he had no tattooed mask around his eyes. His bare, brawny arms carried a lockbox.

"Ho, Tolliver," the priest bellowed as he approached. "Who's this? You brought a team to help you? I didn't think you were *that* old yet."

"Greetings, Kevik," said Tolliver from his seat, forcing a smile. "This is my son, Dantess. And his friend Jyn. Dantess is learning the business. You never know when he may have to take over."

"Your son, eh? I didn't even know you *had* a son, Tolliver. You never talk about him." Kevik eyed Dantess like he was appraising a side of meat. "Do you know who your grandfather was, boy? Did Tolliver bother to tell you?"

Dantess smiled uncomfortably. "I know. Varyon. He gave me this." Dantess held up the hand with the silver ring.

"A ring?" He laughed. "Of everything he could have given you, he chose jewelry? Huh." He looked down at the lockbox in his hands. "All right Varyon's grandson, let's see if you have any more promise than your father. Catch!" Kevik tossed the lockbox to Dantess. He tried to catch the small chest, but it was heavier than expected. He fumbled and dropped it.

Kevik chuckled. "Like father, like son. With hands like that, it's a good thing you're getting into the supply business, rather than guarding our gates. No matter your lineage, I guess not everyone is cut out to be a warrior."

"It was just a box. I slipped," Dantess mumbled, a little defensive. "I've actually trained a bit. I know how to fight."

"Do you? All right, let's see what's what." With a swift motion, Kevik grabbed the boy's arm—too fast for Dantess to react. "Huh. Your reflexes aren't much to speak of. Without those, you need strength, but you've a long way to go to match even the weakest on my squad. You see?" Kevik flexed his other arm, which was loosely the size of a tree trunk. "This is what a warrior looks like."

While undeniably large, Kevik's arms were almost blank—likely because he was new to the temple. Dantess knew that tattoos on a priest's arms indicated rank, usually achieved through victories in combat. The most senior priests looked like they had cultivated an elegant bramble field of intertwining barbs.

Even if Kevik wasn't friendly, he was a priest of War—and that fact alone demanded Dantess' respect. He decided to try a different tack to connect with the priest and maybe even impress the man with his knowledge of War. "I might surprise you," said

Dantess. "If I were on your squad, I bet we could add some wins to those arms. Maybe enough to get you to the Convergence of the Divine!"

The Convergence occurred every hundred years, but it was only a few years away. There wasn't a single priest of War who didn't dream of attending. The most prestigious honor was to command the guard there.

If Dantess meant the comment earnestly or even playfully, that's not the way Kevik took it. He snarled and squeezed Dantess' upper arm like a vice. "You dare speak to *me* that way? A damned faithless, talking about the Convergence as if you knew anything about it?"

"I... I didn't mean..." stammered Dantess.

"Please, Kevik," interjected Tolliver, climbing down from the wagon. "You're one of the most promising young priests here. Everyone knows you'll rise quickly in the ranks." Tolliver's ever-present smile was replaced by an expression of undisguised fear. "I never should have brought my son here, clearly. If you need to punish someone for his insolence, punish me."

Tolliver's speech and terrified expression seemed to calm Kevik down. "As a boon to my favorite delivery man, I'll give the boy a pass." He chuckled. "Who knows? It might be interesting to have Varyon's grandson on my squad. If anyone could turn him into a real man, it's me." He released Dantess and the boy stumbled back a step. "You should test tomorrow if you're so bent on joining the temple. But until then, remember the faithless must know their place. Your mouth is going to get you into trouble you can't walk away from."

Kevik strode over to the waiting laborers and commanded them to take the supplies inside. They scurried to follow his orders.

"What just happened?" Dantess asked his father. "I've spoken to priests of War back in Freethorn Creek, and it never went like that."

Tolliver shook his head, his teeth clenched. He labored to breathe, too angry to speak. Then he growled, "Why are you talking to priests of War? Why would you suggest joining his squad? Is that why you wanted to come here? To join up?"

Dantess stared back at Tolliver. He knew nothing he said could make this better, so for a long moment, neither spoke.

"Load the box on the wagon," said Tolliver. "We're leaving."

Dantess did as instructed. He climbed up into the wagon bed and dropped the strongbox, but when he stepped toward the driver's seat, Tolliver stopped him. "Stay back there for now. I'd like to be alone up here."

The boy did as asked. Jyn climbed into the back and sat with him. As the wagon started rolling toward the gate, Jyn punched him in the shoulder and whispered, "You know, if that big muscleheaded priest over there tried grabbing me like that, I would have pounded him."

Dantess sighed, but grinned despite himself. "I'm sure you could have taken him."

True, Dantess felt gutted, but he couldn't fault Kevik. The man was a priest of War. He embodied Dantess' greatest wish: the god of War called him here and found him worthy.

And Dantess was just a stupid kid with a famous grandfather.

He rubbed his arm where Kevik gripped him and grimaced at the touch. It almost made him wish he hadn't come in the first place.

CHAPTER THREE

WITH MUCH OF the day already lost, the shadows from the forest trees lengthened as the sun dipped lower.

At first, they traveled without speaking. Only the creak of the wagon and the horse's heavy chuffing broke the silence.

Tolliver finally grunted. Without turning around, he said, "I'm a fool, aren't I? You never had any interest in the business. You just wanted to come to War's temple."

"That's not true!" insisted Dantess. "Not entirely, at least. I really wanted to help." He sighed. "But I do wish you didn't hate War so much. What did Grandpa do to make you hate not only him, but his god? A *god!* War's priests do his divine work in this world. That can't be bad."

Tolliver shook his head. "You brought up the Convergence of the Divine to Kevik. Do you really know what it is?"

"Of course, I do. Every hundred years, senior priests from four temples bring their Gifts to an island. Good and Evil debate, Law records, and War protects." Thinking about protection, Dantess picked up one of the fireplace pokers and idly rubbed the smooth metal.

"But *what* do they debate?"

"Laws, right? The rules."

"Yes. Laws that govern the faithless. And who *isn't* invited to the table? The *faithless.*" With that, Tolliver stomped on the toe board under their feet. His passion about this subject took Dantess by surprise.

"But the gods' *Gifts* are there," said Dantess. "The laws are guided by the gods. They know what's best for all of us."

Tolliver scoffed. "The gods don't care about the faithless. Those laws are made by *priests*, who only want to ensure we stay in our place and pay the tithe every month. The only debate is about *how* they punish us."

"But, Da—"

"Wait," said Jyn, interrupting him. She pointed ahead. "What's that on the road? It wasn't there before."

23

Tolliver pulled on the reins and stopped the wagon. He shielded his eyes from the low sun ahead and said, "Fallen tree. It's blocking our way."

The hair on the back of Dantess' neck rose when he realized that they had likely driven into the middle of an ambush. The rumors of bandits in these woods weren't just rumors.

Dantess lifted his poker, but Tolliver shook his head and said, "I'll handle this."

"But this is why we came," said Dantess. He crouched in the wagon bed, his eyes scanning the tree line.

"Until we know what's happening, it's safer for all of us to stay in the wagon."

Jyn, her poker also in hand, pulled on Dantess' sleeve. "It's true. Until we can actually see the threat—"

Jyn's statement was interrupted by a solidly-built man wearing a burlap sack as a mask and carrying an ornate saber. He emerged from the forest and walked atop the downed log until he reached the middle. "Ho, good travelers. Is this old tree in your way?"

"It is," said Tolliver flatly. "What bad luck it dropped to block the only road."

"Exactly," said the man. "These trees are ancient. They can drop at any time. One falling like this can be dreadfully inconvenient. I'd be glad to help you out and get you on your way." He kicked a bit of bark onto the ground. "For some recompense, of course. We all have to make a living."

"Truly helpful people don't usually wear masks to hide their faces. Let me see who I'm dealing with."

"Oh, this?" He touched the burlap sack. "You'd understand why I wear it if I took it off. For now, it stays."

"Regardless," said Tolliver, squinting, "we don't have anything to take. We delivered everything of value."

"Oh, I know. I don't want supplies. Too heavy. No, I'd much rather have the *payment* for those supplies. I want War's gold."

Tolliver sighed. "You may not know this, but people depend on this gold. Not just my family, but the farmers and bakers and craftsmen who entrusted me to ship their goods. You may not pay the tithe anymore, but some of us still have to."

The man jumped down from the tree and swung his saber through the air a few times as he approached the wagon. He executed a flourish with the sword, ending with the tip close to Tolliver's neck. Even if Dantess pulled away in shock, he was surprised that his father didn't even flinch. Dantess could hear his own pulse pounding in his ears, but Tolliver remained stone still.

"I feel for you," said the man. "I do. Think of this as a payment not only to get that tree moved, but to prevent future falls. You'll make up for this one delivery with more later."

Dantess focused on the saber's tip hovering inches from Da's throat. He couldn't watch his father be threatened like this. All of his training led to this moment. He was here to protect Da. He *promised* he would. He couldn't let his fear or the fact that this was his first real fight prevent him from acting.

Dantess grit his teeth, gripped the metal poker tight, and, still crouching in the wagon bed, lurched forward. He swung the poker and knocked the saber away from his father's throat, punctuated by the loud ring of metal striking metal.

Surprised, the man lost his grip and the sword flew behind him onto the ground. While he scrambled for it, Dantess leapt from the wagon, poker held as if he were also armed with a blade. In the fading light, it almost looked like one.

"Leave my father alone. In fact, leave us *all* alone and let us pass," said Dantess, shaking slightly.

The man reclaimed his sword and retreated a few steps. He looked to Tolliver and said, "I don't want to hurt anyone tonight. I just want the gold."

Dantess pressed forward, close enough to smell the sour odor of sweat coming from the bandit's stained shirt, but the man backed away even further.

Is he afraid to fight me? thought Dantess.

He pointed the poker at the man and demanded, "Drop the sword and leave."

The man halted only a step from the felled tree. He craned forward. "Is that a *fireplace poker?*" His shoulders relaxed. He laughed and stuck his saber's point into the ground. "You're either brave or stupid, lad. Coming at me with *that?* Listen to me. Get back in the wagon, or things will end badly for you. Let the adults do business."

When Dantess refused to move, the man exhaled a breath while flapping his lips. He leaned on the hilt of his sword and said, "No more playing around. I'll be clear. Even if you *were* a real threat, there are five men with bows in the trees. They'll kill you all and then we'll take the gold. Don't make me give the order."

Dantess couldn't help it. He whipped his head around, looking up at the trees that surrounded the wagon. He didn't see anything. No bandits. Not even any movement. To the man, he asked, "Is that true? Or are you a liar as well as a thief?"

"He's both," said a deep voice. Kevik, the hulking priest of War from the gatehouse, walked out of the trees from behind the cart. "He only had *two* men in the trees. My squad has already taken them. Now he's all alone."

"Why are *you* here?" asked Tolliver, shocked.

"My squad was assigned as security for tomorrow's auction in Freethorn. I figured I'd get there early. Left right after you. Lucky I did. For you. Not for him." He gestured to the highwayman.

The masked man pulled his sword up and brandished it with both hands, visibly shaking. "Let me go," he said to Kevik. "Please. We just wanted to eat. We have nothing."

"Oh, don't worry about me. No, the kid squaring off with you is none other than the grandson of *Varyon*. He thinks he could be a warrior. I'm anxious to see how he does in a real fight."

"No!" Tolliver pleaded. "My son isn't trained. He doesn't even have a proper weapon."

Dantess gripped the poker tightly. "Don't worry, Da. I... I can do this." *I hope I can. Especially in front of Kevik.*

Kevik laughed, leaned against the wagon, and crossed his arms. "Show me." He gestured to the highwayman. "And him."

With the poker held like a sword, Dantess took a tentative step forward.

"You have to let me run," whispered the highwayman. "There's no way I live if you don't."

Dantess was taken aback. "Surrender, then. There's no shame, not with a priest of War here."

"You don't understand. That's not an option. It won't matter." He squared his shoulders and lifted his blade.

So, the man wanted to fight anyway. Dantess tried to recall how he sparred with Jyn, but nerves emptied his mind of any particular tactic. He flicked his wrist in a quick swing. The masked man parried easily, but didn't counter.

Dantess swung again, wider and stronger. The man backed away just enough to let the swing go by. Again, he did not attack, despite the obvious opportunity.

The boy grew frustrated and nervous. The bandit wasn't even trying. Dantess could sense that he was outmatched, that his opponent was toying with him.

He remembered the lesson Jyn taught him earlier. A poker wasn't a sword, even if his opponent expected him to use it like one. Dantess lunged forward at the man's chest, but then twirled the tool from the middle—just as Jyn had with the tree branch. When the man tried to parry, the bar struck the fingers holding his saber's hilt.

The man flinched, swore, and dropped his weapon. As he bent to retrieve it, Dantess struck the side of his opponent's head with the poker, then whirled it around to smack the other side. The highwayman clutched his head and groaned.

Dantess grinned. Those blows had to have left the man's head ringing. He paused and demanded, "Give up. With a priest here, this fight is pointless now."

The man grunted, slid his foot under the hilt of his blade and—with what seemed like a single motion—kicked it up from the ground, caught it in his other hand, and lunged forward.

Time seemed to stop. Dantess saw the blade coming straight for him. Out of reflex, he raised his hand to block the attack and the fading light of the sun reflected off of his grandfather's ring, right into the eye-holes of the burlap mask. The flash of light caused the man's blade to drift off course. Dantess dodged it by a hair.

What are the odds of that happening? wondered Dantess, but he couldn't waste the time to ponder. Dantess thrust his poker forward again hoping to disarm the man once more. Unfortunately, his opponent had learned the lesson. He simply dodged the thrust and then kicked the boy in the chest, sending Dantess onto the ground. The poker tumbled out of the boy's hand.

Kevik roared with laughter.

Tolliver stood up in his seat. "Dantess, get out of there!" To Kevik, he demanded, "You have to stop this!"

"It's his fight, not mine. He has to learn when not to step up to someone who can put him down."

The highwayman took one step forward and held the saber to Dantess' throat. "I'm sorry, boy. I didn't want this to happen."

Dantess stared at the sword's tip and wondered, *Could I die? In my first fight?* Weirdly, he also thought, *Jyn will be ashamed of me.*

As if summoned by this, Jyn jumped from atop the log and onto the man's back, screaming, "Get away from him, you bastard!" Dantess realized she must have slipped out of the wagon and maneuvered behind the highwayman while everyone was watching the pair fight.

She put her poker around his neck and pulled as hard as she could.

The sword retreated from Dantess' throat. He scuttled back to put some distance between them.

The man choked and pulled at the poker. He twisted back and forth, but Jyn did not relent. Then the man punched behind his own head, and kept punching until his fist connected with Jyn's face. Stunned, Jyn loosened her grip. The man grabbed her hair and threw her off—but not before Jyn dug her fingers into his burlap mask. She tumbled to the ground, but did so holding onto the mask.

Even in the dim light, the black tattoo surrounding the man's eyes was obvious.

Kevik's laughter stopped abruptly. "You're bound to War? A damned deserter!"

The bandit touched his temple and then threw his saber down. "Please, I'll surrender. Please, just let me—"

With a single smooth motion, Kevik pulled out a dagger and hurled it. The hilt appeared between the man's eyes and the blade's tip poked out from the back of his head.

The lifeless body dropped to the ground.

Dantess' jaw dropped, reacting not just to the man's sudden death, but the skill of the attack. He'd never seen someone move so swiftly.

Kevik walked over to the bandit, put his foot against the man's neck, and pulled his dagger free. He wiped the blood on the man's tunic, sheathed the blade, and picked up the saber. "I should have known he came from War. You don't see many faithless with swords like this, and he was comfortable with it. He had training."

"He didn't have to die," mumbled Tolliver. "He was hungry. And desperate."

Dantess looked at his father in shock. "What?"

"Not that it matters," said Kevik, "but he was a traitor. You see the tattoo that brands him as a runaway? He was a dead man the moment he fled the temple."

"What he was, was faithless, with all his choices stripped from him." Tolliver balled his hands into fists. "Tell me, where are his men? The ones in the trees?"

"Dealt with."

"Oh? Have you taken them prisoner?"

Kevik was silent.

"No," said Tolliver. "And they weren't runaways, were they? Did they *all* deserve to die?"

Kevik scowled. "Most people would be grateful for the rescue. Perhaps I should have left *you* to die instead?"

Tolliver looked at Dantess and then Jyn. He sat down and, for a long moment, he just breathed.

Dantess couldn't miss his father's transition. The tightness left his hands and jaw. His eyes dropped. "You're right, priest of War. Your intervention is appreciated. Please convey our thanks to your squad. And to your temple."

A rider, leading a large, black stallion, approached from behind the wagon. She wore a breastplate and chainmail sleeves, like all faithless soldiers. A black tattooed mask surrounded her eyes. "The forest is clear," she informed Kevik. "The rest of the squad has already moved on to Freethorn, as ordered."

Kevik leapt up onto the saddle of the riderless stallion. He looked at home atop the huge beast. "I've had enough of uppity faithless for one day. Let's go." As the horse trotted past Dantess, he called down, "You showed me something today. More than I expected. Maybe fighting for War isn't out of the question for you. As I said, it wouldn't hurt to do some strength training. You can start by moving that tree off the road." He chuckled.

The two horses leapt over the fallen tree and rode off. Soon, the sound of pounding hooves faded away.

"Da, I don't understand. Why did you argue with Kevik? He saved us!" Dantess pointed to the man on the ground. "That man was going to kill me, and you feel sorry for him?"

Tolliver's face darkened. "You practically *dared* that man to kill you! Why did you jump into a fight you couldn't win? What are you trying to prove?"

"I was trying to protect *you!* And besides, Kevik's a *priest.* He wouldn't have let him kill me."

"Dantess, I know you look up to the priests of War, but they're not our protectors." Tolliver pinched the bridge of his nose between two fingers. "Listen, I know these people. They protect the temples. They protect the tithe. With priests of War, it's always '*us* versus *them.*' Do you think any priest includes the faithless in '*us*'? Your grandpa made it clear that even his own family was outside of his relationship to his god. The faithless aren't part of their religion, so to priests, we're not important. We're *expendable.*"

"Expendable? No, priests can't kill a faithless because they *feel* like it." Dantess thought about it. "Can they?"

"You're young. You haven't seen what priests are capable of." Tolliver sighed. "Jyn, help Dantess hitch up the horse to the log. We need to drag it off the road before we attract more bandits. It'll be tomorrow before we get home."

Dantess grumbled, but stopped arguing. He and Jyn wrestled a rope around some of the tree's larger branches and attempted to coerce their horse into pulling it away. "Thank you for jumping in like that," he said to Jyn. "I owe you."

"Sure do. Better remember that." Even with a swelling eye, Jyn was beautiful when she smiled.

The tree was large and uncooperative. His father was right. It might take hours to clear the road.

Dantess hoped that was all he was right about.

CHAPTER FOUR

BARELY TWO HOURS after the sun rose, Tolliver's wagon rolled into the town of Freethorn Creek. It had been a long, tiring night and Jyn slept against Dantess' shoulder in the wagon's bed. He knew he should wake her, but he owed her as much rest as she could get. Besides, he found it comforting as well.

Warren met the wagon on its way in. "Jyn! Are you in there?" He began to run alongside the moving wagon, pounding on the wood. "Jyn, Jyn, Jyyyyyn!"

Dantess gently shook Jyn awake. "Your brother is going crazy trying to get your attention."

"What?" asked Jyn amidst a yawn. Despite the bright sun, the morning air was brisk. "Warren? Quiet down. What time is it?"

"You have to come. A priest of Law took Mama to the square. They're setting up for the debtor auction!"

"They took Mama?" Without waiting for the wagon to stop, Jyn climbed out and landed on the packed dirt road.

"Your family's in debt?" asked Dantess. "Since when?"

She answered in a clipped, anxious tone. "I don't know. She didn't tell me anything." Jyn took her brother's hand and bolted away in the direction of the town square.

Tolliver pulled on the reins, and the horse slowed. "Go. I'll drop off the wagon."

"Could it be a mistake?" Dantess asked his father. "If she's really been taken, what'll happen to her? And what about Jyn and Warren? They don't have anyone else to take care of them." He climbed over the wagon's side.

"We can't do anything for their mother at this point. If she had mentioned that she was in trouble before, maybe..." Tolliver shook his head. "She's a proud woman, and now it's too late." As Dantess jogged off toward the square, Tolliver called out, "Tell Jyn and Warren that we will help them however we can."

Dantess ran through the back streets toward the town square, flanked by progressively better-built and fancier buildings. Some even sported recent coats of paint.

The street emptied into the town square. People had already packed it full, pushing as close as possible to the wooden stage in the square's center. The only other area free of the crowd was the roped-off stands nearby. Those seats were reserved for priests only.

Any other time, kids might have been playing on that stage, or sanctioned actors and musicians could have been performing there—but that's not why it had been constructed.

The stage was a tool of the temples. A raised dais in the center was sometimes used for formal announcements, but there were times when the person standing there wasn't doing so by choice. A sturdy beam overhead and a lever, currently with the handle unscrewed and packed away somewhere, were the only clues that the dais could serve as gallows. It wasn't used much for that purpose—Evil's dungeon was the usual destination of law-breakers—but if a temple demanded a more public end to a criminal, this is where it usually happened.

But today, the stage—decorated with colorful bunting all along the edges as if for a celebration—would serve its main function. It was *auction* day.

Any faithless who weren't up on the wooden stage were watching those who were. The temples encouraged it. The event illustrated the consequences of avoiding the tithe.

A line of ten faithless, many in rags, stood on the well-worn stage. Their hands were bound in front of them and affixed to an iron ring. A rope ran through each ring, stringing all of the prisoners together. The rope had been secured to sturdy beams at either end.

Somewhere in the middle of the line was Jyn's mother, Siriana. She was dressed in the worn, washer-woman's clothes she wore every day. The apron at her front was tattered and soiled, as if she had been dragged here.

Dantess found Jyn and Warren as close to the stage as they could get, a few steps away from the bunting. They were trying to speak to their mother, but a soldier bound to War—the one who supplied Kevik his horse last night—kept the crowd back.

Siriana kept her head down. Her shoulders shook and tears dripped from her face.

Dantess pushed his way through the crowd to Jyn. "Jyn! Are you two all right?"

32

"All right?" asked Jyn, wringing her hands. "My mother is on the auction block. What do you think?" She looked to be on the brink of tears herself.

"Sorry. I didn't mean..." Dantess grimaced. "My da told me to let you know we'd take you in, so no matter what happens, don't worry."

"Telling me not to worry right now is like telling me not to breathe." Jyn threw her hands up. "How did this happen? Ever since our da disappeared, Mama has worked her hands to the bone, washing clothes *every* day, *all* day. Clearly, I started to think about helping out too late."

Warren tugged on Jyn's sleeve. "What's going to happen to Mama?"

"It depends on how big the debt is," answered Jyn, biting her lip.

"Can we pay it? I can go find some money! I'll steal it if I have to!"

"Shush!" She pressed her hands over Warren's mouth. The nearby soldier raised her eyebrow, but said nothing.

Dantess placed his hand on Warren's shoulder. "Once collected by Law, only a temple can buy her debt. Then she'll be its property." He shared a worried look with Jyn.

Warren whispered, "Will she come back?"

"No." Dantess sighed. "I'm sorry, Warren."

"Which temples are here?" asked Jyn.

This was an important question. Only priests who attended could bid, and the temple that purchased a debtor would determine the quality of the rest of their life. Some, like Charity or Good, were known to take care of their bound faithless. Others, not so much.

Arriving priests were seated in the stands, away from the crowd. Some conversed, some stared. It was interesting to see which temples got along with each other. "The priest of Law is here, of course," answered Dantess. "He's chatting with Good. Makes sense—they're allies, and they've got deep pockets. The others look like... Serenity? And Drama, I think. There are a few I don't know, too. Some promising possibilities. If her debt isn't too high, the starting bid won't scare off the smaller temples."

"Those aren't the only ones here," said Jyn.

"No." Dantess didn't have to mention the black-robed priest sitting on his own with his hood pulled up over his eyes, talking to no one. Evil *always* attended. If someone's debt was too much, or none of the other priests bid, Evil was there. Waiting.

They had the deepest pockets of all, and they'd take anyone.

"Has anyone ever escaped?" whispered Warren.

"Some faithless run before Law collects them. Then they have to run forever. But once they get here?" Dantess pointed at War's faithless soldiers stationed around the stage, his finger falling finally on Kevik, who lounged by the stands—the only priest who didn't mind being near Evil. "It would be futile. War guards every auction. No one's ever tried."

The priest of Law approached the dais. He raised his hands to quieten the crowd. "People of Freethorn Creek, welcome to the auction!"

The crowd's reaction was mixed. Many erupted in applause and cheers, but quite a few others grumbled, or at least stayed silent.

After the noise died down, the priest continued. "I must ask you: why do you pay the tithe?" He paused. "You all know the tithe allows us to establish and enforce the Law, provide the healing of Charity, and remove your worst criminals to the dungeons of Evil. But do you pay the tithe to receive these things? Because of what the temples do *for* you?"

The crowd responded, "No!"

"Of course not. You pay the tithe because the gods of Order wish it. This has always been the way, and it will always be so."

The priest gestured to the line of debtors in front of him. "These people refused to pay the tithe. They blasphemed against *every* god of Order, every priest, every temple—from the smallest outpost to the grand halls of Law itself. Can we allow this sacrilege to stand?"

"No!"

"What must happen?" asked the priest.

"The tithe must be paid!" chanted the crowd.

"*What must happen?*" the priest repeated.

The crowd bellowed, even louder, "*The tithe must be paid!*"

Dantess stood nervously and said nothing, but held Jyn's and Warren's hands. He noticed that those shouting the loudest were the richest among the faithless, those who paid the tithe without worry every month.

34

"Yes. The gods demand the tithe, and so it must be paid. In their generosity, these temples," the priest gestured to the stands, "will pay the tithes *for* these people—not just to reconcile *this* debt, but *every* tithe they owe for the rest of their lives. In return, these people will dedicate themselves to the temple's service. It is right and just."

"It is right and just," echoed the crowd.

"Let us begin," said the priest. He pointed at the first man as he read from a parchment. "Our first debtor is a baker. He owes five gold. Who will pay his tithe?"

"Is that Poole?" whispered one of the people standing close to Dantess. "Aw, I'm going to miss his biscuits. Guess we'll have to find another bakery."

One of the priests, dressed in a colorful robe, smiled and raised his hand.

"Five gold to the priest of Merriment. Could be a good fit. Anyone else? He's a baker! That's a trade that every temple can use."

The solitary black-robed priest raised his hand. "Ten."

Disgust passed over the priest of Law's face, and the baker's eyes opened wide. "Ten gold to the priest of Evil. Does anyone else need a baker? Anyone?"

Poole the baker turned to the other priests, urgent need etched into his face. He whispered, "Please..."

"Sold to..." the priest coughed, then continued, "the temple of Evil for ten gold."

The man's face dropped into his hands.

The priest looked down at his parchment. He pointed at the next prisoner, a girl barely sixteen years of age. "Here we have—"

A stately residence at the edge of the square exploded. Out of reflex, Dantess ducked and shielded Warren with his arms.

What was that? thought Dantess, and he clearly wasn't the only one. It seemed the entire crowd screamed at once.

In quick succession, another building burst into flames on a different side of the square. And yet another, closer to the stage. Flames shot out of the windows, and debris from the shattered walls peppered the screaming audience. Flaming fragments caught the bunting, setting it alight.

"Law's mercy!" exclaimed the priest of Law, stepping off the dais and backing away from the slowly-spreading flames.

The crowd was frantic, shoving each other to get away from the fire. It was all Dantess could do to keep the crazed onlookers from crushing himself, Jyn, and Warren. As Dantess searched for a clear exit from the pandemonium, one man, wearing a black scarf around his head that covered his face, wasn't trying to run. He pushed past them and, while everyone was distracted, pulled himself up on stage.

Why don't the guards stop him? wondered Dantess, before the nearby soldier from last night slumped over, an arrow protruding through her neck.

Screams—not of fear, but pain—came from those seated in the stands. A black-scarved mob carrying knives, sticks, and pitchforks charged the priests. Some already lay bleeding in their seats. Others struggled for their lives, attempting to avoid or push away the improvised weapons, but it was clear that the priests were not used to protecting themselves.

Even Kevik seemed overwhelmed. With an arrow lodged in his shoulder, he ducked under the swing of a farmer's scythe and blocked two other attacks from masked men with his bracers, their metal blades striking sparks where they landed.

"This... this is an attack," Dantess yelled to Jyn. "We have to get out of here before we get hurt!"

The black-masked man who pulled himself on stage ignored the approaching fire, jumped onto the dais, and bellowed over the clamor, "We are the Harbingers of Chaos! We bring death to every priest who would enslave the faithless! We bring destruction to every temple that would steal your mothers and fathers and children! We bring freedom from the gods of Order! Join us!" He withdrew a knife from inside his jacket, moved to the line of debtors, and began to saw at the thick rope.

"Look!" Jyn said, pointing on stage. "Maybe this is our chance to free Mama!"

"This won't end well," said Dantess. "Anyone breaking the law *will* get caught." *Or worse,* he thought, remembering his father's words.

As if on cue, before the man could make any real progress, a spear plunged through his chest.

Jyn gasped. "They're still tied together. They're stuck on that stage. They'll *burn!*" She turned to the stage and called, "Mama! I'll help you!"

Dantess grabbed Jyn's arm. "If you help her, they'll think you're one of these terrorists. They'll *kill* you."

"*Someone* has to help them. *No one else* is!" She pointed to the soldiers fighting with black-masked attackers on the ground. "War's priority is to save the priests, not *debtors*. Truth? I'm not leaving without her." Jyn forced her way past a well-dressed merchant, a washerwoman, and three teens who were too enthralled with the spectacle to move. Barely avoiding the flames, she pulled herself up on stage.

Dantess and Warren watched, dumbfounded as Jyn picked up the knife and, like the dead masked man before her, began sawing into the rope.

Before she could cut through, the stage exploded. Flames whipped around the stage's edge and climbed high, smoke billowing into the sky. Even if she could free those people, getting them off the stage unhurt would be difficult.

"Jyn!" Dantess shouted as she covered her mouth and coughed. She shook her head and worked the knife into the rope further.

A nearby soldier ran his sword through a black-scarved fighter. While he tried to extract the blade, he dropped to his knees, breathing hard. Dantess approached him cautiously, hands raised. "Why are you sitting there? You have to save those people trapped on the stage. The fire will kill them."

"Can't," the soldier wheezed, pulling at his sword. "My orders are to deal with the terrorists. Besides, they're probably in league with them. If they stay up there, the problem will solve itself."

Dantess blinked.

"Mama and Jyn are up there!" blurted out Warren.

"Yes," said Dantess, leading Warren away from the guard. "The soldiers aren't going to help."

"*We* have to do something then!" Before Dantess could respond, Warren blurted, "I've got an idea." The young boy bolted away through the crowd toward the stage.

"Warren!" Dantess hissed air between his teeth. "Get back here!" He swore and shoved his way after him, but Warren had a much easier time slipping through the crowd than he did.

People were frantic. Between the fire and pockets of combat, no one seemed to know where to run. Others lashed out. Worried for both Warren and himself, Dantess felt the need to arm himself. He paused at the dead soldier with the arrow in her neck and—after a moment's hesitation—took her sword. Just in case.

When Warren reached the stage, instead of climbing up on it like Jyn—something he wasn't tall enough to do anyway—he dove underneath. Dantess followed Warren by squeezing between two beams suspending the stage.

For a moment, everything was cool, dark, and calm—a moment's respite from the chaos in the square. Then Dantess spotted Warren jumping up and down, reaching up toward the underside of the stage.

"Help me! I'm not tall enough!"

"What are you doing?" asked Dantess, exasperated.

"The door. I can't reach it."

"A door?" He looked up and saw, indeed, a trap door. "The gallows! That trap door opens to the dais." One problem: this wasn't a typical trap door with a simple latch. Instead, a wooden drawbar controlled by the lever above kept the door from swinging down. The bar threaded through two brackets until it reached the lever, where a pin attached them together.

Dantess reached up and tried to push the drawbar back with sheer force, but it didn't budge. It was clear that, without the lever in place and someone pulling that lever from above, the drawbar wouldn't budge.

"Open it! Open it!" said Warren.

"I'm trying." Dantess tried hacking at the bar with his sword. Wood chips flew everywhere, but his effort only marked the bar. It was too thick for him to cut through in any reasonable amount of time.

Despite being under the fire, smoke and heat began to fill the space under the stage. Dantess wiped the sweat from his eyes and shifted his attack to one of the two brackets that held the bar in place. The wood was smaller and thinner than the bar and—if he was right—the brackets were the only things holding it up.

He chopped at the first bracket. With each strike, chunks of wood flew. After the fourth hit, just when his arms were about to quit, the bracket broke. The bar dropped about an inch, held up solely by the second bracket.

"You're doing it! Don't stop now!" yelled Warren, between coughs.

Dantess took a deep breath, summoned what strength he had left, and began to chop away at the remaining bracket. Chips shed everywhere.

While Dantess used his sword like an ax, Warren stood under the trap door. He cupped his hand around his mouth and called up through the inch of space, "Jyn! Jyn! We're here!"

"You'd better move out of the way," said Dantess. Warren backed off and, after one more strike, the bracket exploded into pieces. The drawbar swung down, pivoting on the pin attached to the lever.

Without the drawbar holding it up, the trap door fell open with a crash. Dantess walked under it to find Jyn's astonished face looking down from the stage.

"Jyn!" said Dantess. "Get everyone down through here! Quickly. I'll help!"

Soon, Siriana's legs poked down through the hole. Just as Dantess grabbed her and lowered her to the ground, more people began to climb down. Dantess lost count of the number of people who he caught or who dropped to the ground on their own, but he guessed it was most of those above.

Panting, Jyn landed next to him. "A soldier saw us. He's trying to stop us. Right behind me!"

Dantess tried to push the same hinged trap door he just released back into place. He groaned. "Tell everyone to scatter. Get them away from the fire. There are lots of ways out from under here."

A burly arm slammed into the door and held it slightly open.

He braced himself and pushed on the door, using all his strength to keep it from flying open. "Jyn, go! Take Warren and your mother to my da's shop. I'll meet you there."

Jyn nodded. She grabbed her mother's hand and ran, with Warren following behind.

Somehow, Dantess hadn't anticipated that the soldier would just jump on the trap door. All of the man's weight came crashing down on him, and the door's wooden edge slammed into Dantess' head.

Everything went dark.

Dantess awoke, flat on his back in the square. The smell of burning wood hung so heavy it almost choked him, but the fire appeared to be out. Kevik stood over him while a young woman wrapped the priest's shoulder in a bandage.

"Wherever there's trouble, there's you," the priest of War stated.

Dantess shook his head, still woozy. "Not my fault. Trouble keeps finding me."

The square showed the grisly remains of a battle. At least three buildings were gutted and smoldering from the extinguished fire, and most of the stage was gone. Soldiers of War were dumping black-scarved bodies into a waist-high pile in the center.

Dantess fought the urge to vomit. "Oh no. What happened? Why are they all dead?"

"Friends of yours?" Kevik's eyebrow rose.

"You think I had something to do with this? War help me, I don't know these people. I don't even know what they were trying to do."

"That's obvious: these terrorists were trying to kill priests. And they killed two—*on my watch!*" Kevik stepped forward and loomed over Dantess. "Where are the ones who escaped?"

"There are more?"

"Assuredly. And if I let even one free today, they'll multiply like roaches. I've also got some escaped debtors to track down because of you. Come on, Dantess. You're not a bad kid. It's not too late for you to be on the right side of this. Tell me where they went."

Of course, he knows what I did, thought Dantess. *The soldier that jumped on my head must have told him. How much trouble am I in?*

"I have no idea," said Dantess, coughing. "You have to believe me: I was just trying to save people from burning to death." Even the idea of crossing a priest of War made his insides ache, but he couldn't betray Jyn and Warren. "How would I know where anyone went from here? I was unconscious, remember?"

Kevik tilted his head. "I've got an idea: let's look together. You know this town pretty well, right? I'm sure you can sniff out a few black-scarved, priest-hating cultists. Let's go."

Kevik pulled Dantess up from the ground. Four soldiers of War fell in behind them as they walked out of the main square.

Dantess' stomach knotted. On one hand, he couldn't help but be excited about assisting a priest of War with a mission to capture cultists. On the other hand, that same priest wanted to recapture Jyn's mother.

What am I going to do? he wondered.

○

"I'm not sure where you want me to take you. Everywhere I suggest, you disagree. The town is not that big. I'm going to run out of places to try," said Dantess.

"There's one place I want to look first," answered Kevik. "This way."

They walked purposefully down alleys and streets until they reached the market street close to his da's store. Given that it was market day, haphazardly placed carts and rickety booths made passage difficult—but the usual crowds were absent. Almost no one was shopping.

"Isn't that your da's store? Just up here?" He looked over his shoulder at one of the soldiers tailing them. "That looks like a good place to start our search."

At that moment, Dantess knew Kevik was playing him for a fool. He'd told Jyn to get the debtors to his da's store. The soldier atop the trapdoor must have overheard this and relayed it to Kevik.

As they neared the storefront, Dantess caught a glimpse of Jyn, hiding behind a cart. Relieved that she was well and free, he shook his head ever so slightly and ignored her, hoping she would be smart enough to avoid the store and the attention of this war party.

Kevik approached Tolliver and Son's General Supply store. After motioning for two of his soldiers to stay outside and watch any other exits, he kicked the door open.

Behind his counter, Tolliver startled but quickly composed himself. "Good day, priest of War. I'm glad you came. With the violence in the square today, everyone's on edge. But now that you're here, I feel much safer." Tolliver waved his hands at the shelves stacked with goods and barrels filled with fruit and nuts. "Looking for something in particular? Or are you dropping off my son?"

41

"So, you know what happened in the square." Kevik wandered toward the counter, idly picking up objects from the shelves and setting them back down. "Who told you?"

"My customers. It's all anyone can talk about."

"Customers?" Kevik raised his hands and looked around the empty store. "I don't see anyone."

"Ah. True. They left. What can I do for you, priest of War?"

"I won't intrude on your *busy* day more than necessary. We're searching for the cultists and the escaped debtors. Any idea where they may have gone?"

"None." Tolliver wiped his brow. "But if I see anything, I'll report it immediately."

"If you don't mind, we'll look around. We have to be thorough. You understand."

"Of course. As you can see, there aren't many places to hide here. Unless they're in the apple barrel." He flashed the famous Tolliver grin.

"Ah. I have to follow every lead." Kevik walked to the barrel and tipped it over. Apples spilled everywhere. "Nope. Not a bad apple among them." Kevik waved his hand at his two soldiers who began to tear the store apart, upending boxes and sacks and pushing shelves over.

"Please, you don't have to do that. There's nothing here to find!" pleaded Tolliver.

"Then tell me where to look!" Kevik roared. "I know at least one of the fugitives came here. If they aren't here now, you know where they went!"

Another shelf crashed to the ground in splinters. A soldier emptied a bag of grain all over the wooden floor.

"I don't! I swear! They never came here. Please stop destroying my store! Remember who my father was. I still have friends in the temple!"

Dantess gasped, but covered his mouth. Tolliver never invoked his grandfather, especially to a priest of War. His da must have been desperate.

But why is he so worried? wondered Dantess. *There's no one here.*

Tolliver's threat must have made an impact, because Kevik placed his hands on the counter, leaned forward, and stared into Tolliver's eyes while the carnage continued. "Still trading on your

42

father's name? How long will that work? It's amazing anyone even remembers him. I think the temple needs a new hero."

"You?"

"Could be. After I capture these cultists, maybe." Kevik smiled and leaned back. "This isn't over." He turned around and walked toward the door. "I'm taking your boy, Dantess. Remember he's with me while you're thinking about where those cultists might be."

Dantess was in the midst of exhaling his full lungs in relief when one of the soldiers called out, "Wait!" Kevik spun around to see the man holding a dark bit of fabric. "It's a black scarf." He hissed, "There's blood on it."

The priest of War ran back inside, threw the counter aside, and grabbed Tolliver by his shirt. "You lying piece of faithless trash. They were *here!* Where are they now? Tell me!"

Dantess locked eyes with his father. His expression asked, *What did you do, Da?*

Tolliver clamped his mouth shut, but just for a moment, his eyes flicked to look at the worn mat on the floor.

"Don't hurt my da!" yelled Dantess. He jerked forward, intending to pull Tolliver from danger, but one of the burly soldiers held him back. It didn't require much effort.

"He knows something," Kevik growled. "And he's going to tell me. Even if he needs a new mouth to do it." With Tolliver secure in one hand, Kevik drew out his dagger with the other. Tolliver's eyes opened wide.

We are expendable. His father's words echoed in Dantess' head. He knew what Kevik was capable of. He could still see the dagger split open the skull of a faithless bandit in his mind. Dantess wanted so badly to stay quiet, but he knew without a doubt that Kevik was about to kill his da.

"Wait!" cried Dantess.

Kevik held his dagger inches from Tolliver's throat. "What? You have something to say?"

"No, son," said Tolliver. "Don't get involved." Dantess had never heard such steel in his father's voice.

When Dantess paused, Kevik dragged his knife along Tolliver's neck. The tip left a trail of red, and drips of blood dotted the floor. His da's eyes betrayed his pain, but his expression told the whole story. He was willing to die if it meant saving others.

"Forget about this trash, boy. He's hiding *terrorists*," said Kevik through clenched teeth. "Do you want to serve War someday? Like your grandfather? If you know where those murdering bastards are, it's your *duty* to tell me."

Dantess' face grimaced in anguish. Tears rans down his cheeks. He loved Jyn and Warren, and he knew what betraying their mother would mean, but...

This was his father.

"You'll spare him?" asked Dantess. Kevik's expression was conflicted, but he nodded nonetheless.

Da, I can't let you die. I'm not that strong. I need you.

"There's one more place you can look. I'll tell you. Just leave my father alone. Like you promised."

Kevik smiled, but kept his dagger pressed to Tolliver's throat. "Where?"

Dantess shook himself free of the soldier holding him, walked to the mat, and picked up a corner.

Tolliver closed his eyes and groaned.

Silently weeping, Dantess flipped the rug up to reveal the trap door beneath. The soldier shoved Dantess out of the way, knelt down, and threw the trapdoor open.

The cold storage was packed with people, including Jyn's mother. Their eyes were filled with fear.

"No!" Tolliver thrashed, but Kevik held him like a vice.

"These people can't resist going down a trap door, it seems. Good work, boy." Kevik laughed. "I knew you could come down on the right side of this. You just needed a little motivation." He pointed at the huddled people and motioned to his squad. "Get them out of there."

As the soldiers started to pull the people up from the cold storage, Kevik hauled Tolliver toward the exit by his shirt.

"You said you'd spare him," demanded Dantess.

With a bemused expression, Kevik stopped and turned Tolliver to look at him. "He's still breathing, isn't he? But even Varyon's son has to answer for what he's done."

As Kevik dragged Tolliver away, his da asked simply, "Why?"

Dantess saw the hurt in his father's eyes. He didn't realize it was possible to feel worse than he already did, but guilt struck Dantess like a hammer to the chest.

"Da, I..." he started, but Kevik had already taken his father out the door.

CHAPTER FIVE

"HOW COULD YOU do that to my *mother*?" Jyn punched Dantess in his chest. "To your *own father*?" She hit him again. "You want to be a priest of War so damned bad you're doing their dirty work for them?"

"I'm sorry," said Dantess, looking down at the dirt road outside his father's store. The soldiers kept him inside until now, perhaps to keep him from interfering with their handling of the prisoners. By the time he emerged, most everyone was gone—except for Jyn and Warren. They were happy to see him at first, until he explained what happened.

"You're *sorry*?" She shoved Dantess with all her strength, and he fell onto the packed dirt. "You told me to bring my mother here! Did you know she would be captured? Was that your plan?"

"No! Of course not. Kevik was going to kill Da!"

Jyn crossed her arms. "Didn't you say priests don't kill faithless on a whim?"

"You didn't see the look in Kevik's eyes. He was going to do it, and my da wouldn't say anything to stop it. I couldn't let him die!" Dantess sniffed, trying to keep from crying.

Jyn shook her head, anger in her eyes. "You don't know what Kevik would have done. Maybe Tolliver had a plan. He knows the temple better than you. You were scared. You panicked, and now both your father and my mother are gone."

Warren took his sister's hand and looked up at her. "What do we do now?"

"We get on a horse, and we go to War." Jyn began to walk away with Warren in tow. "Somehow, we have to get our mother back."

Dantess climbed to his feet. "They're at War's temple? My da too?"

Jyn stopped in her tracks and spun around. "All of them. I saw them load everyone in carts while you were inside. The priests are going to interrogate them to find out about those deranged Harbingers of Chaos. You know what that means." Tears trickled down her tanned face. She wiped them away and stared daggers at Dantess, clearly blaming him for making her cry. "If she'd been sold at the auction, she'd be a slave at some temple right now—but at least she'd be safe. Now they think she's one of those cultists. They'll torture her and send her to Evil's dungeons."

"You're right," Dantess said, lifting his gaze from the ground. "And they'll do the same to my da. I'm coming with you."

She held up her palm and her glare kept him at a distance. "Stay away from us. I don't trust you anymore." With that, she pulled Warren away.

"Jyn, please," Dantess called after her. He'd never seen her so angry, and being the cause made his heart ache. "You're my best friend. I can help. I *need* to help."

But Jyn didn't turn around. She entered an alley between two buildings and disappeared from sight.

There was no way Dantess was staying behind, even if Jyn wanted nothing to do with him. He saddled up his da's cart horse and left as soon as he could. It wasn't lost on him that this trip was probably the last thing his da would want him to do.

Riding on the road to the temple of War for hours, Dantess may not have seen Jyn or Warren, but he wasn't alone. He passed other travelers, undoubtedly headed to War for testing day. Those who truly felt the Longing always found their way to War's Gift at the temple. The test was their final obstacle to becoming a priest of War.

A girl and two boys, dressed in well-worn outfits, trudged in the middle of the road. They were so engaged in their conversation, they didn't react to his approach. To Dantess, they looked excited enough to be heading to a party.

Dantess called down, "Rider behind you."

Amiably, they wandered to the road side and waved to him. Dantess slowed and asked, "You all going to War to be tested?"

"Yep." The girl put her hand on the shoulder of the boy next to her. "I'm Locke. He's Motti. And that's Karlo. We made the decision today after the attack at the square. War saved us all from those black-masked bastards."

"Do any of you feel the Longing?"

"Maybe," said Karlo. "We're not sure what it's supposed to feel like."

Motti piped up, "Yeah, I hope I pass, but even if I have to be a soldier, it'll still be fine—as long as I get to fight like that priest did. Did you see him kill those cultists in the square?" He punched and kicked the air.

"You might become a soldier? Does that mean you aren't paying for the test?" asked Dantess.

Locke laughed and rubbed dust from her short-cropped hair. "Do we look like we have the gold for that? Nope. Our fates are in the hands of the god of War."

Dantess nodded. War did not turn away applicants if they couldn't pay. If they succeeded, the fee was forgiven. If they failed, they became bound to the temple, as if it had purchased their debt. To any faithless who liked the idea of combat, the idea of becoming bound to War was attractive enough to test regardless of what the outcome would be. Some even did it when debt was about to force them to the auction so that they could choose which temple would take them instead.

"Good luck to all of you." Dantess waved and spurred his horse on. He needed to get to the temple before War could do anything to his father.

"See you there!" called Locke, waving. To Motti, she asked, "Hey, why didn't *we* get a horse?"

Dantess hurried his horse as much as he could without exhausting it, but still hours passed before he spotted the mountain temple peeking through the trees. Finally, he was near to his goal.

As before, he felt anxious to arrive, but it was mixed with a good dose of trepidation. How would the priests treat him? Would they let him see his father? Could he figure out a way to get the temple to release him?

Once across the barren field, Dantess hitched his horse outside and joined the people filtering into the gatehouse. He knew that the small crowd inside expected to test. Based on the garb worn, like woolen coats intended for a colder climate, many came from faraway places, likely having traveled for weeks. Those with true Longings could ignore the pull for a while, but the compulsion grew with time. Sooner or later, they would have to come—and the closer they approached the Gift, the stronger the Longing became. The only way to mitigate the Longing was by holding a magic artifact blessed by the god, which was only available at the god's temple.

But while some were drawn here, many others wanted to try their luck. Since no one knew if or when their Longing would make itself known, they hoped the test would reveal it, even if they hadn't felt it before.

Despite the urgency of his mission, he couldn't help but reflect on how much he dreamt of being one of these petitioners and, one way or another, joining the ranks of War. Even so, he could imagine the heat of his father's anger just for coming back to the temple, much less during a testing, but he had no choice. He gritted his teeth and walked inside.

After pushing his way through the crowd, searching for his friends, he finally spotted Jyn and Warren at the back. He rushed to meet them.

"Jyn. Warren. I'm so glad to find you."

"Leave us alone. We don't need your help," responded Jyn. It seemed time hadn't softened her feelings toward Dantess.

"Are you sure? Some people here still remember my grandfather. One of them might help me get inside. Or if not, at least get our parents a message."

Jyn crossed her arms. "You have a plan? Fine. Go ahead then. I'll watch."

Maybe she didn't believe he could do anything, but Dantess took her reaction as a good sign. Perhaps it was an opening, the first step toward earning her forgiveness. A few priests of War passed through the crowd holding wooden boards. He approached the nearest one, a priestess with a number of black tattoos on her arms. "Can you help me? My father is inside the temple."

The priestess looked confused. "Inside the temple?"

Kevik approached from behind the guard, a stern look settled across his strong features. "I'll deal with young Dantess here. I know him." Once the priestess nodded and wandered off, he continued, "So, what do you want?"

Dantess groaned to himself. He didn't expect much help from the man who took his father in the first place. "You brought my father and my friends' mother here to the temple. I need to see them."

Kevik shrugged. "Pretty busy day today, what with the testing and all. Come back tomorrow and I'll see what I can do."

Dantess caught a glimpse of Jyn staring at him, arms crossed. He couldn't let Kevik brush him off. "This can't wait. You have to let me speak to them before..."

Kevik laughed. "All right, I won't make you wait. I'll tell you my answer now. Unless you're a priest or bound to the temple, you're not getting in. There are rules. You know that. You'd better get going back to Freethorn. But keep an eye out for bandits."

As Kevik began to turn away, Dantess grabbed Kevik's arm. "Please, Kevik. Have mercy. I didn't even get to say goodbye."

Kevik snarled and pulled his arm out of Dantess' grip. He was about to respond, but stopped himself. Instead, he smiled. "All right."

"What?"

"There's one way I can let you in. You already know it." Kevik held out the board. At the top were the words, *I declare my intent to test at the temple of War. After testing, I will settle accounts with the temple.* Below were carved squares containing the exposed points of small metal nails. About half of those squares were red with blood. "If you test, I'll do everything I can to get you in to see your father."

For a moment, Dantess stood without saying anything. *Test? Me? Could I really?*

But aloud, he said, "Test? I can't. I don't feel the Longing."

"Neither do most of those here." Kevik waved his hand at the group of other applicants. "You've wanted to be a part of War's temple all your life. It's in your blood. Your father didn't have it, but your grandfather did, and maybe you do too. Join up, even if it's just as a soldier. You can't help him from out here."

Dantess paused, conflicted. *Da will be furious if I agree,* Dantess thought. *But he's locked away, and this might be the only way to reach him. Maybe I have no choice.*

He looked back at Jyn. Her face showed shock. "Are you seriously considering this? After they took our parents, you're going to join them?"

"There's no other way in. Do you want to wait out here while they're tortured inside?"

"Do it," said Warren. "You have to get to Mama." Both Jyn and Dantess were surprised at the words.

"But..." Jyn began.

50

Dantess winced, thinking of his father once more. Tolliver was the biggest reason not to test, but also the reason Dantess *had* to. He nodded. "I agree. What do I do?"

Kevik smiled and held out the board. "Put your thumb onto the first open square. This binds your intention in blood. If you renege after this, it will be treated as a failure."

Dantess looked at both Warren and Jyn. Jyn closed her eyes and shook her head, but there was a ferocity in Warren's stare—something he'd never seen in him before. Dantess pressed his thumb to an open square. A sharp pain told him that the pin pricked his skin. Blood flowed onto the wooden surface.

"Done! Stand over there with the other applicants," said Kevik, snatching the board back. "We're going to have some fun here, you and I."

It hadn't sunk in yet, but Dantess knew that moment had changed his life forever. He prayed he did the right thing.

Somewhat stunned, he began to walk to the group of initiates. Jyn watched him leave, and then took Warren's hand. As they began to back away from the crowd, Kevik moved to block them.

"You two, you're the children of one of the debtors we brought in? The woman from Dantess' store?"

"That's right," said Jyn.

Kevik grabbed Jyn by the arm. "You're not going anywhere."

"What do you mean?" said Jyn, shocked and worried.

"The moment your mother escaped, her debt became outstanding. As a fugitive, she has no value, so that debt is passed to her eldest child. To *you*. Knowing how slippery your family is, I think we'll hold you here until the next auction." He motioned for his soldiers to come take her.

"What? No. You can't do this!" Two soldiers grabbed her by the arms. "What will happen to Warren?"

"Not your concern," Kevik responded.

Dantess stepped forward, but a soldier shoved him into the applicants' area. "Jyn!"

Warren reached for Jyn, but Kevik stopped him with one hand. Then, when Jyn was safely on the other side of the gatehouse—out of earshot—he knelt down to speak directly with the boy. "Warren, is it?"

Warren nodded.

"Your family is in trouble. First your mother goes into debt. Then she tries to escape. That was a foolish thing to do. It put your sister in debt and left you alone. That doesn't seem fair, does it?"

Warren shook his head. To his credit, he stayed stone-faced and silent.

"How would you like to save your sister?"

Warren looked up at Kevik with wide, glistening eyes. "How?"

"There's more than one way to pay your mother's debt. Sure, we could auction off your sister, but I'm going to give you the chance to be a man. You, young Warren, could save her right now. All you have to do is test."

"Test? Me?"

"What are you doing?" Dantess raised his voice.

Kevik threw a look back at Dantess. "Keep him quiet." A soldier put his hand on Dantess' shoulder and a finger to his own lips.

"You are the man of your family. It's your duty to protect them. I'm giving you the opportunity to do that. If you test, I'll let your sister go. The debt will be paid."

Even though she couldn't hear what was being said, Jyn saw the exchange. She struggled against her guards. "Let me go!"

Warren winced, watching Jyn fight. Tentatively, he nodded and reached his thumb out toward the board.

"You're doing the right thing, Warren."

The boy pressed his thumb down on an open square, yelped in pain, and pulled his hand back, leaving a red dot on the thirsty wood.

"It's done. Stand over there." Kevik gestured to the group of committed faithless surrounding Dantess. He looked at the board, chuckled, and commented to another nearby priest. "I can mold a boy this young into anything. I've seen other priests get the most ruthless killers on their squads when they start with boys no younger than him."

Confused and scared, Warren ran over to Dantess. Dantess knelt down and hugged him.

"Let her go," said Kevik to the soldiers. "Her brother paid the debt."

Enraged, Jyn ran at Kevik and launched her fist toward him. Kevik sidestepped the attack, grabbed her arm, and rolled her over his hip. She fell hard on the ground.

"Remember, girl: I'm a priest of War. Try that again and I won't be so forgiving," said Kevik. "You'd better leave while you can."

Jyn pulled herself up and spit on the dirt ground. "You tricked my brother into testing. He didn't know what he was doing. Take me instead. I'll test."

Kevik dusted off his breastplate. "It doesn't work that way."

"I can't leave him here alone at War. I *know* what you'll do with him. You have to take me!"

"Why would I want *you?* You're just a headstrong girl—it would take more effort to break you than it's worth—but your brother is malleable. Besides, his intention is bound in blood. He *will* test. Those are the rules."

"Jyn, I'm here," said Dantess. "I'll take care of him."

"Like you took care of my mother? No. *I'll* take care of him. Like I always do." Jyn grabbed Kevik's board and pressed her thumb onto an empty square.

"I guess we'll take you after all," Kevik said. "But you'd better damn well hope you don't end up on my squad." He retrieved the board and waved toward Dantess and Warren. "Stand over there."

Jyn stormed over to Warren, grabbed his hand, and turned away from Dantess.

Dantess sighed and sat down on the hard dirt ground.

This had already been a long day, and it was just getting started.

CHAPTER SIX

THE THREE SAT on the ground for over an hour while other hopefuls filed in. In all, about fourteen people sat with them—a mix of young and old, but mostly teens—all committed to testing.

Jyn and Warren only spoke to each other. They avoided even glancing toward Dantess, even though he looked at no one else. "Hey! It's you from the road," exclaimed Locke, sitting down right next to him. The girl pointed to Jyn and Warren. "Are those friends of yours?" When Dantess nodded, Locke asked, "Mad at you or something?"

"They blame me for being here."

"Blame you? But this is the beginning of a whole new life! If you brought them, they should be thanking you."

Dantess looked up at the girl's dirty but smiling face. A smattering of freckles covered high cheeks, and her green eyes glistened with excitement.

"You're pretty happy to be here," remarked Dantess. "Don't you have parents or loved ones that will miss you?"

"Parents aren't part of my story anymore. Now, these boys are my family." She punched Motti in the shoulder, who screwed up his face and grabbed his upper arm, as if it were the most painful injury he could imagine. Locke chuckled. "Been together for years. We stick fast through everything."

"You might get separated, you know. If you fail. You could go on different squads. And that's if you're lucky. If no one drafts you, you'll end up pulling up weeds from the open field outside. Or cleaning latrines."

"What?" Motti interjected. His long, dark fingers scratched his thin black beard. "You mean we might not fight?"

Interested in Dantess' answer, many of the others in the group looked over at him. Even Jyn and Warren spared a glance.

"Just do well in the combat portion. Even if you don't pass the test, if you catch the eye of a priest and they have space on their squad, they'll ask for you."

"Good to know," said Motti, nodding.

"Hey." Karlo poked Dantess in the shoulder. "How do you know so much about the testing?"

"My grandfather was a priest here, so I was curious. I asked questions of every priest and soldier who would talk with me."

An older man, lean and slightly graying at his temples, bent closer. He kept his voice quiet. "Every temple has a final challenge, the important one. Do you know what War's final test is? I haven't heard anything."

"No," admitted Dantess. He'd often wondered the same thing and was intensely curious. "They're not allowed to tell faithless about it. Not until we've committed. I guess we'll learn all about it soon."

Once the last of the spectators—the faithless who decided not to commit—were escorted out of the gatehouse, Kevik stood in front of the remaining group. "Congratulations." He held up his board. "You have all committed to testing at War's temple. This board may hold the first blood you spill here, but it will not be the last."

Another priest began to hand out leather straps with an ornate golden clasp threaded onto it. The clasp was embellished with the symbol of War: an intricately-inscribed shield.

Kevik held one of the clasps high. "You are being given War's token. This is our badge. If you are experiencing any difficulty resisting the Longing, this will help. You can wear it anywhere on your body. Personally, I wear mine here." Kevik pointed to his waist, where they all saw his clasp attached to a thick, well-cured, and high-grade leather belt. "A priest wears this *always*. My first tip to you: secure it well. You do not want this falling off, especially in combat."

The candidates began to fumble with the straps. Most followed Kevik's example and wore the straps as belts. Some attached them to their upper arms or legs. Once the straps were in place, the faithless leaning against the inner gate let out audible breaths, as if the clasps gave them relief. It was a strong sign that those people felt the Longing.

Dantess wrapped the strap around his waist. When he completed the loop, his heartbeat slowed. Some of the nervousness he'd been carrying in his shoulders loosened. This wasn't relief of the Longing being put at bay, but the clasp felt right. Natural. And he knew, until the moment he was forced to remove it, hope remained that he could be a priest.

Jyn sat still, staring at both her and Warren's straps in her hands.

"Can I help?" asked Dantess.

She shook her head and then placed hers as a headband with the badge on her forehead. The excess leather fell behind her like a ponytail. Dantess could see how the strap would also keep her long hair from her eyes. Afterward, she wrapped Warren's strap over one shoulder and under his opposite arm. Given Warren's small size, it was the most secure way to attach it.

"Finish up and get into a single file line," called out Kevik. "We're entering the temple."

The applicants shuffled into a line facing the exit. One of the priests pulled away a thick wooden bar and pushed open the massive door, revealing a drawbridge spanning a dark, waterless moat. On the other side, there were two obvious paths: the winding road that spiraled up around the plateau and a tunnel that led into its heart.

The priest led the line of faithless across the bridge and into the tunnel. Dantess was glad they weren't walking up the road. It must have stretched for many miles to encircle the entire plateau and would likely require hours if not days to climb.

The sunlight fell away as they entered, but the tunnel was lit by candles placed on small inset shelves on alternating sides of the hall. Holes in the wall opposite the candles opened to parallel corridors, and guards in those corridors were armed with spears and bows. If an enemy used this approach, the guards would see the moment someone passed in front of a candle, and a well-placed spearpoint or arrow would stop the invader.

No spears poked out from the holes in the wall this trip, though—and soon they approached a dark chamber with no exit. The priests crowded everyone inside. Strangely, the floor was constructed of wood, not stone. A voice called out from the darkness, "Brace yourselves."

The whole room lurched into motion. A few people lost their balance and dropped to the floor as the room rose up, first slowly, then with more and more speed. After a few moments, Dantess heard a rumble coming from the walls and noticed large grooves cut into the stone there. The sound grew in volume until counterweights, attached to thick ropes, sped downward in the grooves.

A distant dot of light above them grew with every passing moment. It wasn't long until they reached the opening and the platform beneath their feet slowed to a halt.

Now that the walls had fallen away, they found themselves in an expansive courtyard. Dual fountains flanked their platform, each depicting an identical god of War. Further in, the temple's architecture rose in tiers. Nearby, stands were filled with both priests and bound faithless. All eyes were trained on Dantess and the other applicants. Behind those, high walkways supported by sweeping arches surrounded the courtyard. Spectators also crowded the rails on the walkways, behind which were layers of terraces, arches, and eventually towers and ramparts. Every element was clearly functional, but the artful combination was undeniably beautiful.

There was one other element that dominated the view and mystified Dantess: a huge wooden step pyramid in the center of the courtyard, perhaps a hundred feet across. Its panels were decorated with carved and painted depictions of glorious battles. As a piece of art, and even history, the pyramid was undeniably impressive, flawlessly constructed, and beautifully decorated, but... why? For the space it occupied, Dantess could not divine its purpose, and War was defined by purpose.

Dantess blinked. Despite what brought him here, he realized he had reached his goal. He finally stood within the temple of War. His grandfather walked this ground. Tested here. Trained here. Fought here.

A priest with a wide nose and strong chin emerged through a nearby arch with a few others following closely behind. His ornately-engraved breastplate gleamed like purest gold, which contrasted with his dark skin—although not quite dark enough to hide the intricate black thorn tattoos that flowed across his muscled arms. He wore a bejeweled headpiece that appeared more crown than helmet, but what was most noteworthy was his presence. This man commanded attention and respect just by stepping into the yard. He would have done so even without his gleaming gear.

"Welcome to our temple, young hopefuls." The priest's deep voice echoed off the stone in the courtyard in such a way that everyone heard each word loudly and clearly. "I am Morghaust, High Priest of War. I see you are all wearing your tokens. Does that mean you are ready for the testing to commence?"

Dantess nodded, as did most of the other candidates.

"Then let us begin!" He raised his hands and the crowd cheered. He let the sound fill the courtyard, then lowered his hands, and the crowd quieted as one.

"When the gods of Order created this world," Morghaust began, "it was perfect. But making it wasn't enough. One can spend a life building the highest tower only to have an enemy knock it down in an instant. When the gods looked out over what they created, they also saw the need to defend it.

"The god of War placed a portion of his essence into a Gift and sent that down into the world. It called the strongest, the bravest, the most skilled warriors to come here, to his temple.

"*We* are those warriors. We take up the mantle of defenders of the gods. Charged with our divine mission, we enforce their will. We protect what the gods have made against all who would steal or corrupt or destroy it. We are the world's mightiest force and *nothing* can stand against us."

Cheers rang out from the stands, joined by a few of the more excited applicants, like Motti and Karlo.

"Today, we welcome more warriors into our ranks." He waved his hands toward the group of faithless on the platform. "Do you want this honor?"

Most of the candidates cheered, although Dantess couldn't help but notice Jyn and Warren stayed silent.

"Desire is prized, but wanting to join our mission isn't enough. Are you strong?"

They cheered again.

"Strength is important, but still, it isn't enough. Are you brave?"

Once more, the group cheered—louder now that they knew it was expected.

Morghaust nodded. "We shall see. We shall *all* see." As the entire crowd cheered and whooped, he walked to a tall chair, swept his cape aside, and sat down.

Another priest stepped forward. He was quite a bit younger, but his burly arms were equally covered with the black marks. "I am Kaurridon, the high priest's Hand. It is time to test you all in combat. We will match you with each other in individual bouts."

Kaurridon looked over the line of hopefuls. He pointed to a young man Dantess didn't know. "You shall face off against..." The priest scanned the line again and pointed to Locke. "You. Choose a weapon from the rack and enter the circle."

Both teens sprang up and headed to a rack holding weapons of three types: staves, wooden practice swords, and pairs of thin, fighting sticks. Locke pulled out one of the staves, spun it around a bit, then smiled. Motti and Karlo nodded and waved. The boy grabbed a wooden sword and walked directly into the large white circle in the middle of the courtyard. Locke raced to follow.

"No killing," explained Kaurridon. "The match is over when one of you leaves the ring, surrenders, or is too injured to proceed. Respect yourselves and your opponent. Remember, it is not just *us* who watch. The god of War is watching." He floated his hand up and then jerked it down in a fist. "Begin!"

From the moment they first moved, it was clear neither had trained to fight. Locke swung her staff in large, easy-to-dodge arcs, but the boy failed to take advantage of Locke's recovery. After a particularly wide swing, the boy realized his opportunity. He stuck his sword out and poked Locke in the side. Locke flinched and the crowd cheered. This seemed to spur the boy on, so he pressed his attack, snaking the sword to strike Locke's other side.

Locke groaned and retreated, and the boy followed, refusing to lose the advantage. However, as soon as the boy took one step forward, Locke stuck the staff between the boy's legs and swiveled it. The boy tripped, landed on the ground, and dropped his sword. Locke pounced and rolled him until the boy's head poked outside the ring.

The crowd erupted in applause and cheers. "We have our first winner. Return to the others." Locke returned to cheers and hugs from her two friends. Dantess congratulated her as well. The other boy kicked the dirt at his feet and sat down on his own.

The courtyard fell silent as Kaurridon looked over the applicants. "You." He pointed to the older, graying man. "And you." With his other hand, he pointed to Motti.

Locke whispered to Motti, "Choose the staff. It's got a great reach."

"I don't know. He's old and I'm quick. I think I can win by tiring him out," said Motti.

The man walked to the rack and pulled out the fighting sticks. Motti studied those sticks, and then pulled out another pair. "Good luck, old man," he said. "I've been waiting for this chance for a long time, but I'll try not to hurt you too bad."

If the man heard the words, he didn't react. In fact, his eyes were distant, as if he were listening to a voice only he could hear.

They both walked over to the ring and took positions on either side.

Again, Kaurridon raised his hand, held it there for a moment, and brought it down. "Begin!"

The man's eyes lit up. He looked at the fighting sticks and then threw them away.

Motti was shocked. "Aren't you going to need those?"

"No," said the man, sounding a bit surprised himself. "I don't think so." He walked forward confidently.

By the time the boy held the sticks up in front of him defensively, the man was already upon him. In a blur of motion, the man grabbed Motti's wrists, twisted, and sent the sticks tumbling to the ground. But the motion didn't end there. He spun Motti around, pinned one arm behind him, and then kicked him in the back. Motti found himself stumbling out of the ring.

"What... what just happened?" Motti stammered.

The crowd roared its approval.

"Rejoin your group," instructed Kaurridon.

Motti shambled back to the group, still mystified, and the older man followed.

After Dantess consoled Motti, he sidled up to the winner and asked, "You fought well. Are you trained?"

"No," said the man, shaking his head. "I've never fought before in my life. But I just knew what to do. Like someone was telling me." He looked down at his hands. "And I moved fast. I never moved so fast before."

"Whatever you're doing, keep it up." Dantess patted him on the back, and the man smiled.

"Next match. You." The priest pointed at Dantess. "And you." He pointed at Jyn.

The blood drained from Dantess' face. He had been dreading this possibility. To Jyn, he said, "I can't fight you."

"Of course you can," said Jyn, firmly looking him in the eye for the first time since outside his da's shop. "Because *I* can fight *you*. And I can beat you. I've done it lots of times before."

"I don't want to do this. You're my best friend."

"Then surrender if you want. But if beating you gets me closer to seeing my mother, then that's what I'll do. That's why I'm

60

here." She walked over to the weapon rack and chose a wooden sword.

Dantess stood where he was. Deep in his heart, there was nothing he wanted more than to become a priest of War, but this was not how he fantasized that the test would go. He didn't want to be forced into it because his father and Jyn's mother had been taken prisoner by the same temple he dearly wanted to join, matched up against his best friend, and without ever feeling the Longing. Instead of this being a moment to celebrate, the anguish tied his insides into knots.

Karlo nudged him out of his thoughts. "You're up. You'd better get it together. That girl looks like she's out for blood."

Dantess smiled nervously and nodded. He twisted the ring on his finger and realized that his grandfather would never refuse to fight, no matter who he was matched against. Steeling himself, he walked over to the rack and also chose a practice sword—the weapon they both had the most experience with.

Both walked to the ring. Jyn swung her sword through the air a few times to determine its weight and balance. Dantess looked down at his own sword and sighed.

Kaurridon raised his hand, the crowd hushed, and then he brought it down. "Begin!"

Jyn did not hesitate. She lunged—a direct thrust to Dantess' chest.

Since they were sparring partners, Dantess was familiar with Jyn's fighting style. He knew exactly how to counter: an easy parry, followed by his own thrust. Of course, Jyn knew Dantess equally well. She blocked by swinging the tip of her blade around Dantess' sword and striking it away.

They circled each other.

"I'm sorry you're here," said Dantess.

"It was my choice," she responded, then took a wide swipe at Dantess' head.

He ducked and countered with his own swipe to her side, which she blocked by holding her blade perpendicular to his. "Just the same, I didn't want this for you. I didn't know you'd be taken for your mother's debt. I didn't know Warren would commit."

"Neither did I." She backed up a step, then rolled in front of him and untucked while striking his waist with her sword. The unexpected attack landed and sent Dantess stumbling backward, clutching his midsection while Jyn got to her feet.

61

The crowd cheered at the successful hit. Jyn didn't smile, but kept her eyes locked on Dantess. "I know it's not all your fault, but I'm going to do what I must to move forward. It'll be better for me, Warren, and my mother if I win."

Dantess groaned. That thrust hurt. He placed his hand on his bruised waist, the cold bite of the gold clasp reminding him of War's badge. All priests wore this token. Why? Did it do anything besides blunt the Longing? Did it help a priest fight somehow?

Jyn charged forward with a three-strike attack. Dantess parried and retreated, barely fending her off. He looked down and discovered his feet were inches from the white line of the ring.

Jyn saw it too. That was her plan: keep pushing Dantess until he stepped out. He tried escaping right and then left, but Jyn blocked those positions, trapping him exactly where he was.

Her eyes narrowed. She was about to attack, and he had no room to retreat.

In the sliver of time before Jyn's inevitable lunge, Dantess couldn't stop thinking about his badge. The Longing was the key to using artifacts. While he didn't experience the feeling that everyone described, he figured it wouldn't hurt to try. Just to see. He didn't have anything to lose.

The Longing was supposed to pull someone to War's Gift. If he had to guess, he'd say that the Gift was... inside the wooden pyramid?

That didn't seem right. Why would the Gift be there?

But if it were true, that meant his intuition wasn't just a guess. Upon reflection, he *did* feel a tiny draw there, like a tentative compass in his mind. Maybe it wasn't just wishful thinking.

Could he have the Longing? For real? But if so, why was it so weak?

Jyn lunged forward, ready to finish the match.

The attack triggered something. In an instant between moments, before her sword reached him, time stopped. Visions swam in his head.

In his mind, swords—not his own—attacked and countered. He saw each maneuver and every possible counter or block and every possible counter to that, like a game of Ka, branching out further and further until the final stone was placed to achieve victory.

As if trained by years of practice, his muscles moved on their own. His sword not only blocked the attack, but caught her weapon between his blade and hilt. A twist of his wrist sent Jyn's sword clattering onto the ground.

Her jaw dropped open, but Dantess wasn't done. With surprising speed, he reached out with his other hand, grabbed her shirt, and pulled her forward. He rolled back onto the ground, lifted her up with one leg, and tossed her over his head.

She landed with a dull thump. Outside the ring.

"We have a winner," cried Kaurridon. The crowd erupted in applause, whistles, and cheers. He looked at both children. "Go back to your group."

Dantess offered his hand to Jyn. She lay for a moment, staring at Dantess with an expression of pure shock, then used his hand to pull herself up. Both walked back to the group together.

"What happened out there?" Jyn asked. "You never fought like that before."

Dantess wanted to apologize, but he couldn't bring himself to feel too sorry about winning—and experiencing whatever just happened. "Somehow I saw what I was supposed to do. And I did it like I'd been trained for years."

Jyn's eyes widened even further. "Do you have it? The Longing?"

"I don't know. I can't really explain what happened without it." Inside, Dantess was *exploding*. The Longing! It *had* to be responsible. Why had he never felt it before? If he truly had it, this changed everything!

Karlo, Locke, and Motti shoved their way to Dantess and slapped his back in congratulations.

"You've got some skills," said Karlo.

Kaurridon pointed at Warren, cutting the celebrations short. "You." Then he pointed at a muscular brute of a boy. "And you."

Both Dantess and Jyn couldn't help but blurt out, "What?" The pairing was ridiculous. Warren was a slight, bookish young lad who never got into a fight in his life. The other boy looked like he picked fights on a daily basis. With bears. And won.

Warren's eyes fixed on the older boy who approached the weapons rack. Warren didn't blink. "He's so big," he whispered. "I can't do this."

Dantess whistled low. "It's not fair, but you must. You committed."

"I'm scared."

Jyn took his hand. "Fear is his biggest weapon, but you can't let *that* beat you. What is *your* biggest weapon?"

"I don't know."

"You're stronger than people know." She tapped his head. "Up here."

"How does that help?"

"Think of this as a war game, like you play with your toy soldiers. Come up with a plan." Jyn put both her hands on his shoulders. "He's not smarter than you, right?"

Warren cocked his head, the wheels in his brain turning. Then he nodded and began walking toward the weapons rack.

Dantess was impressed. Today, Warren was showing more backbone than he'd ever suspected the young boy had.

The older boy looked over the rack then swung his gaze to Warren. He laughed, threw up his hands, and entered the ring without choosing anything. "Who needs a weapon?" Some among the audience chuckled. "Come on, runt. Let's do this!"

Warren didn't hurry. Instead, he studied the weapons carefully, finally deciding on the staff. He lifted one from the rack, but had a hard time controlling its weight.

"The staff?" Jyn asked Dantess, gesturing to her brother. "It's taller than him! He can't lift it, much less fight with it. Maybe I was wrong."

Dantess shrugged, but was pleased Jyn was talking to him again. "Give him a chance."

Warren dragged the staff up to the ring and stopped. For a moment, he looked at the ground and panted.

"Already winded from dragging that staff?" said the brute. "Come on. Get in here. This is going to be fun!"

Warren stepped into the ring and dragged the staff over to where he was supposed to stand, leaving a track in the dirt. He tried to lift it into a defensive stance, but the staff kept tipping over.

The brute laughed.

Kaurridon lifted his palm and brought it down. "Begin!"

The older boy sprang at Warren and was upon him in three steps. With one hand, he grabbed the staff from the smaller boy's grasp and tossed it over his shoulder. Warren, dumbstruck, tried to back away, but the brute clasped both hands together in one fist, brought it up over his shoulder, and swung it like a hammer into the side of Warren's head. The impact knocked Warren off of his feet.

The brute raised his arms and took in the crowd's applause. He stepped over to Warren and kicked him in the side. Then kicked him again.

Clutching his head and doubled over, Warren groaned and coughed.

"Surrender, Warren!" Jyn called out, her face etched with worry. "He'll have to stop!"

Warren said nothing, but grabbed the dirt ground and pulled himself away from his opponent. It looked like he was trying to escape the ring by crawling out.

The brute laughed and loomed over Warren. "Not so fast. The show's not over yet!" He grabbed Warren by the back of his shirt, lifted him up, and spun him around. With a huge grin, the older boy cocked his fist back to strike.

Warren flung the dirt he had been holding into the brute's face.

The boy yelped in surprise, dropped Warren, and clutched at his eyes. Warren bolted through the older boy's legs in the direction of his discarded staff.

Blind, the older boy heard Warren scrambling for his weapon. He spun around, but Warren had already reached the staff. Again, he tried to wrestle it under control.

The brute roared in rage and charged.

Instead of using the staff to strike or defend, Warren shoved the far end into the dirt ground, lifted the other, and braced. Everyone could see that, if the brute kept running, he'd hit the end of the staff.

At first, the staff was aimed at the brute's chest, but the weight was too much for Warren to hold up that high. It slipped downward.

The boy slammed into the staff at top speed. The impact shattered the wood. He squealed and fell forward, holding his groin, and collapsed onto the hard dirt.

As one, the crowd winced and moaned in empathy.

Warren was left holding the splintered end of the staff, visibly stunned that his gambit worked. He looked at the brute, who was quivering and groaning in pain. The boy's massive bulk wasn't outside the ring, but one of his feet was close.

So Warren shoved the end of the staff under the brute's leg and tilted it upward. His foot slid down the staff and the toe of his boot broke the line of the ring.

"We have a winner!" announced Kaurridon.

The crowd exploded in applause and cheers. Warren, bruised but smiling, shuffled back to the group while soldiers carted the brute off to a space next to the group and dumped him on the ground.

Jyn hugged Warren. "I can't believe it! You beat that monster. *Alone!*" Warren squirmed a bit, uncomfortable at the public affection, but he smiled regardless.

"How did you think to do that?" asked Dantess.

"I made a plan," Warren said from inside Jyn's embrace. "One of the stories from Mother Nettle's book was about a soldier who used a spear like that to stop a charging horse. I only had a staff and he wasn't a horse, but it worked."

"You're full of surprises."

"I'm so proud of you," said Jyn, squeezing harder.

"Ow. Watch out for my bruises." Warren winced and extracted himself from Jyn's hug. "Dantess, will I have to fight again? That trick won't work twice."

"I don't know, but I don't think it will matter. You already showed them something, so more wins won't make any difference." The faint twinge he now recognized whispered through Dantess' brain, and he turned his head toward the pull. "I think *that's* what everyone should be worried about."

"What?" asked Warren, following Dantess' gaze. "That wooden pyramid thing?"

"Something tells me whatever's in there is our next challenge. That has to be War's final test."

CHAPTER SEVEN

MORE MATCHES PLAYED out. After a while, it became clear which candidates had an aptitude for combat, born through training, natural ability, or the Longing. When everyone had battled at least once, the high priest rose from his chair.

"My thanks to our hopefuls for such an entertaining exhibition. You have shown desire, you have shown strength, and you have shown bravery—some to a surprising degree." He glanced at Warren. "But now I must tell you what you already know: none of these are enough by themselves. A true warrior is chosen by our god, no other.

"It is time for the final test."

Morghaust motioned to the soldiers waiting at his side. Once they gathered others from around the courtyard, they approached the wooden pyramid's four corners. The leader in each group attached a hook and chain to their corner, and the chain was picked up by the line of soldiers behind him. As one, the four groups pulled the corners apart, each sliding in a different cardinal direction. The growing spaces between the enormous wooden pieces revealed glimmers of sunlight reflecting from large metal pieces, but there was much more. Whatever was in there, it was both confusing and awe-inspiring.

"What... what is that?" asked Jyn.

The look on every single one of the hopefuls' faces showed they agreed with Dantess: no one had ever seen its like before.

The soldiers parked the wooden corners in the far ends of the courtyard, leaving behind a huge clockwork creation the size of a large building. The dome-shaped structure was built of levers and bars, plates and spikes, cogs and gears, chains and beams. Every element was of varying colors, sizes, shapes, and materials. It was either a mechanical marvel or monstrosity.

"I don't know," breathed Dantess. "How could anyone even *think* of something like that, much less *build* it?"

The audience was quiet while the high priest approached the mechanism. He stood by a large, round stone plate on the dome near to the ground. It was suspended by six taut, steel chains, which looped through hooks and pulleys until Dantess lost track of them much deeper into the mechanism. In the center of the plate was an indented space in the shape of a shield.

"Anyone can serve War, but only those chosen by our god can join the priesthood. This test separates the chosen from the hopeful. Let us begin!"

The high priest pressed his hand into the circle. He closed his eyes, his brow furrowed, and a bright glow filled the shield. Sparks erupted from the plate's rounded edge everywhere the chains connected. It was as if the chains themselves caught fire with the plate's magic. The glow ran down each chain along its convoluted path. Once the energy touched every corner, the entire mechanism jerked into motion. Many of the hopefuls stepped back in surprise, but the audience erupted in applause, whoops, and cheers.

"Is that thing an artifact?" asked Dantess, slack-jawed. "The *whole thing?* If so, I think he just activated it."

Morghaust cleared his throat. "War's Gift has been placed inside one of thirteen boxes suspended within the test. To pass, all you must do is touch the box that contains the Gift."

Dantess pointed at one of the boxes the high priest referred to. About a foot across, they were all colored a bright red, different from anything else in the mechanism. But when he thought he nailed down the position of one, it moved, often swinging deeper into the puzzle.

It wasn't just the boxes. Whole sections lurched into motion, changed configuration, and lashed out their spikes and bars, which clanged against each other. There were so many moving parts, it was almost impossible to follow the motion of the boxes.

Luckily, not all of the mechanics moved at once. Some sections operated and then stopped as others started up. He couldn't identify any pattern to the motion, couldn't predict what would move, which sections would interact together, and which would stop.

Even to watch from a distance was maddening. Dantess couldn't imagine trying to navigate it from the inside.

"You can enter the test wherever you like," Morghaust continued, his hand still touching the shield indentation. "Follow any path that opens to you. But if you touch the wrong box or leave the test, you fail."

Kaurridon stepped up to the group of candidates. "Go singly or all at once—the test doesn't care. Who will be first?"

No one moved for a few long moments. Finally, Locke stepped up, rubbing her short ginger hair and adjusting her dirty shirt. "I guess I'll give it a go!" She walked toward the mechanism with a jaunty step. She waved at the audience, and when they responded with a cheer, she stopped and did a full forward flip. The crowd loved it.

When she finally reached one of the many open spaces in the dome, she paused. "Which box do I need to touch?"

Kaurridon laughed. "Don't ask me. Ask your Longing. It will always point you to War's Gift."

Locke rolled her eyes. "Ah, right. My Longing," she mumbled. To the crowd, she yelled, "I'll be right back!"

She climbed into the dome like a monkey traversing tree branches. The audience murmured its excitement. She braced herself on the intersection of two bars and leapt up to grab hold of a swinging arm. That arm brought her up to a plate, where she dropped and caught her balance.

Jyn pointed at a red box suspended perhaps fifteen feet above Locke. "She's close to a box already. See?"

Indeed, it appeared that Locke spied it, too. She began climbing up a lattice of crisscrossed pipes—but then the whole section spurred into motion. The lattice tilted back and a metal sphere attached to a chain swirled behind Locke, unseen. Even though the girl lost her footing, she managed to climb with just her hands. She approached within mere feet of the box when the sphere struck her in the shoulder.

"Ow!" The sphere knocked Locke from the lattice. Flailing, she tried to grab onto one of the potential handholds on the way down, but ended up just bashing against the many hard surfaces between her and the ground. Finally, she landed on the dirt beneath the structure, winded and groaning.

The audience moaned and then clapped politely.

Kaurridon nodded. "When you are able, go sit there." He indicated a bench to one side.

With that command, they all knew the bench was the last stop. Those who sat there had failed. They were not chosen.

No one moved, now that they had seen what was waiting for them.

"Anyone else? No? Then there's one more thing for you to consider." Kaurridon snatched up a tarp, uncovering a large hourglass. He picked it up, flipped it over, and placed it on a table next to the high priest's chair. "You have until this glass empties of sand to enter the test. If not, you fail."

Dantess couldn't estimate how long the glass would hold its sand, but the flow was swift. It had its desired effect: three people broke from the group and approached the test.

The audience cheered.

The three candidates attacked the test from different starting points. One dove in the nearest opening. Another, a girl, circled the dome and entered from the far side. The last, the graying man who showed such promise in the matches, climbed up the outside. He found an entrance toward the top and dropped down into it.

Sections of the mechanical maze shifted and rearranged themselves. The first hopeful narrowly avoided being caught between two converging plates. That made Dantess wonder how dangerous this test really was. Could someone actually die inside there?

The girl on the far side showed promise. She used the bars methodically to swing herself up and around obstacles. A set of five metal spears almost struck her, but after they deployed, she used them as a ladder.

The older man's approach was different. He didn't react to threats or obstacles. Instead, he simply wasn't where they deployed—as if he knew where the danger would be, rather than where it was. He soared and flipped and wrestled through the maze like a much younger acrobat. When he launched himself into the air and caught a bar that wasn't there a moment earlier, Dantess felt his breath catch.

The first boy reached for a red box, but when it was inches from his grasp, it swung away from him. He yelled in frustration and extended his arm. In that moment of hesitation, the bar he'd been standing on fell away. He grabbed at a nearby chain, but it was loose. He dropped about five feet before it pulled taut. Somehow, he held on, but regretted it when a nearby canister expelled a cloud of green gas into his face. The boy took one breath, started coughing, lost his grip, and plummeted to the ground, unconscious.

The crowd cheered.

70

The girl was both canny and lucky. She avoided obvious threats and tried to stick to sections of the maze that weren't moving. In one impressive maneuver, she bounded across half of the dome, stepping on gears and bars and even a taut rope. She launched herself at one of the suspended boxes, then caught herself on its chain. With a victory whoop, she slapped her hand on the box.

Everyone watched closely.

The six sides of the box exploded outward and, from inside, a fibrous net enveloped the girl. She cried out, lost her grip, and fell straight to the ground.

"Wrong box, I guess," said Motti.

The older man came to a stop. Instead of flipping and running, he stood on a platform of thin metal mesh.

"What's he doing?" asked Warren. "He'll get creamed if he doesn't keep moving."

"Maybe he's tired," said Karlo.

"I don't know, but I wouldn't bet against him," said Dantess. "He's been one step ahead of the others the whole time."

Indeed, the man twisted once to avoid the arc of an incoming metal hammer, but then lifted his hand straight up. From much deeper in the mechanism, a red box swung all the way to the space above him, right into his hand.

The box glowed red, and the courtyard was filled with the deep, sonorous peal of a massive bell.

"We have our first success!" exclaimed Morghaust.

The audience went crazy. By their cheers and howls, it was obvious they'd been waiting for someone to succeed.

"That's the one! That's the box holding the Gift!" yelled a candidate over the audience's commotion. He ran toward the test in the hopes that he'd be able to track the old man's box and touch it—but as he neared the dome, all the boxes swung toward the center into a large group, shuffled their positions such that no one could follow the location of the correct box, and redeployed into the metal maze. "Oh, crap."

Jyn pointed at the hourglass. "Look! The sand is almost gone." They'd all focused so much on the test that they had neglected the glass.

The entire group scrambled to the dome. They pushed and shoved each other, trying to find an entrance before the sand depleted.

Dantess jumped up onto the dome and climbed. At this point, he couldn't watch out for his friends. There wasn't enough time. He had to enter before it was too late and trust that they would do the same.

Unlike the previous candidates, these ones had to worry about navigating around other people, not just the test. While there were quite a few openings available, many of the hopefuls tried to jam through the nearest possible entrance.

Dantess discovered an aperture between two plates that looked promising. He slipped inside only to see the brute that Warren embarrassed squeeze his bulk in behind him.

"You're following me?" Dantess asked, annoyed.

The brute grinned and nodded. "I saw the way you fought. I think you've got the Longing."

Dantess rolled his eyes. "As long as you don't get in my way."

The brute's conviction aside, Dantess had no idea what to do. The older man who succeeded looked like he predicted the future. How was that possible? Did his Longing help him do that? Looking out at this maze of mechanics and traps, Dantess couldn't decipher it much less predict it.

But the high priest claimed one of those boxes held War's Gift. If Dantess had the Longing, it should tell him which box was his target. He took a moment and delved within for something, anything, that might indicate a direction.

A twinge pointed to a box on the far side of the puzzle.

Dantess was at once both overjoyed at the feeling and disappointed at his own lack of foresight. Why hadn't he checked the Longing *before* he entered? Now he had a long way to go.

He dropped down to a plank supported by springs. It wasn't easy to keep his balance, but he managed to leap up and use a chain to swing to a nearby lattice. The brute kept on his heels.

Screams of fright, frustration, and even agony sounded all around him. Occasional thumps indicated that other hopefuls had already fallen out of the test. But he couldn't focus on them. He needed to figure out how to get himself through this maze.

As he climbed onwards, the bell sounded.

"Success!" called out Morghaust. The audience whooped and hollered.

Already? thought Dantess. *Someone smarter than me chose a better entrance.*

Dantess could feel the movement of the Gift as it was pulled to the center, shuffled, and then replaced into the test somewhere else. But, as luck would have it, the box housing the Gift stopped nearby. He could almost see it from here.

He grabbed a bar above his head, but it buckled, attached only by a hinge on one side. He dropped down into the path of a roller the size of a log. His reflexes quickened, and he bounced on the ball of one foot, flipped over the roller, and caught himself on a set of crossed bars.

Did I just do that? thought Dantess, and then realized: *War's badge must have helped.*

And with that thought, it came to mind that he hadn't consciously tried to use the token yet. Could it do something besides help him fight? He pulled at his twinge and tried to force it through the clasp, if that was even possible.

It was.

In his mind, he saw the test, but also other configurations of the test's components overlaid again and again—possibilities unfolding until his inevitable final winning move.

What he saw wasn't speculation. Instead, he saw the test through different eyes. Many, many eyes. The eyes of every priest of War who had ever tested throughout history. All those thousands and thousands of priests—watching, planning, reacting, winning. They had done the work, and now they were showing Dantess how they did it.

At once, he knew the test wasn't random. It moved purposefully according to how it was built. This gear would move its neighbor, which would pull a trigger, which would launch a wall of spikes, all of which would happen if he touched the handle next to him. Beyond that, he saw each section of the test, how the whole thing would move in certain conditions, and where his path would open once it had.

He realized that the older man hadn't predicted the future. He watched how the test had previously acted and expected the same, because it *always* acted the same.

It was as if he had run the test himself, all of those thousands of times, and now he just had to do it once more.

With renewed confidence, Dantess climbed onto the edge of an expanse filled with vertical poles of differing lengths. He leapt onto one and then another, knowing that the ones he skipped would have toppled or revealed tips of sharpened metal spikes. He did not stop until he was able to grab a hanging chain that pulled him upward.

The brute followed, amazingly limber after his literal run-in with the business end of Warren's staff. He carefully jumped only on the pole ends that Dantess had proven stable. Moments after Dantess grabbed the chain, the brute also grasped the tail end of it.

While the chain pulled both boys up, the loud peal rang out.

"Another priest has found his calling," announced Morghaust. While the audience cheered, inside his head, Dantess cursed. He knew what was about to happen.

Once more, everything changed. The box he'd been tracking, along with all the others, pulled to the center, shuffled, and redeployed into different sections of the test.

While he rode the chain upward, his mind mapped out the possibilities. His current path wasn't viable anymore, but he did see another way forward.

Dantess released the chain and stepped onto a tightly strung wire. He walked across about halfway, and then dropped onto a series of metal beams. As he stepped on them, he counted. Once he reached the fifth, he came upon a shallow trench between the beams—barely deep enough to hold him. His Longing told him what was about to happen, but he had to fight every instinct that told him *not* to lie down in that trench.

The brute followed him onto the wire. After a moment, he lost his balance, dropped down onto the beams, and found Dantess lying in the trench.

"What are you doing? Are you trying to hide from me?" he asked.

"I'm waiting."

"What? You can't wait. We've got to keep moving. Lying around won't get us to the Gift."

"If you need me to tell you the way, you don't have the Longing, and you'll never make it there. That's how this test is designed. You can't cheat it." Dantess turned his head to the side. "Regardless, you have to move on. Now. You won't want to be here soon."

As if on cue, the entire section lurched into motion. The brute's wild eyes took in the nearby moving gears, swinging arms, and closing paths. "Then let me in." The brute reached down to grab Dantess' arm. "Quit hogging all the—"

A huge metal slab rocketed over the trench, slamming into the boy. He yelped at the impact, then screamed as he plummeted to the ground.

The slab also sealed Dantess into the trench. Even knowing what he did about the test, it was hard to ignore that he was trapped in a metal coffin so tight he could not move his arms or turn his head. There was barely enough space to take a breath into his lungs, which was made worse by his quickening heartbeat and rapid breathing.

He couldn't see anything, but sounds and vibrations in the metal around him spoke to parts of the machine moving, rotating, sliding, and locking into a new configuration. Even the slab continued to slide across the opening of the trench. It seemed endless.

When the rest of the mechanism ground to a halt, the slab completed its journey. The far edge slid over and released him from his metal tomb. Dantess pulled himself out and looked up. His plan was not wrong. There, suspended far above, was the red box that held the Gift. His Longing confirmed it.

But there was no path to climb to the box, and no one would be able to jump that high. No one without War's token, anyway.

He channeled the Longing through his token and sprang upwards with strength he'd never before experienced. As he rose through the air, all of his childhood dreams replayed in his head, and he realized they had never been foolish wishes. Each thought had been the Gift calling him without Dantess understanding it.

He reached his hand upward, grasping at a future he thought impossible. He could imagine his grandfather looking down on him and smiling.

At the apex of his leap, his fingertips grazed the red box. The box flashed its glow. The bell sounded. The audience roared and stomped.

His god had summoned him here, to this temple, to the Gift, to this moment. Dantess had finally answered, and by His favor, Dantess became a priest of War.

CHAPTER EIGHT

"CONGRATULATIONS TO THOSE who passed the test."
Morghaust swung his hand to indicate the short line of four
candidates still standing. The remaining thirteen sat on the bench,
including Jyn, Warren, and the three teens Dantess met on the
road. "We welcome you to the priesthood of War. Today, the
temple is stronger with you in its ranks."

The audience cheered the new priests with abandon. After
a few moments, Morghaust lifted his hands. "Before we move on, I
have an announcement to make."

The roar died down, and a curious murmur rippled
through the crowd. This wasn't part of the normal ceremony.

"While all of our new priests are to be celebrated, there is
one in particular I wish to acknowledge. Dantess, would you come
next to me, please?"

Dantess took a quick breath in surprise. His heart
pounding in his chest, he walked to the high priest. Morghaust
gently turned him to face the crowd.

"I suspect most people here may not know that Dantess is
the grandson of one of our most celebrated priests: the legend,
Varyon Tiernocke." The ripple turned into a collective gasp. "I am
pleased to be able to present Varyon's belt, recovered from his last
mission, to his grandson. May it help propel you to the same great
heights in the temple as your grandfather."

Morghaust handed Dantess a beautiful, intricately-
decorated leather belt—clearly the masterwork of a talented artist.
Dantess was overwhelmed. From what he understood, his
grandfather wore this belt during every mission. He wore it on the
mission that killed him. And somehow, it made its way back to
Dantess.

As he took it, Dantess understood that the belt wasn't just
meaningful to him. It had immense historical value to the temple.
The expectations it placed on his shoulders were daunting.

Despite the pressure, he couldn't help but fill with pride.
This was, indeed, his first step on the long path of following in his
grandfather's footsteps.

The crowd applauded, as did many of those standing nearby—but Dantess noticed that one person abstained. Standing on his own, Kevik crossed his arms and glowered at his grandfather's belt.

"To our other new priests, the tokens are yours to keep, although you are welcome to replace the simple straps whenever you wish. What's more, the obligation to pay the temple for your testing has been waived. Welcome to your new home!"

Kaurridon turned to the bench of thirteen failed applicants. "Those of you without War's Longing have accounts that must be settled. If you can pay the fee, please come forward."

Two of the faithless rose from the bench. Kaurridon held out his hand, and the failed candidates each placed a small stack of gold coins in his hand. The priest smiled. "Your accounts are settled. You will be escorted out of the temple. Do not discuss what has happened here."

To drive the point home, Morghaust approached the two and glared at them, his brow furrowed. "On pain of death. Do you understand?"

Both boys sucked in their breath, but nodded. Kaurridon gestured to a nearby soldier who escorted the boys to the lift.

Once they were gone, Morghaust turned to those remaining on the bench. "The rest of you failed, and you do not have the means to make things right. In return for your testing debt and all future tithes, the temple demands your service. We will now determine your place here. Stand."

The eleven faithless stood up from the bench. Warren held Jyn's hand. Both looked nervous. In fact, most of the others did as well.

"One of our priests' primary duties is to train their squads. As new priests, you don't have anyone in your squads yet. We're about to change that."

Kevik uncrossed his arms and interrupted. "High Priest, I ask to be included in this ceremony. Two of my squad were killed in the attack at Freethorne Creek. I need to replace them."

Kaurridon looked to the high priest who paused to think about it. Morghaust nodded.

"You may choose one," Kaurridon said, "and only after our new priests have recruited one each. You can replace your other in a future testing."

"After the new priests? I should choose first. You know I always take the most dangerous assignments," said Kevik.

"That's enough," said Kaurridon, frowning. "You heard the order. Report to me later. We'll discuss your insubordination then."

Kevik said nothing. He crossed his arms again and nodded.

Morghaust turned his stern look to the new priests. "Hopefully, you were all paying attention in the combat trials. You should have enough information to determine if these failed candidates are fit for battle. Choose well. Those you recruit will hold your life in their hands, as well as the lives of their squad-mates.

"If you feel a candidate cannot be molded into a soldier, do not choose them. You will have other chances to add to your squad. Those not chosen will be assigned different tasks in the temple."

"You shall choose in the order you passed the test," said Kaurridon. He held out his hand towards the older man. "Frederik, you were first. Please select one of the candidates."

The graying man stepped forward. He examined the line of children critically, pointed at the girl who entered the test at the same time as he did. "You."

A broad grin broke out on the girl's face. She almost ran over to Frederik's side.

Kaurridon nodded. "Now, Belloci. You finished next. Choose."

A tall, muscular girl put her hand to her chin. "I'll take the eunuch. If he can still walk over here." She pointed to the brute, clearly referring to his bout with Warren. Everyone tittered at the comment, and the boy looked at the ground as he shuffled to her side.

A young boy, perhaps three years Dantess' junior, impatient with the brute's slow progress, announced, "I want—"

Kaurridon put his hand up. "Chester, as a priest of War, you'll need to learn to follow procedure." Once the large boy had reached his spot beside Belloci, Kaurridon finished, "You may choose now."

"Her." Chester pointed at Locke. "The funny one."

Locke almost leapt to Chester's side, even as Kaurridon closed his eyes and rubbed his temples.

"Dantess, you were the last priest to succeed," said Kaurridon. "Take your pick."

There was no doubt in Dantess' mind who he wanted to choose. His hand lifted toward Jyn, but she shook her head.

Confused, he wondered, *Does she still hate me? Is that why she doesn't want to join my squad?*

But the look in Jyn's eyes wasn't hatred. It was fear. She locked gazes with Dantess and then glanced at Warren.

Immediately, Dantess understood. *If I choose Jyn, Kevik will choose Warren. And he'll destroy him. Or turn him into something we won't recognize.*

The decision was heart-rending. He so wanted Jyn by his side. She was his best friend. He trusted her with his life. But how could he leave her frightened, too-young brother to the tender mercies of someone like Kevik—the one who tricked Warren into committing in the first place?

Tears welled in Jyn's eyes. She mouthed the word, *Please.*

Dantess recalled his promise to look after the boy when Warren committed. He couldn't turn his back now. "Warren, I choose you," said Dantess, pointing at the boy holding onto his sister's hand.

Warren looked up at his sister. She smiled, tears trickling down her face, and she hugged him. Then she sent him off to walk to Dantess.

"Interesting," said Kaurridon. "Kevik, you may choose someone now."

"You sure you want that weak little kid, Dantess?" asked Kevik. "I'm willing to take him off your hands and let you choose again. You need someone with some strength to start out your squad, especially if you want to live up to *his* legacy." He gestured to the belt in Dantess' hands.

At once, Dantess knew he had made the right decision. Kevik *did* want Warren, most likely to break him down and rebuild him in his own image. "I'm fine with my choice. Warren has a keen mind and a lot of determination. I'm certain he'll do well in my squad."

Kevik's face darkened. "I was trying to do you a favor. If you want to keep the weakling, fine. Then I'll take his sister. I like a challenge." He pointed to Jyn. "You, get over here."

Jyn's face went white.

With just a few words, he lost Jyn to Kevik. Even though Dantess knew he made the right choice, he couldn't help but regret making that possible.

Jyn's every step toward Kevik looked like she was walking to the gallows, likely remembering Kevik's words to her when she committed: *You'd better damn well hope you don't end up on my squad.*

Dantess' heart sank, thinking about what could become of his best friend.

"Is Tolliver here?" asked Dantess. When the guard looked confused, his first thought was that he was in the wrong place entirely. Someone directed him to the cells when asked, but he found himself turned around a number of times before ending up here. Just to be sure, he added, "He's a prisoner, a shopkeeper from Freethorn Creek, brought in with everyone after the attack on the auction there."

"Tolliver *Tiernocke*? Ah. He's in a cell toward the back." He pointed to one of the last reinforced wooden doors in the hall. "Normally he'd be in with the others, but somebody recognized him as the son of Varyon. I guess that affords him a private cell."

"My thanks."

When Dantess began to walk toward the cell, the guard held his hand up. "He's not supposed to receive visitors."

Dantess' first instinct was to turn around and leave, but then he remembered the badge around his waist and the belt that held it. He gathered up his courage. "Then be sure to turn away anyone who isn't a priest of War. Remove your hand."

The soldier snapped to attention and stepped out of the way. "At your command."

Dantess smiled slyly. He could get used to others following his orders.

The soldier fell in behind him as they walked across a dimly lit hallway. When they neared the cells, the soldier pulled out a key, unlocked a door, and opened it for Dantess. After Dantess entered, he shut the door behind him.

His father lay on a thin mattress atop a flimsy cot. Dim rays of sunlight filtered through the barred window high on the wall. While seeing his da wasn't quite enough to make him cry, the stench wafting from a bucket in the chamber's corner almost brought a tear to his eye. It was a small, sad, smelly room.

He had rehearsed this conversation in his head a number of times. Da would *have* to understand what he did. While Tolliver always wanted his son far away from War, Dantess had no choice but to test. He couldn't leave his father here to rot.

Besides, Dantess succeeded. The god of War called him here. No one could argue with that.

"Da?"

Tolliver sat up in his bed. "Dantess?"

"Da!" Dantess ran over to his father and hugged him.

Tolliver resisted a bit at first, but then hugged him back. "How did you get in here?" Then he saw the belt at Dantess' waist. "Is that my father's belt? With War's badge on it? Are you a priest now?"

Tolliver pushed his son away.

Dantess held his hands out. "Testing was the only way I could get into the temple. I needed to see you, to help you, no matter the outcome." When Tolliver grimaced, Dantess tilted his head. "Did you miss the part where I *passed* the test? I'm a priest. You were always against me joining the temple as a faithless, but becoming a priest means I was summoned by the god of War! It was my destiny. And it means I can actually help you!"

His father frowned. "I tried for years to keep War's claws out of you. You don't even know the lengths I went to. The moment I was out of the way, War pulled you in. I failed." His father turned away.

Dantess shook his head. "How can you argue with this? Passing the test means the Longing would have brought me here sooner or later. It was inevitable. There's nothing you could have done to prevent this. What's more, I can protect you now. I might even be able to get you released."

Tolliver scoffed. "You have no idea what you've stumbled into. You're a new priest. With bare arms. You don't have much more influence than I do. Power is all about rank here. I'm surprised they even let you in to see me."

Dantess' hand went to his belt. "This seems to get some respect. Lots of people remember Grandpa. They say that if I'm half as good as him, I should climb in the ranks quickly."

"My son, you don't know him. Not really. You've heard the stories, but I was there. He's the reason I kept you out of the temple, to prevent you from turning into him. Everyone else here can idolize him, but you shouldn't. I raised you to be a better person than he ever was."

Dantess' jaw dropped. He'd never heard his father be so blunt about his feelings towards Grandpa. "Well, I'm here, and I'm a priest. It's done. Even if I'm new, I'm sure there's something I can do to protect you and everyone else."

"Everyone else?"

"You know. Jyn and Warren's mother. And, um... Jyn and Warren. They tested, too. They're bound to the temple now."

Tolliver's eyebrows shot up. He gripped the edge of his cot as he leaned forward. "They're in here, too? How could you let this happen?"

"I couldn't stop it." Dantess rubbed his forehead. "You know how stubborn Jyn can be. At least Warren is on my squad. But Jyn..."

"What happened to her? Who is she assigned to?"

"Kevik."

Tolliver's face blanched. "Does he have any reason to dislike her?"

Dantess nodded. "I think he chose her to get back at me for taking Warren."

"Kevik's a true priest of War: no mercy and no sympathy for the faithless. On top of that, he's a vindictive bastard."

"But he's still a priest of War. He needs to follow the rules, right? She's not in any real danger?"

Tolliver took Dantess' hand. "Listen to me. I've tried to tell you this before, but you need to actually hear me now. To the priests, the faithless don't matter. Because they lack a connection to the gods, the faithless aren't even people. They're objects that pay the tithe and clean the dishes and die in battle. Faithless who become problems are removed. Not solved, *removed*. That's what they teach here."

The words hung in the air.

Dantess paced back and forth. Finally, he said, "Then I'll protect her myself. War's token makes me invincible. It's like I was trained by every priest ever. And I'm stronger and faster than anyone."

"Stronger and faster than Kevik?" asked Tolliver. "He's a monster to begin with, and did you forget he has a token, too?"

Dantess blew out a breath and rolled his eyes. "Then what? What can I do?"

"I can't believe we're here, and we need to have this conversation." Tolliver rubbed his forehead. "As I said, power comes from rank, but not just yours. You need to cultivate relationships with the people who can actually affect things."

"Who?" Dantess thought about this. "Oh, what about the high priest? He seems to like me. He liked Grandpa, anyway. There's no better rank than high priest!"

"No!" said Tolliver. "Never him. Morghaust is the one that sets the temple's direction. Remember, it's men, not gods, that make the rules. He's the reason priests of War treat us so badly." Tolliver softened his expression. "The Hand of the high priest is a different matter, though. Kaurridon holds his cards close, so I never knew exactly how he felt, but I get the sense that he dislikes Morghaust's policy of hatred and abuse. He might be someone to connect with."

"If he'll even talk to me." Dantess threw up his hands.

"Bide your time. Log some wins. If you catch his eye, he may be open to it. And there's one more person: Withyr. She's been a priestess for a while, part of the establishment. She doesn't necessarily like the faithless—doesn't like much anybody, actually—but we... have a bit of history."

"How are you so tied into this temple?" asked Dantess. "You're not a priest."

"I don't talk about it much, but I was born here. My mother was a soldier in Varyon's squad until she died and Da kicked me out of the temple. While I lived here, I learned a lot about War— and if there's one thing you can count on, the temples of Order don't change. That's by design. The gods don't like change."

Someone pounded on the outside of the cell door. "Time's up. You have to leave."

"I'm going to get you out of here," said Dantess to his father. "Don't worry."

Tolliver put his head in his hand. "What I worry about are the dungeons of Evil. That's where they'll send the Harbingers of Chaos when they're done questioning them. I hid those people in my shop. They think I might be one of them."

"They wouldn't dare send Varyon's son to the dungeons of Evil, would they?"

"I may be Varyon's son, but to Morghaust, I'm just faithless."

"Well, I'm not." Dantess grasped his belt. "You and Jyn's mother aren't going anywhere near Evil while I'm here."

Tolliver lowered his voice. "Know this: the closer you seem to me—a man accused of being part of a group that killed priests— the more vulnerable you are. You're in the game of temple politics now. Don't let your enemies use me against you."

As that sunk in, Dantess began to get a little overwhelmed. He assumed that simply being a great warrior would open his path. He hadn't factored politics into it.

"One more thing," Tolliver continued. "There's nothing I can do to reverse what happened. You're a priest now. It's done, and it will define the rest of your life. But now you have to ask yourself, what kind of priest will you be? Are you here for glory, or do you want to change things? I think we'll soon find out who really raised you: me or your grandfather."

The door opened and the soldier outside stood at attention. "His questioning begins soon. I must ask you to go."

Dantess stood for a moment and then nodded. He was about to hug his da goodbye, but—remembering what his father said—realized the guard would likely tell everyone about the embrace afterward. He couldn't be seen to be too close with him. With reluctance, he walked out of the cell and didn't look back.

Dantess found his friends and the other candidates lined up outside the building that processed newly-bound faithless. Inside, faithless were being tattooed, clothed, equipped, and assigned quarters.

"Did you get in to see your da?" asked Jyn.

"Yes. He's here and doing as well as can be expected," said Dantess.

Warren piped up. "What about Mama? Did you see her, too?"

"No. She's in a group cell with the Harbingers. They won't let anyone near those folks. But I won't rest until I make sure she's safe."

Jyn edged closer to Dantess, her eyes glistening. "Thank you."

"For what?"

"For taking Warren into your squad. For looking out for Mama. I know I was hard on you before, but you're a good friend. You're doing everything you can. And I'm grateful." Jyn wrapped her arms around Dantess and hugged him tightly.

Surprised, Dantess' eyes widened momentarily. He put his arms around her and enjoyed the warmth of the lingering moment.

Until Jyn was ripped away.

"What do you think you're doing, *Boot?*" Kevik held onto Jyn with a one-handed vice-like grip, just like he held Dantess not long ago. He shook her as he spoke. "This is *my* recruit, on *my* squad. She's my property. You don't talk to her. You don't touch her. In fact, you don't even look at her from now on. Am I clear?"

Dantess' mouth opened, but couldn't put a thought together well enough to respond.

"Am I clear? Answer me, *Boot!*"

Dantess could only nod. Warren glanced up at Dantess in shock.

Kevik leaned in and whispered, "Test me on this and see what happens." He dragged Jyn past the queue and into the building to be branded.

As she disappeared through the doorway, Warren tried to follow. "Jyn! *Jyn!*"

Dantess caught the boy and pulled him back. "Quiet. We have to let her go."

"But she's my *sister!*" A tear trickled down Warren's cheek. "I want her back."

"I do, too. But for now, we both have to be strong for her."

"But I'm not strong. I'm not a warrior." Warren sniffed. "I don't want to be here anymore. I want my sister and mother and I want to go *home.*"

Dantess could see Warren's tears starting, but he knew that his recruit breaking down in front of everyone wouldn't help either of them. He knelt down. "Warren, look at me. I know it doesn't feel like it now, but you *are* strong. You proved it today. You may think

I chose you to protect you, but I also saw your potential. I wouldn't want anyone else as the core of my squad."

The words were helpful, but not enough. Dantess knew he had to do something substantial, something that would hopefully propel Warren through the years of suffering that may come.

"Let me prove it." Dantess pulled off his silver ring. "This is Varyon's ring. My da gave it to me because, on the day I was born, grandpa saw the spark of a warrior in me. He told Da he wanted me to have it. I see that same spark in you."

The tears stopped. Warren looked at Dantess in shock.

"Take this ring. If you ever doubt yourself, look at it. The ring is a promise you will live up to." Dantess slipped the gleaming ring onto Warren's finger.

The boy stared at the ring with glassy eyes. "I... I will?"

Dantess put his hand on Warren's shoulder. "I know it."

And, strangely, he did know it.

PART II

THE GAME

CHAPTER NINE

IT HAD BEEN two years since Dantess joined the ranks of priesthood, and in that time, the Harbingers of Chaos' attacks had increased. Reports indicated that they had started assaulting temples now. If that were true, Dantess wanted his squad to be the one selected to protect them.

To do that, his squad had to be better than the others, and the only way there was to train. It wasn't easy breaking down the combat knowledge contained in his token into teachable tactics, but Dantess wanted all six members of his squad prepared for the worst.

It was no secret that Dantess always requested the most dangerous and high-profile missions to speed his climb up the ranks. He wasn't doing it for glory, though.

"Eyes on me," Dantess called out to his squad. A few of them tried to hide their yawns. Dantess had pulled them out of bunks into the training yard just as the sun rose today, but if they were tired because it was so early, he'd quickly wake them up. "Why do we train so hard?"

"To enter the Game of War!" they all answered in unison.

"That's right. It only comes once every hundred years, but that day is coming *fast*. If I don't rank high enough, I can't be selected. And if I'm not selected?"

"None of us play," the squad said.

And I won't be able to free my father and Jyn's mother, thought Dantess. But aloud, he simply yelled, "Line up!"

Once the squad had done so, Dantess pulled Jeremy out to stand beside him. Only slightly nervous, Jeremy held a practice sword in one hand and a wooden dagger in the other. Dantess channeled his Longing into his token and options flooded his view. He chose the most straightforward way to disarm Jeremy to present to his squad.

The move played out in his mind like its own story. He saw the steps, could feel the tug in his muscles—the token wanted to take control—but he needed to *understand* it so he could teach it.

"Squad, eyes on me. Jeremy has two weapons. He can use either of them to attack or defend, but you don't know which will be used for which purpose. Since you can't read his mind, make the decision for him." He caught Jeremy's eyes. "Ready?"

Jeremy tensed and nodded.

Dantess lashed out with a hand closest to the dagger. Jeremy's hand twitched, attempting to block the hand with that dagger—but Dantess was already turning and sidestepping to the opposite side. He grasped Jeremy's sword arm and twisted. The sword clattered to the ground and Dantess stood behind him with the arm caught in a firm grasp.

"Did you see the steps?" Dantess asked. "Feint, roll, grab, twist. Pair off and let me see you try it."

The squad did as he commanded. Warren paired with the new recruit, Fullon. Dantess' friend had changed quite a bit in the last two years. The black tattooed mask over Warren's eyes gave him a more serious and menacing appearance, and while he'd never be a brute, the years of training at War had done much to fill out his spindly frame. He was a half-foot taller and many pounds heavier. Regardless, Warren was still Warren, and his value on Dantess' squad had never relied on his physical skills. Even new, Fullon likely had a physical edge in this matchup.

The pairs went through the motions at half speed with Dantess correcting them when needed. After they traded places, and everyone had a chance to walk through the technique, Dantess noticed the sun had crawled its way to mid-morning. He announced, "All right. Time to spar."

Most of his squad grunted in approval. This was their favorite activity. The pairs grabbed whatever weapons they wanted from the racks and began their practice fights.

Again, Dantess wandered around the grounds to watch them. He was about to encourage Warren to be more aggressive when Soloman cried out in pain and dropped to the ground.

Dantess raced over, shocked. "Motti, what did you do?"

Motti, grinning smugly, stood over Soloman. The older boy on the ground clutched the back of his head and groaned. "I'm sick of losing to him when we spar, so I tried something different." He held up his elbow. "The back of his neck met the overwhelming force of my elbow."

"Is this something I trained you to do?"

90

"Not exactly. But it works, right? I've done it lots of times before I came here. First, you catch their mouth in a fish hook." Motti showed two fingers bent like a hook. "Drag their head around, and then drop the elbow. No one sees it coming."

"This isn't a street brawl, Motti. This is the temple of War. There's no tolerance for dirty tactics or improvisation. You represent *me* when you fight. When you do something like this, you embarrass us all."

"You'd rather I lose?"

"Follow your training, and you won't lose." Dantess pointed to the wall surrounding the yard. "Give me three laps."

Motti shrugged. Even while jogging to the edge of the yard, he still looked pleased with himself.

"Make it six," called out Dantess.

"Dantess?" A young soldier ran up to him, holding out a missive. "Orders."

Dantess took the paper and read it. "Squad, listen up. We've been assigned to the temple of Serenity. They've asked for help, and we're it." He shook the missive at his squad to emphasize his point. "If we do well, this could be the mission that puts us in contention for the Game. Pack up and meet at the lift."

He cupped his hands around his mouth. "Motti! Fall in for now," he yelled. "But however big the temple of Serenity is, you're going to run around it six times."

The rest paused to chuckle, so Dantess added, "All of you, move!"

As Dantess put his clothes to the side, he took a moment to appreciate the colorful, expansive, and impeccably-cultivated gardens of Serenity. The air was heavy with the combined fragrances of countless flowers, most of which he couldn't recognize. This wasn't Dantess' first mission, but it was the first where he had been trusted to defend another temple from the ever-growing threat of the Harbingers of Chaos. Of course, there was no reason to think they would assault this place in particular— but temples, especially the smaller ones, were nervous. Most weren't too proud to ask War for protection. Certainly, Serenity wasn't in any position to defend themselves.

It wasn't easy giving up his breastplate, but it was all part of the plan. Dantess felt vulnerable, sliding on only a loose blue robe—but that's what the priests of Serenity wore. He consoled himself that his squad had it worse. They had only the puffy wrap-shorts, leather sandals, and broad sun hats of Serenity's bound faithless to cover them.

"Seeing you in our priest's garb will inflict disturbance on the others here," said Illistre, the high priestess of Serenity. Her face was like ice—beautiful, hard, and unchanging. She didn't frown—ever—but looked like she wanted to.

Dantess fixed his leather belt around the robe. The open neck showed off his muscular chest. The years of training had done much to increase his strength, speed, and stamina—even without the help of his token. That part of his experience at War's temple, at least, had lived up to his expectations.

"You're saying you don't like us wearing your clothes?" asked Dantess. "Well, I'm not fond of giving up my armor. Neither is my squad. Why don't your faithless wear shirts, at least?"

"The lack of clothes puts them more in touch with their surroundings. They connect with the world in ways you could not understand. I'm sure the experience is lost on you and your squad. Why did you feel the need to wear our clothes again?"

"You're the one who reached out to War, correct? You're worried the Harbingers may attack, loot your tithe, and kill your priests. Well, if they do come and see a bunch of warriors here, they'll wait until we're gone before they try. Do you want that?"

"No, of course not. The plan just seems... unconventional. I thought War's tactics were more steeped in tradition. I can't say I've heard of anything like this before."

Dantess hesitated. He, too, felt a little uncomfortable with this approach. Guile and subterfuge weren't usually part of War's playbook. Priests preferred the tried-and-true tactics of using overwhelming force to assault the enemy on an open battlefield. This felt... sneaky. "Warren? Is that true? Has this never been done before?"

Warren stepped up. "No, not quite. Thaddeus Helstrop, a priest of War some two thousand years ago, infiltrated a collective of pirates by disguising himself and his squad. He used the tactic as a force multiplier. By attacking the enemy from within by surprise, he was able to destroy nearly half of them before they rallied."

"Did he survive?" asked Dantess.

Warren coughed. "Uh, no. But he did kill the leader and slowed the pirate scourge in that area of the world. For a year or so, anyway."

Dantess put his hand on Warren's shoulder. "I trust Warren's read of the situation. His advice may seem unorthodox at times, but I've succeeded more often by listening than not."

"As you say," said the high priestess. "I must take my leave now. I will not wish you peace and tranquility, because they would not serve you—but I do wish you a swift resolution to your mission, and a swift departure."

She glided away, leaving Dantess and Warren to watch in amazement. While they couldn't see her feet beneath her robe, she moved as if they never touched the ground.

Dantess and Warren left the central pagoda where the high priestess meditated and taught. They exited using a well-tended path flanked by foliage on all sides. The dense surrounding trees curved around and above them, giving the impression of a natural tunnel—even though he knew the trees had been carefully shaped to create it. Emerging from the tunnel, they were able to see the temple's many buildings, sticking up from the sprawling open-air gardens like huge toadstools—smooth, white, elongated domes— with no seeming rhyme or reason for their locations.

"Look at this place," Dantess exclaimed as they walked the many winding paths surrounded by perfectly-cultivated topiaries, gardens bursting with flowers of every color, and expertly-carved statues. The quiet of these gardens was soft, enhanced rather than broken by the occasional birdsong and the burble of water coursing through man-made streams and ponds bridged by works of art.

Warren swiveled his head to take it all in. "I know. I've never seen anything like it. Every bend in the path reveals a completely new scene, like a painting. It's nature, but there's nothing wild about any of it. Everything is so controlled."

"What?" Dantess shook his head. "That's not what I meant. How much sheer effort, not to mention *gold*, is necessary to maintain this? Why do they need flowers from all over the world? I don't get it at all. What's the point? A whole temple of gardens?"

Warren shrugged. "I don't know. It's pretty?"

"What's worse, the temple has no standing guards. Even if they did, the layout is impossible to defend. You couldn't have designed a better target for these Harbingers to attack. What was Serenity's plan here?"

"Well, the buildings are decentralized and randomly placed. It's hard to know where to search for valuables. You could spend a whole day looking. The only obvious target is the high priestess' pagoda."

Dantess scoffed. "That won't stop anyone. It just delays the inevitable."

"True. It's not very defensible. I like to look at it all, though. It's calming." After saying this, he noticed a faithless girl pruning a flower bush, and he swung his gaze away suddenly.

"You don't look calm." Dantess chuckled. "Are you uncomfortable with Serenity's workers not wearing any tops? They're just connecting with the world."

Warren cleared his throat and mumbled, "That's fine. Can we patrol elsewhere?"

"Sure. Let's check on the rest of the squad."

They found Motti standing leisurely near to the arch that served as a front gate to the gardens, his sun hat lying on the ground. As soon as he spotted Dantess, he snapped to attention and brought his fist over his heart.

"What are you doing?" demanded Dantess. "I'm a priest of Serenity, right? No one salutes anyone around here."

"Right. Right!" Motti immediately tried to relax, but only succeeded in looking awkward.

Dantess palmed his forehead. "Get that sun hat on your head. You want everyone to see your tattoo?" As Motti grabbed his hat and pulled it down over his eyes, Dantess sighed. "I swear, anyone looking for a soldier here would be hard pressed not to spot one. Now, start pruning that bush and give me an update."

Happy for something to occupy his wandering hands, he squatted next to a bush and began plucking random leaves from it.

"Everyone is still at their posts, but I'm worried we don't have enough people. It's damn hard to establish a perimeter with so few and without looking obvious, and this place is so huge and so open. Jeremy and Solomon are nearby, and the others are roaming."

"Anyone see anything?"

"Not really. Solomon reported some movement in the tree line on the road's edge about an hour ago, but it could have been the wind."

"Where?" asked Dantess. Motti was about to indicate with a finger when Dantess pushed down his hand. "Don't point. Tell me."

"About twenty feet from where the main road ends. To the right."

Dantess channeled his Longing through his token. In response, his eyesight grew sharper. It was as if everything fell away but those particular trees. His view drew closer until he could see every single leaf quaking in the slight wind.

And the black-masked Harbinger hiding behind them.

Dantess' heart leapt. "He's there." Coming to Serenity wasn't wasted time. It was a *true* mission, one that might win him the rank he needed.

Motti's mouth dropped. "You can see someone? A Harbinger? How many?"

"Only one, but that doesn't mean there aren't more. He's waiting for something. Motti, get Solomon and Jeremy. Enter the forest on either side and get behind him."

"Won't he see us?"

"He'll be looking at something else." With that, Dantess strode toward the main road, trying to keep his gait as casual as possible.

"Ho there!" called out Dantess. "Come to see our gardens? They'll... bring you peace... or something. Come on out, my friend."

While Dantess provided a distraction, Motti collected the two other squad mates. They moved away from the main road, but then crossed the open space between them and the forest. Dantess judged that they would be honing in on the Harbinger's position shortly.

Surprisingly, the man didn't run. He stepped out of the tree line. "I'm here to bring you peace, priest of Order. The peace of the dead. And then I'll free those slaves who toil for the temple."

Dantess did not slow. "You Harbingers are definitely single-minded. But not very perceptive."

"No? Then how did I notice your men slipping into the forest behind me? How did I notice that your belt has the token of War on it? You and your men are about as obvious as a blow to the head."

Dantess cursed himself and his grandfather's belt. Of course he should have covered it. He wasn't used to all this sneaking around, and he had to admit, he wasn't great at it. "Fine. I'd prefer to give you an actual blow to the head anyway." With that, Dantess sprang at the black-masked man.

Time slowed. Myriad images swam before his eyes, all of the options presented by the thousands of priests of War before him. He dismissed the fatal paths, preferring to keep the man alive and able to answer questions. He decided on a quick punch to the chest, followed by a kick to his knee. The man grunted as the punch connected, but he avoided the kick, choosing to defend against the more damaging attack. His opponent had training.

Sounds of combat rang out from the forest behind them. "Your soldiers have found my people, it seems. I hope you brought more. Because I did." The man pulled out a dagger and sliced at Dantess, who avoided it easily.

"I know Harbingers. One of my squad is worth a hundred of your dirt-diggers. Can you imagine how many a priest of War is worth?" When the man extended his arm to stab Dantess, he struck the man's wrist and sent the dagger flying into the bushes.

Without his weapon, the man's eyes betrayed his fear. He jerked toward the dagger, but then bolted back into the forest.

"Coward!" Dantess looked back to see Warren still at the gate. "Warren, with me."

"You don't know what's back there," said Warren, standing still. Even after all his training, his fear was obvious. "You'd be running in blind. Maybe I should get the others..."

"The fight is here and now. I don't need the others. I am a priest of War. I am the overwhelming force." Dantess could see his chance to enter the Game disappearing with the Harbinger into the trees.

Grandpa Varyon never backed away from a fight, thought Dantess. *I won't either.*

He ignored Warren and chased after the Harbinger.

Branches whipped at his face and torso, once again making him miss his breastplate. The Harbinger had escaped along an animal trail, allowing for easy tracking. Dantess knew his prey couldn't be too far ahead.

As he passed a nearby tree, a different black-masked man leapt out at him, brandishing a hooked blade. Dantess' reflexes and training kicked in. He caught the swinging arm and dragged it down, which brought the man's face along with it. Once planted on the ground, Dantess struck the back of the man's head. He went still.

But Dantess didn't. Without looking, he kicked up and connected with the chest of another attacker. The man flew back into a tree and grunted at the impact. Dantess wheeled around and struck the man three times in the chest and head before he could even rebound from the tree. The man fell to the ground, senseless.

Dantess cursed these distractions. Each delay increased the leader's lead.

Out of instinct, Dantess grabbed the hooked blade and raced along the path. With each step, he heard his men fighting deeper in the forest, but he trusted them to stay alive. He had trained them himself. For him, it was more important to stay on the trail of his quarry. Capturing one of the leaders of the Harbingers would be an accomplishment that could get attention inside the temple and increase his rank, which would enable him to help his father—still locked away after all this time.

Dantess rounded a bend in the path, and his heightened senses alerted him to a new challenge. Above, two Harbingers balanced in the branches of a tree on either side of the path, waiting to drop a net on top of him. In a moment, he'd be enveloped in its heavy ropes. The holed stones strung on the edges would prevent any escape before they attacked.

Had they set this trap for him? How long had they been preparing this?

Surprisingly, this was not even close to the first time a priest of War had encountered this situation. His token filled his vision with options, and before he could even think, his muscles swung the hooked blade in a mighty arc that cleanly cut through the thick ropes. The net fell around him as he passed through the newly-sliced hole in the center.

The Harbingers above were not expecting that.

Dantess took advantage of their confusion to cut one of the stones from the net's edge. He launched the stone upward at one of the men above, and then threw the blade at the other. A moment later, both thudded onto the forest floor. After checking swiftly to see if the men were disabled, the priest of War resumed the chase.

It wasn't long until the path led into a clearing. Finally, Dantess saw his quarry on the other side, holding a tree and breathing heavily. The man also noticed his pursuer and bolted.

Dantess smiled. The leader was within his grasp.

The priest of War sprinted after him—but his first step landed on nothing: a collection of thin branches and leaves spread over a void. He had been so focused on his target he hadn't noticed the pit trap. Even his lightning-quick reflexes couldn't stop him from plummeting downward into it. When he finally struck the bottom, pain lanced though his leg. His hand felt the sharp stake that penetrated his thigh.

"Shall we talk about how perceptive we are again?" The Harbinger stood at the pit's lip, breathing hard. He removed his mask, revealing a strong chin covered by a closely-trimmed dark beard. "And maybe we should include arrogant as well, yes? You priests of War are all the same. So eager to jump into battle you don't bother to see what you're jumping into." The man pulled away from the opening, but Dantess could still hear him. "A priest of War is a fine prize, but the high priestess of Serenity will be even better—and easy to harvest without your protection. I'll be back to finish you off after."

"Come back, you godless bastard. I'll tear you apart with my bare hands!" There was no answer, and soon even the leader's footsteps faded away.

Dantess tried to rise, but the stake kept him pinned where he was, and the pain that shot through his leg every time he moved was excruciating.

He cursed himself. The man was right. He *was* arrogant. He'd been trained to think of himself as a one-man army, virtually unbeatable in any fight—his token gave him access to every tactic every priest had ever employed—but above tactics was strategy, and he was still vulnerable to those smarter and less impulsive than himself. He knew now that the Harbinger leader had been waiting for him the whole time, just to lead him here.

And with him trapped, the temple was helpless.

What would Varyon think of me now? thought Dantess. *He wouldn't have fallen for such an obvious trap.*

Dantess didn't have the leverage to pull himself off of the stake, so he worked the sharpened stick of wood back and forth in the earth, trying to lever it out of the ground. The pain made him grit his teeth and snarl. After almost blacking out multiple times, the stake came free—still stuck in his leg, but no longer pinning him to the ground. He grabbed a root from the wall of the pit and dragged himself upright with a loud grunt.

"Motti!" he called out. "Solomon! Jeremy! Where are you?"

Only birdsong answered him.

"Motti! Attend me!"

Nothing.

Dantess tensed his muscles to try to leap out of the pit, but the pain in his leg shut that thought right down. He pulled on the root he'd used to stand, but it poked out of the pit wall only about half-way up.

He leaned against the wall. "Motti!" After a moment, he added, "Anyone?"

"Here," Motti's head peaked over the lip of the pit. "How'd you get down there?" Upon seeing the stake in Dantess' leg, he gasped. "You're hurt!"

"Don't worry about that. There's a rope net a bit down the trail. Use it to pull me up. We have to get back to the temple before the Harbingers complete their mission."

"On it." Motti scurried away to follow his orders.

Dantess sighed and hoped it wasn't too late. To his credit, Motti did not dawdle. Soon, Dantess was free of the pit and Motti lent his arm to help the priest limp back to the temple.

"Where is the squad?" asked Dantess.

"Solomon and Jeremy are cleaning up in the forest. We found a knot of Harbingers there, but they weren't well trained. They'll come back when they're done."

"Did you see how many Harbingers got into the temple?"

"No. I was too busy fighting. I was barely able to break away after I heard you."

Dantess grunted at the pain in his leg. "Then we have no idea what's waiting for us there." He released Motti. "Go ahead. You'll be faster. I can walk on my own."

"Are you sure?"

"Of course. Head to the central pagoda. We have to save the high priestess at any cost. That's where the man who trapped me is headed. They want to kill priests more than anything."

Motti nodded and raced ahead.

Dantess stood and tested his leg. It held his weight. The effort was painful, but even with the stake still poking out from his thigh, he felt he could trust his muscle not to buckle. He thought about removing it, but once it was gone, the wound might not stop bleeding.

He staggered through the front arch and into the gardens. At first, they looked just as peaceful as when he first saw them, but when he rounded a corner, three masked Harbingers lay on the ground next to Fullon, his newest squad member. The man's eyes were open. A knife wound in his chest explained why.

"I should have been here," lamented Dantess, his jaw clenched. "You deserved better. At least you should have had your armor to protect you."

Dantess limped from one path to another, trying to keep from getting lost, when sounds of combat rang out nearby. He pushed himself to hurry. A group of four Harbingers surrounded Motti, whose back was against an ancient, braided tree formed of many intertwining trunks that spread into a shared canopy of broad leaves. They were armed with axes and other sharp-looking farming tools. Motti jabbed at them with a spear, keeping them at bay.

Out of reflex, Dantess channeled his Longing through his token and dug deep into its library of tactics. To his surprise, priests of War had found themselves in similar situations with similar wounds. Options lay themselves out in front of him. Once his choice was made, his muscles took charge.

Before anyone knew he was there, Dantess grabbed one of the Harbingers around the throat with one hand and the man's arm with his other. Dantess forced the man to swing the axe he held into the chest of the person standing next to him. Dantess then grabbed the axe himself as he twisted the first man's neck far enough to break it. Finally, the priest of War hurled the axe at a third.

The three Harbingers collapsed within the space of a few moments. The fourth, seeing his comrades down, tried to run, but Motti threw his spear into the man's back, dropping him in his tracks.

"Thank you for the help," Motti said, wiping the sweat from his brow.

But Dantess barely heard him. He was distracted by the braided tree behind Motti. Shifting images surrounded that tree— different flowers, different decorations, different visitors—but the tree was always the same.

He realized other priests of War had seen this tree and, once triggered, his token summoned those memories, some a thousand years old. They showed previous flower arrangements planted in this area, statues and benches that appeared and moved away, and conversations with priests of Serenity. The token didn't limit the available knowledge just to combat. He had access to all of their memories, triggered by familiar places or situations.

It was amazing.

Dantess thought it strange that this ability had never been discussed at War's temple, but he guessed that most priests only found use for the combat training. In truth, it was the token's most obvious and useful trait.

That thought brought him out of his trance. Combat took precedence, especially now. "Keep going," said Dantess. "We've got to get to the central pagoda."

The two trudged to the center of the gardens as fast as they could, but soon realized speed didn't matter.

Warren stood in front of the ring of trees that surrounded the central pagoda. He held a spear out, ready to defend the pagoda from any attack.

"Warren!" Dantess said. "Has anyone gotten this far yet?"

Seeing Dantess, Warren relaxed just a bit. "Well, yes."

"What happened? Are you hurt?"

"No. I didn't want to depend on my own combat skills, so I decided to protect the high priestess another way."

"How?"

Warren moved aside to reveal the Harbinger leader hanging by his foot, stuck in a tree-trap in the entryway. "I realized the only approach to the pagoda is through here, and it's literally a tunnel of trees. With all of this raw material, I thought it would be the perfect site for a trap. And I managed to catch someone. I know I didn't have your permission. Is it all right I did this?"

Dantess slapped Warren on the back. "That's the leader of this little assault group you've got strung up there, and he's alive and kicking."

"The leader?" Warren smiled.

"I guess he wasn't watching where he stepped. I know the feeling." Dantess touched the stake, still in his leg.

Noticing the wound, Warren winced. "Does this make up for my disguise plan? It didn't quite work out as I was hoping."

"Depending on what we get out of him back at the temple, I think it might. This could even be what gets us in the Game. Right now, we have to round up the others. Based on what I've seen, he's the only one with any real training. With him trapped, the others should pose a lot less trouble."

The high priestess glided out from the pagoda. "Has the danger passed?"

"We've cleared the temple and surrounding woods of the Harbingers," said Dantess, tightening the bandage on his thigh. "You and yours should be safe. What are your casualties?"

"Five of our faithless are dead. They threw themselves between the attackers and our priests and priestesses, who are all alive and well. You have done excellent work, priest of War."

"I'm sorry about your bound faithless. Two of my squad were killed as well."

"Don't let it distract you from your victory. They were only faithless, easily replaced. I will send compliments of your work to your temple. I suspect you'll be well rewarded."

Dantess nodded, thankful for her help in raising his rank, but inside he asked himself, *Did she admit that faithless are disposable?*

Just like Dantess, Illistre was faithless once. All priests were. She must have loved someone before she tested here. Did she have friends? Family? How long did it take the priesthood to stop her from caring about them? To change her into someone who could say that?

Did it change everyone?

Will it change me? wondered Dantess.

CHAPTER TEN

THE TATTOO ARTIST, a priest of War named Danzig, dipped his steel pin into the black ink and inserted the pointed rod into a brass tube. "You're gathering quite the collection. Soon, I'll have to hunt for space to add your marks."

Dantess laughed. The comment was like calling ten soldiers an army. "There's plenty of room left. Are you going blind? Maybe you shouldn't be the one to poke me with a needle."

"Quiet." Danzig chuckled. "I can see fine. My point, which you're about to become *very* familiar with," he said as he showed off the needle, "is that you've seen more success than most priests your age. For instance, that Harbinger of Chaos you just brought in? I hear he can actually put a sentence together. We could learn a lot about his cult. It was a real achievement. I'm supposed to give you *two* marks for that mission."

"Two?" Dantess was overjoyed. Two marks were exactly what he needed.

"That's enough to be considered for the Game, right? It's no secret you've been angling for that."

Dantess couldn't hide his smile. "Just barely. Now I need someone to sponsor me." *Like the high priest's Hand,* Dantess finished in his head. After his father suggested Kaurridon, Dantess had tried to catch his eye ever since—but for some reason, he couldn't seem to make a connection. Now could be his moment.

"Ow!" Dantess flinched. The first insertion always hurt the worst, and he hadn't expected it yet.

"I think you just got my point." Danzig smirked. "With prestige comes pain. Now, act like a real warrior while I make you look like one."

"Of course. Sorry. Please go ahead."

The tattoo artist resumed, and Dantess kept his face expressionless. The pain was nothing compared to what each mark represented.

Two more, he thought, astounded. *That makes me the same rank as Kevik.*

He's not going to like that.

It wasn't long until Danzig wrapped up the second mark. As he did, Dantess noticed Jyn walking by the chamber's open door. Without Danzig even knowing she was there, Jyn slowed down, shared a look with Dantess—her large eyes surrounded by the black, tattooed mask, a mixture of menacing and inviting—and jerked her head in the direction she was walking.

Dantess nodded slightly. Jyn smiled and walked away.

He leaned back in the chair, a grin growing on his face. Even though Kevik forbade them from interacting, they weren't breaking any temple rules by doing so. As long as no one found out, Dantess was certain everything would be fine.

"How much longer?" asked Dantess.

"You got somewhere more important to be than here, getting your marks?"

"That's a high bar to clear, but there's someone I have to see."

"Don't worry. I've just finished." Danzig wiped off the skin around the new tattoos. "You're much more fearsome now."

Dantess stood and looked at his arms. He *did* look more fearsome. He was becoming a priest to contend with. "My thanks, Danzig."

"All I ask is that you live up to those marks. With rank comes responsibility. I hope you're ready for it."

"Just another step in following my grandfather's path." He touched his belt and began to walk out of the chamber.

"Grow into the marks you have before chasing his," said Danzig. "You still have a lot to learn."

Dantess waved as he left.

Dantess entered a dark storeroom filled with practice equipment and other boxes, but he knew from experience there was enough room left for two people to meet away from prying eyes. "Are you here?" he asked softly.

"I'm here," said Jyn. She sat on a crate under a small, shuttered window. Only a crack of sunlight escaped through it, but it fell on her face. Dantess could not imagine a more spectacular sight.

If Jyn had been pretty before, now she was beautiful. While still limber and fit, the years had rounded her figure. Her face, once cherubic, now featured her pronounced cheekbones and full lips. No soldier had long hair, so she had cut her flowing brown locks short years ago, but somehow that pulled more attention to her eyes, which hadn't changed: blue and large as a doe's.

Dantess crossed the space and sat next to her. Without a word, they hugged. It made Dantess nervous—Kevik had been clear about how he viewed interaction with her—but he needed to feel close to her. He held her tight.

When they finally broke the embrace, Jyn breathed heavily. "Whew. I guess it has been a while since we've seen each other."

"I missed you," said Dantess.

"Me too. More than I can say." She ran her hand down his muscled arm. When he twitched, she hovered her finger over his fresh tattoo. "Two new marks? Did you take down all the Harbingers single-handedly?"

"Not all of them, but enough, evidently."

Jyn's eyes lit up and she smiled. "Oh! You have the rank to enter the Game, now. The same as Kevik."

"I know. As if he needed any more reason to hate me." Dantess took her hand. "I wish I could figure out a way to get you off of Kevik's squad. Can you imagine training together? Fighting together? Just *being* together without worrying about Kevik seeing us?"

"That's not likely."

"It does happen, though. Squads trade soldiers all the time."

"You know who he would want. The only person he would ask for."

Dantess nodded. "Warren."

"He wants Warren more than ever. It's clear how valuable he's been on your squad. I'm proud of him, but he's attracted a lot of attention. Kevik thinks he's responsible for much of your success."

"He's not wrong. Warren is a strategic genius. He reads everything he can get his hands on. Did you know that he's the one who set the trap that captured the Harbinger I brought in?" Dantess ran a finger over the back of her hand, just as she did with his arm. "But even so, maybe Kevik will come around eventually, and he'll take someone else. Or even two soldiers. Didn't he say that he never really wanted you on his squad in the first place?"

Jyn's face fell. "I think he changed his mind."

"What? Is something wrong?"

Jyn breathed slowly and deeply. "You know that priests sometimes have relationships with their squad members."

"I do," Dantess replied, his jaw tensing. He didn't like where the conversation was going. "My grandmother was on my grandfather's squad when Da was born."

"Right."

Jyn paused again, her brow furrowed. In the silence, Dantess began to get anxious. "And?" he asked.

"So, Kevik has been hinting that he wants something like that with me." Jyn looked down at their clasped hands and tightened her grip.

"No." Dantess' face went white.

"The hints aren't subtle, but he hasn't made any demands yet. I think maybe he wants me to want him, too." Jyn's breath caught. She brought her eyes back up to Dantess' face and he saw her desperation.

"We've got to get you out of there."

A tear rolled down her cheek. "I have no say. I'm faithless. If he orders me, I'm supposed to just agree." She breathed deeply and set her jaw. Fire lit in her eyes. "I won't do that. I won't."

"No. I... I'll figure out something."

"I don't know if you can. But you're sweet for trying." Jyn hugged Dantess again.

Dantess desperately wanted to get her away from Kevik, but right now, he at least wanted her to know how he felt. They had been best friends all their lives, but these last few years of stolen moments made him realize he cared more than that. Definitely more than he'd told her.

What Kevik was planning enraged him. The monster had already taken so much. Now he wanted to steal everything from her. From *them*. Somehow, he had to stop it.

Dantess lifted his head back and looked into her glistening eyes. Even with wet cheeks, she smiled, tilted her head, and closed her eyes.

Is she letting me kiss her? thought Dantess. When Jyn placed her hand on the back of his head, he knew for sure.

With a bursting heart, he pursed his lips and—

"Jyn, what are you doing?" A soldier stood in the doorway, his fingers on the handle.

Jyn pulled out of Dantess' embrace, snapping her hand back. "Roth? How did you find me?"

He shook his head in disgust. "I asked around. Someone saw you come in here. I'm supposed to tell you that our squad is prepping for a mission. But now? Kevik's going to blow his top when he hears about—"

Before Roth could complete his sentence, Dantess sprang across the room, grabbed the man, and slammed him against the wall. Fierce anger and years of fear and desperation took control. "You won't tell anyone about this. Ever." Dantess put his hand around Roth's throat and squeezed.

Roth's eyes bulged. He hit Dantess' arms over and over, but the priest of War didn't even feel the blows.

"Dantess, no!" Jyn cried.

"You heard him," growled Dantess. "He'll tell Kevik, and we know how that will end. I can't let him do that."

Roth tried to talk, or even breathe, but Dantess' grip made both impossible. His resistance grew weaker and weaker.

"It's not his fault. Don't do it. Please," begged Jyn.

"Why not? Happens all the time. Faithless die in battle. Faithless go missing. No one will notice one more gone."

Jyn pulled at Dantess' arms, grunting, "No! You can't!" When she couldn't dislodge him, she stepped back and stared at the muscled warrior priest in shock. "Who are you?"

"What? I mean..." As if waking up, Dantess saw himself choking Roth. He dropped the soldier on the ground, where the man sucked air into his lungs.

Jyn rushed to his side. "Breathe, Roth. It'll be all right. You're all right."

Dantess, still composing himself, knelt down. Even confused a little by his own behavior, he knew what had to happen. "Roth, this is important. You will *not* be all right if you say anything to Kevik about this. Do you believe me?"

Roth stared at Dantess' face with eyes full of fear. He coughed and nodded.

Dantess stood up. He could deal with an enemy's fear, but the shock in Jyn's eyes—that was new. He didn't even know what to make of his own actions. It was all too much for him to handle.

"Jyn, figure out how he's going to explain his condition and take him back to your squad. I need to go."

Jyn did not respond. Instead, she stared at him silently as he exited the storeroom.

Dantess completed a five-move attack against the combat dummy and, on the last strike, broke the staff in half.

Kaurridon, the Hand of the high priest, watched with his arms crossed. Dantess wondered how the man always looked perfect. His breastplate had been shined to mirror brightness, his bracers gleamed like they were new. His hair, on the other hand, was matted and sweaty—as if he had just come from training himself. He chuckled. "Any harder and he wouldn't have a head left."

This was the first time the Hand engaged in small talk with Dantess. Of course, it *had* to be after he'd just broken his weapon, not his finest moment. Embarrassed, Dantess dropped the remaining half of the splintered staff. "I don't think I could hit him harder, so I guess he gets to keep his head."

"Most priests don't celebrate a huge victory by destroying our practice dummies. Are you feeling all right?"

"I'm fine," said Dantess. "But if I could take the opportunity, I was hoping to discuss something with you."

Kaurridon tilted his head, but then he nodded. "Sounds important. Let's go to my office."

"Of course. I need to clean up. I'll be right there," Dantess answered, but Kaurridon was already walking away. He gathered up the pieces of the staff and wondered if he was in any condition to have this conversation. He could still feel Roth's neck in his hands, and Jyn's shock haunted him.

He knew he needed to put his confused feelings to the side for now. After years at the temple, this audience with Kaurridon could be the chance he had been waiting for. Da was depending on him.

He tamped down his feeling of urgency, instead taking his time disposing of the staff and covering the dummy with a heavy tarp. Even after, he did not rush through the temple to get to

Kaurridon's office. Instead, he walked deliberately, collecting his thoughts as his gaze wandered over the architecture.

While the mountain contained a labyrinth of chambers and tunnels beneath his feet—such as the faithless' barracks, the prisons, and the grand library—priests preferred to see the sky. The upper temple was built like a small city atop the plateau. Many sections were open, such as the training fields, expansive courtyards, and even some lovely parks. Dantess ignored those and instead took a turn into a district crowded with buildings, home to armories, taverns, the priests' living quarters, and offices.

The walls were perfectly built—solid and smooth to the touch because of sandstone sheeting—but were broken by the charming balconies supporting rows of open windows. As with everything in the temple of War, function took precedence, but form was not far behind. Even after his years of living here, this place—his home—took his breath away.

The short tour helped to calm his mind. It wasn't long until Dantess reached the building where he knew the Hand kept his office—even though he had yet to visit. He stopped, inhaled and exhaled four deep breaths, and entered. A flight of stairs delivered him to an open door, beyond which Kaurridon sat in a chair on the other side of the chamber.

"Have a seat," said Kaurridon. "Did you know this was your grandfather's office when he was the high priest's Hand?"

Dantess tried to take it all in. It wasn't easy. In contrast with the spartan streets outside, the room was crowded with every War-related object he could think of. A bookcase packed full of ancient editions, scrolls, and bundles of parchments covered one wall, and trophies from past battles, like weapons and banners, hung from the others.

"I knew, but I've never seen it. Are these from his time?" Dantess gestured to some of the weapons.

"Some. Some are from much earlier. He wasn't the only hero called to War." Kaurridon smiled at his own joke.

Dantess stared at a giant, gleaming halberd and wondered, *Who wielded this? What was their story?* On a whim, he channeled his Longing through his token. *Would it work here? Could I see for myself?*

The rush of memories was overwhelming. All at once, the stories and thoughts and conversations of the thousands of priests who ever set foot in this room flooded his view. He couldn't make out a single, individual idea in the collision of so many perspectives.

Dantess brought his hand up to his head and staggered back.

"You're using your token?" asked Kaurridon, perhaps a little impatient at Dantess' foolishness. He pulled out a rock from behind his broad desk constructed of hardwood and steel brackets. "Focus on this stone. Don't look at anything else. It will clear your thoughts."

Dantess did as he was commanded. He studied the stone. Soon, the other images fell away and only the stone remained. "It worked! Is the stone an artifact?"

Kaurridon shook his head. "Of course not. It's just a stone. But it's *my* stone. No other priest has seen it, especially in this room, so no one besides me has any memories of it. Everyone who serves in this office brings something like this, just in case. Until I collect a trophy I truly care about, I just keep this stone." Kaurridon pointed to the simple wooden chair in front of his desk, and Dantess sat down. "I'm surprised you're accessing that ability of your token. The priests that bother are usually much more senior than you. New priests are too fascinated by the combat aspects."

"I stumbled on it during the battle at Serenity. It's amazing. Can you access anyone's memories?"

Kaurridon nodded. "If they were a priest of War, the token remembers what they did. What they saw. What they thought, even. All you need is a trigger."

"I didn't know it could be so overwhelming." Dantess wiped his brow.

"That's the danger of opening yourself up to what's in there. The more you do that, the more your token will show you, and it's not all pleasant. At best, it's a distraction. At worst, you can lose yourself in others' memories. For now, my advice is to stick with combat. That's what it's designed to impart."

"Of course," said Dantess.

Kaurridon leaned back in his chair, still stone-faced. "You're an interesting character. On one hand, your grandfather was Varyon, the legend. On the other hand, your father is in a cell as a suspected sympathizer of the Harbingers of Chaos."

"He's not a sympathizer," Dantess rushed to respond. "He was just in the wrong place at the wrong time. He's no danger to anyone."

Kaurridon lifted an eyebrow. "I know what happened. He wasn't exactly innocent. But I can see how he might have got caught up in something beyond him."

"I managed to keep him and a family friend here at the temple when many of the other prisoners were sent to Evil, but I don't have the rank to release them. In fact, that's partly why I wanted to speak to you." Dantess looked across the desk expectantly.

Kaurridon laughed, but not warmly. "You're still young, so I'm going to excuse your impertinence. You know anyone who opens those cell doors will be responsible for whatever they do in the future. There are damned few priests who would stick their neck out like that for *any* faithless, much less ones they don't know or trust. That won't be me."

Dantess put both his palms in the air. "No, I'd never ask that of you. But normally, it would take me another decade to get the rank necessary to release them."

Kaurridon arched his eyebrow. "And?"

"I'd like you to sponsor me to compete in the Game of War."

The Hand's eyes opened wide, then he laughed again. "You? You've been here for what, two years? You want to compete in the most important tournament in the temple's history?"

"I do." Dantess set steel into his eyes.

Kaurridon's laughter stopped. "You have only just earned enough marks to be considered, although I do admit, achieving such a feat in two years wasn't easy. It required a lot from both you and your squad. Was this your goal the whole time?"

Dantess nodded. "My squad is ready. They've been training for this, too."

"Do you know what the Game *means*? It's not just a competition."

"Of course I do. Is there a priest with any ambition who doesn't? The winner of the Game of War earns the position of Guardian for the Convergence of the Divine."

Kaurridon nodded, a twinkle in his eye. "And what do you know of the Convergence?"

"Every hundred years, priests from Good and Evil bring their Gifts to a secret location to negotiate the laws that govern the faithless. Law, Good's ally, comes to advise and record, and War, Evil's ally, protects the gathering. The Guardian is responsible for that."

"You've been studying," said Kaurridon.

"And I've learned that becoming the Guardian can change a priest's life forever. Many protectors went on to become Hands. A few eventually became high priests."

"So that's it, isn't it?" asked Kaurridon. "You think winning will earn you enough rank to release your father."

Dantess studied Kaurridon's face for any clue about how the man felt about this, but—as with the rest of this conversation— the Hand revealed nothing. He decided to barrel ahead regardless. "Yes. I do. He's been in that cell for two years. I don't think he can last ten more."

The Hand rubbed his chin, and a smile crept onto his face, his first truly warm expression. "I have to admit there are worse choices. You're Varyon's grandson, and you're clearly motivated, but I'm not sponsoring someone who doesn't know what they're getting into." Kaurridon pulled a pile of parchments from his desk and winked. "Let's change that." He carefully laid them out and pointed to the top page. *"This* is the Game of War."

Dantess' eyes opened wide. He couldn't believe it. The difference in Kaurridon's demeanor was astonishing. At first, the Hand was like a wall. Now, he seemed all in.

Maybe this wasn't the first time he considered me? wondered Dantess. *Could he have been waiting for this?*

"Are those the actual rules? We couldn't find anything that discusses how it's played."

"We don't keep these pages in the library. They're locked away and only brought out when needed. The Game is not easy. In fact, while the rules prohibit killing, some priests still don't come back." Kaurridon studied Dantess' face. "Are you still interested?"

"I don't scare easily. Tell me more."

"According to the instructions, you must collect a trophy locked in a room at the top of a tower. The priest who returns with the trophy wins the Game."

"That sounds straightforward."

Kaurridon scoffed. "It will be the most difficult mission you've ever faced. To start, you'll be competing against four other priests sponsored by War's senior leadership, each with at least twelve marks."

"Which I have!"

"You have the minimum, yes. So does Kevik, whom the high priest is sponsoring. I hear there is some friction between you two. Will that be a problem?"

Dantess didn't enjoy the thought of competing against Jyn, but he relished the thought of beating Kevik. "Not for me."

Kaurridon flipped the top sheet to the side. "Each priest is given a chest. Inside each chest is a single key. It says here that you cannot open your *own* chest, but you can open any of the other priests'."

Dantess shook his head. "So, you have to protect your chest while trying to open up the others? How can someone do two things at once?"

"You'll have your squad with you. Early on, the challenge is to allocate your resources to defend *and* attack."

"All right, then what are the keys for?"

"To open the tower. This is where it gets confusing."

"Confusing? It's a tower with a locked door. You need a key to enter, right?"

Kaurridon held up his hand. "It's not that simple. War didn't build the tower. Evidently, when the Game first started, the job was given to Evil, and you know how devious they can be." Kaurridon studied the words on the page in front of him. "Its door is unique. It has five locks on it. You can enter the door by unlocking one, all five, or any number in between. I suppose it depends on how many keys you've managed to collect."

"Why wouldn't you enter as soon as you get one key?"

"The tower is magical. The number of locks you open determines what's on the other side of the door. Use one key, and you'll find it nearly impossible to get to the top. Use five keys and your path will be simple. Do you remember those priests who didn't come back?" Kaurridon held up a single finger. "Most used one key."

Dantess leaned back in his chair, his eyes wide. "All right, different question: why would anyone use *one* key then? Especially if the tower might kill you if you do?"

"Because more than one priest can enter. Each has a unique experience that ends up at the tower's top room. *If* they manage to get there. When someone unlocks the door, it takes the keys they used out of play. Any priest who still wants to win will have to enter with whatever keys are left outside. Even if there's only one."

"Sounds terrifying." Dantess smiled. "I want in."

"Don't get overconfident." Kaurridon returned the smile. "But your enthusiasm has convinced me. I'll sponsor you."

Dantess stood up, beaming. "You won't regret it!"

"See that I don't. The Convergence will be held in a month, so we're preparing for the Game now." Kaurridon handed Dantess a bundle of papers wrapped in twine. "Go over this with your squad. It details everything you'll need to know." He learned back and waved his hand. "Dismissed. I have duties to complete. Tomorrow, I'm going to lose the entire day to guarding the gatehouse."

Dantess stood up and saluted. He knew that, despite his rank, Kaurridon insisted on taking a rotation in guard duty. It was one of the things Dantess admired about him. But he also felt bad for anyone stationed with the Hand. Kaurridon insisted everyone else around him give nothing but their best.

He walked out the door. Before Dantess entered this office, he'd only dreamed about the Game of War. Now, he was one of only five priests in the whole temple who would play!

CHAPTER ELEVEN

"WHAT'S YOUR NAME?" Dantess sat on a wooden stool across from the Harbinger he'd captured, who was chained to a metal ring affixed to the floor of a barren cell. The cell was identical to the others in the bowels of the temple. It had a fitted stone floor just rough enough to be uncomfortable to sit on and stained windowless walls permeated with a permanent smell of despair. War's cells weren't pleasant—which brought to mind his father's years spent in one—but they were a much better alternative to Evil's dungeons.

"Does it matter?" asked the Harbinger. "I'm faithless. That's all you care about."

"Not true at all! I very much care about the temple you attacked and the people you murdered. Lots of faithless *aren't* chained to a cell floor. The difference is, they didn't kill someone on my squad." Dantess had sympathy for the faithless as a whole, but not those that joined the Harbingers.

"Others may not have these chains." He lifted his hands and the metal links clinked. "Not yet. But every faithless is just one bad month away from being sold into slavery."

"That's your justification for murder? The system is unfair? The same system that has worked for thousands of years?"

"Says someone who *takes* the tithe instead of *paying* it."

Dantess crossed his arms. He wasn't comfortable defending the temples on this subject, but he wasn't here to discuss politics with a terrorist. "I'm not going to debate the tithe with you."

"Right." The Harbinger dropped his hands. "There is no debate, and there never will be. That's why we resist. It's our only option. Priests can't collect the tithe if they're dead. They can't sell me to a temple or send me to the dungeons of Evil, either."

Dantess decided to follow this track. Perhaps the man would reveal something about his organization. "So. You want to kill all the priests? That's a pretty big job. You're going to need a lot of Harbingers."

The man smiled. "We're gaining more every day. You can strike me down, but two more will join the cause after me and two more for each of them. There are far more faithless out there than priests. Eventually, we'll rid the world of priests and temples and gods."

This man is insane, thought Dantess.

"A world without priests and... *gods*?" Dantess laughed. "You're a smart man. Capable, too. You know it's impossible. Feeding an impossible dream to ignorant people will just get them killed."

"Impossible?" The man tried to stand up, but the chains kept him hunched. Spittle flew when he screamed, "You're laughing at me, but your arrogance keeps you from seeing what's right in front of you. Ask the people of Seaborn Notch if my dream is so 'impossible'!"

Dantess was taken aback. "What?"

The man shook his head and sat back down on the floor.

"What was that about Seaborn Notch?" Dantess had never even heard of the place. "Where is that?"

The silence that followed was broken by a knock at the door. "Dantess?" The door opened, revealing Warren. "Kevik's squad is returning. You asked me to alert you."

Dantess stared at the prisoner for a few more moments, then rose from his chair. He didn't expect to learn more from the man now anyway. "I'll give you some time to think about your future. If you're more forthcoming, maybe I can find a way to keep you out of the dungeons of Evil."

"Don't bother," the man muttered into his crossed arms. "I've got nothing more to say to you."

"We'll see," said Dantess as he left the cell and closed the door behind him.

Dantess and Warren raced to the lift in the courtyard. Along the way, Warren asked, "Did he say anything?"

"Not much. He mentioned a place called Seaborn Notch. Ever heard of it?"

Warren furrowed his brow. "I think it's a remote port. Hard to get to, surrounded by mountains on one side and water on the other."

"When I said that a world without priests was impossible, he brought up Seaborn Notch. There are priests there, right? Of course there are."

"The only thing I know about the area is that, because it's so far from the temples, pirates tend to frequent the port. But as far as I'm aware, there are priests."

They arrived at the lift just as it groaned to a stop. Kevik's squad began to disembark, but two people were missing: Kevik and Jyn.

Dantess pulled Roth from the group. "Where are they?"

Roth's face blanched. "I didn't say anything. I swear."

"That's not the question I asked you. Where are *Jyn* and *Kevik*?"

"I'll tell you, but not here," Roth muttered. He walked behind a sweeping arch, out of sight from his squad. Dantess and Warren followed. "Last night in camp, Kevik asked Jyn to come to his tent. They were in there for a while..."

"Spit it out."

"All right! I heard some sounds of fighting and then a scream. Jyn came running out, clutching her side. Kevik followed minutes later, limping and angry. When we couldn't find her, he declared Jyn a deserter and that he'd track her down. On his own."

"She's no deserter!" responded Warren.

"I wouldn't have thought so, but she ran," said Roth.

Warren cried, "And it doesn't matter why? What if she had no choice?"

Dantess held up his hand to stop Warren from talking. "That'll be all, Roth. Return to your squad."

Roth saluted and followed his squad into the barracks.

Warren wrung his hands. "We have to get to her before Kevik does!"

Dantess was already walking to the lift. "I agree. I've seen how Kevik deals with deserters. But Jyn's smart. She won't be found easily. I think you and I are much more likely to find her— and if we do, we can protect her."

"Where do we start?"

Dantess gave the signal to the lift operator, and the floor under their feet began to travel down the shaft. "Kevik's mission wasn't far from here. Where do you think Jyn would go if she were trying to hide?"

Almost immediately, Warren answered, "Freethorn Creek."

"That's where we start."

Dantess and Warren approached Freethorn Creek's main thoroughfare, but halted before the horses entered the crowded street. For a fairly isolated town, its proximity to the temple drew some brisk and diverse trade, and market day was in full swing. Stands and tents blocked the road, and shoppers filled whatever space was left between them.

"I know a lot of hiding spots in town, but I'm not sure which Jyn would use—especially after I told Kevik about most of them when we were looking for your mother," said Dantess, patting his horse.

"She wouldn't go to any of those," answered Warren. "Roth said she was holding her side. I think she may be injured."

"Would she go to the sanctuary of Charity? That has to be the first place Kevik would look. And wouldn't they report a deserter from War?"

"No, there's another place where she might find healing."

"Where?"

Warren hesitated. "Maybe Mother Nettle's?"

"Mother Nettle? Why would Jyn go to her camp of thieves?"

Warren raised his eyebrow. "Orphans, you mean. The ones who refuse to live at Charity's sanctuary. Mother Nettle takes care of them. She feeds them, and she heals them when necessary. Jyn and I visited her a lot. I used to play and read to the kids, and Jyn would bring sweets. We were always welcome there. When our mother was busy, it was like a second home to us." Warren smiled and then nodded—as if landing on a conclusion. "Mother Nettle is strange, but she's loyal. I can't think of any better place for Jyn to hide."

"She sounds like someone who isn't fond of Order. Might she be in league with the Harbingers?"

"Mother Nettle?" Warren let a small smile slip out. "Never. Trust me, she'd want nothing to do with them."

"All right. It's worth looking into. Where is she?"

Warren shrugged. "I'm not sure. She doesn't trust anyone, so she stays on the move, and I haven't kept track of her location since I lived here."

"Then how do we find her?"

"Mother Nettle doesn't travel light. She has some favorite sites where she likes to set up her camp—until Law forces her to move on." Warren kicked his horse into motion. "Let's start by checking those."

After two empty locations, Dantess felt discouraged, but Warren refused to quit. The next site was a glen, but riding into it, they heard none of the ruckus they would have expected from an active camp.

"Maybe your information is out of date," said Dantess. "We're wasting time. Does her camp even exist anymore?"

"Wait," said Warren. He pointed to some discarded trash. "There. And over there!" He indicated a cold fire pit and cleared sites for tents. "They were here. Probably not long ago."

"Does that help us?"

"Well, it means the camp still exists. It's possible that they moved because Jyn is with them," said Warren. "Easiest way to keep her safe is to keep her hidden. If Mother Nettle is off the map, she might have gone somewhere we won't be able to stumble upon her."

"Then what can we do?" Dantess kicked at the blackened charcoal of a cook fire. He looked down and picked up the remains of a broken straw doll. "Wait, what about the kids?"

"The orphans? What about them?"

"They're not just orphans—they're thieves. And it's *market day*! They're not lying around in tents. Right now, they're out in the crowds, stealing from shoppers' purses. If we can find one of her kids, they can tell us where Mother Nettle is."

Doubt flashed across Warren's face. "They train to stay inconspicuous. I doubt we'd look into a crowd and just notice one." Warren scratched his chin as he thought. "But maybe we can get one to notice *us*. Or more likely, *you*."

Dantess smiled. "You have a plan?"

"I have a plan," Warren agreed.

It was like he never left. Dantess breathed in the familiar smells of the spice booth, listened to the spirited haggling leaking out of the carpet tent, and enjoyed the many colors of fruit and flowers on display. The street was packed with shoppers. Such was the bustle of a busy market day in Freethorn Creek, and he missed it terribly.

Dantess patted the full purse hanging from his belt. Normally, priests kept their wealth hidden from view, but today, it was on display. The purse hung by a single string—a very tempting prize for a potential thief with a sharp knife. Hopefully, the temptation would be greater than the fear of stealing from a priest of War.

"This better work," muttered Dantess to himself. "I like this pouch."

He scanned the area, looking for anyone out of the ordinary, and realized that most people were staring back at him. While his kind wasn't unheard of in town, priests of War rarely shopped for themselves in the market. People were interested. Which probably meant whoever Dantess was looking for already knew he was here.

A few shoppers brushed by him as he headed to a stand selling fish. Once he reached the stand, he noticed his purse was gone. Dantess whistled once, quick and loud.

Along the side of the street, Warren was already on the move, his eyes tracking the child who had just passed Dantess. While Dantess couldn't see the quarry, he could see Warren—so he changed course and walked parallel to Warren's path.

Not far down the street, Warren motioned to an alley. Both of them walked inside, just in time to see a young girl, perhaps ten years old, round the far corner. They ran after her, and once around, saw her enter another alley, but not before she looked back and noticed her pursuers.

The chase was on!

Dantess channeled his Longing through War's badge, and his speed increased dramatically. He bolted down the alleyway, rounded the corner, and saw the girl trying to wriggle between the bars of a sewer grate. She had short-cropped brown hair under a dirty cap, ragged clothes, and a look of terror in her dark eyes as she became stuck. She was also missing her left arm below the elbow.

"Leave me alone!" The girl struggled with her right hand to push herself through the small space between the bars. Ironically, the bulge in her shirt—clearly Dantess' purse—was likely keeping the girl from slipping through.

"Stop struggling," said Dantess, coming to a stop. "You're going to hurt yourself."

"Raine?" asked Warren as he entered the alley. "Is that you?"

The girl went still. "I'm not Raine anymore. Do you know me?"

"Of course. I'm Warren, remember? I saw you at Mother Nettle's camp a bunch of times growing up. You're bigger now." Warren chuckled. "Too big to fit through that grate. Haven't tried this escape route for a while, I'm guessing?"

Raine frowned. "You look different."

Warren pointed at the dark, tattooed mask surrounding his eyes. "I know. I went to War. So did Dantess here. He's Tolliver's son. I'm in his squad."

Raine turned to Dantess. With almost no inflection, she stated, "You're a priest. Are you going to kill me?"

Dantess almost smirked, but stopped himself. He realized Raine wasn't joking, and the question wasn't farfetched from her perspective. It was actually chilling how matter-of-fact her tone was. "No," he said simply. "I'd like my pouch back, but I'm not going to hurt you. *At all.* I just want to ask you a question."

"Get me out first." Raine struggled a bit more in vain. "Please?"

"Warren, grab on to her. Pull when I say."

Warren took hold of Raine's arm while Dantess braced himself. He channeled his Longing and applied his increased strength to bending the iron bars to make the space wider. The bars groaned, as did Warren, pulling Raine. The girl popped free of the grate, and both she and Warren fell onto the ground.

Dantess could see the calculation in Raine's eyes, determining if she could make an escape, but she must have decided against it. Raine pulled out the purse from her shirt and reluctantly handed it to the priest of War.

Dantess accepted the purse, opened it, and pulled out a single gold coin. "Raine, this is yours if you help us."

"That's not my name anymore. It's Lightfinger. It's because I'm really good at using the hand I have left." She showed off her right hand. "Mother Nettle gave me the name when I got my token." She used her hand to reveal a golden pin on the inside of her worn jacket. Warren and Dantess both looked at it, and then each other. Both were clearly thinking, *Token?*

"What do I have to do for the coin?" she continued.

"Do you remember my sister, Jyn?" asked Warren. When Lightfinger nodded, he continued, "We think she may be with Mother Nettle. Do you know if she is?"

She shrugged.

"Jyn may be in a lot of trouble. Can you take us there?"

"Him, too?" Lightfinger pointed at Dantess. "For only one gold?"

"Me, too." Dantess added another coin to the one in his hand. "Now would *this* be worth the trouble?"

Lightfinger nodded and held out her hand.

Dantess put a coin into that hand, but kept the other. "You get the remainder once we're there. Agreed?"

The girl thought about it, but finally nodded. "I'll take you. But Mother won't like it. If you die, it's not my fault." She started walking down the alleyway.

Dantess and Warren shared a look, then followed after.

Lightfinger led them out of town and into the nearby forest. It was obvious that she was taking an unnecessarily complicated route, perhaps trying to confuse the pair. And, in fact, once she jumped over a ditch and ducked beneath the low branches of a tree, they lost sight of her.

"Wait for us!" said Warren. "You're getting too far ahead!"

Dantess stepped over the ditch and sighed. "I think that was the idea. She wasn't leading us to Mother Nettle. She was trying to lose us in the forest."

They brushed aside the tree branches and found themselves in a dark hollow. Trees overhead blocked the sunlight, leaving them in complete shadow. Lightfinger was nowhere to be seen.

"See?" said Dantess. He took a step ahead and his foot snagged against a hidden wire, which triggered two small blasts on either side of them.

"What was that?" asked Warren, shielding his face.

"I'm not sure, but I don't think those were meant to hurt us." Indeed, whatever they were continued to produce smoke that was quickly filling the hollow.

"*Go back, intruders!*" A loud, deep, warbling voice echoed around them.

"Who said that?" Warren put his hands in front of him, but the smoke made even those hard to see. "Where is it coming from?"

"*You are trespassing in our temple. Turn or be destroyed by the magic of our goddess.*" The voice echoed from everywhere.

"Temple? There's no temple out here," called out Dantess as he took a step forward. As he did, he kicked another hidden wire attached to bells. They jingled.

"*You were warned.*"

A stone flew out from between the trees and struck Dantess' chest. "What?" Then two more hit his back, and yet another struck between Dantess' eyes. *That* one hurt.

"What's happening?" asked Warren.

Before Dantess could stop him, Warren stepped into a nest of bells too, and a barrage of stones pelted both of them. They shielded their faces, but the rocks were sharp and thrown at respectable speed, likely with slingshots. Dantess began to worry that they could be seriously injured.

He grabbed Warren's shoulder and pulled him to the ground. "Down," Dantess whispered. "If we can't see them, they can't see us."

Flat on the ground, Warren called out, "I'm Jyn's brother! She's in trouble and she needs our help. Mother Nettle knows me. Please stop! It's me, Warren!"

The torrent of rocks ceased.

"*Wait there,*" the otherworldly voice said.

Dantess glanced at Warren. "Are you hurt?"

"Bruised, but not injured. I'll have some welts tomorrow."

When the smoke finally began to clear, Dantess became impatient. "We don't have forever to wait. What if Jyn isn't even here at all? This could all be a big waste of time." He climbed to his feet and watched for movement in the trees.

As Warren joined him on his feet, Lightfinger walked out from the tree line. "You should come with me now."

Dantess crossed his arms. "We just got pelted with stones. Why didn't you tell them who we were?"

"Why do you think they stopped?" Lightfinger pointed to herself. "You're lucky I want that last coin." She motioned for them to follow and walked back into the trees.

The pair followed her to a trail, which led to a bored-looking boy holding a large, brass funnel. As they passed, the boy smirked, lifted the funnel to his mouth, and said into it, "*Stay on the path or the magic will get you.*" His words were amplified and warbled just enough to sound otherworldly. He laughed.

The path led into a large clearing full of tents and cooking fires. Dirty children in ragged clothes were everywhere—playing, carrying wood, tending the fires, sewing, feeding younger children, but mostly staring at the new arrivals.

Lightfinger led them to an older girl putting a bandage on a young boy's scratch. She had a large but old burn along the side of her face, which was mostly covered by a scarf. "This is Eversong. You should speak with her."

"Eversong?" said Warren. "I think I played with you a few times, years ago. Your name is Vi, right?"

"Not anymore. My priestess name is Eversong. But I do remember you, Warren. You were terrible at hide-and-fetch. What can I do for you?"

"My sister is missing. You remember Jyn? She was hurt, and she's on the run. We think she may have come to Mother Nettle for refuge. Is she here?"

"Your sister is hiding from a priest of War, and you brought one right into our camp. You're only here because we know you. But we don't know him."

"So she *is* here!" Warren exhaled a breath of relief. "I'm so glad." He gestured to Dantess. "This is not the man who injured her. He's here to help, just like me."

"I don't pretend to understand the politics of War, but if one priest wants to capture someone, don't they all?"

"This is a special case," interjected Dantess. "I know Jyn. I knew her before I joined War. She's my friend. I don't believe she did anything to deserve what Kevik has planned for her."

125

Eversong thought about this and shook her head. Before she could speak, though, Warren cut her off. "Listen, I know Mother Nettle, and she knows me. I spent a big part of my childhood in her camps. I'm sure if I could just speak to her directly, I could clear it all up."

Eversong lifted her eyebrow. "If you wish an audience, I will prepare her. Lightfinger will bring you in when she is ready." Eversong walked across the camp and entered the largest tent.

While they waited, Dantess and Warren looked around. "So many children. More than I remember," said Warren.

Lightfinger nodded. "Parents are auctioned to the temples all the time. The children have to go somewhere."

"Why don't they go to Charity's sanctuary?" asked Dantess. "They can stay there at least until they turn sixteen."

"Charity?" Lightfinger scoffed. "Have you ever been to a sanctuary? Sure, there's food, and they'll pay the tithe, but we feel like dirt the whole time we're there. Even Charity's faithless workers look down on us. We're the dregs. The lowest. Just marking time until we get hauled up onto that auction block ourselves.

"Mother Nettle gives us something to be part of. It may not be entirely legal, and it may not even make sense sometimes, but we have a purpose. We contribute. And she doesn't think we're trash. That's worth a lot." Lightfinger dramatically jumped up, having been poked by a toddler behind her. He tittered and ran away.

While Lightfinger was distracted, Dantess whispered to Warren, "Is Mother Nettle running a temple here? Every child is a priest or priestess?"

"Kind of," said Warren, awkwardly scratching his head. "You heard Lightfinger. It gives the kids some structure, a sense of belonging. But no one takes it too seriously."

"It's sacrilegious," replied Dantess.

"Don't worry. It's all in fun. I was here when she made it all up. I even helped to make Mother Nettle's 'Gift'. You'll see. We'll have a laugh about it."

Eversong poked her head out of the tent, waved her hand, and disappeared back inside. "High Priestess is ready for you now," said Lightfinger. She led them to the large tent.

Dantess and Warren walked inside. They paused to let their eyes adjust to the glare and shine. Many, many polished surfaces reflected the multitude of flaming braziers and candles placed everywhere. At first glance, it appeared the tent held a treasure hoard worth the ransom of a whole temple, but then, Dantess saw that the gold and jewels were but scraps of brass and glass. Far from containing a treasure trove, the tent was instead filled with gleaming refuse.

At the far end, a plump old woman sat on a raised chair. She was decorated with so many jewels and bangles, colorful scarves and feathers, it was difficult to make out the woman behind it all. On her head, she wore a glistening tiara, and on a stand to her side sat what looked like a bulbous collection of gems and coins stuck together in a single mass.

"Who seeks an audience with the high priestess of Glamour?" she asked in a quiet yet still raspy and abrasive voice.

Warren laughed and waved. "Mother Nettle, it's me! Warren!" He strode toward her, sidestepping the sparkly piles to approach. "Wow. I remember when you started this game. The temple of Glamour, where even the lowest faithless could be a priest or priestess. I love it. You've really built it into something!"

"Game?" Mother Nettle frowned more with each step Warren took.

"Of course. 'Glamour' was a joke, right? I mean, you chose the name because it's all an illusion. It's fake." He stepped close to her. "Look at this." He picked up the collection of baubles by her side. "Same 'Gift'. It's grown since we made it, though. Are any of my original pieces in there still? It's hard to tell..."

Warren peered at the clump in his hands, then looked up into the seething face of Mother Nettle.

"You *dare?*"

She slammed her walking stick on a wooden board at her feet, striking like a thunderclap. As Warren's mouth dropped open, two boys appeared in each tent corner behind the chair. They all held bows with arrows drawn.

"You mock my goddess?" she screeched. "You call her a joke? In her own *temple?*"

Warren stepped back, stammering, "I didn't... I didn't mean..."

Two more boys and one girl entered the tent from the rear, also armed with bows and arrows.

"Would any other god tolerate such blasphemy?" roared Mother Nettle, struggling to her feet. "No. Not one of them."

Dantess channeled his Longing through his token. Possibilities swam before his eyes. In every case, he could disable or kill all of his opponents, but he could not find an option where Warren was guaranteed to live.

Mother Nettle raised her hand. The bowstrings groaned under strain as the children drew their arrows back.

Dantess tensed. He was about to spring—to put the least bad option into play—but before he could, the tent door flew open once more.

"Stop!" Jyn stood at the door. "High Priestess, please don't do this!"

Dantess halted his plans. It was Jyn! Here!

Thank War, we found her, thought Dantess.

"They disrespected me!" Mother Nettle cried out. "They disrespected my goddess! And my children! No one does that!"

Jyn strode forward. "This isn't you, High Priestess. You are a healer. A mother. You care for people. You don't kill them."

"But you didn't hear what they said. They called me a *joke!*"

Dantess' mind raced. When Mother Nettle started this camp, she designed a religion to provide her kids with things they were missing: a place to live, a structure to their lives, and a sense of belonging. Since then, she had clearly gone over a tipping point. To her, the temple façade had become real. But her delusion was fragile. It needed something, something she craved for her *and* her children.

Even though it wouldn't cost Dantess anything, it was the most valuable thing he could offer—and only *he* could offer it. He would ask his god for forgiveness later.

Dantess took a deep breath. "High Priestess of Glamour, I am a priest of the god of War. I regret that no one has come before me to welcome you to the pantheon of temples. Your goddess has been overlooked for too long."

"She has?" The anger fell from Mother Nettle's face, replaced with surprise. "She has!"

Dantess slowly walked to her chair as the tip of every arrow followed his movement. The bowstrings creaked with tension. "You have created so much on your own, and as high priestess, you inspire complete loyalty in your priests and priestesses. I am impressed."

Mother Nettle sat back down and nodded, enthralled.

"Most importantly, you have used your powers to build a community that cares for those forgotten by the other temples. Such an achievement deserves respect and recognition." Dantess took the malformed Gift from a stunned Warren's grasp and placed it back on the stand. "I am pleased to offer that to you. And, if I could be so bold..." Dantess held out his hand.

Surprised, Mother Nettle put her hand in his. He leaned down and kissed it.

Mother Nettle smiled and blushed. "This is your friend, Jyn?" When Jyn nodded, Nettle continued, "Such a silver tongue for a priest of *War*."

"He is special," Jyn agreed.

As she retrieved her hand, she gestured to the guards to relax. They dropped their arrow tips down. "You think I don't remember you, Dantess? Tolliver's son? You take after him. He was a good man."

"He still is. He's alive and staying in the temple of War."

"What's he doing there? He's not a priest, too?"

"No. He's a..." Dantess paused, then finally finished with, "guest."

"A faithless guest?" Mother Nettle scoffed. "I know what that means. He's locked up there, isn't he?"

Dantess cleared his throat. "Unfortunately, yes. The priest who's after Jyn is the same one who locked him up. I've been trying to get my father out for years, but it hasn't been easy. Temple politics." Dantess winked. "You understand."

Mother Nettle winked back conspiratorially. "Indeed. Running a temple isn't for the faint-hearted." She gestured to Jyn to approach and took her hand when she did. "Are you feeling better, child?"

Jyn put her other hand on her side. "Yes, thank you."

"And you feel safe leaving with Dantess?"

"I do."

The self-declared high priestess turned to Dantess. "Then I am willing to release her into your care, priest of War. I only ask one thing."

Dantess said, "Yes?"

"Now that you've recognized my goddess, could our temple receive a portion of the tithe? We've struggled for so long to feed so many." The righteous expression of the high priestess dropped, leaving only the pleading eyes of Mother Nettle. "It's only right we should get *some* gold, like every other temple. Yes?"

"Tithe?" Dantess thought on his feet. "I... I'm sorry, but I cannot guarantee any regular delivery of tithe. Those in charge can take years, even decades, to officially recognize a new temple." He pulled out his own full purse. "But I would like to contribute what I can in the meanwhile. Perhaps this might make it less necessary for your children to scrounge—at least, for a time."

Mother Nettle's eyes shone bright as she reached for the purse. Just as Dantess was about to hand it over, he stopped and removed a coin.

"I have to pay my debts first. Lightfinger?"

The one-handed girl walked up. Dantess placed the final coin in her palm. "Are we settled?"

She nodded with a smile. "Good doing business with you." With that, she ran off.

Dantess gave the purse to Mother Nettle, whose eyes grew once she felt the weight. "This is all... gold?" she stammered. "I never... So much... It will feed my children for months. You have my thanks. From us all."

"I've never spent my gold better."

"You must let me give you a gift for your temple. A treasure! Something from our collection!" The old woman waved her hands toward the piles of metal and glass. "Your choice. Anything!"

Dantess looked at the sparkling trash and sighed. "I couldn't possibly take something from—"

"I'll pick for you," said Jyn. She whispered as she passed Dantess, "You'll break her heart if you refuse."

"Of course," agreed Dantess.

Jyn walked among the piles, examining each item carefully, lifting pieces and gently moving some to the side. With each touch, Mother Nettle took in a breath and reached out her hands, as if everything Jyn handled was precious and fragile. Finally, Jyn lifted a small, golden box and exclaimed, "I found it!"

"What is it?" asked Dantess.

Mother Nettle chuckled. "That's a music box, right? If I remember, Jyn herself added it to our collection many years ago." She tapped her head. "Like a steel trap."

"She's right," said Jyn. "This is my old mechanical music box from when I was a little girl. Now you can keep it, to remind you of me when I'm not around."

"It's the perfect gift," said Dantess. Indeed, of everything in this tent, it was likely the only thing he would want. "I'll treasure it. Thank you for your generosity, High Priestess." He bowed to Mother Nettle, who smiled. "We must be going. The sooner we leave, the sooner I can get Jyn to safety."

"As you wish, but you two are always welcome here. And," she paused and glared at Warren for a moment before her smile returned, "even Warren here. No one can say that Glamour's high priestess doesn't have a sense of humor. I didn't get this old without having my patience tested a time or two." She ruffled his hair and, while Warren looked annoyed, he did not complain.

Eversong sidled up to Mother Nettle and whispered in her ear.

"Another priest of War has been spotted in Freethorn Creek," Mother Nettle reported. "I assume it's the one pursuing Jyn? You must be swift. Get her to safety."

"I will," replied Dantess, more worried than he let on. If Kevik had been seen nearby, he could be close.

CHAPTER TWELVE

DANTESS, JYN, AND Warren exited the tent and searched out a quiet corner of the camp. Warren grabbed Jyn and hugged her. Dantess waited until his turn and did the same. When the embrace was done, he asked, "Are you all right?"

"Yes. Mother Nettle was a big help."

Dantess' eyes pleaded. "Then tell me what's going on! What happened with Kevik last night? Why are you running?"

Jyn clenched her teeth and clasped her hands together. "I don't want to talk about this."

"Did he...?" asked Dantess.

She looked down. After a moment, she admitted, "He tried. I refused. When he didn't listen, I refused with a knife. After that, I ran." Jyn looked at Dantess, the pain clear in her eyes. "He would have killed me."

"He can't do that. He can't force you," insisted Warren.

"Not according to the temple rules, but it happens," growled Dantess. "No one believes a faithless' word against a priest, so it's never reported."

"This means I'm a deserter now," said Jyn. "Right? I'm dead."

"No. *I'm* a priest, and I will support you. You saw this coming and you told me before all this. I'll make sure you're heard. We'll go directly to the high priest's Hand. He and I have talked."

Jyn shook her head. "Kevik will never let that happen. Just airing this in the temple would be an embarrassment. And if I'm somehow allowed to live, I'll be right where I started: on his squad. I can't do that!"

Dantess set his jaw and took Jyn's shoulders. "I don't know how, but I'm getting you transferred. They can't refuse me after this! And if that doesn't work, I'll try something else. You're never going back to him."

He knew he would do anything to save her.

Because he loved her.

In that moment, staring into Jyn's face, his heart swelled. The love he felt—likely had *always* felt—was real and undeniable.

Jyn met his gaze. She'd never been so vulnerable, so scared—but despite that, her eyes reflected his love back to him.

She smiled. "Thank you." Jyn lifted her hands to either side of his head, pulled him down, and kissed him.

Pleasantly overwhelmed, Dantess closed his eyes and let the world fall away. He could have stayed in that kiss forever, but just moments after it started, an explosion sounded from somewhere nearby in the forest. Still embracing, they both looked toward the noise.

A distant, warbling yell followed. "*You are trespassing in our temple. Turn or be destroyed by the magic of our goddess.*"

"What was that?" asked Warren.

"It has to be Kevik!" said Dantess, releasing Jyn. "He must have trailed us here."

"You are hard to miss," said Warren. "Lots of people probably saw where we were headed."

Jyn ran deeper into the camp, with the boys following behind. When she found Eversong, she stopped. "You have to get everyone out of here, at least for now. The priest of War that's coming will kill everyone here to find me."

Eversong nodded, ducked into a tent, and emerged with a large bell in hand. She heaved it up and down and the sound carried throughout the camp. This was clearly not the first time those in the camp had heard the bell, because even the smallest children knew their roles. Soon, everyone was scrambling for the forest.

"We should take advantage of this chaos to slip out," said Warren. "But we have to go quickly."

"Then let's go." Dantess took a step toward the forest, but Jyn grabbed his arm.

"Wait a moment." Jyn dragged Dantess back and slipped the music box into his hand. "You almost forgot your gift. Keep it safe, just in case."

"I'll keep you *both* safe, don't worry." After he kissed her again—something he could get used to—they all joined the flood of children racing into the forest.

133

Once back in Freethorn Creek, the trio hurried to the stables so that Dantess and Warren could reclaim their horses.

Jyn hovered around the entrance, watching the street, while the two boys walked inside.

"Isn't that Kevik's horse?" asked Dantess, staring at a black stallion in a stable far away from the others. The stallion pawed at the ground and snorted.

Warren nodded. "Now we definitely know Kevik's on our trail." He cocked his head at Dantess. "What do you think? Should we?"

"Take his horse?" asked Dantess. "We need one for Jyn, and it could be worth it. That might slow him down, at least."

The stable hand, a boy in brown overalls, spoke up. "Due respect, but I'd keep clear. There's a reason Master Carl put him over there. He's a mean one."

Dantess, wary but confident, approached the horse. "Oh, you're not so bad, are you?" The horse was a reflection of its owner, packed with muscle and ready to lash out. Dantess reached one hand toward the horse's head, but jerked it back just in time to avoid losing a finger to its snapping teeth. "All right, that's not a good idea. Lad, do you have a different horse for us? A fast one?"

"Sure. A gold ought to do."

When Dantess reached for his purse, he remembered that he'd given it to Mother Nettle. "I'm out. Warren, did you bring any gold?"

"Two pieces." He closed his eyes. "My savings."

"Give the boy one of them, if you don't mind."

Once Warren tossed the stablehand a coin, the boy walked to a stall containing a spotted pony. It nickered at his approach. He opened the gate, entered the stall, and rubbed the pony's head. "Take Splitter. She's young, but always wants to race. Might come in handy for you, I'm thinking."

"Perfect," said Jyn, walking inside. "Let's saddle up and get moving before Kevik comes for that demon horse of his."

Once they were all ready to ride, Dantess turned to the stable hand. "Whatever you can do to slow down the owner of that beast, I'd appreciate."

"Make trouble for a priest of War? Sounds dangerous." The lad's eyebrow rose. "And expensive."

Dantess glanced at Warren and nodded. Warren sighed, took out his remaining gold coin, and flipped it to the boy.

The stable hand caught the coin and grinned. "I think I'll do him the favor of polishing his saddle and gear. Who knows? I might accidentally misplace it after."

"Perfect." Dantess nodded, then spurred his horse. The three began the ride to War's temple.

Even pushing the horses, the trip was long and tense. The trio reacted to every falling branch or bird flying from a tree as though Kevik were right on their heels, but there was no sign of him.

After hours of riding, both horses and riders were exhausted. Without any visible pursuit, they allowed the horses to trot and rest.

"Does Kevik not realize we're heading back to the temple?" asked Warren. "Maybe he thinks we're hiding you somewhere else?"

"No," said Jyn. "He's coming. He won't take the chance I'll tell what really happened. He may not get punished, but everyone in the temple will know. Kevik wants to be seen as a legendary warrior so badly, he'd do anything to prevent a blemish like that on his record."

"Well, his 'legend' is about to take a pounding, because we're almost there. Do you see?" Dantess pointed to the tip of the temple, poking through the holes in the branches ahead. "Soon we'll be at the open mile. And once we're in the temple, Kevik can't touch you. Kaurridon himself is in the gatehouse today, and he won't let anything happen. Not until you're heard. Those are the rules."

Indeed, it wasn't long until the three left the forest and rode into the clear mile approach to the temple. Dantess had never longed to enter that gatehouse as much as now. Even now, there was no sign of Kevik behind them. In fact, this late, they shared the road with no one.

"The trick with Kevik's saddle must have worked. Gold well spent," said Warren. "One more mile and we're home."

About a quarter of the way there, they heard a commotion behind them. A single rider exited the forest, pushing his black, muscled warhorse so hard, it was a wonder it didn't collapse in its tracks.

He rode bareback, no saddle required.

"It's Kevik!" yelled Dantess. "Ride!"

The three kicked their horses into galloping—but their pursuer still gained. A half mile remained to the temple. They were racing, but the distance between the riders closed faster.

The soldiers at the gate were confused, but they recognized a priest of War was speeding toward them. They pulled the gate open.

"We can do it," Dantess yelled. "The gate is open. It's just a little further."

The black stallion thundered nearer, spraying a wake of foamy spittle and blood from his mouth and wheezing as though it could drop dead at any moment. Kevik either didn't notice or care because he did not slow. Instead, he sat up high on his horse and drew his arm back.

Jyn turned her head to look behind them. "He's so close. What is he—"

Kevik's dagger plunged through her forehead, right between her eyes, in the middle of her black tattooed mask.

Lifeless, Jyn tumbled onto the ground. Her horse whinnied and stopped.

"Jyn!" Dantess' chest tightened, as if Kevik's knife had pierced his heart instead.

He and Warren pulled their horses to a halt. Dantess leapt off and ran to Jyn's side.

I'll keep you safe, don't worry, he'd promised her.

He dropped down and cradled her head in his arm. Her beautiful eyes stared out at nothing. "Jyn?"

But she did not answer. She was gone. Kevik executed Jyn, just as he had the highwayman on the road, two years ago. He stole her life away like she didn't matter.

Soldiers ran out of the gatehouse toward them, but Kevik arrived first. His horse collapsed, most likely dead as well. Kevik jumped free, landing lightly on his feet. As he approached, Kevik brushed dirt from his shoulders, nothing but pride on his face. "That was some throw, huh?"

Dantess gingerly placed Jyn's head on the ground and looked up, his wet eyes blazing with rage, the knuckles of his fists white and shaking.

"Why are you so worked up?" asked Kevik. "She was faithless. They die all the time."

Dantess screamed, a primal sound laden with rage and loss, and launched himself at Kevik. His token raced to provide options of attack, and Dantess took the first one that suggested Kevik's death at the end. He plowed into Kevik's chest and knocked the other warrior down with his shoulder.

But Kevik was no normal opponent. He also had the history of War's priests to help him. As Kevik went down, he kicked up and sent Dantess flying over his head. Dantess landed hard on the road.

Both jumped to their feet. Kevik smiled. "Oh ho! I've been waiting for this. You've had it coming for years, ever since you put on that belt."

Kevik sent a kick toward Dantess' throat, but the token saw it coming and deflected it easily.

"You could have had any faithless you wanted. Why Jyn?" Dantess feinted with a jab, then followed up with a leg sweep that Kevik jumped over. But when Kevik landed, Dantess slammed an elbow into his nose. He felt it crack under the blow.

The larger priest did not like that. A swing of his own struck the side of Dantess' head, hard enough to draw blood. Dantess lifted his hand a bit too slow to block, so Kevik grabbed and twisted it around his back. With his other arm, Kevik enveloped Dantess in a reverse bear hug, pinning Dantess' arms to his side. His massive muscles squeezed, compressing even the golden breastplate beneath.

"Because *you* wanted her," Kevik seethed into Dantess' bloody ear. "Warriors take what they win. *I'm* the better warrior. *I'm* the one they'll write stories about. I deserve *everything* you have."

Dantess fought to breathe. He whipped his head forward and bashed it back into Kevik's already broken nose. Slightly stunned, Kevik loosened his grip. Dantess broke the hold and rolled forward. His token snapped him to his feet and wheeled him around in a defensive stance.

Kevik shook his head and then pointed at Dantess' belt. "You wear that thing like it means something. Are you afraid people might forget that you're Varyon's grandson for one moment if you don't? Because without that, you're *nothing*."

137

"You want what I've got?" wheezed Dantess, holding his bleeding ear with one hand and patting his belt with the other. "Come and take it."

With blood dripping into his mouth, Kevik grinned. "There's *nothing* you have I can't take." But as he was about to move forward, strong arms wrapped around Kevik and pulled him back. Surprised, Dantess watched as two soldiers jumped between the combatants, creating a living barrier.

"What's going on here?" demanded Kaurridon, arriving on the scene surrounded by a number of other priests and soldiers.

"Kevik *murdered* Jyn," said Dantess.

"Jyn?"

"A faithless deserter," said Kevik. "While we were on a mission, she ran away from our camp. The rest of my squad saw it all. I was just tying up loose ends before she could embarrass the temple."

"He tried to force himself on her!" screamed Dantess.

"Was that her story?" asked Kevik, innocently. "Faithless will say anything to justify their crimes. The fact is, she's a deserter, and the punishment for desertion is death."

"She was coming back—"

Kaurridon held up his hand to interrupt. "I will look into this further, but for now, I don't want any problem between you two. Save whatever issues you have for the Game next month."

Kevik's jaw dropped. "What? Dantess is playing? How? He doesn't have the rank!"

"He does now. Didn't you notice? After his last mission, he has the same number of marks as you."

Kevik glowered at Dantess, and then his glare dropped to the belt. "Of course. One more benefit of being Varyon's grandson." He wheeled around, shrugged at his dead horse, and began to walk toward the gatehouse, arms swinging freely.

"You'll never be half the warrior he was, Kevik," yelled Dantess. "And you'll never be a legend. Wishing for it won't make it true."

Kevik didn't even turn back. "Let's revisit that after I beat you in the Game, Boot. Just remember, I *earned* my marks."

Dantess knelt back down beside Jyn. He ripped the dagger out and hurled it as far as he could. It landed a hundred yards away on the barren dirt. He held her head, closed her eyes with his fingers, and wept.

Warren stood next to both of them, but watched Kevik's every step as he left with a cold and calculating glare.

CHAPTER THIRTEEN

"JYN IS DEAD," said Dantess.

The length of time it took his father to raise his head and respond spoke more to his worsening physical condition than his emotional reaction. The years of confinement had not been kind to him. Dantess made sure he was eating, but Tolliver was a shell of the friendly, pudgy man he had been two years ago. His clothes hung from his frame, and Dantess couldn't remember the last time he smiled. Instead, he had a perpetual dull look in his eyes that was growing harder to penetrate.

But this news, at least, brought some concern to his expression. "How?" Tolliver asked.

"Kevik. He... made it impossible for her to stay on his squad, and then killed her for deserting. He might have done it just to get to me."

Tolliver ran his fingers over his gaunt face. "Does her mother know?"

"Warren is telling her. I thought it would be best for the news to come from him."

Tolliver nodded. "How is the boy?"

"I haven't seen him cry yet. He hasn't shown any emotion except hatred, and he's channeling that into planning for the Game. He'd love it if Kevik never made it out of there. I wouldn't be too sad, either."

Tolliver's eyes grew like saucers. "The Game? The Game of *War?*"

Dantess nodded. "Kaurridon is sponsoring me. I'll compete to become the Guardian for the Convergence of the Divine."

For the first time in months, Tolliver was completely present in the conversation. He leaned back, his hand on his head. "I don't believe it."

"Winners of the Game have ascended to the highest ranks in the temple, but..."

"But some players don't make it out. Isn't that what you said?"

"Part of the Game was designed by Evil," admitted Dantess. "When they're involved, the stakes are always high."

After a moment, Tolliver scowled. "You can't play."

"What?"

"Why would you? Glory? A rise in rank? Those are things your grandfather cherished. Have you even thought about what I told you? You're a priest of War, in a position to change things—but all you're chasing after is another win."

"That's not fair," said Dantess. "I'm doing it for you. I could win enough rank to free you and Siriana."

"I'm tired. I've already made peace with being done in this world. But you're not. You have a lifetime left to do so much more, and you'd risk it all by entering this competition?"

"I'm not scared."

Tolliver shook his head. "It's not about fear. You think you're an experienced priest now, but agreeing to this shows how foolhardy you are. First," he held up one finger, "you've been here for two years. Other priests have decades behind them. You may think your token evens you out, but there's no substitute for actual time on the battlefield. You have potential, but you're still naive."

Dantess crossed his arms.

Tolliver held up two fingers. "Second, you'll be competing with Kevik. Given the chance, he'll do *anything* to beat you—and he's capable of it. Do not underestimate him."

Dantess exploded. "How could I not face him after what he did? I'd be exactly what he claims I am: a pretender with a pretty belt."

"The more he's in your head, the more power he has over you. Finally," Tolliver held up a third finger, "you'd be putting your life in the hands of Evil. They may be War's allies, but they revel in death. I'm sure they celebrate every time a priest of War dies in their part of the Game."

"I can handle it. I'm more capable than you know." Dantess puffed his chest out a bit. "Kaurridon thinks I'm ready. He sponsored me."

"Why? For your benefit or his?"

"You told me to trust him!"

"I told you he was likely the priest most friendly to the faithless out of the current leadership, but that's a low bar. If he sponsored such a new priest for this Game, especially after having years to choose someone, he's got his own reasons." Tolliver pulled at his scraggly beard. "It's like he was waiting for you."

Dantess stood up. "Maybe he has his own reasons, but that doesn't mean I don't have mine, too. I don't care how many problems you list. It's worth the risk. I can't let you rot in here ten more years. Look at you! You've already started to give up. You'd never make it."

Tolliver stared at Dantess with sad eyes.

"I won't lose you, too," continued Dantess. "I couldn't take that. Not after Jyn."

Tolliver hobbled to the bars, reached through them, and took Dantess' hand. "I understand. I do. But I can't lose you either. If you play and don't come back…"

Dantess nodded and squeezed his father's hand.

His father sat back on his cot and dropped his chin down. The dull look returned to his eyes. Dantess knew that meant the conversation was over.

He stood and said, "I'll see you soon, Da. I'm going to get you out of here. I promise."

Tolliver did not respond, so Dantess turned and left.

Dantess sat on a padded chair behind his broad desk constructed of an assortment of woods inlaid in intricate patterns. The impressive and expensive piece of furniture was just one luxury of many in his lavish quarters. Pure, clear glass windows ran much of the height of the walls beneath a vaulted ceiling and were framed with rich, red curtains. Paintings and bookshelves flanked a marble mantle fireplace, which Dantess had come to depend on in the coldest months.

The suite of rooms once belonged to his grandfather. Someone responsible for room assignments thought it fitting, so Dantess lived more comfortably than most—more than the priests quartered in the standard single rooms, certainly.

He held Jyn's golden music box in his palm. Like everything else in Mother Nettle's treasure piles, it wasn't particularly valuable. It was small and made of cheap materials, but it was also clearly the work of a talented craftsman. Even old and scuffed, every detail was perfect. Dantess understood why young Jyn would have loved it so.

He wound the key on the back. Then he lifted the lid.

A tiny metal dancer rose from within the box and slowly twirled to a simple but haunting melody. Miniature hands reached up to the sky. Exquisitely-sculpted features on her face expressed an innocent joy. Dantess watched her spin over and over until the tinkling music slowed and finally stopped.

Without the music, she was frozen in place. Lifeless.

He couldn't stop staring at her.

Someone rapped sharply on the door to his suite. "Dantess?"

Dantess closed the lid of the music box and wiped his eyes with his hand. "Come in, Warren."

Warren opened the door, awkwardly carrying an armload of papers and books. He walked inside and dropped them on the desk. "I didn't mean to disturb you."

"It's all right." Dantess placed the box on the corner of the desk. "You want to talk about the Game?"

"Yes, but before that... Something happened. I'm so sorry."

Dantess' attention snapped to Warren. "What?"

"It's about your grandfather's belt."

"My belt?" Dantess' eyes went wide. "What about it?"

"I was trying to clean the blood from it, as you asked. But I didn't do it in my quarters. I did it out in the training yard."

"Why?"

"Because I wanted Kevik and his squad to see it. I wanted to get under his skin." Warren knotted his fists. "After what he did, getting back at Kevik is all I can think about."

"That stunt could have put you in danger."

"I'm fine, but the belt..."

"Just tell me what happened!" Dantess leaned forward.

"Someone distracted me," said Warren. "I only put it down for a moment."

Dantess' face went white. "It's gone?"

Warren nodded. "I looked everywhere. Someone must have taken it."

Dantess sat back and breathed heavily, trying to calm down. "Kevik. Or someone did it for him. He *swore* he'd take what was mine."

"Can we get it back?"

"We can't prove he took it, and Kevik won't admit he has it. Kaurridon made it clear he won't get involved in any dispute between Kevik and me until after the Game." Dantess slammed his fist on the desk. "I can't win with this monster."

"Well, if there's nothing we can do about the belt, maybe we should focus on winning the Game, then," said Warren. "I learned a lot from your packet." He opened the packet and pulled out a large, folded parchment.

As Warren unfolded it, Dantess could see it was a map. "What's this?"

"Every player gets one of these. This is the Game of War. Or, at least, it shows the place it's played." He pointed to a circle in the center. "Evil's tower. The door is on the south side, here."

"What's the scale? The tower doesn't look very big."

"The tower isn't large, but it's tall. Everything I've read says it's bigger on the inside, and the interior changes with every player that enters. But that's not what we're looking at right now." He swept his finger around the area surrounding the tower. "This is where the Game starts. See here? Swamp. River. Ravine. Caves. Hills. Forest. We need to choose the place where we can best defend our chest. All four of the other players are doing the same thing right now."

Dantess studied the variety of available terrain depicted with crude drawings. "How accurate is it?"

"Rough at best, but it will serve us better than you might expect. These maps are actually artifacts of War. When activated, it will show you where all the keys are." Dantess reached forward, but Warren stopped him. "Don't bother. Since no keys are in play yet, you won't see anything marked on the map, but when the game starts, they'll show up here."

"So, there's no hiding the chests from other priests if they can just use their maps to pinpoint them."

"Right. If the chests have keys in them, at least. The goal is to *defend* the chests, not to hide them. But that doesn't stop players from using the environment to their advantage. My research says that players usually drop their chests somewhere deep and inaccessible. In the river. Down the ravine. Under the swamp."

"Something tells me that's not what we're going to do, is it?"

"No," said Warren with a growing smile. He started shuffling through the remainder of the books and papers on the desk. "I discovered something that might help us. If I'm right, we should give the caves a try."

They stayed up late into the night discussing strategy. While the weight of his grief made it hard for Dantess to focus, Warren appeared more driven to win than ever. As always, the boy's analysis was brilliant.

Poring over the most elaborate plan either of them had ever contemplated, Dantess was overwhelmed by and grateful for Warren's acumen—but deep inside, he couldn't help but wonder what price he paid for it. What would have happened if he chose differently after the testing?

Guilt piled onto his sorrow, but he couldn't help it.

If I gave up Warren that day, thought Dantess, *would Jyn still be here?*

Dantess pushed the thought down, wiped his eyes, and returned to the plan, remembering that this was the best chance to save his father.

And perhaps deliver some justice to Kevik.

CHAPTER FOURTEEN

THE DAY WAS here. The Game of War was about to begin. Despite knowing better, Dantess hadn't slept much the night before—the plan kept rolling around in his mind, refusing him rest—but they'd done all they could to prepare. The rest was up to War.

Unlike Dantess, his squad seemed more excited than nervous. So few soldiers competed that they were already talking about their names being written in the history books. All the way to the Game, they bantered and joked with each other about their potential heroics.

Motti was the most rambunctious, always. Often Jeremy and Solomon acted as his audience, who didn't mind egging him on to see how far he'd go. Khalista, on the other hand, had no patience for stupidity and called Motti out on it constantly. For some reason, that didn't bother Motti at all. In fact, he seemed to enjoy her company more than the other boys.

Warren, as usual, kept to himself. He was calm, quiet, and focused.

An hour's march from the temple brought them through a picturesque landscape. The rising sun burned off the last of the morning dew from low, green, rolling hills. Birds and bugs serenaded their journey. Any other day, this trip would have been a pleasant diversion.

In the distance, they could see mountains, a river, a swamp, a forest, and rocky hills—the other landscapes in the Game. Dantess only gave them a passing glance. Instead, he focused on the most important feature of this place: a tall, crooked, black tower—the starting location.

Just in front of the tower, Morghaust, Kaurridon, and the other senior leaders of the temple awaited Dantess and the other four players. Arriving first, he took the opportunity to examine the tower. He had never seen anything like it.

The looming tower was built with black stones, held together with black mortar, topped off with a conical roof covered in black resin. Evil wasn't known for variety in their palette, and for some reason, regardless of the weather elsewhere, the air around the tower was cold. Bitter cold.

The tower's most interesting element was its solitary door at ground level. It was actually five doors, each progressively nested inside the others. The most inner door had an exposed lock and handle, but the others only had metal plates where those things would be. Dantess guessed that other locks might be exposed by unlocking the first.

As Dantess examined the door, a priestess arrived with her squad in tow. It was Withyr, a gruff, burly fighter whose features kind of reminded him of a hawk. She was also the same priestess his father mentioned two years ago, the one with whom Tolliver had some sort of relationship. Perhaps ten years Dantess' senior with twenty marks on her athletic arms, she was smart, ruthless, and solitary. Despite Dantess' efforts to connect with her, Withyr had barely spoken three words to him. He got the sense she didn't like him, but from what he understood, that didn't make him different from most.

"Withyr's the favorite to win," said Motti. "Couldn't get good odds on her if you tried."

"You bet on her?" asked Khalista. "How could you?"

"I didn't say I bet on her, but it doesn't hurt to price out the competitors. Gotta know where the smart money is. Take them, for example." Motti pointed at Glinden and Sorrobask, arriving together and laughing with each other. "Both are here to win, but not as likely to. Decent odds for them, if you had gold you wanted to throw away."

Motti wasn't necessarily wrong. The two priests had logged over seventy missions and thirty marks between them, but weren't considered top competitors. Of the two, Dantess was only worried about Glinden. She was one of the few priestesses that preferred ranged weapons, which was strange since priests tended to rely more on weaponless combat the more they trained, but her fascination made her deadly with them.

"Dantess," called Sorrobask. "I didn't know they allowed spectators. Are you here to cheer me on?" Dantess cleared his throat, but before he could respond, Sorrobask said, "I'm just joking. I know you got bumped up in rank. I'm not saying you cheated, but aren't those tricks your bookworm comes up with beneath you? What you do reflects on your grandfather, after all." He glared at Warren. "Let's keep the Game clean and fair, huh?"

147

Before Dantess could answer, Warren spoke up. "When Dantess wins, he'll do it well within the rules."

Motti leaned toward Khalista and pointed at Warren. "That's why I bet everything I've got on Dantess, right there," he whispered. "Never underestimate one of Warren's plans."

Sorrobask clenched his fists. "You let your squad talk like that to a priest?"

"He was joking," said Dantess. "You love a good joke, right?"

Ready to retort, Sorrobask instead was distracted by the arrival of Kevik and his squad. Once at the tower, Kevik placed his thumbs behind the colorful belt he wore and smiled. Sorrobask burst out laughing. "Speaking of a good joke, is Kevik wearing Varyon's belt? How'd he get a hold of that?"

Without responding, Dantess began to walk toward Kevik, rage boiling up inside him. "This has gone far enough!"

Warren intercepted him and put his hand on his arm. "Wait. What do you think will happen if you attack him?"

"I'll tear his head off."

"And then? What did Kaurridon say about you two fighting before the Game begins?"

Dantess paused and thought about it. "I'd be disqualified." Dantess took a step back. "My father was right. Kevik *is* trying to get in my head."

"Don't let him. Wait until the Game starts. Then we'll deal with Kevik," Warren almost growled with hatred.

"Everyone is here?" projected Morghaust to the crowd. "Good. Just being selected for this group is a great honor, but only one of you will earn the post of Guardian for the Convergence of the Divine.

"You have all chosen your starting positions, and your chests have been delivered there. Feel free to check your maps to confirm."

Warren handed Dantess the map. Dantess channeled his Longing through it and five tiny colored dots appeared scattered over the terrain. There was a red dot in the hills, a green dot in the forest, a yellow dot in the swamp, and a purple dot in the river.

"Nothing surprising there. An even spread." Warren pointed at the blue dot in front of the caves. "That's us."

"When I release you, you will go to your chest. You will have one hour to prepare your defense. After that, we will launch a flare in the sky. That is your signal to start.

"Squads will use only wooden practice weapons. Priests will fight weaponless. Let me be clear: *no one* dies today—at least, not by your hands. We cannot prevent what Evil's tower may do. My advice: guard your life inside there.

"Collect the keys and use them to enter the tower. The more keys you have, the easier your trip to the top will be. Remember, once the door is unlocked, only one priest can enter until it is closed and unlocked again. The player that reaches the upper chamber, obtains the trophy, and returns here to us will win the Game.

"May War bless this battle and grant the best warrior victory. Now go!"

Everyone moved out, each squad heading toward a different part of the terrain. Dantess watched Kevik gather his squad and march them away.

"Where is Kevik headed?" asked Dantess.

Warren watched the direction the priest was leading his troops. "It looks like the hills. Not the place I would have chosen. Harder to defend. But let's focus on our own chest for now. We have a lot of work ahead of us."

The blue dot on Dantess' map led him and his squad of six to a large chest lying outside a cave, one of many cavern openings in the rugged, rocky terrain.

"No! This is not where I told them to put the chest," Warren exclaimed. "We're going to lose precious time moving it." He dove into his collection of notes and mumbled under his breath.

The chest was nothing more than a blue-painted crate—squat and made of some kind of metal—with rope handles on all four sides and a raised plate about the size of a palm embossed with War's shield on the lid.

Dantess knelt down and placed his hand on the plate. It glowed red. "So, I can't open my own chest, but touching this should open any of the others, right?"

149

Warren nodded, distracted by his notes.

"Seems like we should just move the chest into the nearest cave." said Motti, scanning the horizon for any opposition. "It'll be quick and easier to defend in there. Only one entrance."

"No," said Warren. "Every other priest who used these caves assumed it would be straightforward to defend—but in most cases, a chest placed here was the easiest to ransack. No, we need to find the *right* cave."

Solomon leaned down and tugged at the chest by pulling at a handle. It didn't budge. "*War's fury*, that's heavy. How did they even get it here?"

"Don't bother trying to move it on your own," said Warren, flipping through loose papers. "It's built to be heavy, so you can't run it away from the enemy." He pulled out his own hand-drawn map of the area. "Ah! Here we go." He counted the cave markers on his map, then counted them out against the air. "...three, four, five! The cave we want is over there." Warren pointed at a smaller opening further up the hillside.

"Up there?" asked Solomon. "How are we supposed to get it up there?"

"Me," said Dantess. He channeled his Longing through his token, focused the power into his strength, and lifted one end of the chest. Even so, the weight was daunting. "Uh... with a little help." Motti, Solomon, and Jeremy grabbed the remaining handles.

"Quickly," said Warren. "I'll lead the way."

Warren trudged up the hill, leading the struggling group up a rough path to the small cave. As the ground tilted up, most of the weight fell on Dantess—the only person in the squad who could have shouldered it. Together, they managed to reach the cave opening and trot it inside.

"Everyone.... drop!" Dantess and the others let the chest fall to the cave floor. It hit like a boulder.

Motti followed it onto the ground, wheezing heavily. "I never... it's so... I can't... How can it be so *heavy*? There's just a key in there, right?"

As Warren wandered deeper inside, Khalista looked around the tight cavern walls. "It's hard to move in here," she observed. "How are we supposed to defend the chest if we can't fight?"

From further in, Warren called out, "It's here! Come!"

The others squeezed to the back of the cave, where rows of wooden boards were affixed to the rock. Warren stood before the boards, stroking his chin.

"What is this?" asked Motti, surprised.

Warren and Dantess shared a knowing look. "A good sign," said Dantess, stepping closer.

Dantess jammed his fingers between two of the ancient boards and pulled them open. The crumbling wood cracked and splintered, leaving an opening wide enough to walk through. A strange bluish glow from inside reflected off of steel railings that ran along the floor, deep into the tunnel.

"This isn't a cave!" exclaimed Motti.

"No," Warren said with a smile. "It's a *mine*."

"Hey, what do you call these?" Solomon asked as he touched a gleaming crystal embedded in the tunnel wall. Where just a bit of light from the cave mouth touched it, its facets shone like a dim blue star. Others like it poked out of other walls at irregular intervals, also glowing blue.

"Surefire crystals," said Warren, hovering his finger just above another one and watching the blue light play on its tip. "There are veins of it throughout these hills, which is one of the reasons they chose to mine here. The crystals don't glow on their own, but they conduct and amplify light from any source. They can even hold the light for a time. An unbroken vein can take sunlight from the surface and light up caverns miles away."

"They're built-in torches." said Khalista, caressing her own in the wall.

"That's right," agreed Warren. "Miners love them—not to extract, but to illuminate the tunnels. Easy and safe. Better than wandering into a cavern filled with flammable gasses holding a torch. They just had to be careful to dig around the veins."

Motti looked around, his jaw hanging open. "Forget about the stupid crystals. How did you know this mine was here?"

"Research," explained Warren. "There used to be iron ore in these hills, so they dug a mine to extract it and produced a huge maze of tunnels. The entrance is miles away, but it happened to end here where it connected up with this cave. They had no idea it

151

was close to the Game of War's battlefield, nor did they even know what that was."

"Why hasn't anyone else ever used this in the Game?"

"It wasn't here during the last Game of War, but it was still constructed so long ago that no one remembers it. I only found it through some of War's deepest archives no one *ever* reads."

"Except you. You read *everything*," said Motti, chuckling.

Warren shrugged. "I happened upon a mining report that described a tall, black tower—not a common reference. Then I noticed the similarities in the terrain." He smiled. "Of course, once the temple knows this exists, I don't expect them to allow it in the next Game."

"But there's nothing in the rules against it now, so we've got miles to hide the chest! But," mused Solomon, "that doesn't matter much if we can't move it."

"If the inventory lists were correct—" Warren's ears perked up. He held up his hand and said, "Listen."

A sustained screech, like metal scraping against metal, came from deeper in the tunnel. After a moment, Khalista appeared, sitting in a minecart pushed by Jeremy. She asked with a smirk, "Anybody want a ride?"

A distant explosion echoed from outside the cave.

"That's the official flare. The hour's up," noted Dantess. "I have to get out there and gather some keys for myself. Do you have this under control, Warren? Can I count on you to defend my chest?"

Warren looked shocked. "Me? In charge? Without you here?"

"Naturally. There's no one I can depend on more."

"Yeah," said Motti. "You made all the plans. Why wouldn't you be in command?"

"If that's what you think is best," said Warren, standing a little straighter. "I'll do it."

Dantess slapped his shoulder. "I know you won't let me down. I have faith in all of you."

As Dantess turned to leave, Motti called out, "Um, we appreciate the faith, but could we get a little more muscle before you go? We still have to get the chest into the minecart."

Dantess laughed. "Of course."

Dantess hadn't explored many swamps—and for good reason: he hated them. Swamps were like ponds, if ponds were covered with muck and rotting vegetation and smelled like an upside-down graveyard. Dantess pushed through a batch of twisted vines as he trudged further into the waist-deep fetid water toward the yellow dot on his map. Up ahead, the surface was broken only by the occasional huge lily pad and floating bushes.

He checked his map again and verified he was nearing the dot. In fact, he estimated he should have been almost on top of it. So where were the soldiers? Not seeing the chest wasn't surprising—he knew it would be hidden under the surface somewhere—but not spotting its defenders made him cautious.

He put his map away, slowed his steps, and kept his hands out. When his foot struck something large, metal, and heavy, he smiled.

Then his legs were pulled out from under him.

His head flew backward under the water. He gulped some of it in surprise, the rotten, brackish taste flooding his mouth and nostrils, before he realized that his legs had been caught in a loop of vines and tugged tight. Dantess pumped his arms to push his head over the surface just in time to see a collection of bushes rise upwards, the faces of soldiers poking out underneath, camouflaged until the trap was sprung. The nearest two soldiers held onto the vines wrapped around his legs and heaved, sending Dantess back into the water.

Dantess pumped his arms again, but when his face broke the surface this time, it met the business end of a staff. The soldiers had surrounded him. He knew that, if he didn't stop them, their combined attacks would render him unconscious and put him out of the Game.

They're just soldiers, Dantess thought to himself, back under the water. *A priest would have taken better advantage of my blunder by now.*

Calming himself, he channeled his Longing through his token. His reflexes sped up. His endurance increased, giving him more time between breaths. Plans unfolded in front of him.

He saw how the soldiers would act and react in his mind.

Once he broke the vines, the soldiers would know they'd lost their only real advantage, and once they pulled up the slack and saw the broken end, the soldiers panicked. He heard the slaps of the squad stabbing the water randomly, hoping for a lucky strike but hitting nothing.

Dantess maneuvered himself, watching for a stab near enough to drag one of the soldiers under the water, screaming.

Once another dropped, the remaining four grouped together, backs facing each other, hoping that they could counter an attack no matter where it came from. They left only enough room between them to move freely.

That small space between them is where Dantess rose up. First, he reached high, grabbed two helmets, and bashed them against each other with concussive force. Then he kicked out the legs from the third soldier, slammed his other foot onto the man's head, and used it as a springboard to grab the remaining soldier's neck and compress the blood going to his brain. After a small struggle, the man collapsed in the priest's arms.

Even though he lost some time, Dantess made sure the heads of every unconscious soldier were safely above the water line.

Area secured, Dantess groped around for the metal chest. He found it again easily. When his palm touched the plate on the lid, he could see the white glow even through the brackish water—and once the glow disappeared, so did the plate. He reached within to feel a cavity, and at its bottom, a small smooth piece of metal.

He raised his hand above the water, clutching a yellow key.

One down, he thought as he slipped the key into his right bracer. *So far, not too difficult—but how many more dare I collect? How far can I push my luck?*

He set off towards the next dot, green this time. He grinned. *If this is how the other priests are protecting their keys, maybe pretty far.*

As Dantess jogged to the next closest area, he saw himself—marked with a moving yellow dot—on the map.

All the other priests can see the key I'm holding on the move, he thought. *They can track me down as easily as any of the chests. The more I gather, the more attractive a target I am.*

There was no time to worry about that. At least none of the other keys appeared to be moving, which meant he might be in the lead. So far, at least.

The edge of a densely packed woods came into view and at a dead run, it wasn't long until he entered it. The map showed that the green dot was still deep inside.

These were ancient woods, long past their days of being lush. Many of the trees were dead or dying. Dry branches and logs lay everywhere, along with twigs and leaves that snapped and crunched with each step. It would be difficult to sneak up on anyone in this forest.

Dantess kept his footsteps as quiet as possible while still moving quickly. When he estimated he was about a hundred yards away from the dot, a whistle erupted from the top of a nearby tree. It was answered by another whistle deeper in the forest, and another deeper still.

I've been spotted, Dantess realized. *What does that mean?*

Dantess abandoned stealth and began to run—but still careful to avoid any rope or pit traps. He'd had his fill of those.

He glimpsed a flicker of light up ahead, and then he smelled smoke. Had the soldiers here started a fire? In *this* dry forest? Did they have a death wish?

"Stay back, Dantess." A soldier, one of Sorrobask's squad, called out to him. He stood in front of a roaring bonfire, perhaps ten feet high.

"What have you done?" asked Dantess, slowing down.

"We may not be able to keep you from the chest, but that fire will. You'll never get to it now. You might as well leave."

Even though the bonfire was in the middle of a clearing, it was still close enough to the surrounding trees to be dangerous. "Listen to me: you need to leave now, and take your squad with you! I heard the whistles. You have men in those trees."

"So?"

Dantess pointed to the fire. Already, the wind was pushing the rising flames to one side. After a moment of licking a dry tree nearby, the fire jumped onto the dead wood. "This whole forest is about to burn. Save your squad!"

"I can't leave the chest for you," said the soldier. "Sorrobask will have my hide."

"Was the fire his idea?"

The flames caught all of the nearby trees, and the light wind was carrying it toward the rest of the squad. The soldier looked around in panic. "Yes."

"Despite what he might have said, Sorrobask won't kill you, but this fire will—as well as your squad. Go save them while there's still time."

The man's face blanched. He tore off, screaming, "The forest is ablaze! Retreat! Retreat!"

Dantess wiped the sweat from his brow. He could feel the heat from the fire even from here, but he couldn't just leave the chest. If only he could just figure out how to extract such a heavy object from the middle of that blaze.

It was out of reach. Could he use something to pull it out? He had nothing that could snag the handle or anything that could drag it.

The fire spread. One side of the clearing was fully aflame. Soon, even as fast as he could run, he would be in danger of getting caught here.

If he couldn't pull the chest, could he *push* it?

Dantess looked around and discovered a log. He grabbed it, leveled it at the center of the bonfire, and charged. The log was mostly hollow, something he discovered when it splintered against the heavy metal chest like a collection of toothpicks. If anything, the log fueled the fire while moving the chest not an inch.

Dantess swore. He searched for something more solid and found a deadfall tree leaning against its neighbors. It was light enough to maneuver, but perhaps sturdy enough to withstand what he was about to ask of it. He pushed the deadfall to the ground, lined it up with the chest in the bonfire, and shoved it forward. The tree struck the chest. Neither moved, but the tree stayed intact.

Dantess channeled his Longing through his token. He focused his increased strength on heaving that tree and the chest forward, before the fire destroyed his improvised battering ram. He pushed and the chest budged. With renewed hope, he pushed again and the chest moved forward.

The deadfall caught fire, and the flames began to crawl towards his hands.

Dantess screamed his frustration at the blaze whooshing and crackling all around him now. The heat burned his cheeks and sweat poured into his stinging eyes, but still he pushed. With one final effort, he shoved the tree forward so hard and so far he almost stepped into the bonfire himself. The chest slid back with the shove, the ashes and sticks beneath helping it along.

He ran around to the back of the fire and found that the chest was almost clear. Clear enough, anyway. He was about to slap his hand onto the raised plate, but realized the fire had likely made it hot enough to burn skin.

But he had no time.

Dantess sucked in his breath and touched his left hand onto the scalding-hot plate anyway. Pain shot up his arm, but he kept his sizzling palm in place until the white glow pulsed and disappeared. It seemed like forever.

With his right hand, he dug the key out and tossed the hot metal onto the ground. While he gritted his teeth and clutched his left palm, he kicked dirt over the green key, trying to cool it down. When he reasoned he couldn't wait any longer, he snatched it up and sprinted out of the burning woods, barely escaping the fire that closed off his exit.

With this success, he couldn't help but wonder where the other priests were. He'd only seen their squads so far.

I shouldn't worry about finding them, he thought. *Now that I have two keys, they'll likely come to me.*

Leaving the inferno behind him, Dantess nursed his aching palm as he examined the map. He noticed that his own key in the caves hadn't moved.

Dantess smiled. The more time Warren and his squad gave him, the more likely he'd be able to collect the other keys.

How many do I really need? he asked himself. *If I enter now, I'll have the jump on everyone.*

But there would still be three keys out there.

Dantess weighed the risk and decided, *Maybe just one more. With three, I'll have an advantage against anyone who comes after.*

The next closest was in the hills—Kevik's red key—so he jogged toward it.

Soon he learned that the term 'hills' underplayed the immensity of these natural sandstone pillars and monstrous edifices. Some could even be labeled as small mountains.

Of course, Kevik's key was at the top of one of the larger mounds, so Dantess started hiking. With every step, he was acutely aware that, while he knew where he was heading, every other priest with a map knew exactly where he was, too.

Dantess arrived at a thirty-foot high vertical cliff. He couldn't believe someone had lifted the chest up there, but his map didn't lie. The chest was close, perhaps right over the lip.

With a quick survey of the terrain for Kevik's squad, Dantess began to climb up the porous stone.

"It's you. I was hoping it would be you," Kevik's voice called down from above. Dantess looked up and saw Kevik standing on the lip of the cliff. "Two keys already, eh?" he continued. "Good work."

Hanging on the cliff wall, Dantess asked, "You stayed here yourself? Don't you trust your squad to guard your chest?"

"Oh, you want my chest?" Kevik laughed. "All right." The priest disappeared, but then Dantess heard him grunting. The edge of the chest inched over the cliff. "Here you go."

Realization struck. Dantess began to scramble down the cliff, but it was too late. Kevik's impressive strength heaved the chest over the side. It slammed onto Dantess, knocking him to the ground and pinning him there.

The impact was painful, but worse, the sheer weight on his torso refused to let him breathe. After flailing his arms, he tried to get them under the chest and push it off, but he had no leverage.

Kevik jumped down and landed next to him. "You never could catch a stupid lockbox." He laughed and knelt close to Dantess' strained face. "You wanted my chest, and now you've got it. So take the key!"

Dantess' mouth opened and closed, but, without breath, he couldn't say a word.

"All right, I'll help." Kevik grabbed Dantess' hand, jerked it up, and slapped the palm onto the plate on the lid. As he held it there, the plate pulsed white and disappeared. Kevik released Dantess' hand, reached into the cavity, and removed the red key.

"So that's what a key looks like. Thanks for your help. I couldn't have opened it without you. Now how about the other two you collected?" He searched and discovered the two keys hidden in Dantess' bracer. "Excellent!"

Again, Dantess' mouth worked but was voiceless. He felt dizzy. Black spots swam in his vision. Without air, Dantess started to fade.

"I thought your belt was a prize, but you know, three keys are even better. You just gave me the *Game*." Kevik laughed as he walked away, but the sound was muffled and echoed. "You should have listened to me when I told you: there's *nothing* you have that I can't take."

In the precious minutes he had left, Dantess channeled his Longing through his token. He used his strength to push on the chest as hard as he could. He wriggled, but it didn't move. He tried to force a breath into his lungs. Nothing worked.

The moment before he lost consciousness, he swore he saw Jyn, who stood over him, shook her head, and said, "Dumbass."

CHAPTER FIFTEEN

WARREN KNEW THAT despite his exhaustive research and preparation, defending the chest against priests would be difficult—but not impossible. Everyone knew that priests of War were nigh invincible, but regardless of what the temple wished them to believe, they weren't *gods*. From Warren's time there, he knew that priests were people, and people had flaws. People could be defeated.

It just required a good enough plan.

"Someone's coming!" Motti called from the cave mouth.

Warren stood by the entrance to the mines at the back of the cave. "Who is it?"

"Well, it's a he, and he's not Kevik or Dantess, so it has to be Sorrobask."

"What's he doing?"

"Exploring all of the caves one by one. He knows the key is somewhere in here, but he hasn't a clue how to get in." Motti chuckled. "Whoops, sorry, not that one. Try again."

"We can't do anything to hide this entrance, so it's only a matter of time until he discovers it. Let's get moving and alert the others."

Motti ran back to Warren and together they jogged down the tunnel. Soon, they would see if their hard work would pay off.

"A damned *mine*?" Sorrobask stuck his head through the broken boards.

Warren watched from around the tunnel's corner as Sorrobask stepped through the opening, stood just inside, and shook his head.

"This isn't fair play. If you choose the caves, you put your chest in a *cave*. You don't hide it in... whatever this place is. A mine? How big is it?" Sorrobask consulted his map. "Oh, for War's sake, someone's stolen my key, and they're on the move. I'd better hurry. So where is *this* one?" He traced his finger on the map, looked around at his surroundings, and then called out, "Fine. Even in a mine, you can't hide it. I have a map, remember? And now I'm mad."

He secured the map and walked into the crystal-lit tunnel with purpose, the blue light glimmering on his shining breastplate.

Warren scurried away, trying to stay out of sight and hoping that the mine itself would slow his pursuer down. When they first entered here, even his squad paused to stare more than once. Knowing the crystals were here hadn't prepared him for the sights that awaited them further in.

The hand-carved mine tunnels followed the now-depleted vein of iron ore, but they did so alongside natural caverns, which meant that the tunnels sometimes intersected open spaces. The miners built bridges to span these openings and support the minecarts transporting the valuable ore. In those breaks, visitors could look into glorious caverns that were sometimes covered with glowing and sparkling surefire crystals of all different colors. It reminded Warren of Mother Nettle's treasure hoard. The crystals weren't rare enough to be valuable, but they were breathtaking nonetheless. He could almost be convinced that, like Mother Nettle's fantasy, the caverns were temples filled with the riches of long-forgotten gods.

Warren scrambled across the rails that bridged one of the many gaps, praying he wouldn't lose his balance or become distracted by the deposits of multicolored crystals. They were mesmerizing. Any other time, he could have stared for hours. Pulsing swaths of color flowed and broke like waves of an ocean against a beach, affected by the light striking the origin crystals at the surface. The waves, ebbing and flowing, told the story of how the clouds overhead covered and revealed the sun.

The winding tunnels and their gaps would force Sorrobask to move slowly. There were dozens of dead ends that his map wouldn't help him avoid and, even on the main path, countless places to hide just off the track where an ambush could be waiting. Unless the priest was completely reckless, he'd have to take his time.

Warren hurried, just in case.

"He's on his way." Warren's voice echoed from the walls of the enormous chamber, hundreds of feet up and down, lit by the rainbow of crystals in the walls. There was no reply, as expected.

He walked out from a tunnel and onto a suspended track that led to a central pillar of rock in the middle of the space. The support, perhaps ten feet across, sprouted many other suspended tracks on every side, at every level, up and down. These tracks led to other tunnels on the cave walls.

According to his maps, this chamber was a central collection point where this whole wing of the mine brought its ore. The pillar acted as a lift. The section of track inside could be rotated to match the orientation of the suspended bridges. When a cart was placed there, it could be lifted to other levels or all the way to the surface where ore was offloaded and shipped elsewhere.

Warren knew that this is where Sorrobask's map would lead him: straight to the chest's location. That said, the map's information was limited. It provided a bird's-eye view. Someone reading it wouldn't know the *depth* of the chest's location, which offered Warren options.

He ran to the central pillar. The lift was on his level. In the center of its tracks was the minecart he knew would be waiting for him.

He placed his hands on the cart. He wasn't the strongest squad member, but he believed he could play his part in the plan. Warren looked over his shoulder and spotted movement from the tunnel he just left.

Sorrobask stood on the suspended track, turning his map one way and then another. "It's here. It's got to be. Somewhere here." He looked up and saw the central column. "What is *that*?"

His footsteps echoed as he walked across the track. "All right, whoever's squad is hidden around here, just launch your attack now so we can get it out of the way."

Sweating and nervous, Warren put all his weight into pushing the minecart on the track leading away from the approaching priest. The ancient wheels screeched their defiance, but began rolling—slowly at first but picking up speed with each passing moment.

"I see it!" said Sorrobask. "Are you trying to *run away* with the chest?" He laughed. "You think you and that minecart are faster than me?"

162

The priest tore after the minecart, but the track under Warren's cart sloped down, and its weight increased its speed. Soon Warren was no longer pushing it, but racing to keep up.

With huge strides, Sorrobask caught up to the cart before it entered the far tunnel, leapt over it, and used his Longing-enhanced strength to bring it to a halt. Warren knew better than to push against him.

"What was the point of that? You just slowed me down a bit," Sorrobask said to Warren as they both caught their breaths. "You'd better hope all of this didn't delay me too long." The priest looked into the cart and saw a pile of rocks. He dug through them, but found only more rocks underneath. "Where's the chest?"

Warren smiled, turned back to the enormous chamber behind him, and yelled, "Now!" The word carried throughout the cavern. In response, five other minecarts rolled outward from the central column on five different tracks on five different levels, each pushed by another squad member.

"What? Wait..." Sorrobask paused as the minecarts rolled off in every direction. "Which cart has the chest?"

"That's a good question," said Warren.

After thinking for a moment, Sorrobask pulled out his map. "Which way is the dot moving? I can't tell." He rotated and shook it, but that didn't seem to help.

"The scale of your map is too large to track small movements. By the time you can determine direction, the chest will be long gone and you won't know which tunnel leads to it. By the way, some of those tunnels have slopes that go for miles." He crossed his arms. "Maybe you should just choose one and catch it before it goes too far. There's a one in five chance you'll be right."

Sorrobask screamed, "You faithless pissant! This is another one of your damned tricks. You think you can cheat *me*?"

Warren tried not to look smug. "Cheat?"

"You act like war is some puzzle to be solved. No. War is won on the battlefield, not in your books. War is won with *this*." Sorrobask slapped his bicep.

"What's worse," continued Sorrobask, "you've infected Dantess. He's Varyon's *grandson*. He should be the best of us—an inspiration. But instead of fighting like a warrior, he listens to you."

Warren held himself still, knowing better than to respond.

"I heard what happened at Serenity. You told him to dress up like a pacifist and set traps like a coward, didn't you? He's supposed to be a *leader*, but he's an embarrassment. You make him weak."

Warren felt the anger seething from the priest of War. He stepped back from the onslaught of words, but then found his own strength. "You're wrong. War isn't just about brute strength. Throughout history, the best priests of War were strategic geniuses. What you call tricks, I call good planning. And right now, my plan is taking the chest far away from you. You may be *strong*, but *smart* will beat that every time."

"Oh, yeah?" Sorrobask grabbed the collar of Warren's breastplate and held him out over the side of the suspended track. "What do you think of 'strong,' now?"

Warren struggled. He looked down at the drop and swallowed.

"Which cart has the chest?" demanded the priest of War.

"You... you wouldn't drop me," stammered Warren. "It's against the rules."

"Faithless die all the time. Especially in a mine like this. Accidents happen."

Those words, so eerily similar to what Kevik said when he murdered Jyn, struck him to his core. Fear shut down his resistance. All of Warren's instincts told him that this man was about to kill him, and there was only one thing he could do to stop it.

"Last chance," Sorrobask said, his grip loosening.

"I'll tell you," said Warren. "Put me down and I'll tell you."

Sorrobask chuckled. "Tell me first, otherwise you won't like how far I put you down."

"The chest is in *none* of the carts."

The priest's jaw dropped. "None of them? You sneaky bastard." He threw Warren onto the tracks. "Take me to it."

Warren climbed to his feet and began walking to the lift. He had no choice.

Warren pulled the lever on the platform and the lift dropped down. He and the priest standing next to him passed exit after exit with suspended bridges that led to tunnels on walls all around them.

"How far are we going?" asked Sorrobask.

"All the way down. It won't take long."

When they arrived at the bottom of the chamber, the lift stopped. Exits led onto the cavern floor, but there was nothing unusual in sight.

"Where is the chest?" asked the priest. "You'd better not be stalling me."

"Wait." Warren turned a crank. After a few turns, it locked into position with a loud clunk. "There's more space beneath us. I just had to switch it over to go further."

"More?" Sorrobask whistled. "Thank War you're taking me there. I'd never have found it on my own."

"I know."

The lift shuddered into motion and dropped down into the chamber's floor. For a few moments, stone blocked the exits and cloaked the platform in darkness—but it wasn't long until the familiar glow of the crystals returned. The pair dropped into what looked like a storage area containing rock piles, crates, and minecarts in various stages of disrepair. Before they reached the bottom, however, Warren pulled hard on the lever and held it fast. The round platform stopped about two feet above the floor.

Sorrobask looked suspicious. "Why'd you stop?"

"Because the chest is hidden in the machinery below the floor. If you want to access it, I need to keep the platform suspended."

Sorrobask palmed his forehead. "That's *genius*. I can see why Dantess is tempted to use your tricks. But remember, in the end, I beat you. My *strength* made you give all of this up." He jumped down onto the stone floor and looked into the void beneath the platform. "It's dark in there. I can't see the chest."

Warren nodded. "One of the reasons it's a perfect hiding spot. Take a crystal in if you like."

"Good idea." Sorrobask broke off a nub of glowing yellow crystal that was in reach, climbed inside the mechanism, and began searching among the gears and rods. "Where is it exactly?"

Warren declined to answer. Instead, he released the lever. The platform dropped the last two feet, sealing off the space beneath.

"What? What did you do? Open this up!" Sorrobask's muffled voice leaked through the cracks between the boards of the reinforced platform. When Warren didn't respond, the wood shook with powerful repeated blows from beneath.

"This reinforced platform was designed to carry tons of ore. I suspect it will withstand even the mighty strength of an angry priest of War."

"I'll destroy you, faithless scum. Open it up now!"

Warren walked off the platform. "You know, there's a way to rig the mechanism from inside there and lift the platform. With only a little bit of knowledge, you could escape on your own."

Sorrobask struck the wood again. And again. And again. "You can't do this!" he screamed. "It's not allowed!"

"I know the rules of the Game, priest of War. Murder isn't allowed, but trapping you is fine. Encouraged, even."

Warren strolled over to one of the discarded minecarts, wiped away the layer of rocks on top, and revealed the raised plate of the chest.

"Here's something you clearly didn't learn in your training: strength can win the battle," Warren said, "but planning wins the war."

CHAPTER SIXTEEN

"IDIOT. HOW'D YOU end up under there?" asked Jyn. Every word sounded further and further away in Dantess' head. The chest on top of him felt like it had the weight of the world inside it, and it was relentless. He was on the edge of slipping out of consciousness.

Dantess' mouth moved silently. He tried to ask Jyn to forgive him. She was dead because of him, and now he was going to join her. Maybe she was here to escort his spirit away.

To his surprise, the massive weight lifted from his chest. Dantess desperately pulled air into his lungs. Each breath was exquisite. With the third, he was able to say, "What...?"

"Move," Jyn grunted. "This chest is heavy."

But it wasn't Jyn. Now that he could breathe, he realized that the person hovering over him was a well-muscled priestess of War, and she had lifted one end of the chest far enough up to take pressure off of Dantess. As quickly as he could, Dantess dragged himself from underneath and, just as his feet cleared, the chest came crashing back down.

"Where are your keys? Tell me you still have them." After noticing the missing plate on the chest, the priestess with the prominent nose pulled out her map and examined it. "You *lost* them? That was the only reason I was tracking you. Who beat me to them?"

He wasn't thinking clearly, but the breastplate, the hawkish features, the insults...

"Withyr?" asked Dantess, still light-headed.

"No, *I'm* Withyr, dumbass. Who took your keys? I bet it was Kevik, right?"

Dantess nodded and tried to sit up. "Yes. Th... thank you for..."

"Rules of the Game. No one dies. I'm surprised Kevik left you here like that."

"It's not..." Dantess paused while he breathed, "out of character."

"Maybe he thought you were strong enough to free yourself? I don't know. But I *do* know he has three keys now and is on his way to the tower." She folded and placed her map behind her belt. "I'm going to stop him." She looked at Dantess and smirked. "Feel free to nap. Or whatever." Without another word, she ran off.

Dantess, feeling like an idiot indeed—for getting himself trapped, as well as losing his keys and likely the Game—collapsed back on the dirt ground and clutched at a rib that might have been broken. At the moment, anything more than breathing was beyond him.

Dantess caught up to Withyr leaning against a tree halfway to the tower. She was studying her map.

"What happened?" asked Dantess as he stopped next to her.

"I couldn't catch him. Kevik entered the tower with his three keys. They're out of play. See?" She held her map up to Dantess. Indeed, the red, green, and yellow dots had disappeared. Only the purple and blue dots remained, both approximately where they started. "That's it. I'm done."

"He entered with my three keys," said Dantess. "Anyone who comes after will have a harder time getting to the top."

"Does that even matter? He's got more keys *and* a head start. I've got nothing. By the time I collect any of the other keys out there, he'll already have his hands on the trophy."

"You don't know that. Anything could happen in Evil's tower."

"Sounds like wishful thinking."

Dantess shook his head. "Even if it is, I can't give up now. I have too much at stake."

Withyr smiled, her eyes narrow. "Oh? How badly do you want this? Are you willing to deal?"

"Deal? Is that allowed?"

"Why not? Alliances are always part of war."

Dantess thought about this. "What do you have in mind?"

"You're blue, right?" When Dantess nodded, she continued, "There are two keys left: yours and mine. The only way we catch up to Kevik is if we get those keys now. I can't get mine, but I can help *you* get it. And you can do the same with yours. That way we can each enter with one key as quickly as possible."

"One key? I heard that priests who enter with one key don't come out."

"Trying with one key is better than giving up. Unless you want to give me both keys?"

"No. I told you, I need this."

"Then it's one key for each of us. Deal?" Withyr held out her hand.

Dantess shook it. "I hope you survive."

"I will. I always do. You, on the other hand, can't even seem to conquer a stationary object. I'm betting on the tower." She shrugged. "My key is closer. We'll get that one first. Let's move."

Together, they ran toward the river.

"This isn't just a river. Your chest is in the *rapids*." Dantess gestured to the fast-flowing current coursing around the many sharp boulders sticking up from the surface. "How'd you even get it in there?"

"Wait," said Withyr. She put two fingers in her mouth and let out a sharp whistle. Heads raised from bushes on both sides of the river, including one soldier hidden near to them. Many of them held baskets. Inside the nearest was a frantic, black, writhing blur of teeth and claws. "Any attempts yet?" she asked.

The soldier shook his head. "Can't wait to see what these will do, though. They're spitting mad."

"What are *those*?" Dantess demanded.

"They're called rippers," said Withyr. "Nasty reptiles. Fast and mean. Not easy to catch, but my squad has spent months practicing for today." Withyr smiled. "They're amphibious, carnivorous, and they love to hunt for prey in rivers like this."

Dantess' jaw dropped. "You were going to release those beasts on anyone who tried to get your chest?"

"Those were the standing orders I gave my squad. It's not easy to fight the current to get the key. I figured it would be harder still while fighting off a few dozen rippers. You should thank War we've got a deal."

"Have you considered they might be, I don't know, *fatal*?"

"If a few rippers can kill a priest of War, that priest has no business competing in the Game. Don't you agree?"

Dantess wiped his brow and blew a loud breath. "I'm glad I don't have to find out. Now how am I supposed to get to the chest—without dealing with your irritable friends?"

Withyr handed Dantess a rope. "Tie this around your waist." Once he did so, she walked uphill to the top of a small fall in the rapids. From where they stood, rocks extended into the river about halfway across. "Follow me."

Fighting to keep their feet, they waded to the center where Withyr grabbed the rope. "Once I'm braced, I can lower you to the chest. You won't have to swim at all. It's almost too easy. Ready?"

Dantess nodded. He climbed over the fall's lip. Almost immediately, his feet slipped but Withyr kept a firm grip on the rope. Hand over hand, she allowed the current to pull him down the river.

Dantess fought to keep his head above water, but having the rope helped him stay in control. For a moment, he reflected on how odd this situation was. He was putting his safety into the hands of an opponent in this game, but desperate times bred desperate alliances.

Soon, Dantess felt the metal box under his feet. "Stop! It's right here."

Withyr stopped feeding the rope and looped it twice around her hands to keep it from slipping.

Dantess took a big breath, dove down, and felt the lid of the chest for the raised plate. Once he found it, he pressed his palm down, fished around in the hole that opened, and grabbed the purple key. He kicked up off the chest and broke the water's surface. "I've got it. Pull me up."

"Right." Grunting, Withyr heaved with one hand and then the other. Dantess felt himself jerking upstream, scraping against the sharp rocks but making solid progress. He knew that pulling something as heavy as himself against the powerful current wasn't an easy job. It spoke to Withyr's considerable strength.

When Dantess had almost reached the top, Withyr stopped pulling. "Hand me the key," she said.

"What?"

"You heard me," she said, as she strained. "Hurry up. It's not easy to keep the river from sweeping you away."

"How about you pull me up and we discuss this?"

"Nope. Once you have my key out there, you might decide to run off and leave me to battle your squad to get the other. The new deal is that I'll keep my key and help you get yours."

"That forces me to trust *you* then."

She shrugged. "Yeah, that's true. It's definitely more appealing from my perspective. But I'm also the one who can release you and then dump dozens of rippers in that river. You're not in a position to negotiate. What do you say?"

With reluctance, Dantess handed up the purple key. Withyr smiled, took the key, and placed it in her bracer. For a long moment, she stared at Dantess. Both knew she could simply release the rope and be done with him—but instead, she grabbed Dantess' hand and pulled him up. Together, they waded back to shore.

"Let's move this along," Withyr said, breathing hard. "You need a key too, right?"

Dantess nodded. "Right." In truth, Dantess admired the way Withyr was playing the game. She was smart and capable and a tad ruthless. He had no choice but to trust her, because she held all the cards—but in a game with no allies, he was glad she was working with him, rather than against him.

Dantess led Withyr through the caverns of the depleted mine. More than once, he had to drag her away from the spectacular displays of flowing light. "These crystals are amazing," Withyr said, breaking off a few different-colored stones from the ground. They held their light, even in her palm. "How did you know all this was here?"

"Research," said Dantess. "There's someone on my squad that reads *everything*." Dantess also grabbed three of the blue crystals. It was Jyn's favorite color.

"Just blue? That's boring," said Withyr, admiring her own multicolored collection. "At least take this to remember me by. Since I'm purple in this Game." She handed him a purple crystal. "It's like blue, but better."

To be polite, Dantess nodded and put the purple stone in a different pocket, away from Jyn's. "My thanks. We should get moving."

When the pair entered the huge chamber with all the suspended tracks, he called out to his squad. Motti appeared behind him. "Why is *she* here?" he asked.

"For the moment, we're working together. Where's Warren?"

"Down there." Motti pointed down to the floor, far below. When Dantess looked startled, he added, "Don't worry. He didn't fall. He took the lift down, but it's still there." Motti put his hands on his hips and stared downward. "We don't dare bring it back up. Warren let us know that, if it didn't come back up, he used it to trap a priest."

Withyr's expression was both shocked and amused. She laughed and asked, "Who'd you catch?"

"Sorrobask," answered Motti.

She clapped once. "I should have guessed." To Dantess, she added, "He's not the brightest gem in the cave. Still, good work to your squad! Capturing a priest isn't easy. I mean, Kevik captured you—and I guess I kind of did too—but these are just faithless, after all."

Dantess ignored her. "Are you telling me they're at the bottom, Motti? With the chest?"

Motti sent a sideways glance at Withyr, but nodded.

"No lift, huh?" said Withyr. "Then let's take the shortcut down." With that, Withyr jumped off the suspended track.

Dantess reached out to her in alarm, but she landed on another track below. Then she jumped to a deeper track, and another deeper still. Dantess shrugged at Motti, channeled his Longing into his token to increase his agility, and followed her.

It wasn't long until they both stood at the lip of the final hole leading to the storage basement. "Down there?" asked Withyr.

Dantess nodded. "That's my understanding."

Both dropped down and landed on the wooden platform with a loud thump. Warren, resting nearby, jerked up.

"You startled me," said Warren as he snapped his hand back from atop a minecart. "What are you doing here? And why is Withyr here?"

"Kevik entered the tower with three keys," said Dantess. "Withyr and I are working together to get two keys as quickly as possible, so we can get in there after him. With her help, I opened her chest. Now she's here to open mine."

A pounding came from underneath their feet. "Who's up there? Let me out!"

"Is that Sorrobask under there?" said Withyr, chuckling. "We can't let you out. How else would you learn your lesson? And you *surely* need some schooling. Only an idiot would get caught like that." She pounded her own foot on the platform. "Now, shut up. The adults have work to do up here." She pointed to the minecart next to Warren. "Your chest is in there, I assume?"

Warren looked to Dantess with misgiving, but the priest nodded, so he presented it to her with his hands as he walked away from it.

"I haven't actually opened a chest yet." She glanced up at Dantess. "It's exciting."

As Withyr approached the chest, Warren took Dantess aside. "Is this wise?" he whispered. "Teaming up with another player?"

"I didn't have a choice. It was the only way to get a key and get into the tower quickly enough to have a chance to beat Kevik."

Withyr wiped away the rocks to reveal the raised plate.

"So you have her key, she gets your key, and you both use one to enter?" Warren continued. "Sounds risky. In a lot of ways."

"No, she's got her own key. And now she's going to give me mine."

Warren's eyes grew wide. "But then what's stopping her from—"

"Nice dealing with you," said Withyr as she leapt straight up through the hole in the ceiling. The chest's plate was gone and so was its key.

"Not again!" said Dantess, alarmed. "She has both keys!"

Dantess channeled his Longing through his token, and tensed. Before he jumped, Warren said, "Wait, I need to tell you something about Kevik!"

But Dantess was already pushing off the ground. As he flew upward through the hole, he heard Warren's distant voice calling out, "Get it back!"

Dantess bounded from track to track, trying to catch up to Withyr, but she was a priestess of War at the top of her game. If anything, she pulled away from Dantess—especially after one jump when Dantess missed the landing and was forced to grab onto the track to keep from plummeting to the ground. The time it took to lift himself up was time Withyr used to increase her lead.

He finally made his way to the exit tunnel and hoped that his knowledge of the mines would give him an advantage. He channeled his Longing into his speed and raced through the maze of caverns—but when he arrived at the cave exit, he saw Withyr already a half mile nearer to the tower.

"Withyr!" Dantess called out, breathing hard. "Stop!"

She didn't turn or slow, so Dantess continued his pursuit.

The marsh passed by on one side, the burned-out forest on the other, and the black tower in the distance grew larger with every passing minute. Still, he was no closer to overtaking Withyr. He began to despair that he could prevent her from entering with the two keys.

Inevitably, Withyr arrived at the door first. With his enhanced vision, Dantess could see her inserting the blue key as he approached. The first keyhole swallowed the key, a handle popped out from the door beneath it, and the metal plate on the door sliver to its right slid open to reveal a second keyhole. Her options at this point were to pull the handle and open the single-key door, or insert the second key and unlock the next nested door.

"Wait. Don't use the second key!" Dantess called out. Remembering what his da told him about the pair's shared history, he added, "Please! I *have* to enter. It's the only way I can save my father!"

Withyr paused, the purple key inches away from the second keyhole. "Your father?" she yelled back.

She stopped? Surprised, Dantess continued, "My da. Tolliver. Varyon's son. He's locked up because of me." Dantess slowed his run as he arrived at the tower door. "And he's dying in his cell. He won't survive the years I'd need until I have the rank to release him."

"But if you win the Game..." Her hand dropped back from the keyhole.

174

"Yes." Dantess walked closer. "I can get him out."

"I didn't know you were doing this for him."

"Why does that matter to you?" Dantess kept walking, steadily closing the distance between them.

"Stay back." Withyr held her hand up, keeping Dantess where he was. "Make a move, and I'll enter before you can do anything."

Dantess stood his ground and listened.

Withyr sighed. "When I was young, your father worked in the stables. I joked that he should help me win some stupid horse race. Day of the race, my main competitor fell off his horse. They checked his gear and found the harness had been tampered with."

"My da did that? For you?"

"I didn't ask him to. Not directly. Regardless, to affect the outcome of a competition is to defy the will of War. Varyon banished Tolliver from the temple. I think he would have killed him if Tolliver hadn't been his son."

Dantess was amazed. "He lost everything."

"I thought maybe Tolliver was rebelling against his father. He hated it here. Regardless, I never forgot what he did. Even if it was wrong, he did it for me." Withyr looked at the key in her hand.

The last player in the game, Glinden—having approached while both Withyr and Dantess were distracted—slammed into Withyr and knocked her to the ground. They rolled around as they wrestled for the key.

"Give it over!" Glinden demanded.

Dantess looked at the door. There was nothing blocking it. He could enter now. The first of the nested doors was already unlocked. It was what he was promised. But...

He channeled the Longing. Options spread out over his vision and he chose the first that offered what he wanted. From behind Glinden, Dantess slipped his hand under her arm and behind her head. He used his leverage to pull her from the grapple and hurl her over his hip. She landed with a thud a few feet away.

"Leave off," said Dantess. "This is between Withyr and me."

Glinden growled, "I've got *no keys*. According to my map, the only two left in the game are here. If I don't get these, I won't get in."

Back on her feet, Withyr sighed and flipped Dantess the purple key. "Take both. You'll have a better chance to save your da.

175

Make sure to tell him the debt's paid." She squared off with Glinden, who was getting back up. "I'll keep this one from getting in the way."

"You're working together?" screamed Glinden. "That's not fair!"

Dantess inserted the purple key into the second keyhole, and the key disappeared inside it. The first handle collapsed back into the door, and another, just under the second keyhole, popped out. As a metal plate covered the second hole, another uncovered the third—but Dantess knew he wouldn't be using that one.

Withyr blocked a flurry of Glinden's attacks. Almost casually, she said to Dantess, "I want to win, but I want to make sure Kevik loses *more*. I know what he does to women. With rank, it'll be worse. You're taking my chance, so make it count."

He used the handle to pull the second door open. "I will. I promise."

Dantess stepped through the doorway and into the cold black void that awaited him.

CHAPTER SEVENTEEN

THE DOOR SLAMMED shut behind him, but it wasn't the same wooden door he unlocked outside the tower. This door was steel, set into a wall of crossed metal bars containing a lock with two keyholes. The space beyond the bars was dark.

Shouldn't that way lead back outside? was Dantess' first thought. Noticing that the other walls and ceiling were also made of crossed steel bars, his second was, *Did I walk into a trap?*

There were no lamps or torches or windows, or even any sun or sky through the bars above him, but Dantess could see by virtue of a dim ambient light with no obvious source. It seemed limited to this room. Spaces beyond the bars in any direction were completely dark.

Dantess returned to the door and pulled on it. It was locked shut. Even with his enhanced strength, the door did not budge. After giving up the effort, he noticed a plaque next to the door that read:

> *Within these walls,*
> *A priest of War,*
> *Finds what he brought,*
> *No less, no more.*

Dantess, confused, walked deeper into the room, but the dim light wasn't much to navigate by. In fact, only two steps in, he almost tripped on a large stone laying on the rough floor. Squinting, he realized that there were a number of these stones about.

He returned to the wall of bars and felt his way along it until he reached the corner after about twenty feet. He continued along that wall until he arrived at another door, this one with three keyholes and the same plaque beside it.

Another door? he thought. *But with a different number of keyholes?*

Dantess continued his slow journey, eventually making his way to the next corner. After walking a few steps along the new wall, he accidentally kicked something.

But this was no rock. It certainly smelled much worse than that.

A furry, hulking shape snorted and then exploded into motion. It jumped at him with incredible ferocity. Out of reflex, Dantess leapt back into the corner and slammed against the hard, metal bars. The shape lunged forward and swiped at him with a huge taloned claw. It rang off of his armored chest plate and made his bruised ribs ache. Even though his flesh was spared, he could feel the strength of the creature behind it.

In the split-second following, Dantess channeled his Longing through the token. Even without fully understanding the anatomy of his opponent, he was able to apply his increased speed and choose an effective counter. He struck at its midsection with a mighty blow that knocked it back a few feet, and followed up with two powerful kicks that sent it to the ground.

It rolled away.

Dantess looked around for movement, but saw nothing. He stepped forward just as the huge furry beast launched itself from behind a boulder. It struck him in the side and knocked him against the bars once again. This time, his head struck metal and, for a moment, he was senseless.

The claws attacked him repeatedly and swiftly. Most rebounded off of his chest plate, but a few raked across his leg and shoulder.

He dove back into his token and asked, *What can I do?*

The plan was immediate and specific: strike *here* along the "neck"—or at least somewhere toward the top—and then *here* and *here* at seemingly random places in the midst of the furry mass.

Before the thing shifted and Dantess lost his bearings, he launched his attack. With each hit, the thing buckled a little more. At the last strike, it dropped like a stone, let out a strained gurgle, and expired.

At first, Dantess was amazed at how effective the attack turned out to be, but then realized that previous priests must have fought this thing and prevailed. Once more, he marveled at how powerful a weapon the token of War proved to be.

Even more cautious, Dantess continued his exploration of the room. It was square. There were four doors, one on each wall and each with a different number of keyholes ranging from two to five. Finally, he inched out into the center of the room and found yet another door in the floor. This one had a singular keyhole.

There's no way out except these doors, Dantess thought. *But they all require keys to open. I don't have any more keys. I used mine to enter the tower.*

Dantess sat on a rock and thought further. *If I need keys but don't have them, maybe I can find some.* With this in mind, Dantess began to search the room. He ran his hands on the floor, especially along the barred walls. He lifted rocks and felt beneath them. He even searched the furry body of the creature he'd killed.

Nothing.

Then he remembered: *This place was designed by Evil. Where would priests of Evil hide some keys? What would be the most horrific place to make me search?*

Dantess found a fist-sized rock and smashed it against a boulder. He picked up a knife-edged fragment and, after taking a big breath, used it to slice into the fuzzy corpse. Disgusted but determined, he reached into the entrails and began to search. A few squishy minutes later, he touched something small and metal. He pulled out a key. Another few minutes of rummaging through entrails produced one more.

But that was it. No matter how long or thoroughly he searched, two keys were all there was to find: one purple and one blue.

Now that he had two keys, it followed that he could use them to leave. Maybe the two-key door led to a two-key path to the top? He approached the door with the two keyholes. As he inserted each key, it disappeared. Once both keys were gone, the door unlocked and slid open.

Dantess walked through into the black.

The door slammed shut behind him. As expected, this door was steel, set into a wall of bars. When he looked back, he saw that the door had a lock with two keyholes and the plaque next to it contained the familiar verse.

And just as before, a dim, ambient light with no obvious source lit this room littered with rocks and boulders.

"Huh," said Dantess.

A loud growl erupted from the far corner. One of the dark shapes leapt up and began to bound its way straight at Dantess.

This time, Dantess had the opportunity to channel his Longing through his token and react. His token assumed this was the same type of creature he defeated before. As the fuzzy creature neared, he struck the three vulnerable spots almost simultaneously. The creature's momentum sent the furry bulk directly into Dantess and bowled him over. For a moment, Dantess struggled to escape from the dead weight of fur and claws and muscle.

Once free, Dantess searched the room. It was exactly the same as the one he left. It had the same doors with the same number of keyholes, the same plaques, and the same rocks—even the one he smashed.

But it was dark. Maybe the room just seemed similar because it had the same design.

After searching the room and finding no keys, he steeled himself, found another sharp rock, and sliced into the creature. The keys were exactly where he found them before.

"One more time," Dantess said to himself. "Let's see what happens."

He took the blue and purple keys and put them into the two-keyhole lock. When the door opened, he walked through.

The two-keyhole door slammed shut behind him. The plaque next to it contained the familiar verse. A dim, ambient light lit the scattered rocks and boulders.

"Damn it," said Dantess.

"UH?" A muttered growl came from the far side of the room. "AGAIN?" A furry shape shuffled up, growled, and began its approach.

"Wait! You can talk?"

The creature stopped. "YUH." Its voice sounded like the mix of a jungle cat, a bear, and a bucket of rocks.

"No! Stop! Wouldn't you rather talk than fight?"

The creature tilted its 'head'. "NUH. LIKE FIGHT." It raised its claws again.

"But I always kill you, right? Wouldn't talking be better?"

The furry monstrosity tilted its head—maybe its torso?—the other way. After a moment, it said, "YUH?"

This is so weird, Dantess thought. But aloud, he said, "Great. So, this is the same room. Every time?"

"YUH. MY ROOM. TWO KEY."

"And if I keep using two keys to leave here, I'll keep ending up back here?"

The creature scratched its front with the knife-like claws. "YUH."

"So how do I *actually* leave? How do I get to the top of the tower?"

The creature held up one of its many appendages. One at a time, five claws popped out from it.

"Are you saying I need five keys? I don't have five." Dantess sighed. "I only have the two. And they're inside you, evidently."

"MORE KEYS IN YOU? I LOOK." The creature started to stretch out a few too many limbs with joints that bent ways that were just wrong. Then it crouched down, preparing to leap.

"Wait," said Dantess. "If we fight, I'll just keep killing you over and over. It's senseless."

"NUH. MY JOB. FIGHT YOU AND OTHER."

"Other? You fought Kevik?"

The creature performed what could be interpreted as a shrug. "YUH."

"How did Kevik get into the two-key room? And *why* would he do that?"

Perhaps that was one question too much, because the creature didn't answer. Instead, it grabbed itself and started shaking.

Dantess edged away. "Are you all right?"

"JOB!" the creature roared and leapt forward.

Almost absently, Dantess let the token take control of his actions. He struck the creature's vulnerable spots in quick succession, and it dropped to the ground with a gurgle.

Dantess sighed, picked up the exact same rock he used previously, and cut open the beast. After only a little searching around, he pulled out the two keys.

"Two keys," said Dantess. "Again."

I wish Warren was here, he thought. *He'd figure out what to do.*

Dantess sat down and pondered. *How would Warren solve this? He'd definitely stop doing the same thing over and over. He'd try something unexpected.*

He stared at the two keys in his palm.

So, what would happen if I don't use both of them? Kevik must have done that. He came here into the two-key room even though he had three keys. But that would mean, Dantess stepped over to the door on the floor with one keyhole, *I'd have to go into the one-key room.*

It was a fact that every priest who played the Game knew. Those that enter the tower with one key sometimes never leave.

Dantess suspected he was about to find out why.

He inserted the purple key into the one-keyhole lock. The door unlocked and slid open, revealing a dark pit. Dantess put the remaining blue key into his bracer.

After he took a moment to gather his courage, Dantess dropped down into the inky hole.

In pure blackness, he fell onto a hard floor. One foot landed awkwardly on a stone, and he rolled his ankle. Dantess grunted and fell to the floor, clutching his aching heel.

He couldn't see a thing, but he could hear something: a hiss, as if smoke made a sound while it coursed through the air, never diminishing.

It circled him. He could hear the hiss floating on one side and then another.

"Prieeeessssst. Welcoooome."

"You can talk, too?" Dantess asked.

There were no words in response, but the hissing continued to circle and perhaps draw closer.

Dantess waved his hands in front of his face, but could not see them at all. "Stay back, whatever you are."

"Jooooin meeeeee." The words seemed to come from everywhere.

Something brushed against his face, like the tickle of a breeze. Dantess jerked back. While he felt no pain, he touched his cheek and found a bloody cut there. He swore he could hear wheezing laughter in the air.

Dantess wasn't normally fearful of the dark, but the thought of fighting an unseen enemy terrified him. His token could not help him fight something he couldn't see. What was he supposed to do without any light?

Something brushed against his hand and left it wet with his blood. Anything that could cut this deep without pain had to be razor sharp. He could lose a finger and not know it. "What... what do you want?"

"Yoooou don't neeeeeeed blooooood. *I* will beeeee yoooour blooooood, prieeeeest. Beeeeeetter thaaaan blooooood."

Fear pushed Dantess to panic. He was defenseless unless he could see what he was up against. If only he had a torch or...

Inspired, he rooted around in his pocket and felt the loose rocks inside: the surefire crystals from the mines! Hurriedly, he pulled out the three blue crystals and held them up.

Their blue glow had diminished from when he first took them—the stored sunlight wouldn't last forever—but the crystals threw out enough illumination to light up the small area around him. Dantess gasped. A thin tendril of flowing smoke hovered inches from his eye. As the light struck the smoke, however, the tendril solidified, then crackled and singed. Flakes fell as the tendril began to collapse into ash.

Dantess pushed the crystals further away from him, following the tendril. About two feet away, he found the base: a thick stream of mist sprouting a number of other thin tendrils. Under the light, the stream coagulated into the dark oily skin of a serpent whose surface hissed and popped as if it were cooking.

An airy scream flooded the room. The section of ropy, burning meat dropped to the ground, but was still connected to something larger, something out of sight.

"Suuuuunliiiiight?" something moaned.

"You don't like the sun, even from a crystal?" Dantess lifted himself using a nearby boulder and waved the crystals to reveal more of the mist-being.

It thrashed in the light, but couldn't seem to flow away from the damaged piece of itself. The scalded section was solid enough to act like an anchor.

"Let's get a better look at you, shall we?" Hobbling, Dantess followed the larger stream. Like hairs along the surface, the little tendrils fried and disintegrated, leaving the trunk to solidify, burn, and fall heavily onto the ground. If it was a snake, it was much longer than any he'd seen before—perhaps twenty feet or more. He started to wonder if it ever ended.

"Keeeeeeep awaaaaay." The voice was localized now, coming from something he approached. Finally, the crystals lit up a large reptilian head. A webbed collar framed a snout and teeth like a crocodile's. As the light brushed against its face, the tongue lashed back and forth. "Yoooou willlll paaaay..."

The head dropped to the ground, still hissing and bubbling. Its eyes sizzled and popped, spraying goo everywhere.

"Disgusting," muttered Dantess. On a hunch, he grabbed its massive jaw and forced it apart until it cracked. He reached into its gullet and pulled out two keys.

"Two keys!" Dantess checked his bracer and found the single key there. "I have *three* now. I can move up!"

With purpose, Dantess began to search for a wall. He couldn't see far with the weak light from his crystals, but the distance he walked meant it was clearly a much bigger space than the two-key room he came from. His ankle pained him with every step, and the trip required quite a few to reach the wall of bars.

When he finally located a door, it had a lock with three keyholes. And he had three keys!

"Let's see where this takes me." Dantess inserted the keys, one by one, into the lock. When the third key disappeared, the door slid open. Dantess limped into the dark opening.

The three-keyhole door slammed shut behind him as he walked into a well-lit room. In fact, having just left total darkness, Dantess had to squint and shield his eyes until they adjusted. During this, he heard a tapping or clicking noise. It was constant and everywhere.

"Another priest?" a squeaky voice piped up, strangely sounding like it was being spoken through chattering teeth. "It's a feast!"

"Flesh and meat, a chance to eat!" another voice, slightly deeper, chattered back.

It looked like a small child, but with a larger, flatter head and lean limbs of pure muscle. Whatever it was opened and closed its horrible sharp-toothed grin as if it were always chewing as it launched itself at his head. "So hungry!"

Dantess tried to swat it away, but it grabbed onto his arm and sunk those needle-like, chattering teeth into his flesh.

From behind, another imp grabbed onto his back and began climbing up to his head. "So hungry!"

"Get away, you pipsqueak demons!" Dantess bashed the first against the closest boulder. At first, the imp ignored the impact and continued to scissor his teeth into Dantess' arm, but on the third swat, the creature fell to the ground, senseless.

By that time, the imp on his back had climbed up to his neck. He covered Dantess' eyes with his bony hands and bit into his ear.

Dantess screamed in fury and pain. He channeled his Longing through his token and increased his speed and strength. So enhanced, he took hold of each of the imp's arms and pulled them away. Its chattering head only came off of Dantess' ear with a piece of it still in his mouth. Enraged, Dantess pulled on those arms until they detached from the imp's body. He grabbed its torso, looked into the deranged eyes of the imp, and saw no pain, no hesitation—only incessant hunger. Atop chattering teeth.

That's when Dantess noticed the room was filled with the vile creatures. Their chattering teeth sounded like a hard rain. Their eyes were all trained on him. "So hungry! So hungry! So hungry!" they chanted.

"More! More! I'm so hungry!" The armless imp in his hands squirmed and bit the air.

When the creatures surged forward, Dantess defended himself by using his imp as a blunt instrument. He clubbed flying imps out of the air. He bashed the creatures crawling toward his legs. Through all of this, his weapon never stopped chattering.

"You want to chew on something?" asked Dantess. "Chew on this!"

He pressed his imp's face against the chest of one that was climbing up a nearby boulder. His weapon did not disappoint. It took a few impressive bites of his fellow monster.

"Hey!" the imp in his hands cried out. "Xrrrth tastes good!"

"He does?" inquired many of the other imps.

"No, I don't!" said the imp with the bite marks in his chest. "Yuuloth is lying. Stay away!"

Four or five imps swarmed atop poor Xrrrth. "So hungry!" the other imps sang out as they tore into their meal.

Another licked its teeth. "Klywth tastes good too!"

"So does Ghzlth!"

"Joplth doesn't fight as hard as a priest!"

Soon, Dantess found himself kicking and pushing only a few stragglers away. All the other imps were engaged in a feeding frenzy, fighting and biting and eating each other. Blood and gore flew everywhere.

After a while, the incessant tapping of teeth and the chants of 'so hungry' stopped. Dantess limped around the room, stomping on whatever imps were still chattering. With a sigh, he began to search through the revolting remains.

Inside two of the dead imps, he found a key each—but no more.

No matter how hard he looked, there were only two keys, blue and purple.

"I'm down a key? After all this, I still only get two keys back?"

He limped over to the plaque and read it again.

Within these walls,
A priest of War,
Finds what he brought,
No less, no more.

He stared at the blue and purple keys in his hands. They were the same ones he used to enter the tower—no less, no more.

How was he supposed to get five keys if he'd only be able to collect two from each room he entered?

Weary and hurt, Dantess cleared the remains of an imp off a boulder, clutched his injured arm, and sat down. He knew what he had to do, but that didn't make him feel any better about doing it. In fact, he felt defeated already.

"I have to go back to the one-key room. Back to that mist snake thing. In order to get five keys, I have to kill it three more times. I'll never last." He dropped his head into his hands.

"And it knows I'm coming."

CHAPTER EIGHTEEN

DANTESS HAD HIS crystals in hand before he ever dropped back into the one-key room's complete darkness. This time, the landing was still painful, but it didn't injure him further. The crystals' blue glow was dim and growing dimmer with each passing moment. He needed to work quickly.

"Come on out," said Dantess, waving the crystals back and forth. "Let's get this over with."

But his words were met with silence. He couldn't even hear the hissing he expected to hang in the air. The only sound was the crunch of his own footsteps as he used his limited light to navigate through this garden of rocks and boulders.

"You're here somewhere. I'll find you."

"I'm right here," a rough masculine voice said just beyond the light.

"I'm right here," another voice added behind Dantess.

"...right here." The words repeated many more times in different parts of the room.

Confused, Dantess took a step forward and held the crystals out. A priest of War stood in front of him—but even in the dim blue light, Dantess could see the man wasn't well. Portions of his body were decayed or missing. His breastplate, cape, and even the style of his boots hadn't been seen in the temple for hundreds of years.

"Who are you?" Dantess asked.

The priest worked his mouth slowly, as if unused to speaking. "I'm you."

The words echoed throughout the room.

"Let me by. I have to kill the mist snake."

The priest cocked his head. From everywhere at once came the word "No."

Much quicker than Dantess expected, the priest lunged at him, but the attack was clumsy and easily parried. Dantess channeled his Longing and the token laid out his options, but even injured, he almost didn't feel the need for it. Whatever training this man once had, he wasn't using it now.

A few jabs at the man's head sent him stumbling back, but then another attack came from behind. His token had been anticipating it. He ducked, balanced on his good leg, and swept out the feet from the priest back there.

Two more priests came from the sides, and the first one he knocked away came back for more. These few priests were starting to add up to a mob, and Dantess realized their lack of training didn't matter. If enough of them swarmed him at once, he could be overwhelmed, especially weakened and injured as he was.

Dantess grabbed the first priest and twisted—his plan was to get behind him and use him as a shield against the others—but when he did, he noticed a smoke tendril lodged into a wound at the base of his skull. As the blue light from his crystals hit the tendril, the smoke filament crusted and burned away into ash. The priest fell from Dantess' arms onto the ground like a rag doll. Whatever kept him on his feet was gone.

"So that's what you meant, you sick monster," said Dantess. "You wanted to be my blood. You're the blood of all these poor priests left behind here, aren't you?"

Three more priests surged forward. Again, the attacks were clumsy, but Dantess was tired and wounded. They managed to land enough blows to create an opening. One of them plowed into Dantess, sent him sprawling on the ground, and landed on top of him with his hands wrapped around Dantess' throat. At first, Dantess tried to pull those hands off, but they were as cold and strong as stone—so instead, he held the crystals behind the dead priest's head. A puff of ash later and the priest collapsed lifeless atop Dantess.

He couldn't help but chuckle. Now that he knew their weakness, he would be able to render them all back to the corpses they truly were. But before he could escape from under the heavy body, someone grabbed his hand carrying the crystals. He clasped his fist shut, but strong fingers forced it open and took the stones.

"No!" screamed Dantess as he saw three blue points of light fly away into the black.

In the resulting darkness, Dantess pushed the dead weight off his body with all his might. He struggled to his feet and blindly lashed out against attacks that didn't come. The priests had retreated, and in their place, the familiar hiss circled around him.

"Jooooin meeeeeee," said the wind.

188

A tickle to the back of his neck forced him to jump forward. Dantess pressed his hand there, and it came back wet with blood. His heart dropped. That was the place the tendrils entered the corpses to animate them. He couldn't let that happen to him.

He began to run in the direction of the tossed crystals. Maybe he could recover them.

The wind laughed as he stumbled and tripped over the bodies and boulders in his path. Each time, he scrambled to his feet and limped on.

Soon, he ran headlong into the wall of bars and realized, if the stones were tossed here, they would have flown beyond the wall, completely and utterly lost.

He pressed his back against the wall and slid down. He had no plan. The hissing grew louder.

"Jooooooin meeeeeee."

Yes, he was scared. Yes, he felt sorry for himself. But it wasn't just his life at stake. Others depended on him. Warren needed his protection at the temple. His da wouldn't survive the death of his son.

The hissing grew closer. It was almost upon him.

Even Withyr put her faith in him to stop Kevik from winning and perpetuating his violence and hatred. Withyr gave him her chance. He promised to make that chance count.

But he remembered that it wasn't all she gave him.

In the mines, she also gave him a *crystal*. A single purple crystal.

Frantically, Dantess rooted around in his other pocket and brought forth an extremely dim purple surefire crystal. The light barely illuminated a few inches from his hand, but it was enough to reveal five slim tendrils reaching for his head.

The light was too dim to burn away the tendrils, but the ghostly filaments solidified and halted their approach.

Dantess pulled himself up and shuffled forth, holding the crystal as close to the tendrils as possible to force them into solid shape. He hoped their source was not far away.

More than once, the whisper-tickles continued upon exposed places on his body—his legs, his arms, his face—but each time, he swung the crystal to the spot and froze the offending tendril in place.

With each step, he grew weaker. By the time he reached the snake's trunk, he was covered with too many cuts to count and a

189

trail of blood behind him. As with the tendrils, the single crystal did not cook the main stalk of the serpent, but it did force it to become solid. Those solid sections still served to anchor the beast.

Dantess limped along the trunk, occasionally waving the crystal around like he was shooing flies to halt the tendrils, but he always brought it back to the body of the serpent.

"Yooooooour liiiiiiight is weeeeeeak," said a voice from up ahead.

"It's strong enough," whispered Dantess. "I hope."

Finally, he reached the webbed collar of the head. The dim light made the mist form solid, but it was still more formidable than any snake he'd ever even heard of.

"If I caaaaan't possesssss yooooooou, I'll eeeeeeat yooooooou."

The newly-solid snout opened, showing off its sharp teeth. Dantess had no doubt that its bite could rip off a limb or tear him open. He channeled his Longing to give him enough stamina to stay standing.

And to do one more thing.

He grabbed the snout with one hand and plunged the one holding the purple surefire crystal as deep into the serpent's mouth as it would go. Then he opened his fist.

With both his hand and the crystal deep inside the mouth of the creature, the world plunged into darkness. Dantess took a moment in the stillness to pray to the god of War for protection. And if not that, then salvation.

After a short burbling sound, the serpent's head exploded.

Dantess collapsed onto the ground and, by the dim purple glow of the newly exposed crystal, passed out.

When he awoke, the crystal was so dim, it was hard to see the difference between it and the dark. He didn't know how much longer it would keep any light at all.

He found his hand still lodged in the serpent's mouth, so he used it to root around and find the two keys.

That gave him three.

He needed two more.

How was he supposed to gather two more? His light was almost out. He barely had enough strength to stand. And to get the keys, he'd have to kill a reanimated mist-snake twice more?

He couldn't do it. It wasn't possible.

As he sat and considered, he asked himself what that meant. If he gave up, he'd become another corpse on the ground, another soldier for this thing to reanimate when it activated again in a hundred years.

Like a bolt of lightning, he realized, "The corpses! A few of them must have come from the two-key room, like I did. As the verse says, 'A priest of War finds what he brought.' They're also priests or War—or at least, they were when they entered."

Dantess staggered to his feet and, holding the dim purple crystal out like a dying lantern, began to search for corpses of ancient priests.

It didn't take long. He tripped over one almost immediately—but this one had nothing, or had nothing left. He was actually missing quite a few body parts. The next one was a disappointment as well.

The light from his crystal had almost extinguished. Was he wasting his time?

After searching two more corpses, he was overjoyed to find a key under a priestess' belt. "Yes! I have four. I only need one more!"

And as luck would have it, the next priest had a key hidden in his bracer. "Five keys. I have *five* keys now." He could hardly believe it. "So, where's the five-key door?"

He stumbled to the wall and followed it, hand over hand. The crystal's light flickered and went dark so he continued in the blackness. When he reached a door, he felt three keyholes on the lock and sighed. That meant the five-key door was on the opposite side of the room.

He followed the wall around the room. He hung on the wall when his ankle pained him, but he kept moving. He was weak from lack of blood, but he kept moving. His mind conjured enemies in the dark that told him to quit—threatened him if he didn't—but he kept moving.

After what seemed like hours, he arrived at the five-key door.

Dantess had already spent so long in the tower. He couldn't imagine that Kevik hadn't already won the Game. His opponent *started* with three keys. He probably never even had to face the mist snake.

With almost no hope, he felt for the keyholes and placed his keys inside one by one. When the door slid open, he breathed deeply and stepped through.

The five-keyhole door shut behind Dantess, but not into a wall made of steel bars. Instead, this room was built from black stone and lit by torches. There was a plaque by the door. This plaque, however, contained a different verse:

> *So many chests,*
> *Each holds a key,*
> *But only one,*
> *Will set you free.*

The room was round, as if the curvature of the tower defined the outer wall. It wrapped around a central pillar that made the space feel like a large corridor that curved out of sight to the left and right.

Apart from a path down the middle, every open space held a chest. There were big chests and small chests. Chests of every color and material. Chests on the floor, chests in stacks, chests on shelves. Far too many chests to count.

"Arrghhhh! War should burn down this tower and everything in it," swore a voice from out of sight, around the curve to the right. "Stupid keys. Stupid chests. Stupid Game."

Dantess couldn't fail to recognize that voice. *Stupid... Kevik?* he thought. *He's still here? He hasn't won yet. I still have a chance!*

Even so, there was nothing he could do about his physical state. Dantess could barely stay up on his feet. If Kevik was healthier—and he likely was—a fight between them would be no contest.

Dantess looked around for any place to hide and recover, but chests filled every space. He was about to open one of the larger chests to see if there was room inside when Kevik walked around the curve.

"Dantess? How'd you get in here?" He looked over Dantess' wounds and whistled. "You are a mess. Let me guess: your opponent got it worse? I don't think that's possible, unless he's a corpse."

"Quite a few corpses, actually," Dantess answered, holding himself up on a chest and wondering, *Why isn't Kevik attacking me?* He continued, "You didn't visit the one-key room, I take it?"

"Nope, and seeing you makes me glad I didn't. Once I figured it all out, a few trips to the two-key room gave me the keys I needed to get here. I didn't want to risk whatever's in the one-key room."

"Good call. If I entered with my three keys, I would have done the same."

"You still sore about me taking your keys?" Kevik chuckled. "You got here eventually, didn't you?"

"I did." Dantess pulled himself up to his feet. "But you arrived hours before me. Why are you still here?"

Kevik thought about this, and then answered, "I'll show you." He walked down the curved path to the right. When Dantess was about to lose sight of him, Kevik turned and beckoned. "Come on. If you can still walk."

Trying to look as hale as possible, Dantess shuffled after Kevik. Once around the bend, he saw the end of the curved tunnel, the only place not covered with chests: a plain, rock wall. The only feature on that wall was a door with a single keyhole.

Next to the door was a pile of keys. Dantess had never seen so many in one place. They were all different sizes, shapes, and colors. Some had jewels in the head, some were made of gold or lead or iron. Some weren't even metal, but carved of wood, ivory, or even entire gemstones.

"So, the trophy needed to win the Game is...?" asked Dantess.

"It's the damned key to open this door, yes."

"You tried all of these?"

"Yep." Kevik pointed to another, larger pile in the corner. "And those."

Dantess gasped. "There can't be this many chests!"

"You haven't explored this place yet. If you go right from the entrance, you end up here. If you go left, you can follow the circle forever. I don't know how it works, but I haven't found an end. And I looked." Kevik shook his head. "The whole tower is filled with chests and more chests forever."

Dantess laughed. "You can't figure it out. You can't find the right key."

Kevik grunted. "That's obvious."

"And you think I might, which is why you didn't attack me when I first arrived."

"Can't hurt to have two people looking, right? We can hash it all out when we have the right key."

As much as Dantess wanted to put Kevik down, he knew he needed to look at this as an opportunity to recover. He was in no shape for a fight. "All right. I assume you've cleaned out all the chests close to the door?"

"Hours ago."

"Then I'll explore. I need to know more about this place."

Kevik held out his hand toward the path. "After you."

For a while, Kevik shadowed Dantess, keeping an eye on him. Every so often, Dantess would lean down and tilt open a chest to find it empty. In doing this, he discovered the chests were immovable, locked into their places in the hall. Then he would shuffle a little further and repeat.

Kevik began to grow impatient. "I tried all these keys already. Hurry up." When Dantess continued to amble down the path, Kevik threw up his hands. "You're too *slow*. We'll be here for a hundred years at this pace. I don't know what I was expecting from you, but you're like an old man." He shoved Dantess into the chests and stormed off further along the path. "No damned help at all."

Finally, Dantess was *alone*. He levered himself up, groaned at the pain of doing so, and considered the problem. There were thousands of chests here, and—according to the verse on the plaque—only one held the key that would open the door.

The task seemed impossible. Indeed, Kevik's lack of progress while brute-forcing a solution reinforced that idea.

But it *couldn't* be impossible. He knew this because, every hundred years, a priest of War won the Game. Each of those winners found the key. They figured it out.

And, he realized, *that* was the answer.

He didn't need to solve the problem. He only needed someone to have solved it.

Will it work? thought Dantess. *I'm not just looking for a memory. I'm looking for a strategy.*

Dantess channeled his Longing into his token, and the room burst into motion. He could visualize priests checking the chests, removing the keys, and bringing them to the door—but that wasn't what he wanted. He needed the kind of foretelling he received in War's testing. Which of these chests would lead to victory?

The answer: none of them. He had to search elsewhere.

At least my token is giving me an answer, thought Dantess. *That, in itself, is encouraging.*

As he shuffled along the path, he wondered why Kevik never thought to use his token this way. Then he remembered Kaurridon's explanation that most priests never look beyond the token's natural ability to help them fight. The rest wasn't interesting enough to discover and explore.

Dantess tottered along, scanning the nearby chests using his token. Priests in the past opened them all, as the crowd of figures in his view attested, but none of them found the correct key.

Kevik approached along the path to the door, carrying an armful of keys to try. As they passed each other, Kevik bumped him into the chests again. That was getting annoying.

Cursing and finding his feet again, Dantess continued along the path. When it felt like he'd made a full circle, he was astonished to see the curving hall did not end. Even though Kevik already explained this, Dantess had a hard time believing it. There was no slope, no portal of any kind, and yet the hallway extended onward. Even so, he didn't have time to marvel at Evil's architectural tricks. He asked his token if any of these chests contained the key, but the answer was always no.

Even though it was hard to keep track, Dantess estimated he had walked about three complete circuits around the center when his token identified a tiny chest on an upper shelf as the one holding the trophy: the special key needed to open the final door. Dantess gasped and clambered to it, tipped open the lid, and discovered the chest was empty.

Empty.

What did that mean? If he assumed all the chests contained keys at the beginning, then the only person who could have removed it was Kevik. The door was still locked when

Dantess arrived, which meant that Kevik must have *just* taken it. In fact, it was likely in Kevik's latest armload of keys to try.

Which meant Dantess had to hurry, otherwise Kevik would open the door soon and leave him trapped here.

Dantess' urgency almost pushed him to race back to the exit right away, but he forced himself to slow and think it through. He wasn't ready yet, and he needed to be.

First, Dantess focused on the chest. He replayed the memory of a priest who removed the contents and, as he hoped, Dantess saw it: an ornate key carved from a single large ruby and braced with gold. Now he knew what the trophy looked like.

Next, he walked a few paces down the path and began flipping open chests until he found one that Kevik hadn't scavenged. It contained an iron key graven with a golden hawk.

That would work perfectly.

"No, no, no. Damn these keys," cursed Kevik. He rattled one in the lock, threw it on the pile on the floor, and inserted another from the diminishing collection in the crook of his arm.

Dantess hobbled in, took a seat on one of the larger chests, and waited.

Kevik noticed him. "I don't see a pile of keys in your arms. You found something more specific?"

"I got tired, so I figured I'd watch you for a while. You know, gather some more information."

Kevik narrowed his eyes. "No. You're not just resting. You *found* the key and you're waiting for me to leave to use it. Where is it?"

Dantess dropped his hand behind his back. "If I had the key—and I'm not saying I do—you think I would just hand it over? It's my trophy, right? If it's correct, I earned it."

Kevik laughed. He dropped the bunch of keys in his arms on the ground. "You haven't figured out yet that there's *nothing* I can't take from you?"

And that's when Dantess saw the ruby-red key clatter to the floor, along with about two dozen other keys that Kevik had yet to try. His plan was working—he knew Kevik couldn't resist the chance to steal something of value from Dantess—but he also knew the worst part was coming up.

Dantess channeled his Longing through his token, trying to enhance his stamina and speed, but it was like propping up a fallen tent with a piece of straw. His body wasn't responding. He was too weak to fight someone like Kevik.

Kevik took a step forward and grabbed Dantess' arm. He pulled the hand Dantess hid behind his back, forced his fist open, and saw the hawk-graven key in his palm.

"Ah. That's what I thought. Thanks again for gathering my keys for me."

While Kevik was looking at the key, Dantess balled up his other fist and jabbed at Kevik's throat. Surprised, Kevik choked for a moment, but then his token kicked in. Kevik grabbed Dantess, lifted him up, and flipped him backward over his head.

Both men landed on their backs, but Dantess took the brunt of the impact. He groaned—hurt, but still conscious. Just as important, the hawk-graven key remained in Dantess' hand. When the two fighters locked eyes, Dantess knew he had already lost this fight, so he hurled the key as far down the hallway as he could.

Kevik rose to his feet, snarled, and kicked Dantess in the head. Dantess dropped back to the ground, eyes closed. To Kevik, he appeared to have passed out—but as his opponent walked toward the hawk-graven key, Dantess summoned enough strength to grab the ruby key from the floor, open a tiny chest right next to it, and slip it in. After that, he didn't have to fake losing consciousness.

Dantess woke to Kevik sitting on a chest, staring at him. He realized Kevik had shoved him into a corner away from the door.

"Your key didn't work," said Kevik. "Whatever you thought you figured out, you were wrong."

"There was always that chance," agreed Dantess, holding his bruised rib, aggravated by Kevik's body slam.

"But you know *something*," Kevik looked at him like a hungry wolf. "Tell me what you were thinking. I'm going mad trying all these thousands of keys."

"Why would I tell you anything?"

Kevik stood up and looked over Dantess' many wounds. He shrugged and said, "I don't know how much more punishment you can take, Dantess."

"What?" asked Dantess. "You're going to kill me? That's against the rules of the Game. Not only that, it's against the rules of the temple."

Kevik tilted his head. "I'm not going to kill you—I mean, you'll technically be alive—but you may have trouble walking. Or feeding yourself. You can lie around in your grandfather's luxurious quarters as people feed you mashed food while I guard the Convergence." He stepped forward and towered over Dantess. "Or, you can tell me how to win and walk out of here."

Strangely, Dantess had trouble focusing on those words. Instead, sitting in front of Kevik, he found himself looking directly at his grandfather's belt around the priest's waist. To Dantess, seeing that belt refreshed the memories of all of Kevik's crimes— not just stealing the belt, but imprisoning his father and murdering Jyn.

And that's when Dantess noticed the slight tear in the belt. The merest notch. Was that there before?

"You've taken enough from me, Kevik." Dantess channeled his Longing through his token. He asked for a little strength, a little speed, to add to his own rage and determination. His hand shot forward and he grabbed the belt.

"What?" Kevik gasped.

Dantess pulled at the tear and, to his surprise, the belt ripped easily and completely. With a snap, he slid it from around Kevik's waist, token and all.

Kevik's jaw dropped. "Uh..." He stood awkwardly, like he didn't know what to do with his muscular limbs.

Had Kevik become so dependent on his token that he couldn't function without it?

Dantess asked his own token for plans, anything he could do in his weakened state. He chose one of the few options and allowed it to put his muscles into play. His good leg kicked out toward Kevik's knee.

Any other time, Kevik would have blocked and countered before the blow connected, but now Kevik didn't react at all. The kick landed and his leg collapsed under him.

"Poor Kevik. You should have trained instead of just relying on your token."

With Kevik on the floor, Dantess kicked again and struck his opponent's head with his boot.

His senses scrambled, Kevik tried to back away. He started to rise, but his injured knee buckled and sent him down again, so he tried crawling.

Dantess pulled himself up. Everything hurt, but he steadied himself on a chest and hobbled forward, grasping his grandfather's belt in his fist.

Kevik stopped crawling. "I need..." he muttered. "I mean, the token is mine so... you shouldn't... can I...?" He turned back to Dantess. "Please?"

"No." Dantess struck a nerve cluster on the side of Kevik's neck. He dropped to the floor, unconscious.

Dantess held the belt with a grasp so tight, it shook. Here was Kevik, helpless. Dantess could do anything to him. The man was at his mercy.

Instead, Dantess limped to the tiny chest on the floor, removed the ruby key from inside, and approached the exit.

"War, let this be the right key," he prayed.

He inserted the key and turned it. The lock produced a loud *thunk* as the tumblers moved into place. The door cracked open, now free on its hinges. Sunlight spilled in through that crack.

With a shaking hand, Dantess removed the key from the lock. He pulled the door open and covered his eyes from the intense sun. After a moment, he realized the door opened to the front of the tower.

Warren and his squad stood on the green grass field. In fact, all of the squads were there, along with Withyr, Glinden, and even Sorrobask, who flanked the temple's senior leadership.

Dantess removed Kevik's token from his grandfather's belt, tossed it onto Kevik's unconscious body, and stepped out of the tower into the light.

Everyone broke out into applause. Warren whooped and cheered. A beaming Kaurridon prodded the high priest in jest and then approached Dantess.

Kaurridon held out his hand. "The trophy?"

Dantess gently placed the ruby key into his palm.

Kaurridon grabbed Dantess' other hand and shook it. "Congratulations, my boy. You are the winner of the Game of War."

Dantess smiled and nodded, blinking at the bright sun.

After that nightmare, he won. He actually won.

He won for his father. He won for Jyn.

He won for himself.

Maybe even his grandfather would be proud of him.

The relief washed over him, and Dantess realized he couldn't take another step. He let himself collapse into a deep, dark slumber.

PART III

THE LEGEND

CHAPTER NINETEEN

Seaborn Notch, five years ago...

TWYLA WASN'T SHY, but her confidence didn't come from being tall, graceful, or pretty like some other girls. Instead, she was short, awkward, and had a slightly-too-large nose, thin lips, and dirty brown hair that looked like straw and stuck out at all angles. None of that stopped her from being both loud and persistent. Throughout her fourteen years, the world hadn't been kind to her, so sometimes she just felt like screaming back at it.

"Why are we doing this?" asked Muk, balking at climbing the rough road that wound uphill through a forest of twisted trees. "We're not supposed to go this way, right, Han?" Muk, a boy slightly younger than Twyla, always sucked the fun out of everything. He constantly tagged along after Hanlow, his older brother—which was infuriating because Hanlow only agreed to come after hours of Twyla's badgering. Twyla had a crush on the older boy, but getting him alone was next to impossible.

Hanlow nodded. "You're leading us to Shattered Peak, aren't you? Even getting near that old village is forbidden by the temples. If the stories are real, Chaos will curse us just for stepping foot there."

Twyla lifted an eyebrow. "Really? You're scared of stories?"

"No," Hanlow scoffed. "But it doesn't matter. It's getting late. Twyla, you may not have parents in Seaborn Notch to come home to, but ours will be worried."

The remark stung. Twyla wasn't an orphan exactly, but she might as well have been. Her father died when she was young and her mother had been auctioned away to the temple of Evil when they fell into debt two years ago. The local sanctuary of Charity gave her a place to sleep and paid her tithe, but only until she turned sixteen. According to law, after that, she was on her own.

Twyla shrugged off the comment. "Admit it. You're scared. Well, I've stepped my feet in there a bunch of times on my own, and I haven't been cursed once!"

"Are you sure about that?" joked Muk. "Have you seen yourself lately?"

Hanlow shushed his brother. "Don't be mean, Muk. All right, we'll see the village. *Quickly*, and then we go. I kinda always wanted to, but I never got up the nerve."

"That's the spirit." She got a sly look in her eye and pointed over Hanlow's shoulder. "Behind you, I meant. There are *lots* of spirits around here. That's what happens when a whole village burns down with everyone in it!"

Muk and Hanlow both whipped their heads around to look behind them. Twyla laughed, picked a yellow wildflower, and skipped further down the overgrown road that wound through the deep woods.

"Are there really spirits here?" whispered Muk to his brother.

Hanlow shook his head. "She's joking. Come on." The two boys followed her.

Some minutes later, the trees thinned. The road leveled out and entered the remains of a burned-out village. While some bits and pieces of charred wood remained, most of the evidence that there were once buildings here had decayed into dust. The soft crunch of the children's footsteps seemed loud and out of place in the complete stillness. Even the wind was silent.

"I don't like this," said Muk.

"Me neither," agreed Hanlow.

"Hold on. The buildings toward the center are more intact. The stone ones didn't burn." Twyla picked up her pace. "Come on. Let me show you."

Soon, they entered the central square. Twyla was correct. While ruins of the wooden buildings poked up from the dirt like rotten teeth surrounding the square, several stone structures still stood, including a centrally-located well.

The actual Shattered Peak overshadowed everything, so known because the mountain's top appeared broken. The village that shared the name was located against the cliff-face beneath it.

"Why is the mountain missing its top?" asked Muk.

Twyla shook her head. "I don't know. So they could call it Shattered Peak?"

"It's scary. This whole place is. I want to go."

"If you're scared of mountains, you should be less scared of one without a top. Like, four-fifths as scared." She turned to

Hanlow, pointed at one of the stone buildings that still had four mostly-intact walls, and said, "That's my father's old house. He used to lead the village. Do you want to see it?"

"Your *father's* house?" asked Hanlow, surprised. "You lived here?"

"Are you a spirit?" said Muk.

"Shut up, Muk." Twyla began to walk toward the house's remains. "I don't remember any of this. I was too young. My mother told me we all lived here once, but she had taken me to visit Seaborn Notch when it happened. We were lucky, I guess. Except for Da."

"I didn't know anyone survived from this village."

"I don't normally tell people," Twyla said as she gingerly stepped into the ruined building. "No one seems to react well to anything associated with this place."

Within the stone walls, she walked to the stout chair that still stood in the middle of the room, the only piece of furniture left. Then she wiped away dirt from the stone floor, revealing a large carving of a three-eyed raven. In fact, most surfaces here were covered with similar mysterious carvings of hellish images. They were strange. She was fairly certain her father hadn't carved them, so she wondered if someone had done so after the fire.

She was about to point out a few interesting carvings to the boys—knowing the pictures would scare Muk even more—when she realized they hadn't followed her inside.

Twyla huffed and turned around. She began to pick her way out through the rubble when she heard the clink of chains and an unfamiliar voice.

"Faithless aren't allowed here," said a deep voice from the square. Twyla knelt down and hid behind the door frame. She could see the back of a hooded, black-robed man, holding a length of chain whose other end was wrapped around the waist of a girl. The girl wore tattered clothing and a tight, metal collar. She pulled against the chain toward Twyla's hiding place. Her eyes were distant, though, as if straining to reach something far behind Twyla. But the chained girl's strength was nothing compared to the man in black, who stood fast and stared at Hanlow and Muk.

"*Spirits!*" Muk whispered to his brother.

"They're not spirits," responded Hanlow. To the robed man, he stammered, "We... we're just lost."

The man waited.

"We're trying to get home," Hanlow continued. "Could you point us to Seaborn Notch?"

After a moment, the man pointed in the direction of the secluded shipping town where Twyla and the boys started their trip.

Hanlow blew out the breath he'd been holding. "Thank you. We'll go then."

They're going to abandon me here? thought Twyla, feeling a mixture of anger and fear.

Emboldened by the permission to leave, Muk couldn't help but blurt out, "If you're not spirits, who's that girl with the metal collar? Why is she on a chain?" Hanlow slapped his hand over his brother's mouth.

The man's hood tilted a bit. Then he laughed. "You've got a curious mind, lad. So I'll tell you." While the boys stood transfixed, the man took his end of the chain and wrapped it around the still-sturdy supports of the square's well, leaving the girl pulling against it like a leashed dog. "The girl's name is Quin. She's been bad. Her collar is just a tool, one of many magic artifacts given to us priests by our god. It helps to keep bad people under control."

Muk pulled down Hanlow's hand and, to his brother's shock, kept talking. "Is the collar working? Seems like she'd run away 'cept for that chain."

"That's because of her Longing," the man explained, as he ensured the chain wouldn't slip free. "People pulled by a Longing don't listen to reason. They have to go to whatever's calling them, no matter what. The collar, and even its threat of death, won't stop them."

"I thought only priests had Longings."

"Priests of *Order*. Like me. But little Quin is attracted to *Chaos*. We haven't had someone at the temple drawn to Chaos for years. When I realized that's what Quin was chasing, I knew I had to bring her here. Do you know the stories about this place?"

"Kind of," said Muk.

"Many years ago, someone here discovered an artifact of Chaos. To protect everyone against its corruption, we came here to remove it. But we were too late.

"In the hands of someone drawn to Chaos, the power of the artifact was unleashed. It corrupted the whole village, made them sick. They were dying. To keep the corruption from spreading, Varyon—the legendary priest of War—destroyed everything here.

206

Burned it to the ground. He died himself in the process, but his sacrifice saved everyone else, including you and your families!

"Unfortunately, no one could find the artifact in the remains of the village. It could have been anywhere, looked like anything, and only someone drawn to Chaos could have sniffed it out. We had to leave it behind. Until now. Until Quin. She'll find it for me."

"Aren't you scared Chaos will infect you?" asked Hanlow.

"An artifact of Chaos is powerless in the hands of a priest of Evil. Once I have it, it can't corrupt anyone."

"Evil? You're a priest of Evil?"

"Yes, of course. Of all the temples of Order, we are charged with guarding against Chaos." The man slid back his hood. From the back, Twyla couldn't see his face, only his tightly-cropped gray hair. But she noticed that he wore a strap covering his eyes, tied behind his head.

"Why are you wearing a blindfold?" asked Muk.

"Oh, don't worry. I can see fine. It's another magic artifact. What do you think of it? Do you notice anything special about it?"

Muk peered at it. "It's got buttons."

"They kind of look like eyes," said Hanlow. "Are they... moving?"

"They are," agreed the man. "It's my collection. See how many I have? Can you spot any empty spaces?"

"There's a few I think, but... wait..." Muk gasped and brought his hands up to his face. "What happened? I can't see!"

Nodding, the priest of Evil said, "Of course not. When you do bad things with your eyes, you can't be trusted with them." The priest swiveled his head back and forth. "Ah, young eyes are so sharp, so clear. I appreciate you adding to my collection, both of you."

The man pulled his cowl back up over his head. "It's a shame you didn't leave when you had the chance. That would have saved me time and effort. But you noticed Quin's *collar*. You even *asked* about it! You must understand, faithless can't know about our slaves. That would spoil the popular notion that anyone can become a priest of Evil."

Hanlow was on his knees, feeling around with his outstretched hands. There was blank skin on his face where his eyes once were. "Muk! Where are you? Everything's black."

The man grabbed Hanlow by the hair, pulled the boy's head back, and admired his handiwork. "I wouldn't curse you to a life without sight, lad. That would be inhuman." He lifted his other hand adorned with a series of metal rings along every finger but the thumb, each ring connected to the next by a tiny chain.

As the rings began to glow red, Twyla covered her eyes. Even though she didn't see the blow land, she couldn't escape the sounds. The muffled scream. The squishy impact. And the dull thud of Hanlow's body dropping to the ground.

"Han!" cried Muk. He stood still for a moment, and then bolted straight into the side of the well. The collision sent him stumbling backward, where he collapsed on the ground. While the man chuckled and moved to hover over Muk, Twyla backed away deeper into the building, tears running down her cheeks. She couldn't endure any more of this horrible scene, and she didn't dare let the priest discover that she had been watching.

What could she do?

Nothing. She was faithless. She was powerless. She could only hope not to be discovered.

Her muscles froze with fear while the priest reclaimed the chain and causally resumed his journey, following Quin toward the mountain like he would a hound. When Twyla couldn't hear them anymore, she inched out of the house, holding her breath, in case he might hear it.

She snuck toward the village exit, to the road leading to Seaborn Notch. A few minutes more and she'd be far away from that horrible man, but then she passed the bodies of Han and Muck.

Her friends came here only because she insisted. And now they were dead.

Twyla knew they shouldn't have come to this forbidden place and that was her fault, but *no one* deserved a priest of Evil killing them like he was taking out the trash. Priests didn't value faithless lives, but she'd never seen one of them kill like that. He even seemed to take pleasure in it.

She tried to walk by, but the memory of her mother, taken by Evil, haunted her too. After seeing that poor slave girl, Twyla was sure she knew what had happened to her. If her mother was still alive, she was undoubtedly wearing one of those collars.

No one else would hold him accountable. Any priest could do anything he wanted to any faithless. Priests could take them as slaves. Or steal their eyes. Or murder them.

Twyla stopped.

She was terrified. She had no idea what she could do, but she refused to run away from this monster. To let him get away with what he did.

Twyla turned back and began to follow the priest. If she didn't end up dying, somehow, she'd make him pay.

On previous trips, Twyla had wandered everywhere in the village, and still she hadn't discovered the narrow path up the cliff face, hidden by some stubborn trees and rock formations. But, somehow, Quin wriggled her way through the obstacles and up the path, pulling the priest along behind her.

"Ah!" said the priest. "A secret path up the cliff? How could we have missed that? Well, my little lost villager, you couldn't have taken the artifact too far. My hound will find you, wherever you ended up." He chuckled to himself.

Twyla followed the pair as near as she could without giving herself away.

When the path leveled out, the priest made camp. He gave Quin some water and a little food that she barely noticed, tied the chain to a tree, and made himself comfortable as night fell.

Cold, tired, and hungry, Twyla crouched behind a nearby rock outcropping and watched the priest. Hefting a sharp stone she found by her foot, she tried to convince herself she would never get a better opportunity to kill the man she assumed was sleeping inside that hood. But she had never killed anyone before, much less a priest. And the sound of Hanlow's death kept replaying in her mind. Her fear and hesitancy turned minutes into hours.

While Twyla struggled to act, Quin never stopped struggling with the chain leash, not even to rest or sleep. Twyla guessed whatever her Longing pulled her to, it must have been close.

Finally, the sun broke over the horizon.

Twyla didn't have much time left.

If she couldn't bring herself to attack the priest directly, maybe she could cause some chaos, which might lead to opportunity. Before the priest could rouse, Twyla snuck to the tree and carefully unwrapped the chain—not an easy task given that Quin would not stop pulling at it. When the chain slipped free, Twyla jumped behind her rock and Quin bolted up a rocky path, dragging the noisy chain behind her.

"What?" The priest's head popped up just as the last links disappeared around a boulder. "Curse you! Come back here!" He pushed himself to his feet and ran after Quin.

Twyla kept on his heels. As distracted as the priest was, he never looked back.

More than once, the priest stumbled over his robe or paused while he negotiated a hard climb. Each time, Twyla's heart jumped into her throat, and she dropped to the ground. So far, he hadn't noticed her, but she knew her luck could change at any moment.

After a half an hour of this, the priest heaved himself over a crest. "Finally," he said as he pulled back his hood and sucked air into his lungs. "You... stopped."

Twyla caught up and peeked over the rock lip. They were close to the summit, at the bottom of a tiny canyon. Rough walls rose up on either side, as if something plowed out a channel through the mountain's peak. A picturesque spring in the center of the canyon fed a waterfall on the far cliff edge.

The slave girl stood waist deep in the spring—no longer running, but holding a dark, porous rock the size of a man's fist in both hands.

"What do you have there? A rock? If it called you here, it must be what I'm looking for." The priest held out his hand. "Give it over, Quin. Now."

The girl shook her head violently. She pulled the rock to her chest.

Worried, the priest cleared his throat and held up his rings. "You know how the collar works. I won't ask again."

The girl's eyes widened. Shivering, she started to hold out the rock, but then snapped it back to her chest. Quin closed her eyes and dropped her chin.

"Your choice. Goodbye, little slave girl."

There was no mistaking what the priest had planned. After all this poor girl endured, her reward would be a horrible death at the hands of this monster. And Twyla couldn't help but see her mother's fate in Quin.

It was too much.

Before she knew what she was doing, Twyla launched herself at the priest. She wasn't far away—only a step or two—so she hoped maybe she could strike with her sharp rock before he even knew what hit him.

Lightning quick, the priest grabbed Twyla's wrist holding the rock. "What do we have here? Another faithless?" He tapped the band circling his head, covered with the unsettling, independently-rolling eyes. "Not a good idea to sneak up on someone with eyes in the back of his head."

Twyla averted her gaze from the strap. She saw what happened to Hanlow and Muk when they looked at it.

"No time to play. I've got more important things to do." As Twyla struggled in the priest's iron grip, the rings on his other hand began to glow red. He cocked his fist back and Twyla winced.

A loud, rasping croak drew their attention to Quin. From her expression, it seemed the girl's fear had been replaced with anger. She held the misshapen rock toward the priest, but not as an offering. As the two stared, a golden light sparked deep within the pockmarked rock, and from one of the holes, a glowing mote snaked out.

The mote floated through the air leaving a beautiful serpentine trail, an afterimage of curves and spirals. It hovered and circled as if contemplating its next move, then shot straight at the priest's glowing rings.

The rings exploded.

The priest shrieked. He released Twyla and cupped his scorched hand with the other. "What did that wretch do to me?"

Twyla ran through the spring pool to Quin, who looked just as shocked and confused as Twyla felt. Along the way, she almost tripped over some bones just under the water—perhaps those of whoever brought the artifact here.

Regaining his composure, the priest called out. "Look at me, Quin. You don't know what you're doing, but I can help you. Just look at me." He raised his voice. "Look at my eyes!"

"No! Don't..." Twyla called out, but it was too late. By the time Twlya reached Quin, her eyes were gone, replaced with flat patches of skin. "Oh, no."

Quin croaked again, a sound full of fear and despair. Twyla hugged her close, and Quin returned the embrace.

"Too late, little faithless. She's powerless now. In my experience, you can't fight what you can't see." The priest groaned. "You know, that witless slave actually hurt me. And she destroyed my rings!" He laughed. "It's a good thing I have another artifact. Without that, I'd be chasing my *own* Longing."

Ignoring her own tears, Twyla squeezed her eyes shut and held on to Quin. She knew she was just one glance away from losing her own sight. "Your rock destroyed his rings," Twyla whispered. "Maybe you can do it again? To his other artifact? Even without seeing him?"

Quin shivered and shook her head.

"I'm tired," complained the priest. "I'm sure you are too. We all just climbed up a mountain. Let's end this. Turn around, little faithless. You have to look at me sometime."

Twyla heard the priest wading into the spring. He was just behind her.

"Please try," whispered Twyla. "He's there. Right in front of you! You have to! He'll kill us both."

Quin's forehead knotted. She held out the stone.

A quiet spark emerged from the rock and traced through the air with its golden trail. It wandered out and up, curving and slicing, almost randomly.

The priest drew in a breath and froze in place, inches from Twyla's back. Then he retreated a step.

As if making up its mind, the spark shot straight to the priest's blindfold. And just like the rings, it exploded. The priest screamed in pain.

Twyla steeled herself and glanced behind her. The priest clutched his face and thrashed in the water, scraps of the leather strap floating beside him.

"You faithless pieces of garbage! I'll kill you!" He lashed out with his fists, but connected with nothing. With his hands away from his face, Twyla noticed he, too, lacked proper eyes— perhaps the price for using that horrible artifact of Evil. But now, without the strap, he was as blind as his victims.

"How dare you think..." He swung wildly at nothing, then shook his head. "When I get my hands on..." He trailed off, his eyeless face swiveling back and forth.

Twyla continued to hold Quin while she watched the priest with fascination.

"I have... I have to go," the priest mumbled. He splashed through the spring to its edge. "I have to get to..." Without even slowing, he tumbled into a steep, rocky slope that fed into the mountain's waterfall.

The priest screamed as he plummeted, but those cries were quickly drowned out by the rushing water.

"He's gone. He's gone," said Twyla while stroking Quin's blond hair. "He just walked off the cliff." She thought about it. "I guess that was the fastest way to the Gift of Evil. At least his Longing thought so."

Twyla pulled back a little to look at Quin's eyeless face. "So, your name is Quin?"

Quin nodded.

"Nice to meet you. I'm Twyla. We're friends now."

Quin smiled and nodded again.

"I don't have many friends, so you're special. I'll tell you what: I'll take care of you if you take care of me, too."

Quin nodded emphatically.

"I like you. You're a great listener."

Twyla led Quin out of the spring and began to retrace their path out of the canyon. When Quin stumbled, Twyla caught her. "Don't worry. *I'll* be your eyes from now on." Noticing the collar, she added, "And I can *definitely* talk enough for both of us. You just keep your rock ready, in case we have to deal with any other priests. There could be more of them looking for it, after all." Twyla thought about it. "I think the stories about Chaos are meant to scare us. There's nothing corrupting about that rock, but I can see why *priests* would be afraid of it.

"I've never even heard of anything that could destroy an artifact of Order like that. That's kind of amazing. And powerful. *Really* powerful.

"You know, something like that could change the world."

CHAPTER TWENTY

"YOU NEED TO wake up," said Warren, gently shaking Dantess.

Dantess blinked. Even lying in his comfortable bed in his spacious quarters, he felt terrible. His wounds were treated and bandaged, but his aches ran deep. He remembered having some crazy and disturbing dreams, but they were already fleeing his mind. "How long did I sleep?"

"Three days. Off and on." Warren pulled the blanket down. "I would have let you sleep more, but Kaurridon demanded to speak to you in his office."

"Now?"

"He's been asking for you all three days, but I put him off. Now it's an order. You have to go."

Dantess swung his legs over the side of the bed and tried to put weight on them. The room spun around him, and he sat back, lightheaded. "Give me some time. I don't think I can stand, much less walk."

"If you don't go now, he'll send soldiers to collect you."

This woke Dantess up. "Soldiers? Why? What happened?"

"No time," said Warren on his way out the door. "Get dressed, and then I'll walk you to his office. I'll be outside. Hurry."

Warren offered his arm, but Dantess walked on his own, despite the pain. Together, they approached the building that housed Kaurridon's office.

Dantess didn't know what he expected after his win, but he didn't think the occasional congratulations from others in the temple would have been out of place. Instead, priests ignored him and soldiers avoided him. Even the faithless looked down at the ground as they passed.

"What's going on, Warren? Why is everyone acting like I'm a criminal?"

"I'm not sure. No one's telling me anything." They reached the entrance, and Warren opened the door for him. "But I have an idea, and if I'm right, I'm so sorry."

As Dantess entered, he asked, "What does that mean?" But Warren closed the door and left with the question hanging.

Without a better plan, Dantess shuffled up to Kaurridon's place of work, once his grandfather's office. Kaurridon sat behind his deck, writing up a report.

"Hand? You sent for me?" said Dantess.

"Sit." Kaurridon's expression betrayed nothing, save that the man was not happy.

Dantess was happy to rest on the proffered chair, no matter how hard and uncomfortable it was.

Kaurridon opened a drawer and reached inside. "We have something to discuss." With that, Kaurridon dumped the two pieces of Varyon's colorful belt on the desk.

"My grandfather's belt? That's what this is about?"

"Yes." The Hand said nothing else, leaving it to Dantess to fill the silence.

Dantess thought he might understand Kaurridon's pique. "I'm sorry for destroying such an important piece of history. It was quite meaningful to me, too."

Kaurridon leaned in. "You admit you did this?"

"Well, yes. Kevik stole the belt from me and then used it in the Game. When I got the chance, I tried to reclaim it. That's when it broke. It's not against the rules to separate a priest from his token—although most priests protect their tokens better."

"It *is* against the rules to sabotage a priest's equipment, though." Kaurridon flipped over the belt, showing the back of both pieces. "This leather was scored—cut almost all of the way through from the inside—before Kevik ever put it on."

Dantess' jaw dropped. "Cut?"

"No question. Subverting the will of our god, especially in a competition like the Game of War, is a serious crime. What do you say to that?"

"I had no idea." Dantess ran his finger over the edge of the scored leather. "I certainly didn't know anything about it."

"You tore the belt off as if you did. We need to be clear. Are you saying you didn't cut it?"

Dantess lifted the piece of the belt, glaring at the cut. "Of course not. *Never*. Not only would that have been against the

215

rules, it was my *grandfather's* belt. I'd sooner cut my own arm off."

The Hand leaned forward. "Then who did it?"

"How would I...?" But then Dantess' thoughts broke through the haze of three days of sleep. Who would cut the belt deliberately? Who knew ahead of time that Kevik would use the belt in the Game?

The belt fell from his fingers. *Warren.*

Warren left the belt out to be taken. He knew Kevik couldn't resist stealing and then flaunting it in the most public display possible.

What was more, at the mine, Warren told Dantess to 'get it back.' Dantess thought he was referring to the tower key Withyr stole—but Warren prefaced the comment by saying it was about Kevik. Warren wasn't talking about the key. He was talking about the belt.

The boy never went into a mission without a plan, and, after Kevik killed Jyn, he would have done anything to ensure the priest's defeat.

Even break the rules.

Kaurridon saw the realization in Dantess' eyes. "Dantess, you are the grandson of Varyon. You have more potential than any priest I've seen for years. You won the Game, and with the rank you receive, you could rise to great heights—even order your father's release! Tell me who did this." He looked into Dantess' eyes with a steel gaze. "*Convince* me you weren't involved."

"And if I do?" said Dantess. "What would happen to them?"

"They're faithless, aren't they? Maybe one of your squad? Even if Kevik weren't calling for blood, you know how Morghaust feels."

So. They'd kill Warren, like they almost did to his father when Da helped Withyr in her competition.

What was the alternative? Dantess would lose everything the win was supposed to give him: the rank, the position of protecting the Convergence, and his place in the temple's history—a chance to show everyone he deserved Varyon's legacy. And most important: he wouldn't be able to release his father from his cell.

But he couldn't send Warren to his death. Especially not after losing Jyn.

"No," said Dantess. He closed his eyes. "I can't."

Kaurridon frowned. "Are you sure? Someone has to answer for this."

"I... I take full responsibility." Dantess rubbed his temples and grimaced.

Kaurridon growled and slammed his fists on the desk, startling Dantess. "This isn't how it was supposed to go. I backed you, and you *failed* me. Now, I have to award the win to *Kevik*. He'll get the rank and the position."

"What about me?" asked Dantess.

"You?" Kaurridon stood up behind the desk. "If you're taking responsibility for this crime, then I should lock you up. Put you in a cell next to your da. How does that sound?"

Dantess' heart sank. "You'd be in your rights."

"You're an *idiot*, Dantess." Kaurridon picked up a book and hurled it at the wall. He stood there for a moment, panting. "But it's because you're young. Too young. You don't truly know what it means to be a priest of War yet. It's my fault you failed. I should never have entered you in the Game. You weren't ready."

Dantess stayed silent.

Kaurridon sat back down. "I'm not going to lock you up. From this moment, you are stripped of all rank. We can't take back your marks, so you'll wear sleeves like a soldier from now on."

"And the Convergence?"

Kaurridon laughed, but there was no mirth there. "Maybe I'll tell you how it went when I return in two weeks." He waved to the door and returned to the report on his desk. "But for now, get out of my sight."

Warren wasn't waiting outside for him, which was best. Dantess didn't know if he could contain the anger boiling up towards his friend.

He cut my grandfather's belt? Dantess thought.

The world fell away from him as he walked. People might have spoken to him, but he didn't hear.

He cheated. He cost me the Game.

He stumbled through the temple grounds, aimlessly. He was dimly aware of soldiers training in the sun's heat, groups of priests laughing with each other, life continuing on as if everything hadn't just completely fallen apart.

My father is doomed to that damned cell for the rest of his life.

An open door right in front of him led to a popular taproom. To Dantess, this seemed like as good of a destination as any.

And the man who killed Jyn won everything.

Dantess entered and sat at a table. As expected, the room was empty of patrons. "A cup," he said to the room.

"Dantess?" Palie, a bound faithless, looked up from cleaning the floor. "I don't see you here often. And at this early hour? What would you like?"

"I already said: a cup. Fill it up with something. Then do it again. And again."

Palie nodded and did as he was commanded.

It was dark outside when a group of priests and soldiers, led by a boisterous Kevik, burst into the room. They were all laughing far too loudly. "A round of drinks to celebrate the winner of the Game of War!" Kevik called out. His group answered him with a cheer.

As Kevik strode toward the bar, his gaze ignored the handful of other patrons at the tables and instead landed on the priest sitting alone toward the back: Dantess.

"Look!" Kevik announced to his friends. "It's Dantess, up and about! Truly, I wouldn't have won the Game of War without this man. Please, Palie, give him a drink from me. Everybody should be drinking!"

"I have my own drink," mumbled Dantess into his cup.

Kevik walked up to Dantess and stood over him. "But I owe you! If you hadn't cheated, it might be *you* guarding the Convergence. Now, you can sit here all day and drink and drink. Maybe that was your plan from the beginning?"

Dantess stood up, a little wobbly. "Leave me alone, Kevik."

"Wait. I notice a problem. You're out of uniform." Kevik looked at Dantess' bare arms. "Didn't you lose all your rank? Aren't you supposed to be wearing sleeves to cover your undeserved marks, like a faithless?" Kevik turned to his group. "Roth?"

One of the soldiers stepped out of the group. "Yes?"

"Give Dantess your shirt. We can't have him walking around the temple looking like a priest with any rank. That would be against the rules, and I'm sure Dantess doesn't want to break any more rules. I can't even imagine what more they would do to punish him."

Roth hesitated, but then unbuckled his chest plate. As he removed it, Dantess tried to leave, but Kevik stepped to block him. The hulking priest put up one finger and nodded, as if asking Dantess to wait a moment.

Finally, a bare-chested and embarrassed Roth handed his chainmail shirt over to Kevik.

Dantess and Kevik locked gazes. Smirking, Kevik said, "How can we expect our faithless to follow the rules if we don't show them a good example?" He offered the shirt to Dantess. "Wear the shirt. Otherwise, I'll be forced to take you to a cell myself."

Dantess fumed. He even channeled his Longing through his token and watched the options fill his vision. But he ignored them.

As much as Dantess wanted to fight, he was in no shape to do so, and he knew nothing good would come of it. And worse, Kevik was right.

Without saying a word, Dantess unbuckled his breastplate and let it drop to the floor. He snatched the chainmail shirt from Kevik's hand and put it on, wincing as his injuries reminded him how hurt he truly was.

"There!" Kevik presented Dantess to the room with a grand gesture. "Now no one would think you're a high-ranking priest. You're just barely a step above a soldier. Right, Boot?" When Dantess did not answer, he repeated, "Right?"

"That's enough, Kevik." Dantess grabbed his breastplate and pushed himself out of the corner he was trapped in. Smiling, Kevik let him go.

When Dantess was a step away from the exit, Kevik called to him in a more serious tone. "You never learn, Dantess. There's nothing I can't take from you. *Nothing.*"

Dantess looked over his shoulder and said, "I hope you're satisfied. You've taken it all."

"Oh, I don't know about that. You'd be surprised." Kevik winked.

Dantess stumbled out the door, dragging his breastplate and listening to Kevik's laughter echo in his head.

"You look like garbage thrown out by other garbage. But I suppose that's appropriate."

Without seeing her, Dantess almost ran into Withyr while walking through a small park back to his rooms. She stood in his way in the middle of the path.

"Can I..." Dantess closed his eyes, breathed heavily, and tried to steady his spinning head. "Can I get through, please?"

"On your way to something important? Something else you can screw up?" Withyr stood her ground.

"No. I just want to go to bed." Dantess put his face in his hands. "Look, I'm sorry about the Game. I didn't mean—"

"You're *sorry?* I gave up my chance for you! Look how that worked out!" Withyr counted on her gloved hand. "I sat out of the only Game that mattered in my lifetime. Tolliver is still in a cell, and that bastard Kevik is in charge of guarding the Convergence. All because you *cheated!*" Withyr shook her head. "I don't even understand how you could do that. You're a *priest of War!* Priests don't break rules."

"You don't understand. It's not that simple."

"No, it *is* that simple. You're a disgrace to the temple. I never should have trusted you." She grabbed Dantess with one hand and balled up her other into a fist. Dantess did not resist, and when she smelled the ale on his breath, her face screwed up in disgust. "You're not worth my attention."

She shoved him against a low, stone fence close to the path. As Withyr stormed off, Dantess slid down into a bush and fell into a stupor.

Dantess woke up, blinking away the bright late-morning sun. His whole body hurt, but not just from his injuries. As he rose, he realized that he spent all night sleeping in a bush.

Things could not get any worse, thought Dantess.

He rubbed his eyes, trying to calm the pounding in his head. He picked up his breastplate and concentrated on putting one foot in front of the other to get his aching body back to his rooms. And, more specifically, his bed.

He was steps from his door when he saw the person he wanted to talk to the least, standing there, waiting.

"I couldn't find you anywhere!" exclaimed Warren. "Where were you?"

"Get out of my way." Dantess pushed the lad aside—maybe a little harder than necessary—and entered his room.

Warren rebounded from the wall and followed him in. "We have to talk."

"No. We don't. Leave me be, Warren. I have to rest."

"But you have to know—"

"Be *quiet!*" bellowed Dantess. "Don't talk to me. Right now, I can't stand the sight of myself. Imagine how I feel about you!"

Warren's mouth opened and closed, but no words emerged.

"Get out of here." Dantess shoved Warren out the door, but before the priest could close it, Warren shoved his foot in the crack.

Dantess seethed, "How dare you? I'm injured, but you don't want to push me. Not now. I don't know what I'll do."

"No, please," Warren's face twisted in anguish. "It's not about me. I *tried* to find you. It's Kevik. He used his new rank to bully through his own orders. He's taken the prisoners with him to Convergence Island. He's planning on transferring them over to Evil so they can take them to the dungeons."

Dantess let the door fall open. His face went white. "The Harbinger. The sympathizers. But not..."

Warren nodded, tears now dripping down his face. "My mother and your father."

Ignoring his aches and nausea, Dantess bounded out of his quarters. He tore through the temple grounds until he reached his father's cell. The door was open, revealing an empty room.

Warren finally caught up, wheezing. "I told... you. He's gone."

"How long?"

"Kevik left early this morning, along with most of the other priests. Everyone headed to the port to board the ship to Convergence Island. It's been hours."

"Gather the squad. And horses. We have to catch them before they set sail. If my da gets on that ship, I'll never see him again."

Warren nodded, wiped away his tears, and ran off.

Now Dantess knew what Kevik was referring to. There *was* something else he could take.

Dantess thought he hit rock-bottom, but then he realized life can always get worse.

CHAPTER TWENTY-ONE

NIGHT FELL BEFORE Dantess' squad rode into Victor's Folly, a bustling shipping town. Ships arrived here day and night from distant ports, looking to offload their goods. The port's docks were large enough to accommodate even the tallest frigates, and its taverns were specialized enough to service even the most demanding crews.

They passed through the shopping district, noted for its colorful and elegantly appointed wooden buildings, now closed and locked up tight for the night. The road then led them into the tavern district, which was just entering into their busiest time—made obvious by the raucous laughter and music that spilled out of the slightly rougher establishments. Finally, they arrived at the docks. Many huge schooners were anchored just inside the bay, but these famed docks also had room for a number of large ships at once.

One of those was a frigate named Righteous Fury. War's ship.

But it was already pulling out to sea.

Dantess leapt from his horse and ran toward the dock. "No! You can't leave!" He dropped to the ground and watched the ornate letters of 'Righteous Fury', already far enough away to be hard to read, shrink further as the ship's sails caught the wind. "Come back. Please."

The other riders stopped, their sweaty horses breathing hard. Warren dropped down and approached Dantess. "We tried. We couldn't have ridden harder."

"We missed it by minutes," Dantess moaned.

"What are your orders?" asked Motti, also dismounting.

"Orders?" Dantess thought for a long moment. "If I can't stop that ship from leaving with my da on it, then I have to stop Evil from taking him off that island."

"How?" asked Motti.

Dantess stood up, still staring at the Fury. "Motti, take the others, stable the horses, and wait for me. I'll be back." He began walking down the docks.

"What are you going to do?"

Without turning, Dantess answered, "Find another ship."

It was hard enough to get anyone aboard the large ships to even acknowledge him, but even so, those that did announced that they could not negotiate passage. They instructed him to speak with the ship's captain—and without fail, those captains were slaking their thirsts at the Frisky Zephyr, a nearby tavern, while their crews readied their ships.

When Dantess approached the Zephyr, two massive toughs at the door tipped their hats and opened the door for him without a word. The tavern's common room was covered in recently polished hardwoods and was packed with tables surrounded by well-dressed sailors. Many of them lifted their perfectly-blown glasses filled with imported wines and ales in salute at Dantess' entrance. By the reception, it was clear these people had done business with War's temple before.

He walked to the bar. The proprietor finished serving a mustachioed man in a long frilly coat and wide-brimmed black hat and rushed over. "Welcome to the Frisky Zephyr. A finer establishment you'll not find on the wharf—especially friendly to priests of War. How can I help you?"

"I need transport. Can you point me to someone who has a boat?"

The man chuckled. "No boats here. Only ships." He smiled. "The Zephyr is a captains-only tavern frequented by those of some of the most prestigious vessels at dock. I'm sure someone here can help. Where do you need to go?"

By now, a number of captains were listening in. Dantess could feel them trying to weigh him up, to get an idea of how much gold they could shake out of him. He was lucky he filled his coin pouch before leaving the temple.

"The island hosting the Convergence of the Divine."

Murmurs of disappointment traveled like a wave through the crowd. Most turned back to their tables or stared into their glasses. Evidently, the potential reward of a priest's gold wasn't enough to keep these captains interested.

"Didn't a ship bound for the island just leave? Loaded with almost a whole temple of priests?" asked the bartender.

"That's right. The Righteous Fury."

"I assume you missed it?"

"I did," agreed Dantess. "So, who can take me?"

"No one here," said the mustachioed man in the black hat. "No one knows where it *is*—except the captain of the Fury, and he already left."

Dantess swore to himself. It made sense that the location of the island was secret. No matter what security War provided, the Convergence of the Divine was a tempting target—especially for a group like the Harbingers. Not only would it be packed with priests, but also the Gifts from four religions.

Including the Gift of War, that his Longing would never fail to locate.

Indeed, he explored his Longing and found that it pointed out to sea in the direction of the Righteous Fury.

Dantess smiled. "Turns out that's not a problem. I can find it. I mean, I know the way."

A tall woman in a leather-belted, velvet surcoat with a feathered trim and high black boots asked, "Has this trip been authorized by your high priest?"

As much as he wanted to, Dantess couldn't bring himself to lie about that. "No, but it's important."

"Important enough to sever my relationship with the temples, the bulk of my business? To get me and my crew locked up?" The woman scoffed. "I don't care how much gold you're offering. I want no part of it."

"Any of you?" asked Dantess.

Without responding, the captains all returned to their conversations, sipping from their fancy glasses.

The bartender slid a glass to Dantess. It was filled with a plum-colored liquid. "That will be three gold."

Dantess was still fighting the headache from yesterday's binge. He wasn't in the mood to repeat it. But even so, "Three gold? For a drink? And I didn't even order... whatever that is."

The man lifted the drink to reveal a folded parchment underneath then dropped the glass down again. "Three gold. It's what you need."

Dantess narrowed his eyes. The bartender shrugged and began to pull the drink away, but Dantess grabbed his hand. He

225

pulled out his pouch, counted three coins, and placed them on the counter.

As the bartender collected the coins, Dantess shrugged and tilted the glass into his mouth. He was pleasantly surprised to discover it was an excellent wine from the Errant Moors. Of course, no glass of wine was worth three gold coins, but at least it was better than the rotgut he swilled yesterday.

He opened the parchment. It contained only four words.

Bloody Hook
Captain Sacquidge

Dantess raised an eyebrow, but the bartender nodded.

"I hope that drink put things into perspective for you," he said. "We don't need trouble here. No *reputable* captain will take you where you want to go. I'm sorry."

With that, Dantess drained the last drop of wine from his glass and set it down on the bar. He nodded and left with the note clutched in his hand.

The Bloody Hook didn't look like the name of a ship, so Dantess went searching for another tavern. But it wasn't a tavern either. Not exactly.

Dantess walked past almost every single tavern sign, but found no Bloody Hooks in the bunch. In front of a decrepit, ramshackle building, quite far off the main road—fittingly called Scraping the Barrel—the tough at the door took a look at the parchment and held out his hand. Dantess sighed and put a gold coin into his palm. The big man smiled and thrust his thumb to point Dantess to a crack between the tavern and a smithy next door.

He tried to measure his excitement, but this was the first indication that anyone recognized the name at all.

Once Dantess squeezed inside the crack, shimmied alongside the building into a fenced area, and pushed his way through a pile of trash, the space opened into a dark abandoned alley. The buildings on either side weren't marked. Or inhabited, possibly.

This can't be right, Dantess thought. *No one would willingly come back here. Certainly not a ship captain.*

But then Dantess heard a smash and a groan from deeper in the alley. While keeping his eyes open for danger, he jogged toward the commotion.

The alley wasn't straight. In fact, it seemed to follow the haphazard construction of the larger buildings, hastily-made shacks, and random piles of everything. He felt like he was navigating War's test again, just trying to reach the unmistakable sounds of combat.

Once he brushed aside a red-painted tarp, the alley opened up into an intersection of many alleys—but the main path continued on to a sharp bend ahead. The walls were covered with tarps, old flags, and a few torn sails, all dyed or painted red.

The Bloody Hook, thought Dantess. *It's not a tavern. It's just a bend in an alley.*

Dantess knew he had the right place because it was filled with a ring of dangerous-looking sailors, most holding frothy flagons in their fists and screaming either encouragement or creative profanities at two men fighting in the center.

One of those men was a monster—Dantess couldn't see a neck for all of the muscle packed on his arms and shoulders—but despite his mass, he moved with ease. The other man was wiry and quick and only showed a little fear.

The crowd encouraged him. He flipped and slid and circled, laughing as he showed off his tricks. A few times, he scored a few strikes at the monster's head and back.

When the man got a little too close, the brute moved faster than expected and grabbed the man's arm. With his other hand, he grasped his opponent's neck, lifted him up off his feet, and slammed him down on the ground. Everyone heard the man's back pop at the impact.

"Enough?" asked the tightly-wrapped bag of muscles.

The man struggled. He twisted and pulled at the iron grip around his neck, but after a moment, sighed and tapped twice on the monster's arm.

The grip released and the massive sailor took a step back. The other man pushed off the ground and nursed his back while limping into the crowd. There were a few angry remarks, but most of the others seemed supportive that he lasted as long as he did. Gold changed hands from upset to smiling faces.

"Who's that?" said a sailor, staring at Dantess.

All eyes turned to look at him, still on the edge of the alley. One of the sailors piped up. "Looks like a priest of War. But I've never seen one wear sleeves like that."

Dantess cleared his throat. "I'm looking for a man named Sacquidge. Is he here?"

At the name's mention, the monster from the fight stopped in his tracks, turned around, and announced in a low, rough voice, "That's *Captain* Sacquidge. Why?"

"I need transport somewhere. I was told that *Captain* Sacquidge was the man to see about it. The destination is a bit... problematic."

The man shook his head. "No passengers on this trip. Try again next year."

"I can't wait a year." Dantess took a step forward. "Is this about gold? I can pay."

With that step, sailors around Dantess pulled away. The brute's gaze locked with Dantess'.

"What? What?" A short, stocky woman with a weathered face and tall cap appeared to wake up from a drunken slumber atop a barrel. "Did someone say..." Her eyes fell on Dantess. "A priest of War! With gold in his pocket?"

Most of the crowd's conversation quieted. For some reason, they wanted to hear what this short, drunken sailor had to say.

The woman dropped down from the barrel and stepped forward, grinning from ear to ear and swinging a half-empty mug. "Oh, this is going to be *so* good. *I'm* Captain Sacquidge." She bowed unsteadily then pointed to the burly man who spoke for her. "This is my first mate, Navar. Tell me, why would a priest of War find himself slumming down here in the Bloody Hook?"

"I'm looking for passage. I was told to ask for you."

"Passage? I don't do that." She burped. "But, to be honest, I don't care what you want. I want to see you fight. Navar loves to fight priests of War. Don't you, Navar?"

Navar was silent.

"I'm not here to fight," said Dantess.

The captain's expression was comically startled. "A priest of War who doesn't want to fight? That's a first. Don't you all think you're invincible? Come on. You don't come to the Bloody Hook unless you're prepared to fight! Right?" The crowd cheered as she took a swig from her mug. "Let me be clear, you're *going* to fight. Either just Navar, or all of us."

A rumble traveled through the crowd. Evidently, they liked that idea.

Dantess swallowed. "You're threatening a priest of War? How brazen are you? Law will dismantle this place."

"We have an arrangement with the watch." She gestured around to the rough crowd in the alley. "These are hard-working, tithe-paying sailors who need to blow off some steam between long voyages. We could do it in the better parts of town, but we don't. We come here to the Bloody Hook. The upper class is so happy we don't show up at their prissy, polished establishments, they supply us with grog and keep Law away. Everyone's happy to stay where they belong. Except *you*."

Dantess began to sweat. There were a lot of people here, and he was not in top form. He channeled his Longing through his token. Possibilities flashed over his vision. "You don't want this fight, Captain. Nor should anyone here."

"Oh, I *do*. More than anything."

Dantess couldn't understand why this captain wanted him to fight her mate so badly. The reason most priests considered themselves unbeatable was because it was true. Even sore and wounded, Dantess feared no opponent, no matter who they were.

"One bout?" asked Dantess. "Against your first mate? And if I win, you'll get me and my squad to where we need to go?"

The captain looked to her expressionless first mate, who still hadn't moved a muscle. "Agreed. But lose and I'll take your gold. All of it."

"I expected as much." Dantess moved to the center of the alley. Strength flowed to his sore limbs from his token.

Captain Sacquidge ambled up to Dantess on her short legs. "Despite the alley's name, no one dies here. Kill my man and you'll have to kill every sailor here to escape. You want to quit? You tap out. Understood?"

Dantess nodded. Despite his wounds, and the pounding in his head, and bone-deep weariness, he wasn't worried. "Your first mate is a good fighter, no question—but he's just one man. I'm a priest of War. We don't lose."

"'Assume victory and invite defeat.' You'd do well to remember that." With a glint in her eye, she stepped back and waved her first mate into the circle. "Show him, Navar."

Navar stepped into the circle and removed his shirt, revealing a beautiful tapestry of tattoos covering his chest and arms. Ships sailed through stormy waters near to voluptuous sirens and merfolk, fighting monsters as big as the ships themselves. Swords and spears and flames and flowers and piles of treasure filled every open space. But isolated in the middle of his chest, a bird with three eyes and knives for talons hovered. No other tattoo dared touch it.

As Dantess channeled his Longing through the token to prepare, he encountered a surprise reaction: confusion, panic, and fear. That image tapped into something deep and primal. It dug a hole into his spirit through which madness flowed: the bird flew vanguard, leading a serpent large enough to squeeze and crush the entire world, a spider dripping plague from its fangs, a mist that corrupted anything it touched, and fire—unending, burning torment.

Dantess stumbled backwards. He couldn't make sense of his own thoughts. He couldn't focus enough to separate reality from this unrelenting series of nightmares.

A powerful punch landed in the middle of his chest, throwing Dantess to the ground.

What was happening?

Dantess tried to struggle to his feet, but took a swift kick to the mid-section, which sent him spinning away, holding his side.

"That doesn't look like winning to me," Captain Sacquidge joked to the sailor next to her.

Dantess pulled on his token to shore up his strength and speed. He sprang to his feet and allowed it to push his muscles into a complicated attack that promised to disable Navar, but as soon as he got even the tiniest glimpse of the tattoo on his opponent's chest, the images overwhelmed him. His whole thought process broke down. He couldn't focus on anything, much less the tactic his token suggested.

A kick connected with his head. A follow-up swept his legs from under him, and Dantess collapsed on the ground again. He couldn't even consider defending himself.

What were these images? He'd never seen anything like them. They weren't *his* thoughts. They seemed like dreams, or memories of dreams, but not his.

That was it. He realized that they *must* be someone else's memories, likely those of a troubled and long-dead priest.

Triggered by the three-eyed bird, his token summoned them and served them up as if they were Dantess' own, forcing his own struggle to maintain his sanity. It wasn't just distracting. It was debilitating.

"Enough?" asked Navar.

Sore, tired, and more than a little rattled, Dantess pulled himself up. "Not yet." This time, he did not use his token. Without its power flowing through him, he glanced up to Navar's chest and winced, but was not assaulted by the nightmares.

He could focus once again—but now, he had to fight without his token. Could he beat this opponent with only his natural ability?

Dantess squared off against Navar. He thought back to all of his training sessions with his squad, when he broke down the techniques into understandable chunks. Now, he just had to remember and use them without the advantage of his token.

Navar casually launched his fist towards Dantess' head. Dantess blocked the attack and countered with two punches to the man's midsection. The first mate chuffed in surprise, then smiled. "You can think? You can fight?"

"I can. Want to tap out?" It was hard for Dantess to hold his sore limbs up in a defensive stance. Without his token, he was exhausted.

"Oh, no," said Navar. "We're just getting started."

Navar sprang at Dantess, grabbed his shoulders, and tackled him to the ground. Dantess knew the counter well. He kicked up and used his opponent's momentum to send him flying overhead. Navar landed hard behind him.

While Dantess lay for a moment, trying to catch his breath, Navar jumped up. Seeing Dantess still lying on his back, he brought his foot up to stomp on the priest's head.

Dantess barely rolled away as Navar's foot slammed onto empty ground. He kept rolling as Navar stomped away at where his head had been only split seconds before.

While he rolled, Dantess realized how much he had come to depend on his token to fight. At this point, he usually knew exactly what would happen, what moves he would need to defeat his opponent. He always visualized the conclusion and waited for reality to catch up. But now, he had no idea what to do or what the outcome would be.

As Navar attempted another stomp, on instinct, Dantess grabbed the sailor's leg as it came down, and he pulled it to the side. This tipped Navar over and dropped him to the ground.

As both men rose, Navar pounded Dantess with three lightning-fast jabs to the midsection followed by a solid uppercut. Dantess dropped to one knee and shook his head, blood dripping from his mouth.

Seeing Dantess' condition, Navar smiled, as fresh as when he started. As if he had no concerns, he dropped his guard and turned away to his captain. "How much more? The boy can barely stay upright."

Captain Sacquidge laughed. "I like this lad, but he needs a little more convincing to quit. So stop talking and convince him!"

The first mate was right. Dantess admitted to himself that, without his token, he couldn't defeat Navar.

Not if he fought the way he'd been trained, at least.

But if not that, then what?

Navar's turned head reminded Dantess of something Motti did in a training session. Something the boy used in street brawls. What did Motti call it? A *fishhook*?

When Dantess dressed him down, Motti responded with, *You'd rather I lose?*

No, thought Dantess now. *I can't afford to lose.*

While Navar was distracted, Dantess stepped forward, bent two fingers, and hooked them into his opponent's mouth, inside his cheek. Navar's eyes widened in surprise, but before he could react, Dantess wrenched the man's head around, forcing Navar to lose his balance.

Control a man's head, and you control all of him, Dantess thought, impressed with the effectiveness of this approach. *No wonder Motti liked this trick.*

He used his hook to pull the first mate down to one knee and then dropped the elbow of his other arm onto the back of his neck with as much force as he could muster.

Stunned, Navar fell to the ground. Dantess wrapped his arm around his neck in a hold that he knew would cut off blood to the man's brain. "Enough?" he asked.

It took a few moments before Navar realized the position he was in. Once he did, he tapped twice on Dantess' arm. Dantess released him, and the man collapsed.

"That's it," Dantess wheezed. "He surrendered. I won."

The captain looked at Dantess with new respect and nodded. "You did. I can't believe it, but you did. Let it not be said that Captain Sacquidge reneged on a bet. I'll take you where you want to go."

"Wait, what?" said a sailor standing nearby. "The priest wasn't supposed to win! Navar never loses."

Another sailor added, "I'm not going to pay off my bet. He cheated. Those weren't War moves. Is he even a real priest?"

"I think he is, and priests have gold. Lots. If Sacquidge doesn't want it, I say *we* take it." A sailor stepped forward into the ring.

"Wait a moment," said Captain Sacquidge, looking cross. "We had a deal. He won. He's free to leave."

"He didn't make any deal with me!" said the sailor. "How about all of you? Do you want all that gold walking out of the Bloody Hook?"

The crowd chanted a resounding, "No!"

"Look at him! The priest is so weak he's about to fall over. Let's take it!" The sailor lunged forward, but a hard, wooden mug flew through the air and slammed into the side of his head. He tumbled to the ground.

"Shame. Waste of good ale." Captain Sacquidge shook her head. "Navar? You awake?"

Indeed, her first mate was on his feet. He nodded and came to the captain's side.

"This man is a guest of our ship now." She turned to Dantess with a smile, but also a glint of determination in her eye. "Ten gold gets you there alive. Agreed?"

Dantess nodded.

"There's more of us than them," another sailor cried. "The priest's gold belongs to us all!" The mob surged forward.

Dantess found that, as long as Navar's tattoo was out of sight, he was able to use his token to fuel his strength and stamina. With its help, he managed to fend off each wave of attack as the sailors crowded in.

At his back, he heard Navar punching, pushing, and even throwing sailors away. He was grateful the man was on his side now.

Even the captain was surprisingly light on her feet. She produced a walking stick and wielded it with talent and purpose.

Any sailor that got too close ended up with the business end poked hard into a rib—or worse, an eye.

But there were too many, and the crowd knew it. They pressed the three back. Dantess realized it was only a matter of time until his strength would completely give out.

"Fan out. Protect Dantess!" The cry came from behind the mob. Soon, fighting broke out everywhere—and it didn't involve the three.

Between blows, Dantess spotted his squad interspersed in the crowd. Motti brought down a burly sailor with the training Dantess drummed into his head. Khalista fended off two opponents and dropped them with two smooth motions.

With War's soldiers in the mix, it wasn't long until the alley was clear of aggressive sailors. They were all either lying unconscious on the ground or fleeing somewhere far away.

Warren approached. "I'm sorry it took me this long to gather the squad. I wish we could have been here earlier."

"You followed me?" Dantess asked as he felt the Longing drain from his token, leaving him weak and unsteady.

"You didn't explicitly order me not to." Warren cleared his throat. "And I was concerned. You have an issue with me, but that doesn't mean you shouldn't trust your squad to have your back."

The rest of his squad nodded their agreement.

"I guess a little initiative isn't..." Dantess wasn't just tired— he was lightheaded, "...always a bad..." The alley spun around him. He couldn't stay on his feet.

But as Dantess dropped, Warren caught him. "Don't worry. We've got you."

CHAPTER TWENTY-TWO

DANTESS WOKE TO find the world still spinning. No, it wasn't *spinning* anymore—it was *rocking*. He lay in a rope hammock suspended between two wooden beams in what seemed to be a ship's hold, crowded with crates, barrels, and even a wooden cage or two holding goats. The wood creaked as the ship rocked back and forth. For that, he was thankful for the hammock. In a bed, he might have rolled out.

"You're awake. I'm so relieved," said Warren, sitting on a box near the hammock.

Dantess yawned and stretched his sore limbs, pointedly not responding to Warren.

"We looked you over," continued Warren. "None of us could find anything seriously wrong, so we were hoping you'd wake up on your own. You did." Warren rubbed his hands. "Now that you're awake, can you please tell me what happened? I saw the fight. Something was wrong. Even on your worst day, even as wounded as you were, Navar shouldn't have posed any trouble for you. You're a priest of War!"

Dantess grunted and almost ordered Warren to leave him alone. He tried to maintain the anger that drove him since his punishment at the temple, but he couldn't do it. The fight in the alley sapped all of his strength, and, truth be told, Warren's arrival with the squad saved him at the end.

What was more, he couldn't ignore that he wasn't the only one in pain. Warren lost his mother at the same time Dantess lost his da.

Dantess sighed and decided it was easier to forgive. He knew he would eventually, anyway. He had to admit that sooner was better, because Dantess dearly wanted to discuss this mystery with the boy. He had no other confidant.

"I couldn't use my token against Navar."

"What?" asked Warren. "Why?"

"Every time I tried, his tattoo triggered some kind of insane memories. They were overwhelming."

Warren's eyes grew wide. "He shut you out of your own token?" Dantess could see the wheels spinning in Warren's head. The lad blew out a breath and continued, "That's a powerful tactic: leveraging some weakness in the long history of priests to eliminate the benefits of the token. What's the origin of the tattoo?"

"Navar isn't very talkative. He didn't mention where it came from."

"I meant the image. Whose memories did it access? Can you activate your token and search for it?"

Dantess chuckled. "I know you love the idea of burrowing into research, but the token doesn't work like that. Those memories and experiences are triggered. I'd need to see the tattoo again while the token is active to learn more, and I'm not planning on doing that anytime soon."

"Understandable. So, you had to fight him without your token? As hurt as you were?"

"I guess so." Dantess leaned back and smiled. "As much as I hate to, I have to admit Motti's sneaky street fighting came in handy."

"But why? You could have tapped out. Why push yourself when you were already in bad shape? We could have found another way."

"I don't know if that's true," said Dantess. "Regardless, I couldn't stomach the thought of losing again. Especially after the Game."

Warren sighed. "I'm so sorry. I'd understand if you could never trust me again. But I needed you to win. I needed you to beat that murderer, Kevik. His own greed and entitlement gave me the perfect—"

"Don't say it," interrupted Dantess. "The moment you actually admit it, I don't think I'll be able to cover for you anymore. It would be against the rules."

"I understand. You're a priest. You can't break the rules."

"It's hard enough now not to turn you in, but..."

"Yes?" Warren leaned forward on his box.

Dantess cleared his throat. "You're my friend. I don't have many of those." He omitted the word *'left'* at the end, but it was implied.

"Then that's the last we'll say about the matter. Except... I'm sorry about your grandfather's belt. I know it meant a lot to you."

Dantess winced. "I've lost a lot lately. We both have. I expect you to work twice as hard to help me get back what we can!"

"Of course." Warren stood up. "I owe you my life. That debt will never be repaid." He held out his hand to Dantess. "Are you feeling up to taking a tour of Captain Sacquidge's boat?"

Dantess grabbed the hand and used it to pull himself out of the hammock. Every motion was painful, but it was a pain that told him he was healing. "I think you're supposed to call it a ship."

"Uh, I don't know about that. Wait until you get the tour to decide if the 'Mourning Glory' is a ship."

Once on deck, Dantess realized that the hold was the biggest area on the Glory. The captain sat on the raised aft while Navar—thankfully wearing a shirt—manned the helm below. Dantess' squad had scattered along the deck, trying to stay out of the way of the two other crew members who seemed to be engaged in a synchronized dance of chores—like refastening the rigs, orienting the single sail, and scanning the horizon—and who didn't appreciate the obstacles.

Warren was right. The Glory was afloat. It had a crew. It had a sail. But it was nothing like the huge vessels War hired for transport. Dantess had never been aboard a boat so small.

Before moving on, Dantess took the briefest opportunity to close his eyes to feel the gentle push of the sea breeze. That, along with the sounds of rushing water, the smell of salt, and the slow rock of the deck under his feet was calming, and he enjoyed the moment of serenity. Unlike some other priests who hated to travel by water—even became sick doing so—he found that sailing agreed with him.

Being here reminded him how much the sea called him. He couldn't remember a time when it hadn't. Even his father remarked on it, years ago.

Eyes open, he looked out over the waves and saw chalk-white cliffs only a few miles off the side, topped with lush green trees. He'd never sailed along this coast, and the view was breathtaking. "We're so close to land?"

"According to the captain, it's safer than the open sea, for a lot of reasons," replied Warren.

"Where are we headed? I didn't tell the captain where we needed to sail."

"True. After the ruckus in Victor's Folly, she thought it best to leave the area while you recovered."

Dantess searched his Longing and realized that, with each passing moment, they were sailing further and further away from the Gift of War. He rolled his eyes and said, "Of course. Some deal I made, huh? We ended up on a tiny boat that's headed in the wrong direction. We started with two weeks until the end of the Convergence, and now we're burning days while my father and your mother are being taken away from us."

"So, let's change that." Warren gestured to the gray-haired captain relaxing at the aft. "Tell the captain where we need to go."

When Dantess looked up at her, the captain tipped her hat. Dantess took the cue and climbed up the wooden ladder to the raised platform.

The captain took a long, carved pipe from her mouth. "Back with the living? Never seen a man as tired as you after that fight."

"I've had a rough week."

She laughed, a loud and infectious sound. Dantess couldn't help but smile at it. "I see that. But what's worse, you decided to drag *me* into your week. I was happy sitting in an alley and watching drunks beat each other up while I won a bit of gold. Speaking of, you owe me ten pieces." She flipped off her hat and held it out to Dantess.

"I don't know how it would have gone if my squad hadn't shown up, but you and Navar earned this gold." He opened his pouch, counted out ten pieces, and dropped them in the captain's hat. "But our bet was about getting me and my squad where we need to go: Convergence Island."

"Convergence Island?" Sacquidge removed the coins, pocketed them, and replaced her hat on her head. "Are you joking?"

"No. It's a matter of life and death. I have to get there."

"Where, exactly? Do you know where the island is? Because I don't. No one does."

Dantess closed his eyes, asked his Longing for a direction, and then pointed out to the open sea.

The captain looked at Dantess' hand and broke out into another laughing fit. It took a few minutes for her to calm herself. "You didn't think to mention this *before* I agreed to the bet?"

"You would have agreed anyway. That's how certain you were that you'd win."

The captain replaced the pipe in her mouth. "True."

"So, can you turn this boat in the right direction? We've already lost too much time."

The captain took a long draw from her pipe and leisurely blew out a plume of white smoke. "Have you sailed these waters before?"

"Not often."

"But when you did, it was on a ship like the Fury, right?"

Dantess nodded.

"A magnificent ship, no question. Pirates avoid temple ships like the Fury for good reason, but the Glory?"

"Ah," said Dantess, starting to understand where the captain was leading.

The captain rubbed the wooden railing in front of her with affection. "For her purpose, there's no better vessel than my Mourning Glory. She's faster than you might think, she can hold cargo that you'd never find if you searched for a month, and she can slip through shallows others can't navigate. But she's no war ship."

Dantess nodded. "She's an easy target."

"Aye. Which is why we can't venture into open waters. It's full of predators. Close to shore, we can run where the big ships can't chase."

Dantess thought about this. "What if I were to guarantee your safety?"

"Lad, you're a force on land, to be sure—but a warship could sink us before it got anywhere close. Your guarantee wouldn't protect us. Especially from the Sea King."

"The Sea King?"

"You've not heard of the Sea King? You are landbound, aren't you? His fleet owns these waters. Even some of the remote coastal towns. You don't sail anywhere around here without giving him his due."

Dantess' eyebrows rose. "*Towns?* How is that possible? Law would stop him."

"You'd think so, but once the priests left, the Sea King moved in. The residents don't seem to mind."

The words, said so casually, hit Dantess like bricks. "Priests left their towns? Where did they go?"

The captain shrugged. "Just gone. One town empties and then the next. Usually small towns, up and down the coast."

Dantess thought back to his discussion with the Harbinger of Chaos and remembered the place he mentioned. "Is one of them Seaborn Notch?"

The captain pointed her pipe at Dantess. "Aye. In fact, it's said that's where the Sea King makes his home."

Dantess leaned against the back railing and watched the Glory's wake while he turned all of the facts over in his mind. "So, the big ships won't defy the temples. And the others are too scared of the Sea King. That about right?"

"Aye."

Dantess turned back to the captain and nodded. "How far to Seaborn Notch?"

"If the wind is with us, about a day. Why?"

"My high priest is already out to sea, so logically there's only one other person who can guarantee safe passage."

The captain's jaw dropped open, and her pipe fell into her hand. "No."

"I need to pay the Sea King a visit."

"My young friend, one does not *visit* the Sea King. If anything, one is *dragged* in front of him." The Captain jabbed her pipe at Dantess to emphasize the point. "Right before something much worse happens."

Dantess puffed out his chest a bit. "If he tries, he'll find out I'm not some sailor he can bully."

"No, you're a *priest*, heading to a town where all priests have vanished."

"I'm a priest of *War*," Dantess corrected. "What priests disappeared from these towns? Law? Charity? And probably the dregs of those temples, if they were assigned to these backwater towns. I am the grandson of *Varyon*, one of the most celebrated warriors in our history. The Sea King won't have dealt with my kind before."

The captain took another puff. "I knew priests of War were overly confident. I didn't know how foolhardy they could be."

Dantess frowned. "Captain, you promised to take me where I need to go. Or are you a woman who reneges on her bets?"

"Never, and let no one say so." The captain stood up and looked Dantess square in the eyes. "I'll take you there, but it'll take more than ten gold to keep you alive after that."

"We're going to the *Sea King?*" Warren sat on his favorite crate in the hold. Somehow, he voiced the question with his mouth hanging open.

"Yes. Captain Sacquidge explained that if we sail into open waters, one of his pirate fleet could capture us—or even sink us, if they were so inclined. The only way to ensure we get there in one piece is to ask for safe passage."

Without closing his mouth, Warren continued, "We're going to ask *him* for permission to sail to Convergence Island?"

"I just said that. Hopefully, it'll only be a question of price."

"And we're going to look for him in Seaborn Notch, a place where all the priests somehow disappeared? Maybe the home of both a pirate lord *and* the Harbingers of Chaos?"

"I admit the plan sounds a little crazy when you say it like that."

"It doesn't matter how I say it," said Warren, shaking his head. "It's just crazy."

Dantess leaned back into his hammock with a grimace. "I don't see an alternative, do you? We *have* to get to our parents before they're shipped off to Evil. Regardless, I'm a priest of *War*. I'm not afraid of the Harbingers. I'm not afraid of the Sea King. With the power of my god behind me," he said with a groan as he lifted himself into a more comfortable position, "I'm invincible, remember?"

Warren rolled his eyes. "Invincible, huh? And tired and hurt and desperate. But you're right that I can't think of an alternative. One more question, though: if everything somehow goes perfectly and we manage to get to Convergence Island, what happens then? How are we going to free our parents?"

Dantess' eyelids drooped. "You expect me to do *all* the planning? I'm tired." He yawned. "I'm sure you'll come up with something."

"Right." Warren pinched the bridge of his nose and blew out a loud breath. "I'll let you sleep. You should be as rested as possible whenever you face certain doom."

Dantess grinned. "Couldn't hurt." He closed his eyes and fell asleep before Warren could respond.

Dantess would have enjoyed the voyage much more if a clock didn't keep ticking in his head, reminding him that his father's time was running out. Despite that, Dantess couldn't stop staring at the rushing water and the towering cliffs.

"Seaborn Notch ahead!" The call came from one of the crewmembers. Strangely, Dantess couldn't see the port. In fact, all he saw was a striking change in the landscape: the cliffside jutted out quite far into the water. A few large ships were anchored in the sea around an opening in the cliff towering above them: a slim, vertical cut.

Captain Sacquidge gestured at the opening. "That's the Notch. The port is named after it."

"The town is in there?" asked Dantess, and the captain nodded. "How can this be a port? Ships can't possibly get through that passage." The cliff sides were impossibly tall and quite narrow, both impressive and daunting.

"Ships like that one?" The captain pointed to one of the galleons moored outside. "Wouldn't advise it. But a *boat* can. Right?" The captain winked. "Navar, take us in."

Navar steered the Glory in between the towering walls of rock. Dantess held his breath as the hull of the boat almost scraped against the sides, but missed by inches.

The captain noticed Dantess' concern. "Don't worry. Navar was born here. Sailed in and out of the Notch more times than I can count. He could navigate us through in his sleep."

The sun fell away behind the rock walls, and without the sun, the air cooled. As Navar carefully navigated through the passage, Dantess found himself hugging his arms, ironically happy for his shirt sleeves. But it wasn't long until the ship emerged on the far side of the Notch into a massive cove perhaps five miles wide. The sun reappeared, showing a smattering of boats fishing safely inside the cliff walls.

Dantess' eyes were drawn to the sprawling and seemingly randomly-constructed collection of wooden docks and walkways, which seemed to lead everywhere, including along the cliff wall and even into caverns. Walkways, ramps, and ladders provided passage to multiple levels of a number of wooden buildings, but it was almost impossible to follow one path to its completion. It wound around and connected with and jumped over so many other walkways, he imagined it easy to get lost here. Even the first glimpse of this town promised that it was a place of secrets.

The Glory caught the slight wind inside the cove and sailed toward one of the empty docks, others already populated with vessels about Glory's size and a few longboats from the ships moored outside. Hands stood ready to catch the lines and guide the boat in. For a while, Dantess watched the men at work—a few pulling the lines and others using wooden poles to keep the Glory from ramming the dock—but then he realized that many others both on the docks and shore weren't watching the boat come in. They were looking at *him*, pointing and chattering excitedly. A few children stared with wide eyes, then ran off at top speed. As a priest of War, Dantess was used to being the center of attention—he kind of expected it—but this was a level of enthusiasm he hadn't experienced.

"What's that all about, captain?" asked Dantess.

"You're a novel sight, lad. Remember, there haven't been any priests here in Seaborn Notch for a while." She pointed her pipe at the running children and chuckled. "I wouldn't be surprised if the entire town knew about you before you stepped onto land."

Dantess cursed under his breath. Priests of War were brash and obvious, trained to use their imposing appearance and reputation to put others on their heels. And Warren's failed plan at Serenity left a bad taste in his mouth about concealing his identity.

Even so, he lost his chance to keep a low profile.

The Glory settled into place, and the dock workers tied off the lines.

"What's your plan now?" asked the captain.

"I'm not sure, but you've been a great help, Captain." Dantess pulled out his pouch and removed five coins. "This is for getting us here."

The captain's eyebrow rose. Once the coins hit her palm, she looked at them and said, "Ach, you're a good lad. I can't just cast you into the devil's den alone. I don't know the Sea King, but I know people who do. I'll talk to some of them." Captain Sacquidge pointed to a wooden building with a large sign surrounded by painted flowers. "In the meantime, that's the Primrose Boarding House. My crew usually unwind in their taproom. It's as safe as you get on the docks here. Navar can show you. I'll meet you there when I know something."

"Thank you, Captain. I don't know what to say."

The captain chuckled. "Your gold does all the talking. Besides, it doesn't hurt to have a friend in the priesthood, says me." She smiled and added, "Anywhere but *here*, of course."

As Navar led Dantess and his squad through the maze of walkways, Dantess couldn't help but notice the pointed glances from every single person they saw. Only the children were excited. The adults stared daggers.

The docks weren't all there was to Seaborn Notch, but it was a big part—and a rough one. Quite a few of the ramshackle wooden buildings were in some state of disrepair, and colorful, seafaring folk flowed in and out of them, looking ready for trouble.

The obvious exception was the Primrose Boarding House. The exterior was in top repair—one might even call it pretty. As if taunting the murderous sailors clumping on the docks, an older but fit woman balanced one-footed on a slim ledge, stretching to hold a watering can up to an overflowing flower box beneath the building's sign. She wore breeches painted with various pastel colors and a pink woolen shirt with sleeves bound with leather cords.

"Afternoon, Rose," said Navar, passing underneath.

Rose swung herself to a trellis, also covered in flowers, and climbed down to the wooden walkway below. When she did, her eyes took in Dantess and narrowed. "Navar! Good to see you again. But what are you thinking, bringing a *priest* to my door? Did you lose a bet?"

He shrugged and jerked his thumb to the group. "This is Dantess, priest of War. Can we wait inside for the captain? Her request."

Rose set the watering can down, put her hands on her hips, and stared Dantess in the eye. He could tell that Rose was deeply conflicted. "You're lucky it's Captain Sacquidge asking, otherwise I'd send you on your way. Your kind isn't good for business." She gritted her teeth and jabbed her finger at Navar. "If I let them in, you will keep them out of trouble. I don't need a damned priest of War in my place itching for a fight. It's on you. Understood?"

It was so strange, as a priest, to be treated as undesirable. Everywhere else in the world, priests were received as honored guests—sought after and deferred to, or at least feared. Here, he was a magnet for trouble. At best.

But he couldn't change all of that now. Dantess swallowed his indignation and nodded as Navar did the same. With a scowl, Rose said, "Follow me." She wheeled and walked inside the front doors.

Navar led them all inside the Primrose's open doors. The interior was wooden, but tastefully painted with pastel colors and punctuated with urns, boxes, and vases overflowing with flowers. It wasn't even evening yet, but patrons still filled about half the tables. Upon Dantess' arrival, conversation stopped and all eyes turned to watch him.

He and his squad shuffled their way through the silent diners. A few smiling girls continued serving and chatting until the commotion resumed, although most kept at least one eye on Dantess and his squad. Finally, they reached an open table and sat down. Soon, a girl approached Navar with a mug of ale, smiling warmly at him. "Nice to see you. Here's your usual," she said, placing the drink beside him.

"They seem to know you here," said Dantess.

Navar took a long swig from the mug. "Born and raised." He winked at the serving girl, who blushed and twirled off.

"No priests in Seaborn Notch, eh?" asked Dantess. "How long?"

Navar held three fingers while taking another swig.

"Three years?" Dantess turned to Warren and asked, "How is it that we haven't heard about this before now?"

"These remote towns don't communicate much with the temples," said Warren. "Especially when they're so cut off. Between the mountains and pirate activity, there isn't a lot of temple traffic here."

Dantess sipped from his mug. It contained a surprisingly tasty ale. "So, three years without the tithe?"

Navar nodded. "No tithe. Tribute."

"A tribute? To whom?"

"The Sea King."

Dantess fumed for a moment and steadied himself. He couldn't figure out what to be angrier about: a whole town of tithe deadbeats or a man who collected money like he was his own temple. "How'd he pull that off?"

"People do what they're told. Priests aren't here, but the Sea King offers supplies and safety."

"It's sacrilege. It's not part of Order's plan."

Navar shrugged. "That's life in Seaborn Notch."

Now Dantess understood the looks they received when walking here. After escaping the tithe for years, one would want to avoid anyone representing the temples. They might want to collect.

Worse, the Sea King might react the same way. And, if he felt threatened, he probably wouldn't stop with a dirty look.

After about an hour, Captain Sacquidge arrived at the taproom, accompanied by a young woman. She wore a cloak that covered everything but her head. Her nose was a bit too large for her face, and her dirty brown hair stuck out at all angles. While she wasn't pretty, she carried herself with confidence.

When she saw Dantess, her brown eyes locked with his. Dantess didn't know what to make of her intensity.

"Dantess, I have good news," said Captain Sacquidge. "Honestly, I didn't expect this, but the Sea King has agreed to meet with you." She gestured to the girl. "This is Twyla. She represents the Sea King."

"A girl?" asked Dantess, surprised that the Sea King would send someone so young.

"Not *a* girl. *This* girl," said Twyla. "Is that a problem?"

Dantess was taken aback with the girl's forthrightness. With just a few words, she clearly differentiated herself from most other faithless. Perhaps living in Seaborn Notch inspired such independence.

"Of course not. But are we supposed to negotiate with *you?*"

Twyla laughed. "I'm here to take you to him." When some of the squad began to rise from their chairs, she held out her hands and added, "But only when the moon is at its zenith."

"Where are we going? To his lair?" asked Warren. "That won't be safe."

"No, don't worry," said Twyla. "It's a neutral location. I'm sure that, as a priest of War, you'll appreciate the place. It was my suggestion."

Between bites of a turkey leg, Navar mumbled, "Shattered Peak."

While Twyla's smile didn't leave her mouth, her eyes froze in panic. "What? Why would you say that?"

Navar paused his gnawing and said, "Obvious. That village is where the massacre happened. Because of that priest of War. Varyon, right?"

"Varyon was my grandfather. You're talking about the battle of Shattered Peak! That was *here?*" asked Dantess "He saved everyone here from Chaos. He was a hero and one of the greatest priests of War ever."

"I heard it differently." Navar put the leg down. "You want to go? I've been there. I can take you."

"We have to wait for the moon!" demanded Twyla.

"No, we *have* to go now," said Dantess, rising from his chair.

Warren nodded. "To make sure it's not a trap." He glanced at Twyla. "I'm sure you understand."

Twyla huffed as the squad rose from the table and followed Navar out of the door, but she wasn't far behind.

Dantess couldn't believe it. Despite these being the most desperate of circumstances, he was on his way to visit the place that established his grandfather's reputation as the hero of Shattered Peak.

It was a dream come true!

CHAPTER TWENTY-THREE

IF NAVAR HADN'T been leading the way, Dantess would not have been able to follow the steep and overgrown road to Shattered Peak.

"Does anyone live in the village?" asked Dantess. "This road doesn't look like it has been used in years."

Even though he asked Navar, Twyla spoke up. "The temples declared it forbidden. No one was allowed here. Even so, it's not very liveable anymore. Some people even say it's haunted."

"Haunted?"

Twyla narrowed her eyes. "Once you've seen it, you'll understand."

The group walked along the forgotten road until the sun began to dip on the horizon. As it did, it fell behind a mountain missing its peak.

"That must be the actual Shattered Peak!" Dantess knew he wasn't carrying himself with the dignity expected of a priest of War, but he couldn't help it. "It's amazing. Is it natural?"

"Always been like that, far as I know," answered Navar. "Village isn't far now."

Soon, they entered the village's outskirts, but it was hard to tell. Some stone pieces suggested where building foundations may be, but plants had overgrown anything that may have been left. Silence covered the whole area like a smothering blanket, broken only by their footsteps.

"This is it?" asked Dantess. "What happened to the buildings?"

Twyla stepped next to him. "You don't know? Burned. Almost all of them. Many of those buildings burned with people still inside."

They continued walking in the strange hush. Ahead, a stone well stood in the middle of the village square. Unlike the rubble remaining from most of the surrounding buildings, the well-fitted rings of stone were intact and solid.

The captain, tired from walking so far, tripped and landed on the ground. The impact made her swear, which startled everyone. Out of instinct, Dantess channeled his Longing through his token. Once he realized the source of the sound, he swung his gaze back to the well.

But he was no longer looking through his own eyes.

Crouched behind the wall that surrounded the village square, Varyon stared at the well. "Are you sure this is necessary, Xevout? The whole plan is too underhanded for my taste. We should deal with this situation head-on."

"This is *Evil's* mission, priest of War. You're here only to protect me." A black-cloaked priest of Evil pulled out a metal sphere wrapped by two perpendicular rings of silver. He continued in a whisper, "My high priest made it clear that someone in this village has an artifact of Chaos, but we don't know who. If you run in there and start killing people one by one, the person we really want could slip out. This is the only way to ensure *all* the villagers die. We'll find the Chaos artifact after mine has done its work."

The man in black stood up, lit only by a dim moon. "This late, no one should be awake, but if anyone sees me, kill them before they can alert anyone else." He strode to the well and, seeing no villagers, held up the sphere. After a moment of concentration, the core took on a dull green glow and the metal bands began to rotate around it, quicker and quicker. Xevout smiled, held the device over the well, and dropped it.

It hit the water with a distant splash and a faint sizzle.

When the man returned without incident, Varyon asked, "How long?"

"The well is the only water source, and they all have to drink sometime. When they do, it might take a while for them to react. Within a couple of days, they'll all be affected. Until then, we need to block all paths from the village. No one enters or leaves until this is done."

"As you say." Varyon waved to his squad. They began to fan out in the forest behind them. "Such a charming village. It's a shame."

"A village of *faithless*. There are lots more."

"Of course." Varyon placed his hand on Xevout's shoulder. "Let's move to a safe distance."

Dantess stopped channeling his Longing, and the images faded.

"Dantess?" asked Warren. "Are you all right? Did you see something?"

"My grandfather was here." Dantess rubbed his temples. "But he wasn't leading a battle against the forces of Chaos. He was with a priest of Evil who did something..."

"You can see what happened?" asked Twyla. "All that time ago? How?"

"My token. It allows me to see what other priests of War saw."

Twyla stepped closer. "So, you know what happened here? What *really* happened?"

"I don't know. A bit. I'm not sure I understand it. It was the start of a mission—"

"Follow me if you want to know how it ended." Twyla walked toward one of the only standing buildings, a stone house at the head of the square.

Dantess hesitated.

"Do you care about the truth, Dantess, priest of War?" asked Twyla, once she had reached the doorway. "Do you want to see why we call this the massacre of Shattered Peak, or would you rather stay safe in the warm, comforting legend you were taught?"

After a moment, he took a deep breath and walked one slow step at a time toward the doorway.

"This was my father's house. He was the leader of this village. Take a look." Twyla walked inside.

Dantess stopped a pace from the broken door frame. From this vantage, he could see a single chair sitting in the middle of the floor.

"Dantess, are you sure you want to do this?" asked Warren. "You don't have to."

It was too late. He already channeled his Longing through the token.

A soldier stood in front of the door, next to Dantess' grandfather. "Many of the villagers are dead, but we haven't found the artifact anywhere."

"Someone in this damned village must have the artifact of Chaos!" said Xevout, standing on his other side, looking agitated. "Why can't your men find it? Or you? Be *useful* for once!"

"Watch your mouth, Xevout. Maybe none of the villagers have it. Have you thought of that? Maybe your high priest didn't know what he was talking about. Maybe we killed all these people for nothing."

"No. It's here somewhere. *Someone* has it. Someone *used* it. Whoever it is, they won't drop it or hide it. They can't! Chaos won't let them."

Varyon grabbed the priest of Evil by his robe. "This was *your* plan, *your* mission, right? The failure will be yours, too."

"It's here, I swear," said Xevout, nervously. "Ask the village leader. He knows everyone who lives here. He'll know who has it."

Varyon turned to one of his soldiers. "The leader is inside?"

The soldier nodded. "So far, he hasn't said a word."

"I'll ask him. I can be persuasive."

The soldier stepped out of the way to reveal a young man bound to a chair, sitting in the middle of the small house. His chin was on his chest, and he was breathing hard through his nose.

"So, you're the leader of this quaint little village," said Varyon, walking inside. "By now, you must know that we're looking for someone with an artifact of Chaos. You know how dangerous it is. It infects people with its dark magic. *Your* people. They're dying. If you tell me who has it, we can destroy it before it does any more damage."

The man lifted his chin, anger and madness in his eyes. But he said nothing. He just kept breathing quickly and heavily through his nose, his jaw shut tight.

"You need to tell me. You know everyone here. Surely, someone found something recently, something strange and unnatural? And then people started dying, right? I can stop this," he lied. "Just tell me."

The man simply stared into Varyon's eyes and breathed.

The priest of War's patience disappeared. He lunged forward and grabbed the man's jaw. He screamed into the village

251

leader's face, "You *will* talk to me. You *will* tell me what I want to—"

The village leader spat out a mouthful of water into Varyon's gaping mouth. Shocked, Varyon dropped the man's jaw, sputtered, and stepped back. "What was that?"

"A taste of what you fed to all of us," said the leader, now frothing. "No artifact of Chaos infected us. It was *you* and that priest of Evil. You poisoned our well. Everyone who drank from it went mad and then died. It's happening to me, too—but at least I'll take you with me!"

Varyon began to shake with rage. He drew back his fist and slammed it through the man's chest. The village leader choked for a moment or two and then closed his eyes, his head lolling.

"I want this village in flames," Varyon screamed to his soldiers. "If we can't find the damned artifact, we'll burn the place down around it."

As his squad nodded and ran off to light torches, Varyon turned to Xevout and hissed, "What will happen to me? What will this horrid magic of Evil do?"

"Well," began Xevout, "you're a priest of Order. You're very strong, and you can use your token to increase your resistance and endurance." He took a step back.

Varyon grabbed him. "Will I live?" When Xevout stammered, Varyon continued, "Damn it, *will I live?*"

"No. Even a drop is fatal. The poison will eat away at your brain. You'll go insane. You'll lose your grasp on reality, and then you will expire. It's just a matter of time."

The priest of War hurled Xevout away. He screamed in frustration—and a touch of madness.

Dantess dropped to the ground. His eyes were empty—not shocked, not afraid, just empty. Everything he believed in crumbled before his eyes. "He did it. He killed everyone. And they were just villagers, not agents of Chaos. People. Innocents."

"He killed my father, didn't he?" asked Twyla.

Dantess looked up into her face. "Yes. Your father had the last laugh, though. He poisoned my grandfather with the same water they gave to all the villagers."

"Water from our well?" Her gaze swung to the well in the square. "And then what?"

Dantess nodded, looking around at the places where buildings once stood. "He burned it all."

"Why?"

"They were convinced someone here had an artifact of Chaos. They said it would infect everyone. Kill everyone. According to the legend I know, my grandfather stopped the artifact from being taken out of here and spreading to the rest of the world."

"Your legend is wrong," Twyla said with a cold laugh. "It was a massacre. That's all. Your grandfather murdered a village of faithless, and your temple turned him into a martyr. A hero."

Dantess pulled himself up by grabbing the door frame. As he was about to enter the house, to sit on the chair inside, Navar called out from behind, "Do not go in there."

Dantess turned his head. "Why?"

Navar patted his chest. "My tattoo."

"What about it?"

The first mate pointed to the house. "It's inside the house. I saw it once, and I couldn't unsee it. It's the most terrifying thing I've ever come across, so I put it on my chest to scare others. You know what this does to priests of War. Heed me and steer clear."

Despair and betrayal pushed him on. Dantess had to see it through. He needed to understand it all. He needed to know how his grandfather's story really ended.

He walked into the house.

Every surface, even stone, was covered in carvings. One of the largest pictures, the three-eyed raven from Navar's chest, was etched onto the floor.

Driven by some kind of self-destructive need to hurt himself—to punish himself for believing the propaganda of his temple—and a need to know the truth, he channeled his Longing through his token.

The walls, covered with Varyon's etchings, were lit by the fires raging in the village outside. The priest of Evil's body lay slumped in a corner of the room. The soldiers of his squad were piled outside the door, also dead. Varyon had done them the favor of saving them all from what was enveloping the world by killing them first. They may not have found the artifact, but he knew Chaos was coming nonetheless.

While he was still able, he kept carving images of monsters on the wall. Those pictures would be his warning to those who came after. It was a record of all of the horrors that awaited the living.

Soon, Chaos would take him too. He could feel its hot, fetid breath, the burning touch of its claws and spikes, and the endless terror it injected directly into his spirit.

And the flames. Everywhere, the searing flames.

He wouldn't give it the satisfaction. It was here, right behind him, but also everywhere. There was no escape. Clumsily, he took the knife he was using to carve the pictures on the wall and dragged it across his own throat.

Dantess collapsed on the floor, shaking. Without a knife, he felt around blindly for anything within reach and discovered a rock. With purpose, he pulled it across his throat three times, pulling beads of blood from his skin, before Warren grabbed his arm and snatched the stone away.

"Dantess, wake up! Snap out of it! This isn't you."

Dantess looked at Warren with bottomless despair in his eyes. "There's no escape."

"No, that's your grandfather talking, but he's long gone. Stop channeling. Be *here* with me. *Now.*"

Those two words broke through the torrent of monstrous images: *stop channeling*. And he did. He let the Longing flow out of him, and his token went inert.

Once more, Dantess was back in the stone house surrounded by only carvings, not nightmares come to life. But the images in his head lingered, accompanied by the memory of that irresistible need to take his own life. Anguish twisted his face and he fell into Warren's arms, sobbing.

"You're here. You're safe," whispered Warren. "Thank War you don't carry a weapon."

After a while, when the others began to wonder what was happening, Dantess and Warren walked out of the house.

"Is everything all right? asked Motti.

"No," said Dantess, flatly. "Everything I thought I knew was a lie."

Twyla crossed her arms. "I'm surprised. I would have sworn that at least the priests of War knew the truth. I thought they just lied to everyone else."

Dantess turned to Twyla. "You knew all of this?"

"I knew the legend of Varyon was a lie, fabricated by the temples to cover up this massacre. I'm not sure why they did it, though. It's not like the temples would do anything differently, even if people were to find out. When did a village of faithless lives ever stop the temples from doing anything they wanted?"

"That's a cold way to see it. But... you may be right." Dantess wiped his eyes. "I think the lie wasn't meant to cover up the massacre. It covered up the mission's failure. Think about it. A priest of Evil used his magic to poison a priest of War, and that priest of War killed everyone and then himself. The truth could have soured the alliance between War and Evil."

Dantess staggered over to the well and looked down. "Also, if the faithless knew, they'd suspect that priests were fallible—and especially, that priests of War were vulnerable. Worst of all, it might have been over *nothing*. They never found an artifact of Chaos. Who knows if it ever existed?"

Warren grabbed Dantess by the shoulders and hissed, "Stop this. Not *here*. You're saying too much."

A call came from the other side of the square. It was Khalista. "Movement on the road, coming to the village. The Sea King's party is here. At least seven of them. They're early. Lucky we got here first."

Dantess nodded to Warren and tried to pull himself together. "Squad, positions. I want coverage around this square. Don't let us get surrounded."

It didn't take long before a group of colorfully-garbed sailors strolled into the square. Six of them were rough-looking and weather-beaten, with sabers at their hips and crossbows at the ready. The seventh was shorter and slighter, covered by a dark cloak and hood. The slim hand that poked out, held by one of the sailors, was that of a girl—even though the hood kept her face in darkness.

255

Twyla cried out, "Quin!" She raced to the shorter figure and wrapped her in a tight hug. Afterward, she stayed with her in the line of sailors, holding hands.

One of the sailors stepped forward. The man, in his middle years, was solidly-built, with only the start of a potbelly in an otherwise fit physique. His brown hair was tinged with gray at the temples, but hard to see beneath a black swooping hat home to a crown of feathers. Unlike the others, he wore a saber on his back, attached to a leather strap over the shoulder of his long green coat with gold trim and buttons.

The man was handsome, sporting a well-groomed moustache and beard that ended in a short braid. They framed a warm smile that never left his face. From his air, there was no question that this man was in charge.

"I see you arrived here early." He tapped his head. "Smart. Trying to avoid an ambush. I should know better than to match strategies with a priest of War. Forgive me if I'm out of practice. We haven't seen a priest of War here in years. Decades maybe." He looked at his men. "We haven't seen a priest at all in a while, have we?" The other sailors laughed. "When I heard you were visiting, I knew I had to meet you in person."

Even shaken, Dantess thought this man seemed entirely too comfortable. Faced with a priest of War, he should have been more nervous. It spoke to his confidence, which made Dantess wary.

"You are the Sea King?" asked Dantess. "The pirate lord of these waters?"

Captain Sacquidge winced.

But the Sea King laughed. "A pirate? I'm just a successful businessman. I ship products where they need to go. I'm a merchant of everything from foodstuffs and other supplies to rare and luxurious items, and I'm fortunate enough to have a fleet to help. You should appreciate my story. I'm an example of how the faithless can thrive in this world."

Dantess crossed his arms. "Seems you thrive in lawlessness. The lack of priests here suits you."

"It's true. I do what I can to provide these people some stability in the temples' absence. Is that why you're here? To discuss local government? If so, I find that topic boring. There are other things that demand my attention." He looked over at Twyla and Quin. Twyla met his gaze, as if awaiting orders.

256

Dantess thought about this, then replied, "No, that's not it. I need your help."

Again, the Sea King laughed. "*You* need *my* help? A priest of War? A one-man army? What can this simple sailor possibly do to help you?"

"I have to get to Convergence Island as quickly as possible. It's important."

The Sea King paused a moment, surprised. "You mean the island hosting the once-in-a-hundred-years Convergence of the Divine? Where the high-and-mighty priests create rules to control the faithless?"

"That's right. My trip isn't sanctioned by the temples, so no ship will take me. Everyone else is scared of running afoul of your fleet. So, I ask you, what is the price of passage?"

"You know where the island is?" asked the Sea King, with a serious edge to his voice.

"No, but since my god's Gift is there, my Longing does."

The Sea King raised his eyebrow and rubbed his chin, a smile creeping onto his face. In the pause, Twyla stepped forward—still holding Quin's hand—but the handsome pirate shook his head slightly at her. Twyla frowned and stepped back.

"I'll do it," said the Sea King.

"You'll permit Captain Sacquidge to take me there?"

The Sea King raised his hands and smiled. "No, better. I'll take you there myself!"

Dantess raised an eyebrow. "On your ship?"

"My *flagship*, yes. If speed is of the essence, there's nothing faster than the Leviathan. And no one would dare stop us."

"And the price?" asked Dantess, hooking his eyebrow.

"How much gold do you have?"

Dantess took out his coin pouch. The Sea King did not wait for him to open and count it. Instead, he gestured for Dantess to toss it over. Frowning, Dantess lobbed the pouch to the Sea King's feet. The man snatched it up, weighed it in his hand, and smiled. "This will do for now." He gestured to his men. "Let's be off. No time to waste, eh? Our priest of War is on a mission!"

The line of sailors and the two girls turned and began to walk out of the village. Dantess swirled his hand in the air, and his squad converged on him. As a group, they began to follow the pirates out.

Warren stepped close to Dantess and whispered, "I don't trust him. No matter what he says, he's not doing it for the gold."

"Don't underestimate the power of a bulging coin pouch." Dantess rubbed his neck where the rock had torn at it. "There's more gold in there than most faithless see in a lifetime."

Warren shook his head. "I don't understand why Twyla is with him. She and the other girl don't seem like pirates. None of this adds up."

"She's an orphan. Maybe the other girl is, too? Perhaps the Sea King took them in."

Warren studied the back of the Sea King. "He's too confident, especially when addressing a priest of War. I don't like it. Isn't there any other way?"

"I don't see one. Not in time, anyway. He's our only option. Besides, he betrays War at his peril."

Even if the Sea King showed no fear at all, the man had to respect the power of his god.

Didn't he?

At this hour, the docks were quiet except for the soft lap of the water against the moored boats and the occasional clang of a bell buoy somewhere in the cove. Some of the Sea King's crew along with Twyla and Quin piled into one of the longboats while others prepared a second one for boarding.

"Dantess, are you sure you want to do this?" asked Captain Sacquidge softly. "I don't care how much gold you gave him. The Sea King doesn't do anything that isn't in his own interest. He wants something, and it's not the same thing you do."

"What choice do I have? He's the only path between here and where I need to go—and I *have* to get there soon. If not, my father and Warren's mother will be shipped off to the dungeons of Evil. I can't let that happen."

The captain looked at Dantess with respect. "You're doing this for your father? Dantess, you're a rare breed. Not many priests would enter the lion's den to save any faithless, even if they're related."

Navar grabbed his hand and shook it firmly. "Protect yourself, my friend."

Dantess smiled. "I'm a priest of War. If he betrays me, he will regret it."

The first longboat launched, and the one remaining was already half-full. The Sea King sat at the rudder. He gestured to Dantess. "Climb aboard. We have to leave."

Dantess approached but saw only two empty seats. "How am I supposed to fit my squad into this boat?"

"Your squad isn't coming," said the Sea King. "Just you."

Motti, standing close, piped up. "What? No!"

"You paid for *your* passage, not theirs. Get in."

Warren stepped forward. "I won't stay behind. It's my mother at stake, too!"

At that, the Sea King lifted an eyebrow, but he didn't respond.

Dantess locked gazes with the Sea King. "Warren is coming. That's non-negotiable. Otherwise, we have a problem."

The Sea King pulled at his beard for a moment, then looked at the crew of the boat. Dantess couldn't tell what affected him, but his demeanor shifted. When he looked back, he wore a smile, but it looked a touch more nervous than before. "We can squeeze in one more. Make no mistake: there will be payment for this."

"I have no doubt of that." He turned to Captain Sacquidge and asked, "Can you take my squad back to the temple? You'll be compensated when you get there." Before the captain could respond, he continued, "Motti, I trust you to keep everyone safe. I'll meet you there if... when we're done."

Both Warren and Dantess took a moment to say their goodbyes to the squad. At the end, Warren hugged and whispered something to Motti before both he and Dantess stepped into the longboat. Navar untied the mooring lines and threw them into the boat and then shoved it away with his foot.

As the longboat pulled away, Dantess saw Motti speaking to both Captain Sacquidge and his first mate. The captain responded emphatically by waving her hands. Navar just nodded.

Even though they were obviously smugglers and probably on the wrong side of the law most of their lives, he liked the pair. He hoped he would see them again someday.

CHAPTER TWENTY-FOUR

THE TWO LONGBOATS exited the Notch and rowed out to sea. It wasn't long until they spotted tiny lights hanging in the darkness. As they approached, Dantess realized that the glowing specks were lanterns—and there were a lot of them.

Dantess always thought War's frigate, the Righteous Fury, was the pinnacle of ship making, but the Leviathan put it to shame. It was a four-masted galleon with rows of cannon ports, not only along the sides, but also on the aft. Dantess had never seen a ship so large. It looked like the kind of ship that would rule the seas.

"Impressive," whispered Dantess.

"Don't see many ships like the Leviathan, do you?" asked the Sea King.

"I didn't know a ship could be so big. It's a floating fortress. Four masts?"

The Sea King smiled. "She's not as maneuverable as a frigate, but even full of cargo, I'd match her speed against any other ship."

By the time Dantess' longboat sidled up to the Leviathan, most of the passengers on the first boat had already climbed up the rope ladder. The two that were left were rigging it to ropes attached to a spar in order to haul it aboard. Once the second boat was secure, Dantess grabbed the ladder and started his ascent.

It was not a short climb. The side of the Leviathan was higher than most buildings. He passed by one row of closed cannon ports and then another. And then another. The firepower this ship represented explained why no one crossed the Sea King in his own waters.

A clean-shaven man with close-cut hair stood at the top, drying his hands on his gray vest. He helped Dantess aboard, then did the same for Warren. Warren whistled when his feet touched the deck. "Amazing. Who built this? I'd love to see its plans."

The man in the gray vest did not answer. In fact, his expression didn't change at all. "Stand here, please." He indicated a place next to the ladder.

The rest of the crew moved like an organized dance-troop, preparing the ship for travel. There were men and women everywhere: on the main deck, in the sails, coming in and out of the lower decks. It clearly took a lot of people to crew such a floating fortress.

Dantess and Warren stood where they were told until the Sea King pulled himself aboard.

The Sea King smiled broadly. "My first mate Clay will get your friend stowed away. I need you with me. We have to figure out where we're going, right?" The Sea King turned to the man in the gray vest, who nodded back at him.

As the first mate began to lead Warren away, Dantess tensed. "Take care with my soldier," he warned the first mate.

"Your man will be fine," said the Sea King. "As long as we settle his payment at some point, of course." With a wink, he gestured to the aft and began to walk.

Dantess followed him along the main deck and into the doors leading to the spacious rooms in the aft of the ship.

Compared to every single living space Dantess had ever seen on a ship, the captain's room was a palace. Large windows on the far wall looked out over the water. The furniture and trappings were rich and luxurious, adorned with hanging curtains and golden ropes—although the room was not crowded with them. Given the quarters were located on a ship, almost everything was affixed, stowed, or could be at a moment's notice. Unsecured items tended to fly about during a storm, dangerous if they were breakable.

The Sea King maneuvered himself behind a large desk. A number of maps were already unrolled upon it. The captain looked down and smoothed the map out. "So, my new friend, where are we going? Point it out."

Dantess shook his head. "My Longing doesn't work that way. I can't show you where the island is on a map. I only know the direction to my god's Gift." He summoned his Longing, turned, and lifted his hand to point at the Gift—directly out the starboard wall of the quarters.

"Just a direction?" The captain scowled. "That's not as useful as you might think. Ships rarely sail in a straight line."

"Why is that?"

"Navigating the ocean is an art. You have to know the sea, embrace her gifts like winds and currents, and avoid her wrath.

You haven't lived until you've come out the other side of a hurricane. But beyond that, it's wise to avoid enemy waters."

"Enemy waters?" asked Dantess.

The captain smiled. "We might be the biggest ship in the sea, but we're not the only one."

Dantess shrugged. "A direction is all I can offer."

"You waving your finger around also isn't particularly precise. A single degree off now will lead to us missing your island by miles."

"Then it's a good thing I'm traveling with you. I can offer the direction as many times as you need to make sure we don't stray off course."

"Looks like you are my assistant navigator while you're aboard, then," said the Sea King. "Can you at least let me know how far away it is?"

"It must be at least a few days of sailing. It took us that long to reach Seaborn Notch, and we headed the wrong way the whole time. But we *must* get there before the Convergence has ended. We only have about ten days left."

"Good to know. Remember, there's no faster ship than the Leviathan."

As the captain began to draw lines along the intended course, he said, "I'll call you if I need clarification, priest of War. Feel free to rest. We will be at sea for some time."

Dantess nodded, took his leave, and met Clay outside the captain's quarters. The first mate led him down a staircase past multiple decks full of cannons until they ended at the ship's lower berth. There, he opened up a door to a small, unventilated room. Warren was already in the single, hard bunk. He was snoring.

"Both of us?" asked Dantess.

"You can sleep in shifts, if you want," said Clay. "But this is the space we have for you right now." He walked off briskly, leaving Dantess standing there.

Dantess sat on the floor. He couldn't sleep anyway. Too much had happened just in the last day to put it all out of his head. The images from Shattered Peak haunted him, and he couldn't stop thinking about what Varyon did to those poor villagers.

Especially to Twyla's father.

Dantess rooted around in Warren's pack and discovered a small carving knife. While Warren slept, the priest of War idly etched a few lines into the wooden floorboards.

When the sun came up, Dantess left his sleeping
companion and decided to tour the ship. As soon as he was on
deck, he consulted his Longing. The Leviathan was headed in
roughly the right direction, but a slight course correction would
help. As the captain explained, even a small problem now would
lead to a large one eventually.

On the way to the ship's helm, he came upon Twyla,
leaning against the railing and looking out at the rushing sea.
"Good morning, Twyla."

She furrowed her brow, nodded once, and said nothing. In
fact, the tightness in her lips led Dantess to believe she might be
ill.

"Are you all right?" asked Dantess.

"I'm fine. I just need to..." She swallowed. "I need to..." She
bent over the railing and vomited into the water.

Dantess chuckled. "Sailing doesn't agree with you. It
happens to lots of people, but mostly folk who live on land. Be
honest with me. You're no sailor, and neither is Quin. What is your
connection to the Sea King?"

After Twyla's retching softened into labored breathing, she
asked, "What business is it of yours, priest of War?" She wiped her
mouth.

He could sense her anger, probably made worse by her
sickness. The memory of his grandfather questioning her father
flitted through his head, and he realized how insensitive he was
being. "You're right. I didn't mean to interrogate you." Dantess
leaned against the railing as well. "In fact, I wanted to apologize."

"Apologize? To a faithless?"

"We're both *people*. I used to think I was special—not
because I'm a priest, but because my grandfather was so special.
He's a legend. Everyone reveres his name at the temple.

"After what I learned at Shattered Peak, I'm not proud. Not
anymore. His Longing didn't make him a better person. It just
gave him power, and he abused it.

"I'm sorry about what happened to your father, and to
everyone else in the village. They didn't deserve that."

While Dantess spoke, Twyla's jaw dropped. After he was done, she looked like she was going to say something, but then bent over the railing again and coughed.

"I hope you feel better, Twyla." Dantess turned and walked away. As he did, he caught Twyla looking at him with narrowed eyes.

He didn't blame her. Whatever hatred she held toward him, Dantess had it coming. He walked on, his hand twitching.

After checking in with the helm, he decided to wake Warren. Together, they explored the ship and ended up at the bow where Clay was scanning the horizon with a spyglass—often along the ship's aft.

"You won't find the island back there," said Dantess. "We're headed in the right direction. Finally." He pointed forward and noticed a smudge in the air ahead.

"I'm not looking for your island. I'm keeping an eye out for other ships. Last night's lookout reported he saw a ship behind us." Clay looked through the glass again. "But I don't see anything now."

"Why so nervous? The Sea King controls these waters, right?"

"Not *these* waters. We've been sailing in Mary Bones' territory for half a day."

Warren arched his eyebrow. "Who or what is Mary Bones?"

"She sails the Coming Storm, a formidable frigate—maybe the most fearsome vessel afloat, second only to the Leviathan. And she's convinced our captain has a treasure she'd love to get her hands on."

"Does he?"

"Probably. The captain has collected quite a few treasures in his career." Clay lowered the spyglass. "Even so, she'd never dare come after us. The Storm is no match for our cannons."

Now Dantess could see that the smudge ahead was a fog bank, starting to envelope the horizon—and the Leviathan was headed straight into it. "Fog ahead. Will it be a problem?"

"Shouldn't be. It doesn't affect your Longing, right?"

264

"No, but it might affect your spyglass. Hard to use cannons on a ship you can't see."

"Don't worry. We've dealt with fog before," said Clay. "We'll keep a few extra eyes out." He turned to walk away, but Dantess grabbed his arm to stop him.

"Clay, why is your captain doing this?'

The man's eyebrow arched. "Doing what?"

"Putting his whole ship at risk to get me to that island. Am I supposed to believe it's only for a bit of gold?"

Clay stood for a moment with his gaze locked with Dantess', then he answered, "He wants a seat at the table."

Dantess was taken aback. He released Clay's arm. "What?"

"At the Convergence, the priests determine the laws that govern the faithless. Why shouldn't a faithless be there, too? The Sea King has accomplished what no other faithless has done: govern the places where the priests have abandoned. Who better to represent us to the priests? Maybe make things better for all of us?"

Dantess put his hand on his forehead. "He wants to influence the proceedings? He thinks the priests will listen to him? To a faithless? To a *notorious pirate?* Listen to me: if he sets foot on that island, the best thing he can hope for is to be locked up."

"The captain may have an unshakable amount of self-confidence, but he can actually be quite persuasive. He's convinced he can make a difference. To him, to all of us, it's worth the risk. How often do the faithless get such an opportunity? The Convergence happens once every hundred years and, on *that* day, *you* show up. It's fate."

"Your captain is far more idealistic than I gave him credit for."

Clay shrugged. "He's a man of the people, and he believes the people deserve something better." With that, he turned around and walked toward the aft.

After he had left, Dantess asked Warren, "What do you think?"

"It's a more interesting argument than the gold, but less compelling. We know he likes gold, but politics?"

"Not politics, *power*. Governing Seaborn Notch and the other towns gave him a taste, and he knows it's just a matter of time until the temples shut him down. He wants to make it permanent. His ego has convinced him that the priests will listen to him."

The fog crept over the deck. The two stared into the thick of it off the prow.

"Still, this is different," said Warren. "Clay's rhetoric didn't sound like it was coming from a pirate."

"What do you mean?"

"He sounded like a Harbinger. Who, exactly, are we taking to Convergence Island?"

Dantess scoffed. "If they're Harbingers, the last place they'd want to be is an island teeming with priests of War."

The briny mist wrapped around them, stealing their view and leaving them in muffled silence.

When they returned to their cramped quarters, it was late. Warren insisted Dantess lie down in the bunk while he sat on the floor. "You're still healing, and it has been days since you slept."

"It's hard to sleep. I can't stop the images from Shattered Peak from racing through my head."

"Like these?" Warren pointed to the floor next to him. A collection of faces, demons, and beasts were etched into the boards. "Did you carve them?"

"I don't really remember, but given that we're the only ones staying in the room, I suppose it's either me or you—and *you* didn't relive the trauma of your grandfather's mental breakdown and suicide recently, did you?"

Warren shook his head. "I'm worried about you. I know that wasn't easy to go through. It has to be even harder to shake off."

"I don't know if I *should* shake it off," said Dantess, running a hand through his hair. "The things my grandfather did to those poor people. Someone has to pay."

"Not *you*. You didn't do those things. Your grandfather did. You feel the way you do because you're not like him. You care."

Dantess lay on the bunk and stared at the ceiling, thinking about this.

And then everything went crazy.

A huge metal spear, perhaps five feet long, broke through the hull and sent splintered wood flying throughout the room. The spear's tip missed Warren's head by inches and dropped to the ground, trailing a thick chain behind it.

Curious, Warren reached for it, but Dantess pulled him back. "Don't touch it!"

As if on cue, four rods snapped out from the end of the spear, then the chain yanked the mechanism back tight against the wall. The whole ship lurched in that direction.

"We're being boarded!" cried out Dantess. "We have to get to the top deck!"

Dantess pushed himself off the bunk and toward the door, trying his best to keep his balance as the ship tilted back and forth. The hallway was chaotic. Sailors crowded the halls in front of the stairs.

"Make way!" Dantess pushed through the crowd. Even so, progress wasn't quick. By the time he and Warren climbed the stairs and reached the top deck, they entered a war zone.

Another enormous ship had secured itself to the Leviathan's port side with chains and hooks. Sailors from the enemy ship, covered in skeletal war paint, swarmed onto the deck—even swinging over using ropes from the rigging. The Leviathan's crew were fighting the enemy on their own ship, and they were everywhere.

Dantess noticed Clay, squaring off with a man with a skull painted on his face. With an ease obviously born of practice, he ran his opponent through with his sword. Seeing Dantess, Clay pulled his sword from the man now lying on the deck and pointed it up to the flag of the other boat. It depicted a skeleton riding a storm cloud. "That's the Coming Storm. Came on us at night in the fog. We didn't see them in time to use the cannons, and now it's too late."

A flaming projectile arched from the Storm and struck the Leviathan's center mast. The mainsail burst into flames.

Clay's face went white. "Men, save the sail or the ship is next!" He charged off to lead his crew to put out the fire.

"We have to defend this ship," Dantess said to Warren. "We'll never get to the island if it sinks first."

Warren nodded and they both entered the fight.

Dantess channeled his Longing through his token. At first, it was hard to choose from the overwhelming number of targets, but then he instructed his token to start with the closest dozen.

His token choreographed a dance for him: a flurry of action. Dantess took the first skull-faced sailor's sword and then his consciousness within the first few seconds—and then two more fell moments after. Dantess picked one of them up and hurled the man into three compatriots, knocking them to the floor. Warren followed up and made sure they didn't rise soon.

He dodged sword thrusts from both the front and rear, then followed up with a solid kick that knocked the first over the side and into the water, and a shove that threw the other into the stairway. The man tumbled down multiple decks of hard, wooden steps.

The stairs made him think of the others who were quartered down there, namely Twyla and Quin. For a moment, he hoped they had been able to secure a hiding place out of harm's way. That hope was dashed when he heard a girl's scream.

On the foredeck, a skull-faced pirate grabbed Twyla around the neck. She held Quin's hands as two other pirates dragged the girl from her. When Quin lost her grip and the others pulled her away, Twyla tried to scream again, but the chokehold stifled it.

The pirate brought his knife up, ready to plunge it into her breast.

Dantess was too far away to help her himself, so he looked frantically for anything he could use. He jumped to the railing and pulled out a heavy, wooden belaying pin—normally used to secure ropes and sails—and hurled it at the pirate.

The pin struck the pirate square between his eyes. He dropped both the knife and Twyla.

Dantess raced to her, fending off a few pirate attacks along the way. He arrived at the same time as the Sea King, expertly wielding his saber to clear his own path to Twyla.

"Are you all right?" asked Dantess,

"No!" Twyla was almost in tears. "They have Quin! They took her!"

The Sea King grabbed Dantess by the shoulder and locked gazes with him. "You have to get her back." His tone was urgent.

"Get her back? I thought you'd care more about your ship."

"No. *She's* why we were attacked. Mary can't have her." When Dantess hesitated, he pointed at Warren and said, "This is the payment for your man's passage. Get Quin back! Alive!"

Dantess thought about this and nodded. "Warren, look after Twyla. Get her back in her room if you can. I'm off to recover Quin."

He raced to the railing and leapt over the chasm between the two boats. He landed on the Storm's deck in front of a group of skull-faced pirates ready to cross over themselves. No wonder the Sea King asked Dantess to rescue Quin. Anyone else would have been overwhelmed.

"A priest of War?" said one of the pirates. For the moment, they were dumbstruck.

"Strange times, I'll admit," said Dantess. He let his token take control and soon the pirates were lying scattered about their own deck, senseless.

Dantess spotted the two pirates dragging Quin into the captain's quarters in the ship's aft. He raced after them.

A loud blast heralded a fist-sized iron ball slamming into his torso. It threw him off of his feet into the railing closest to the Leviathan. He wheeled over it and barely managed to cling to the rail with a single hand.

"What was that?" he groaned. His ribs ached. He could tell the only thing that saved him was his breastplate and the strength enhanced by his token.

He looked up and saw a swivel gun nearby, a mini-cannon mounted on the ship's railings.

Of course they have swivel guns, he thought. *And I didn't bother to notice.*

Dantess must have been struck by one on the far side of the ship, which meant that the closer one was already loaded and ready to fire. And it was trained where his hand held the railing.

His instincts told him to release his grip just as the gun fired. The railing exploded into pieces.

War, please don't let the two ships bump together with me between them, he prayed.

Dantess dropped like a stone between the two ships' hulls. He trailed his fingertips along the wooden surface, hoping for anything to grab onto. Precious moments flitted away until his right hand abruptly felt a chain, one of those connecting the two ships. Out of reflex, he grasped it, and the sudden halt almost dislocated his shoulder. He screamed in pain, but held on.

After a moment, he swung his other hand up to the chain. By focusing his Longing on strength, he managed to use the chain to climb in through the open cannon port from which the Storm had fired the ship-catcher. He let go only when he could fall onto the gun deck.

No one was expecting an invasion from their gun deck—so the deck was full of cannons, but no pirates.

Dantess collapsed on the floor and took a moment to breathe. His shoulder throbbed, but still worked. He had to keep going. He had no idea why these people wanted Quin, but he needed to return her safely. Every moment she was in Mary's clutches, the likelihood of doing that dropped.

Dantess pushed himself to his feet, ran to the stairs, and raced up. In the chaos up top, he hoped he could get from the stairs to the captain's quarters unseen, but he was willing to sacrifice stealth for speed. As long as they didn't have enough time to train those swivel guns on him again.

When he reached the main deck, he poked his head up. The entrance to the captain's quarters wasn't far, but it was guarded by the two menacing pirates who took Quin. The two swivel guns were manned, but no one was looking in his direction.

Dantess leapt from the stairs and charged the entrance. His token walked him through the moves to defeat the two guards, even with his injured shoulder. First, he kicked one of the pirates' knees. He felt the man's kneecap shatter and the guard dropped. Dantess disarmed the other with the tried-and-true method he taught to his squad. The move swung Dantess around behind his opponent. He was locking his chokehold when something struck both of them, throwing them backward. Together, they slammed against the doors and crashed through into the quarters beyond.

Dantess shook his head, looked down at the pirate lying on top of him, and realized an iron ball—no doubt from the main deck's swivel gun—had penetrated through the man's chest and stopped only when it hit Dantess' armor. He pushed the man off of him and rolled to the side, ensuring he was out of sight of the gunner.

"A priest of War? On the Sea King's ship? That's unbelievable." A woman's voice came from the far side of the quarters. Dantess looked over to see someone standing behind

Quin, holding the girl in front of her. The woman wore no hat, and her hair was dark and wild, curling and flaring out like a storm over cunning, sea-blue eyes. Her ears and nose were pierced with multiple steel rings. Dantess reasoned that this must have been Mary Bones.

"Quin?" said Dantess. "Don't worry. I'm here to rescue you."

Mary Bones laughed. "*You? Rescue her?* Don't you know what she is?"

"A prisoner of a bloodthirsty pirate, looks like."

"Looks are deceiving." She pulled back Quin's hood and revealed that the girl was blind. Not just blind, but missing her eyes. Blank patches of skin covered the places where her eyes should have been.

Mary whispered something into Quin's ear and followed with, "Do it!"

But Quin shook her head. She let out a croaking sob, like Dantess only ever heard from Evil's slaves. And that's when Dantess noticed the steel collar around her neck.

She *was* a slave from Evil!

There was much more to Quin's story than Dantess knew, and it worried him.

"It doesn't matter who or what she is," said Dantess. "I'm taking her back to the Leviathan. I made a deal."

Mary wrapped one arm around Quin's throat and began to pull out a dagger from a scabbard at her hip. "I'll kill her before I let the Sea King take her back."

Quin let out an enraged howl. She brought up both hands and clawed at Mary's face. A finger caught on her nose ring. Mary's eyes opened wide as Quin pulled it down with all her might and tore the ring out.

Mary screamed, let go of Quin, and clutched at her bloody face. By that time, Dantess was already in the air. His kick sent her sprawling. When she landed, she did not move.

"Good work, Quin. Now, we have to leave. I'm going to carry you. Are you good with that?"

Quin nodded and even smiled a bit. He grabbed her up, carefully inched his way to the entrance, and poked his head out. At first, he was happy just to see the swivel guns unmanned. Then he realized that most of the crew on deck had come from the

Leviathan. Mary Bones' sailors were either lying on the deck senseless or awake but bound.

The Sea King won. He had taken the Coming Storm.

And Dantess was about to deliver Quin back onto his ship.

As much as he needed Warren with him, there was no doubt in Dantess' mind that the Sea King got the better of this deal.

PART IV

THE CONVERGENCE

CHAPTER TWENTY-FIVE

THE MORNING SUN was half above the horizon by the time the crew from the Coming Storm had been shackled in the Leviathan's hold, and the Sea King's men were in place to command the enemy ship. Dantess, Warren, Twyla, and Quin stood with the Sea King as he admired the Storm from his own foredeck, newly detached and beginning to catch the wind.

"She's no Leviathan," said the captain, "but the Coming Storm will make a wonderful addition to my fleet. And removing Mary Bones from the seas? Priceless."

"Be honest," said Dantess. "Was that one of the reasons you brought me aboard? To help you take out a competitor?"

The Sea King shrugged. "The possibility may have crossed my mind. But from this point, you don't need to worry about fending off enemy attacks. It should be clear sailing until we reach your island." The Sea King slapped Dantess on the back and began to walk to the aft.

"Wait," called out Dantess. "I just have a few more questions. Mary Bones said some things that don't sit right with me. About Quin."

The Sea King stopped in his tracks and slowly turned back. "Are you sure you want to do this now?"

"What do you mean? Of course I'm sure."

The Sea King sighed. "Clay?" The first mate came running up. "What's ahead of us?"

Clay unrolled a map he held in his hand, perhaps anticipating this request. "It's a little clearer now." He pointed to a specific spot on the map. "The way we're headed, there's only a few islands it could be at this point. We won't know which specific one until we get closer." He rolled up the map. "Now is as good a time as any, I suppose."

Dantess narrowed his eyes. "Time for what?"

"To answer your questions, of course. You want to know why Twyla and Quin sail with us when they're not sailors. You want to know why Mary Bones risked so much to steal the girl from my ship, and why I asked you to retrieve her. Right?"

Confused, the priest of War nodded.

"You've undoubtedly noticed Quin is not a normal girl. She's special, and not in the obvious ways. You see, she holds the artifact of Chaos from Shattered Peak—the one your grandfather was supposed to track down. And you won't believe what it does!"

Dantess' breath caught as he took a step back. "You all need to get away from Quin right now. An artifact of Chaos can be deadly!"

"Oh, don't worry. Us faithless have nothing to fear," said the captain, smiling. "Priests of Order on the other hand..."

Warren stepped next to Dantess. "We had a deal! Safe passage. Whatever she has—"

"I took you as far as I could." The captain pointed to Dantess. "*You* were the one who insisted on knowing what was going on. I knew we couldn't hide this forever. In fact, I'm surprised it took you this long to ask, but I understand. You had a lot on your mind. You want to know about Quin? Girl, go ahead and show him."

Twyla put her hand on Quin's shoulder and said, "It's all right. Show them."

Quin felt inside her cloak and removed a fist-sized chunk of rock. It did not look like an artifact. It wasn't even a particularly notable stone.

Dantess channeled his Longing through his token. Possibilities flooded his view. Off the top, he could see at least sixteen ways to kill the Sea King.

But the Sea King wasn't the threat. It was Quin. Could he bring himself to attack the girl?

"It's time for Quin to earn her keep, Twyla," the captain said. "Let her know."

Warren raised his hands. To Twyla, he cried, "You can't! Dantess saved your lives—both of you!"

Twyla frowned and closed her eyes. When she looked up, her eyes contained steel, but tears as well. "You're a priest. You're Varyon's grandson, even—and he *killed* my father. I'm sorry, Dantess, but this was the deal we made with the Sea King." She wiped her eyes. "Go ahead, Quin. Use the rock."

Terror pushed Dantess into action, overcoming his hesitancy. He let his token take control.

Everything seemed to flow in slow motion. By the time he took two steps toward Quin, a glowing spark emerged from her dark stone. It traced a curling path of fire in the air. After two loops, it shot forth and left a glowing line directly to Dantess' token. When the glowing mote touched the metal, the token exploded into pieces.

Dantess' momentum kept him stumbling forward, but he dropped to the deck.

My token! thought Dantess. *It's gone.*

As if awoken from slumber, his Longing screamed in his brain. He'd never felt the full, naked force of its call, even before his testing. It was the most powerful sensation he'd ever experienced.

"What did you do?" cried Warren.

The Sea King put his hands on his hips. "Quin's rock destroys artifacts of Order. It leaves priests helpless. Like Dantess here." He knelt down next to him. "A priest of War without his token isn't much of a Warrior."

Clay drew his sword, but the captain shook his head. "No, no. Stand down. This is the best part. We're at sea! I've been looking forward to this!"

Dantess climbed unsteadily to his feet. The unfiltered pull of his Gift demanded he come, but he fought it. "This is why those towns don't have priests," he said, trying to focus on anything but the call.

"You're still asking questions? All right. I'll answer—for as long as you can ask." The Sea King put his hands on the girls' shoulders. "Twyla and Quin sail with us when we visit a new town. They help us clear out the priests and establish our own rule. I knew you folk were getting rich collecting the tithe, but I had no idea how much! Now those freed faithless pay the gold to me."

"And the Harbingers?" Dantess put his hand on a mast, trying to keep from chasing after the unrelenting pull.

"Who knew that clearing out a few towns of priests would inspire a movement? As far as I'm concerned, they're a distraction, but one I'm thankful for. As long as they're out there, they take attention away from what I'm doing."

"Why?" Dantess couldn't help it. He began to shuffle toward the railing. "Why did you agree to take me? Regardless of what Clay said, you don't just want a seat at the table."

"Isn't it obvious? Quin can destroy artifacts of Order, and what will we find there? What is calling you right now?"

"No," groaned Dantess. "The Gifts."

277

"Yes! The Gifts of the four most powerful religions. Guarded by priests entirely reliant on their tokens." The Sea King laughed. "Imagine a world without those temples! It will be anarchy. It will be perfect."

Dantess reached the railing. He gripped it with white knuckles, but his Gift called him. It was out there. He wanted—no he *needed*—to go to it. No matter what. With a helpless glance to Warren, he leapt over the rail and into the sea.

When Dantess hit the water, his chain mail shirt and heavy metal breastplate dragged him under. Even his Longing-obsessed brain knew he couldn't swim if he was sinking, so he struggled to pull them off as he dropped like dead weight.

Finally, the breastplate came loose. He cast it away and dragged the heavy chain-linked shirt over his head. When he was free of the weight, he pumped his legs to swim toward the surface.

It was so far away. He barely saw the glimmer of sunlight from above. But he kept fighting, knowing that giving up wouldn't get him to his Gift—and that was all that mattered.

Perhaps ten yards from the surface, he saw something impact the water from above, followed by another object. The first floated, but the second dropped like a stone. As it reached him, he recognized the swiftly sinking object as Warren.

Dantess grabbed him and undid the buckles on his breastplate. Warren loosened the other side and, together, they pulled off the armor and his shirt. Both kicked upward.

When his head broke the surface, Dantess drew huge, desperate breaths of air into his lungs. Warren appeared right after, also coughing and sputtering.

The Leviathan was already distant. Its sails, full with the strong wind, sped the ship toward Convergence Island.

"I have to go," said Dantess. He'd already spent too long here. He needed to reach the Gift.

"No!" said Warren. "You'll drown. Hold on to this barrel. It was all I could grab before I jumped."

The barrel bobbed next to them. Warren grabbed the rim.

But Dantess ignored it. "I can't wait... I have to... the Gift... it's this way..."

Just as he began to swim in the direction of the Leviathan, Warren grabbed him with his free hand. "You'll die! I won't let you die!"

The morning sun glinted off of Warren's hand.

No. Not his hand. A ring.

Something about that ring pierced through the single-minded haze of his Longing. The ring, his grandfather's ring, the one he gave to Warren on their testing day, wasn't just a band of metal. He could sense it.

It had power.

Warren noticed that Dantess had stopped struggling and was staring at his hand. "What? The ring? Do you want it?"

"It's... it's an artifact," Dantess sputtered. "I never knew. It's an artifact of War."

Warren treaded water for the moment it took to slip the ring from his finger. "Take it! Take it!" He held it toward Dantess.

The second Dantess touched the ring, the Longing receded. He could control the urge. He could think. He slipped it on his finger and exhaled in relief. "You saved me, Warren."

Warren kept his grip on the barrel and hugged Dantess with his free arm. "Thank War your grandfather's ring was an artifact. You didn't know?"

"I didn't." Dantess grabbed onto the barrel's rim. "My da gave it to me when I was young. He didn't tell me."

With that thought, he abruptly understood why he never felt the call of War's Longing before he tested. The ring blunted it. Had his father known? Had that been his plan all along, to keep him from joining the temple?

They bobbed in the middle of the ocean, hanging onto a barrel, no land in sight anywhere.

Dantess gazed at the blue expanse. "Now that I'm not swimming to my death, what can we do?"

"Pray," said Warren.

After an hour, Dantess and Warren grew tired of pulling the barrel in the direction of Convergence Island.

"This isn't getting us anywhere," said Dantess. "I don't think we're measurably closer to the island."

"That's not the point," said Warren. "The exercise is keeping us from freezing."

"I can't keep it up. Without my token, I don't know which is going to give out first: my grip or my legs."

"Even without your token, you're in better shape than most. You can hold out. I know you can."

"Until what?"

"Until... until our prayers are answered. Hopefully." Warren turned and scanned the horizon behind them. "Remember that Clay mentioned spotting a boat trailing the Leviathan?"

Dantess spat out a mouthful of water after dipping too low. "I thought that was the Coming Storm."

"Maybe. But I'm hoping it was something else." Warren took a deep breath. "I didn't want to say anything to get your hopes up, but I might have... suggested... to Motti that they follow us in the Mourning Glory."

"But I ordered them back to the temple!"

"That's what you said to *Captain Sacquidge,* but you ordered Motti only to keep the squad safe, which I'm sure he did. I just suggested an alternate route to do that."

"You could have put them all in danger."

"With the Sea King focused on our trip, he wouldn't be patrolling his wake. I figured it would be safe for the Mourning Glory to follow."

"That wasn't your decision to make. You countermanded my orders," said Dantess flatly.

"Not technically. Besides, you weren't thinking straight after Shattered Peak. It was obvious the Sea King couldn't be trusted, but in that state, you would have agreed to anything."

Dantess scowled. "How can I trust you if you always have your own agenda? That same reasoning lost me the Game of War."

"That was different, and I regret it more than I can say. I did this because I care about you. I owe you everything. I'd give up my own life to keep you safe." Warren huffed. "Do you really want to argue about this when the Mourning Glory may be our *only* hope to survive?"

Dantess went silent, so Warren quieted too. For a while, the only sound was the lapping of the waves against the barrel and the chattering of their teeth.

More than once, Dantess found himself slipping away. The cold and exhaustion, combined with lack of sleep, made it hard to keep his eyes open.

Wouldn't it be easier to drop? he thought. *I'm so tired. Why bother fighting?*

"Stay with me, Dantess." Warren shook him.

Dantess' chattering teeth made it hard to talk. "I w-w-want to rest."

"No. You need to stay awake."

"Why? I g-g-gave the location of the Gifts to the one p-person in the world who can destroy them. What's the p-p-point now?"

As he said that, a dot appeared on the horizon.

"*That's* the point! It's a ship. I know it is. Just hang on!"

Indeed, as the dot grew closer, it became obvious it was a single-sail boat.

"It's the Mourning Glory!" said Warren. "It has to be! What other boat that size would be crazy enough to cross the open sea?"

But when it closed to a mile out, it became clear that the boat would miss them by a huge margin.

"Hey! Over here!" Warren called out. "We're here!" He waved one hand with all the energy he could muster.

The boat did not change course. If it continued, it would miss them completely.

"Dantess," Warren begged. "The ship is there. You have to help me. They're not going to see us. They're going to pass us by!"

Dantess' eyes were closed. All his energy was focused in the single hand holding on to the barrel. And he didn't know how long that would last.

"There's a boat right there! You need to help me signal it."

He heard Warren's words. Still, it was hard to break the apathy he'd settled into. Even if they were rescued, what was the point? Dantess had doomed the world with his selfish quest.

Warren slapped Dantess across the face. It prompted no reaction, so he did it again. "Wake up!" When Dantess' eyes stayed closed, he drew his hand back for one more strike, but Dantess grabbed it before it could land.

281

"S-s-stop, or you'll regret it," growled Dantess. His anger burned away the fog that he'd been drifting in.

"The boat! It's there! Now!" He raised his hand again and waved to it. "Hello! We're over here!" His voice was rough and quiet from thirst.

Dantess saw the boat. It looked like the Mourning Glory, and it was close to passing them by. With a sigh, Dantess summoned up what energy he could, raised his hand, and croaked out, "We're here." He waved his hand back and forth. "Look over here! See us!"

They didn't. He put everything he had into one more bellow. "*See me!*"

With the last syllable, Dantess felt his Longing stir. And, more than was natural, the ring on his raised hand caught the sunlight. It shone like a flare.

A few moments later, they heard the distant cry of multiple voices on the boat's deck carry over the water's surface. The prow came about to point towards the two.

"They saw us!" said Warren. "They're coming!"

Once, Dantess might have given his dead grandfather credit for the ring's miraculous glow. He would have thought Varyon was looking out for him. Now, he knew the ring was just another artifact.

Just another lie.

Motti hauled Dantess and Warren aboard the Mourning Glory, drenching the deck in seawater. Warren clasped Motti in a hug. His teeth chattering, he said, "You made it! I thought for sure you'd lost us."

"We almost did," said Motti. "Especially here at the end. Thank War we saw that flash! What was that?"

Shivering, Dantess said nothing but held up his ring. The squad all nodded. They knew of Warren's ring, although they were a little surprised to see it on Dantess' finger.

Captain Sacquidge took a pull from her pipe and blew a ring of white smoke. "We kept following the same direction as close as we could. When that fog rolled in, I thought for certain we'd never see you again, but then the Leviathan caught fire in the middle of it. The flames lit up the fog like a signal torch we couldn't miss."

"What *was* that?" Khalista asked. "What happened to you two? How did you end up in the ocean clinging to a barrel?"

"It's a long story, but an exciting one," started Warren. "Let me tell you—"

Dantess held up his hand, interrupting Warren. "My thanks, Captain, for rescuing us. I need a little time alone to rest and warm up a bit. Can I use your hold again?"

"Of course," said the captain, surprised. "But what of your mission?"

"We still have much to do," said Warren, firmly. "The Sea King is on the way to Convergence Island with a weapon that destroys artifacts of Order. He destroyed Dantess' token with it!"

Dantess winced. "That's true. I'm not much of a priest of War anymore. I don't have rank or a token or even gold to pay you to take us back. Maybe they'll compensate you when we return, if the temple is still there. Do you know the way from here?"

"We can't just go back!" exclaimed Warren. "Not only do we still have to save our parents, but now we need to save the world from the anarchy that the Sea King will unleash!"

"I'm done, Warren." Dantess' shoulders slumped. He looked at the deck. "Everything I've tried to do just made things worse. But you do what you want. You don't listen to my orders anyway. Maybe you never should have." With the rest of the squad and crew staring in disbelief, Dantess climbed down into the hold.

He crawled into the rope hammock, pulled a blanket over his shivering torso, and closed his eyes.

But sleep still eluded him. The dark just summoned his grandfather's tormenting images.

His hands twitched.

It was funny. He had tried to live up to Varyon's legacy all his life. Now he'd never escape it.

"You've been busy," said Warren.

Dantess had pushed the hold's spare cargo to the corners. In the space he'd cleared, he methodically carved monstrous images using the sharp edge of a pike pole on the hold's wooden floor and walls.

"What do you want?" Dantess asked without looking up. He continued to scratch the lines of a figure covered in flames.

"The captain would like confirmation of our course. You're the only one who knows where the Gift is."

"So," Dantess stopped, "you decided to ignore me again. Why am I not surprised?"

"When you gave us those orders, that wasn't you. This," Warren gestured to the carved images throughout the hold, "is not you."

"It *is* me. I am Varyon's grandson after all." Dantess returned to his carving.

"No. I know you. I've known you longer than anyone. You're not a quitter. Especially with the stakes so high."

Dantess looked up again, tears trickling down his cheeks. "That's why I need to quit! Every decision I make turns out to be the worst thing I could do. What happened when I showed Kevik where my father hid those Harbingers? Our parents were taken prisoner. How about testing at War? Jyn followed me into the temple and died! And then, entering the Game when I wasn't ready? I lost everything I had left."

"But—" began Warren.

"And I can't stop making it all worse! I tried to save my father, and what did I accomplish? I discovered my grandfather wasn't a hero. Instead, he was a raving murderer whose delusions are now burned into my brain. And then I pointed the Sea King toward the Gifts of the four most powerful religions at the one time they're vulnerable." Dantess paused to catch his breath. "I don't blame you, Warren. *Of course* you ignore my orders. Given my history, that's probably the wisest course of action."

For a moment, neither boy spoke. The only sound was the scratching of the pike pole blade on wood.

"Dantess," Warren began, "you are not your grandfather, neither your idealized image of him nor the person you discovered him to be. You are also not your father, who made his own choices and is more responsible for his fate than you. Your problem is you've been trying to live up to both of them without realizing who *you* are."

Warren knelt beside him. "You aren't the worst parts of those two, you're the *best* of them. You're a priest with the power that title gives you, but who still cares about *everyone*, including the faithless. You risk everything to help those in the most need. You gave hope to Mother Nettle when others would have killed her dreams. You chased after the slim chance we could save our parents, even knowing the odds were against us. Not once have you sought glory or riches like others in the priesthood. You've done *everything* for others.

"There's a reason you inspire loyalty in those closest to you. Your squad would follow you to the ends of the world. My sister *loved* you. I would *die* for you. Do you think we'd feel that way about some idiot who screws everything up?"

Dantess stopped carving. He looked up at Warren with new tears in his eyes.

Warren continued. "You're not perfect—War knows none of us are—but you can still make a difference. Without you, all we have are the Keviks and Sea Kings and Morghausts of the world deciding our fates. Do you want to leave the future up to them?"

Dantess dropped the pike blade from his hand. "No."

"Neither do I."

"I'm not a proper priest without my token." Dantess stood up.

"Your token isn't what makes you special. We need you leading us. We *all* need you."

Dantess wiped his eyes. "What can I do?"

"You can start by telling the captain where we need to sail."

Dantess wore one of Navar's shirts as he stood on deck. It fit him loosely, but felt much better than the chain mail insult he'd been wearing for days. He still had no idea what he would find on Convergence Island, nor how he and his squad could save his parents or the Gifts, but Warren's words had convinced him that, if he did nothing, nothing good would happen.

"Land ahead!" a crewman cried from the bow. "And two ships!"

Captain Sacquidge snapped a spyglass up to her eye. "It's the Leviathan squaring off against another vessel." She peered closer. "Both ships are damaged."

"What is the other vessel?" asked Dantess.

285

"A frigate." She leaned forward. "The Righteous Fury. No question."

Even this far away, the repeating thunder of the Leviathan's cannons carried over the water.

"Do you think our parents are aboard that ship?" said Warren.

Dantess squinted, but couldn't make out what was happening, only tiny flashes and the thin trail of rising smoke. "Likely. The Convergence isn't over. I doubt they'd transfer prisoners to Evil until the event was done." He turned to the captain. "Is there anything we can do?"

Sacquidge scoffed. "Keeping away is our best bet. The Glory has no cannons. We'd just give them another target." To Navar, she called, "Avoid the area. Get us to the island beyond without getting anywhere near to the fight."

"Aye," responded Navar. He swung the helm, and the ship banked to port.

"What's happening?" asked Warren.

Sacquidge put the glass back to her eye. "They're trading broadsides." After a series of blasts, she flinched. "The Leviathan's cannons are devastating. The Fury is aflame. Still sailing, though. It looks like..."

"What?" demanded Dantess.

"The Fury is using her maneuverability to swing around behind the Leviathan. Compared to that behemoth, she can pivot on a mark. Maybe she'll get an opportunity to—"

"No," said Dantess, his eyes opening wide. "They can't do that. The Leviathan has rear cannons."

They all heard the explosion of three rows of cannons tearing through the Fury's hull.

The captain's jaw dropped. "The Fury is listing. Two masts gone, the other aflame. The crew is leaping off. It's done for."

"Prisoners are still locked up in there," said Warren. "They'll burn. Or drown. Can we rescue them? Please?"

"By the time we reached them, they'd be dead already," Sacquidge replied. "And so would we. I just pray the Leviathan is too distracted to see us."

While the Glory sailed far around the Leviathan and the smoking wreck of the Righteous Fury, the island became more visible. It wasn't a paradise of beaches as Dantess had expected. Instead, the whole island seemed to be made of countless rocky outcroppings sticking up from the water. Some touched at the top in natural bridges, but most stood separately from each other. Those stone spires grew in width and height towards the island's center until they merged into a mountain of stone.

In all, the island was a desolate collection of rocks. There were no signs of life anywhere.

"Are you sure that's the right island?" asked Sacquidge. "There are no beaches. No docks. Nothing but rock."

"It's Convergence Island," Dantess answered in a dead tone. "My Longing confirms it. And the..." He paused to swallow, hard. "...Fury being here does, too."

"We don't know if our parents were aboard. And even if they were," Warren swallowed, "we have to keep moving forward. They're not the only people we're fighting for."

Captain Sacquidge swung her spyglass back to the Leviathan. "They've launched a longboat. Two longboats. Looks like they're going to try to use them to navigate that rocky mess. It's certainly too tight to take the Leviathan in."

"How about us?" asked Dantess.

"What do you mean?"

"The Leviathan's too large to enter, but what about the Glory? Can we fit? If we can get to the council before them, we can warn them about what's coming. The Glory is much faster than a longboat, and my Longing will guide us in."

Captain Sacquidge raised her eyebrow. "Navar? You perform miracles back at Seaborn Notch, but do you think you can squeeze the Glory into that maze of rocks?"

"Channels look deep enough. Shouldn't be a problem," Navar answered.

"Then take us in," said the captain. "But be careful."

Navar scoffed and headed toward the forest of stone towers.

As the Glory began to slip into one of the many openings between the stone spires, the lookout yelled, "Two more ships behind us! They're rounding on the Leviathan."

Dantess asked for the captain's spyglass and scanned for the ships. "It's the Tranquility and the Seven Stars—two of the other temple ships, from Good and Law. They're frigates, too."

"I wish them better luck than the Fury," said Warren. "Maybe they can rescue survivors from the wreckage."

"Maybe," said Dantess, but he knew, by the time they'd be able to do so, anyone still aboard the Fury would be dead.

"Where's Evil's ship?" asked Warren.

"That's a good question. It's not unlike them to hide. Priests of Evil tend to rely on War for protection. Hence the alliance."

"Which way?" called Navar from the helm. "This is a maze!"

Indeed, the rocky outcroppings became both more numerous and varied in shapes and sizes the deeper the Glory penetrated. Some stuck up on their own, some connected with others, some larger ones even had tunnels that curved out of sight.

"The tunnel to port," answered Dantess. "Enter that, if you can."

"You sure there's an exit?" asked Navar.

"My Longing tells me that's the way. But it can't tell me if we'll fit."

Navar chuckled. "I'll make us fit." His smile fell when the hull rubbed against one of the rocky sides with a screech. "Sorry."

The captain winced at the sound. "Each time we scrape anything, I'm adding thirty gold to your tab, priest of War."

"Worth it," said Dantess.

The stones seemed endless, and each maneuver was a nerve-wrenching scrape through passages never meant for passage. Dantess suspected there were few pilots capable of navigating these tight channels, but he had faith in Navar. Still, he wondered what would happen if they ever found themselves in a dead end with no way to turn. He prayed his Longing would not lead them astray.

Through breaks in the rock forest, Dantess used the spyglass to try and spot the battle behind them. While he failed at that, he did discover something unexpected.

"That's a mast," said Dantess, "See, up there? But its flag doesn't look like it belongs to any of the three ships we know of."

"Is it Evil's ship?" asked Warren.

"I don't think so." Once the wind unfurled the flag enough, Dantess recognized it: a skeleton riding a storm cloud. "No, it's the Coming Storm! The Sea King must have brought both ships."

"What's it doing? Is it joining the battle against the Tranquility and the Seven Stars?"

"It's headed the other way. Maybe it's searching for another way in?"

"Or maybe it's searching for Evil's ship," said Warren. "If I were the Sea King, I wouldn't want another enemy ship at my back out here. They're securing the island."

"The Leviathan must be pretty confident if it doesn't even want the Storm's help against two frigates."

"Maybe the Sea King is overconfident. Let's hope."

Soon, the breaks in the rock canopy all but disappeared. Now, the Glory sailed through one cavern after another. They left the sunlight behind, so the crew lit lanterns and torches.

"I can't see far enough ahead to keep sailing," said Navar.

The captain called out, "Drop the sail. We'll use poles to keep us from the sides. The current seems to be going in our direction."

They took down the mainsail. Everyone except Dantess picked up a pole and stationed themselves around the deck, pushing the Glory away from the cavern walls and shoving them deeper into the tunnel. Dantess took a lantern and stood on the bow, holding it out and peering into the stony darkness.

"Are we getting close?" called the captain.

"I think so," answered Dantess. "Starboard turn ahead, into that tunnel!"

Navar wrenched the helm to point the rudder to starboard, and his squad heaved against the cavern wall on the left. As they entered, Dantess pushed against the tunnel opening with his hand. Together, they nudged the prow into the tunnel with only a couple of major scrapes.

"This is getting expensive, priest of War," said Sacquidge.

But Dantess wasn't listening. Not only did the sweet song of his Longing fill his spirit, but he could see with his own eyes that the tunnel ahead opened up to a huge cavern. A column of otherworldly, slowly pulsing light poured from a circular hole in the ceiling down into the water below.

They were here. They had made it.

The Convergence of the Divine!

CHAPTER TWENTY-SIX

MUCH OF THE cavern was dark, but reflections from the fountain of light sparkled along the water and revealed the edges of the expansive pool.

"The Gift is up there," said Dantess, pointing to the hole in the ceiling.

"That may be, but it's a hundred feet up," said the captain. "There must be another way."

"How about that?" asked Warren. He indicated a landing not far from the tunnel they used to enter. About six longboats were already tied off there. The landing led to a dark tunnel—carved, not natural, and crowned with the symbol of War atop the entrance.

"Did the Sea King beat us here?" asked Motti.

Warren shook his head. "No, those are longboats from the Fury. I think each temple has their own landing. This is War's. Evil, Good, and Law must be elsewhere in the cavern."

"Navar, get me close enough to the landing so I can swim, then move away," said Dantess. "I'm going in, alone. If it all goes wrong—not unlikely, I suspect—then I want you far enough away that you can escape if anyone else comes back through."

"You're not going alone." Warren crossed his arms, and the squad nodded.

"I am. Faithless aren't allowed at the meeting. If you came, any of you, they wouldn't listen to me." Dantess placed his hand on Warren's shoulder. "You know I'm right."

Warren locked gazes with Dantess, but then looked down, nodding.

The Glory swung towards the landing. "This is as close as I get," said Navar. "Go if you're going."

Each of his squad came and hugged Dantess. The last was Warren. When he was close, he whispered, "They won't want to hear what you have to say. They may not even believe you. Make them."

Dantess broke the hug, nodded, and leapt over the railing into the dark water. As the Glory drifted away from the landing, Dantess swam to it, pulled himself up, and walked into the tunnel.

The tunnel was dark, but he could still see—perhaps from the light behind him, or from dim light bouncing around the corners ahead. The tunnel took him on a journey of halls, stairs, and ramps. After a while, he wasn't sure how high he climbed, but by the growing amount of light after each turn, he knew the meeting chamber couldn't be far.

Soon, he came upon a huge archway constructed of massive stone blocks. For a moment, he hid behind the lowest block simply to stare at the wonder of the chamber beyond.

The room was massive and round and appeared like a domed amphitheater. Along the edges were carved stone stands, in which priests sat, watching. Each temple took a quadrant of the room—Evil in one quarter, War in another, Good and Law in their own as well.

In the center, a table—also carved from the rock—encircled a hole in the center of the floor, the hole he'd seen from below. High priests and their top-ranking assistants sat at that table and spoke to each other with animation.

None of this was what Dantess stared at.

Above the table hung a massive metal brace in the shape of a cross, encrusted with surefire crystals. At each of the four ends of the cross, the four Gifts were affixed: the red crown of War, the black diamond of Evil, the perfect, white pearl of Good, and the yellow, multi-faceted ring of Law. The surefire crystals transferred light from the pulsing Gifts through the brace, up its chain, and into crystals embedded throughout the ceiling.

The effect was astonishing.

Dantess had only ever seen the random patterns of sunlight striking naturally-occurring crystals in the mines, and that by itself was spellbinding. But everything about this display was purposeful, from the placement of each crystal to the light that flowed from the Gifts.

At times, the light from one Gift would outshine the others and it would slowly overtake the pattern on the ceiling. After watching for mere moments, Dantess realized the incredible mosaic above acted like an animated illustration of the discussion taking place below—victories, defeats, feints, agreements, all lit by the power of the gods.

It was the most sacred thing Dantess had ever witnessed. It was overwhelming. How could he interrupt it?

Even distracted by the scenery, Dantess couldn't miss Morghaust's imposing figure, his gleaming breastplate reflecting the colors of the crystals above. He slammed his hand down onto the table. "How long will we allow the faithless to use the law to their advantage? The Harbingers of Chaos prove that any one of them is capable of turning against us. By law, every priest *must* have the right to exterminate any faithless for whatever reason. Any less puts priests in danger."

The crown above glowed red and the light flowed into the ceiling.

"But, Morghaust, do you trust *every* priest to judge the faithless?" responded the woman with a thin pointed nose and golden robes. Dantess recognized her as Solitri, the high priestess of Good. "I've known priests who would be... overzealous with such power."

The light of the white pearl infiltrated the cracks of the red blaze.

"Every priest was called by their god," Morghaust responded. "We are the gods' voice in the world. Even the least of us should be able to render judgment!"

Sar Kooris, the high priest of Evil, tapped at the table idly with his long-nailed finger, the noise clearly annoying Solitri. He rose from his seat and chimed in. "I agree. The laws that prevent us from doing what comes naturally are quite annoying."

"You have free rein inside your temple, Kooris," said Vanrose, the high priest of Law. "There are more than enough victims there for you. Outside, you *must* follow the law."

The high priestess of Good spread her hands. "Morghaust, you know as well as I how much latitude we have to deal with the faithless. Our gods trust the judgment of their high priests, as long as we keep everything stable. Perhaps the Harbingers of Chaos' movement is a reaction to the temples being *too* harsh in our treatment of the faithless."

"*Too harsh?*" bellowed Marghaust. "It's our *softness* that has inspired the Harbingers. They push the boundaries to see how much they can get away with. A purge would not be out of order. Rid the faithless towns and cities of any Harbinger influence. Then we'll have stability."

Dantess shook off the trance brought on by both the conversation and show of lights. He knew time was running out. He gathered his courage and stepped forward, his footsteps echoing throughout the chamber. "Forgive me, but I must interrupt," Dantess choked out in a subdued voice.

With everyone's attention on the table, no one noticed Dantess.

"A purge would lessen the tithe," said Vanrose. "Is that something you would risk? It would affect us all."

"Long-term stability over a short-term lack of gold?" said Morghaust. "I find that acceptable. Agreed?"

"Agreed," said Sar Kooris.

Dantess cleared his throat. "Excuse me. I *must* have your attention."

All eyes turned to look at Dantess. Kevik, sitting in the stands, shot up and began to work his way around those seated in front of him, his eyes blazing with hatred and determination.

"Who is that?" asked the high priest of Law.

Kaurridon, silent until now, stood up from his seat at the table. "Is that you, Dantess? How did you get here? Where is your armor?"

"I apologize for the interruption, but I don't have time for explanations. The Convergence is under attack. The Sea King is here. He's already sunk the Righteous Fury. Everyone aboard is dead."

The crowd gasped.

Kaurridon clutched the edge of the table and bowed his head. "Are you sure?"

"There was nothing I could do." Dantess' breath caught. "My father was on that ship."

Kaurridon shook his head. "No. The prisoners—including your father—were transferred to Evil's vessel."

"They're alive?" For a moment, Dantess allowed hope to rise in his chest, but that moment was enough for Kevik to cross the space and plow his shoulder into Dantess' back. They both slid forward on the floor toward the round table in the center.

"You dare come here?" Kevik straddled Dantess' back and slammed his head into the stone floor. "You interrupt these sacred proceedings?" He slammed it again. "*I'm* the Guardian. Protecting the Convergence is *my* duty, remember?" He leaned in to whisper, "You're not going to make me look like a fool."

Dantess was dazed. Blood trickled from his nose and lip.

"You're killing him, Kevik," said Kaurridon. "He's not fighting back. In fact, I don't think he even has his token."

Kevik stood and dragged Dantess up from the floor. "He was never much of a priest of War. It makes sense he lost his token. It will make this so much easier."

Kevik pulled back his fist and slammed it into Dantess' face. The force sent him tumbling onto the table behind him. The priests seated there all scrambled out of the way.

Kevik pointed to Dantess. "He cheated in the Game of War. He disrupted the Convergence. His father is a Harbinger sympathizer! If those pirates are out there, he probably led them here! How many rules does he have to break until everyone realizes what I do? He's no priest. He's a disgrace. He's a traitor."

Dantess shook his head, groaned, and crawled backwards on the table, away from Kevik.

Kevik laughed and grabbed his leg. "No one's going to stop me, Boot. I'm going to finish you in front of everyone."

The look in Kevik's eyes convinced Dantess that he was serious. Kevik was about to kill him. In desperation, Dantess raised his hand. "You're wrong. I *am* a priest. So says *War*."

He channeled his Longing through his ring. The light from the Gifts above reflected from it in a bright flash that blinded not only Kevik, but everyone else in the room as well.

Kevik's grip loosened enough for Dantess to scramble free, but Kevik launched himself on the table after him. Dantess kept backing away until he found himself at the other edge of the table.

Dantess looked around at the priests filling the room and found only the chaos he'd introduced into the Convergence. There was no support there. No one would listen to him now. With nowhere else to go, he leaned back and dropped through the hole in the floor toward the distant water below.

And prayed he'd survive the fall.

The water's impact hurt worse than any of Kevik's blows. It was almost impossible to hold his breath while he struggled to reach the surface. He commanded his limbs to push him upward, and somehow, they did. When he broached the surface, he sucked air into his desperate lungs.

"Captain! Warren!" Dantess sputtered. "Are you here?"

"Here!" Warren replied, not too far away. "We're coming."

The Glory drifted over and, when they were close enough, Warren pulled Dantess onto the deck.

"What happened?" asked Motti.

"The worst you could imagine," said Dantess, collapsing on the deck and holding his bleeding head. "So far, my record of screwing everything up is intact. In fact, the only good outcome is that I got away from—"

Something heavy splashed next to the boat.

"What was that?" asked Warren.

Even in his breastplate armor, Kevik broke through the surface, breathing easily.

Warren stepped between the huddled Dantess and Kevik, still in the water. "Protect Dantess!" The squad surrounded him.

In only a few strokes, Kevik reached the boat. He removed his favorite dagger, plunged it into the hull, and used it to pull himself up to the deck. Leisurely, he reclaimed the dagger, stood, and addressed Dantess' squad. "Get out of my way."

His squad fought admirably. Some even landed a few blows. But they never had a chance against Kevik. As the boat drifted underneath the pillar of light, one by one, Dantess' squad fell.

Warren was the last standing. "You bastard. You killed my sister. I'll do the same to you if I can."

"Your sister," said Kevik, kicking Khalista in the head to ensure she stayed down. "Who was she again?"

Warren screamed and launched himself at Kevik, who sidestepped his attack and struck the back of his neck. Warren dropped like a sack of potatoes.

"Anyone else?" asked Kevik. "I think you're out of squad members."

"Even so." Navar kicked Kevik in the back. As the priest of War went sprawling, Navar removed his shirt. "There's something you should see, priest of War."

Kevik growled, turned, and looked at the three-eyed bird on Navar's chest. His eyes went wide. "What... what is that?"

Navar walked up and kicked Kevik in the head. "A memory for you." He straddled Kevik with his chest in full view. "Look at it.

Learn your history." He pounded Kevik's face, whose expression was one of desperation and madness.

"No, stop! Make it stop!" Kevik yelled, shaking.

"I will." Navar punched Kevik in the nose, breaking it. It spurted a fountain of blood.

Kevik stopped shaking for a moment. In between Navar's blows, he covered his hands with his own blood and then smeared them onto Navar's tattoo. It wasn't long until the bird was effectively covered.

Kevik smiled. "Your trick doesn't work anymore." He used both fists to punch Navar in the chest. Navar flew up over the deck and into the water.

Face dripping red, Kevik staggered up.

Dantess stood on the deck directly under the shower of light from above, next to the hatch leading down to the hold.

Kevik saw him. "It's just you and me, Dantess. Finally. You have to admit, after everything, that I'm better than you. I want to hear the grandson of the great Varyon say I'm the best Warrior in history before you die."

"You're strong, Kevik," said Dantess, "and fast. You with your token and me without, I can't beat you."

"So, you admit it? You give up?"

"No." Seeing Kevik fight Navar reminded Dantess of one thing: sometimes the token of War could be a vulnerability. Dantess stepped to the Glory's open hatch and jumped down.

Kevik growled. "Just admit it so I can kill you!" He jumped into the hatch after Dantess...

...and found himself in the middle of a room covered with monstrous carvings. The column of light pouring in through the hatch highlighted every etching on every surface: floors, walls—even on the crates. No matter where Kevik looked, he could not escape them.

Kevik screamed. He grabbed his head in his hands. "What... What are these?"

"My grandfather's gift to all priests. Tucked away in a corner of your token is madness, just waiting to be summoned."

Kevik collapsed on the ground, shaking. "It's horrible. They're coming for me. For us all! There's no escape."

"Welcome to my world, Kevik."

Kevik grimaced, closed his eyes, and rose to one knee.

Dantess kicked him in the jaw, sending him back onto the ground. Out of reflex, Kevik opened his eyes. The carving of a giant flaming spider greeted him from the floor, and he screamed again.

"You can fight me, Kevik. Just stop using your token. I don't have one, so prove you're better. Fight me on even terms."

Kevik rose again, eyes open. "I can do that. I don't need the token to beat you."

Dantess nodded. Even tired and injured, he wanted this fight more than anything. Here was the man who had done everything he could to ruin, hurt, and destroy Dantess and everyone he held dear.

He locked up his father.

He assaulted and killed Jyn.

Dantess pulled from all of his training sessions with his squad. He had drummed countless techniques into their heads. Even without his token, he had a repertoire of options at his command.

When he launched his attack, it was obvious Kevik hadn't done the same work. The first punch landed without problem. The second slipped by a clumsy block. And the feint that followed opened up an opportunity for a devastating kick in the midsection that knocked Kevik across the hold.

"Where's your training, Kevik? Haven't you ever fought without your crutch?"

Kevik launched himself at Dantess, but without his token's enhanced speed, he moved like a lumbering bull. His target turned and dodged, just as Kevik was about to slam into him. Instead, Kevik collided with the wall.

"You're slower than the token has tricked you into thinking. And weaker. You're no legend. You're not even the best Warrior here."

Kevik rose, slower this time and bleeding from new wounds. "You see my marks? My rank says I'm the best. Better than you!" He pushed himself up using a crate.

"Not without your token." Dantess' fist connected with Kevik's jaw with an uppercut that plowed Kevik back into the wall. "You've lost, Kevik."

"Not to you. Never to you." He pushed himself up again. "I'm a priest! The token is the power of my god flowing through my veins! It's my birthright! Why should I fight without it?" Strength seemed to return to his limbs. He pulled his dagger from

298

his boot and leapt forward. The attacks were so swift, Dantess couldn't avoid a slash to his shoulder. "See? I can beat you!"

But then Kevik saw the three-eyed bird carved on the floor. His eyes opened wide and then went blank. "It's here. It's everywhere. Chaos will take us all!"

He threw himself back against the wall, his gaze staring at unseen horrors, the dagger gripped tight in his hand.

Dantess thought about telling Kevik to stop channeling, but it was too late. He made his choice, and he knew what waited for him when he did so. While Dantess watched, Kevik dragged the dagger across his own throat, then collapsed to the floor, eyes still staring.

Dantess waited as Kevik gurgled his last few breaths. He walked over, closed Kevik's eyes, and removed his token.

His mission far from over, despite everything that happened, one thing hadn't changed: Dantess was a priest of War.

He would need that token for what was coming next.

CHAPTER TWENTY-SEVEN

DANTESS SHOOK WARREN awake. The boy opened his eyes and noticed the token on Dantess' belt. "Is that Kevik's? Is he...?"

"Dead," said Dantess. "By his own hand and with the dagger he used to kill Jyn. He channeled through his token even though he knew what would happen. That's how much he couldn't bear to lose."

"Is everyone all right?"

"Everyone aboard is alive. Hurt, but alive." Dantess stood up. "And what's more, our parents are alive, too."

"They weren't killed on the Fury?" Warren's face broke into a smile.

"No. They were transferred to Evil's ship."

Warren's face fell again. "But Evil's ship is being hunted by the Coming Storm. If it finds her..."

"Exactly." Dantess began to pace. "What should I do? If we wait here, we might be able to help defend against the Sea King and Quin, but the priests up there are probably already coming for us. They think I'm a traitor. If they catch me—especially if they see Kevik's body—I'm done for." Dantess looked around the cavern. "And every minute our parents spend locked up aboard Evil's ship, they're vulnerable."

Warren thought about this. "Why did we come to Convergence Island?"

"To save our parents."

"We thought they were dead, and they're not—but they *will* be if we don't move quickly. We can come back to help after we've rescued them."

Dantess struggled with this, but then nodded. "I agree. It's too dangerous to stay, and they need our help. But how do we find the ship?"

"I have an idea about that. The Righteous Fury was sailing out there." He pointed to the tunnel they entered through. "They would have dropped anchor as close to War's landing as possible. Good's landing is there," he pointed to the left, at another exit tunnel next to a collection of docked longboats, "and Law's landing is there." He pointed to the right at a third dock. "Remember when they came to attack the Leviathan? Extend the line outside the island, and those were their starting positions.

"Evil's landing should be over there." He pointed across the cavern to the far side. "If I'm correct, their ship would anchor as close to that landing as they could get. That passage next to the landing should lead us right to them."

"If they haven't moved," said Dantess. "Or hid."

Warren shrugged. "But at least we'll have a starting point to search from."

"Captain? If you would, let's see where that tunnel leads." Dantess pointed to the exit cave on the far side.

"Navar?" Captain Sacquidge called out. "You up to it?"

Navar—bruised and wet, but standing tall behind the helm—nodded. "Get on the poles, you lot. It's going to be tight."

As the boat was about to cross into the tight cavern ahead, Dantess turned to Warren. "One more concern: how are we going to extract our parents from Evil's ship? I won't attack them. They're just priests following the law."

"They're not just priests, they're priests of *Evil*," said Warren. "And priests of Evil are greedy. I have an idea. If I'm right about how much they value their tithe, they might just hand our parents over."

Those aboard the Mourning Glory were familiar with what awaited them: a maze of passages and outcroppings with no room to spare.

"Which way?" cried out Navar, more than once.

"Your best judgment, Navar," responded Dantess. "My Longing points the way in, not out."

After several minutes, Sacquidge said in a harsh whisper, "Quiet!" She trained the spyglass above the tops of the spires. "The Coming Storm is out there."

"Is that good?" whispered Warren. "Does that mean that they're still searching for Evil's ship?"

"No idea," murmured Dantess. As he said this, he spied a spot of black that looked out of place against the gray rocks, visible only from within the stone forest, not without. He waved to get

Navar's attention and pointed to the harsh turn they'd have to make in order to steer the boat closer.

Navar sighed and spun the wheel to port. The boat tilted sharply, throwing a few squad members off their feet. When the boat leveled out, it drifted toward an open area sheltered and obscured by the spires, but big enough to hold the ship named the Scorpion, Evil's schooner. No surprise to Dantess, it had been painted completely black.

Dantess waved, channeling his Longing to his ring. The flash alerted the crew on the Scorpion's deck who looked nervous and wary, but did not make any threatening moves. Navar managed to swing the Glory close enough for Dantess to use his enhanced agility to leap up to the Scorpion's deck.

He had missed his token's abilities.

A woman, features hidden deep inside the cowl of a black robe, met him. "I'm Wayfurl, priestess of Evil. You're a priest of War?"

"I am. My name is Dantess."

"I thought by that jump you might be, but now I can see your token. Where is your breastplate?"

Dantess shrugged. "Lost to the depths. It's hard to swim with armor."

She nodded and pulled back her cowl. Wayfurl's plump face was almost cherubic, but with harsh black eyebrows. The combination made her smile a bit disconcerting. "You should take it off before you dive in next time. Regardless, can you tell me why that frigate is patrolling right outside of the island rocks? And why your Righteous Fury hasn't dealt with it? Isn't War supposed to protect us?"

"That frigate is the Coming Storm. Very dangerous and not the only enemy ship here. The Righteous Fury was sunk by the pirate galleon Leviathan, currently battling Good and Law's ships on the other side of the island—at least it was. I don't know how they fare. But that's not why I'm here."

"No?" Wayfurl's eyebrow rose.

"I need two of the prisoners you have aboard: Tolliver Tiernocke and Siriana Horner. They were transferred from War. Please release them to me."

Wayfurl crossed her arms and tilted her head. "You mean the Harbinger sympathizers? Why would I do that?"

"They're important. I need to make sure they're safe."

She laughed. "They're headed to the dungeons. For our guests there, 'safe' isn't on the menu."

Dantess took a deep breath. He had practiced this conversation with Warren countless times on their short trip here, but he was still nervous. "Are you the highest-ranking priestess aboard?"

She frowned and crossed her arms. "I am."

Dantess put his hand on her shoulder and led her aside. "It's important your crew does not hear what I'm about to tell you."

"Oh?"

"Believe me, you will prefer it that way. In fact, you're going to hand those two prisoners over, or *everyone* will hear. Including the leadership of the temples."

"Are you threatening me, priest of War?" She smiled coldly, perhaps not taking him seriously. Dantess couldn't blame her. A priest of War showing up on her ship, lacking armor and backup, and making outrageous demands of a senior priestess of Evil seemed ridiculous, even to him.

"Yes." Dantess locked gazes with her. Her flippant attitude drained just a little, faced with the steel in his eyes. "Evil receives a large portion of the tithe because you protect the temples against Chaos, correct?"

"Yes, we're tasked with guarding the vault of Chaos. What are you getting at?"

"Ah, but the job isn't limited to the vault, is it? You're supposed to track down any artifacts of Chaos out in the world before they can threaten us." He leaned in. "How much do you know about Shattered Peak?"

Wayfurl's eyes narrowed. "Ancient history. There *was* an artifact of Chaos there, but the great hero Varyon—a priest of War—gave his life to destroy it before it was taken into the world. Maybe you know of him?"

Dantess winced at the name. "He was my grandfather. I was *just* at Shattered Peak. I saw what happened through his eyes. They poisoned and then burned down the village, but still didn't *find* the artifact much less *destroy* it. In fact, it's on its way here right now."

The priestess of Evil's face drained of color. "No."

"The damned thing *destroys* artifacts of *Order*, and they're bringing it here to the Convergence of the Divine. Your

303

priesthood's failure to protect the temples has put all four *Gifts* in peril. Even if we manage to stop this attack, Evil will never live this down. You not only left it there to be used against us, but you *lied* about it!

"After such incompetence," Dantess continued, "those duties will be taken away. Your tithe will be given to another temple. The Convergence of the Divine is just the time and place to strip Evil of your authority."

"You wouldn't dare!" Wayfurl panted. "War is Evil's ally!"

"Give me the prisoners or I swear this will happen."

"All of this over two faithless prisoners? Why are they so important?"

"Does it matter?" Dantess asked. "Hand them over."

Wayfurl stared into Dantess' eyes, taking his measure. "Fol?" As she called the name, a priest of Evil approached. "Remove Tolliver Tiernocke and Siriana Horner from our hold and bring them here."

"The prisoners?" the man asked, astonished.

"Now," she replied.

The priest scuttled off. Within minutes, he returned with the pair, pulling one along with each arm.

Siriana, her scraggly hair falling over her emaciated face, struggled weakly—but as soon as she saw Dantess, she brightened. "Dantess?"

Tolliver looked much worse, shuffling forward as if he had truly lost all hope. He didn't even react when Siriana said Dantess' name—either not hearing or too far gone to notice.

"Da?" asked Dantess.

After a moment, Tolliver looked up. Gradually, his droopy eyes focused and his scowl lightened. "Son? Is it you? How?"

Dantess couldn't help it. He grabbed them both in a hug. "I'm taking you out of here. I don't know exactly what will happen next, but I'll protect you with my life no matter what."

"That's our end of the bargain, then. Where are you going now?" asked Wayfurl.

"Back to the Convergence. I have to try to prevent the Sea King from using the artifact." Dantess handed his father down to Motti, who helped him aboard. Then he assisted Siriana the same way. When he was done, Wayfurl was waiting for her turn. Dantess looked at her in surprise.

"I'm going, too. I don't trust you not to say anything to the high priests. And besides, it's my temple's responsibility to stop this, right? Help me aboard."

With a shrug, he grabbed the priestess' hand, lowered her down to the Glory, and then jumped aboard himself.

"Let's go back, Navar."

"Sure," Navar answered. "I don't think I've scraped *all* of the wood from the hull yet."

Captain Sacquidge growled. "You're buying me a new boat after all this is over, priest of War."

The Glory managed to keep its hull intact during the return trip. Navar was definitely improving with practice. When they arrived in the large, central chamber, Captain Sacquidge peered through her spyglass and announced, "The Leviathan's longboats are at War's landing." She lowered the glass and looked at Dantess. "And they're empty."

"The Sea King is inside the meeting room already? I thought it would take him longer to navigate that stone maze without the Longing to guide him." Dantess leapt over the railing into the water and swam to Evil's landing. Many splashes followed him. He guessed the others were not going to be dissuaded from joining him this time. Given what was probably happening up there, he doubted anyone would notice a few more arrivals.

Boosted by his token, he sprinted through the entrance tunnel and up the convoluted passage. It wasn't long until he reached the grand archway that opened into the meeting room.

On the opposite side of the room, the Sea King stood with Quin and Twyla. His pirate crew flanked them. From the looks of surprise on everyone else's faces, the new visitors had just arrived.

"Greetings, o mighty priests," began the Sea King, looking over the assembled council and audience. "So *many* priests in one place. You, who hold so much power over us faithless. I'm so glad I caught you before you wrapped up the Convergence. I don't think I could wait another hundred years to catch the next one."

"You are faithless?" Morghaust stood up from his chair. "And you're *here*?" He peered at the invaders. "Are you the one who sank the Righteous Fury? If so, I'm glad you came. We will have words."

Priests of War were already jumping down from the stands closest to the Sea King. They moved to intercept the pirates, but Morghaust held his hand up. The priests of War stopped in their tracks.

"No law prevents me from dispensing justice here, faithless scum. Have you or your men ever fought a priest of War? Just one equals hundreds of your kind. Imagine what the high priest can do to you." The high priest stepped forward. "Scratch that, I'll show you instead."

The Sea King winked. "Twyla, if you please?"

Twyla put her hand on Quin's shoulder and turned her to face Morghaust. "Just one priest, straight ahead. You feel him?"

Quin nodded.

While Morghaust screamed a war cry and ran forward, Quin held out her rock. A glowing spark popped out from one of its pockmarks. It floated in the air, wandered like a drunk firefly, then shot straight at Morghaust's token. The metal exploded.

Everyone in the room gasped. The crown above pulsed red with an intensity that almost covered the entire ceiling of surefire crystals with the ominous color.

Morghaust stopped. The expression on his face no longer showed anger, but confusion instead. "What... happened?"

"That was your token disappearing from existence," said the Sea King. "We have an artifact of Chaos that erases Order from the world. We'll start with your tokens and finish with your Gifts. The time of your rule has passed."

"My... Gift?" Morghaust turned away from the Sea King to the quickly pulsing red crown suspended above the floor. "But I... need that."

The Sea King tilted his head to his first mate. Clay nodded, stepped forward, and ran his sword through Morghaust's back.

Every priest in the room drew in their breath.

"Good riddance," a voice said beside Dantess. It was his father, just now arriving behind him. Warren and the rest of the squad filed in, along with Wayfurl, the priestess from the Scorpion.

"He was still a man," said Dantess.

"He was a *priest*," responded Tolliver. "And one of the *worst* of them."

"Did she just destroy his token?" Wayfurl asked.

Dantess nodded. "Yes. And she's going to destroy the Gifts."

Wayfurl's jaw dropped. "Isn't there any way to stop her?"

Dantess stared at Wayfurl, thinking. Then he swung his gaze to Twyla and Quin. "Maybe."

"No!" Tolliver grabbed Dantess' shoulder with an intensity he didn't expect. "Let her do it."

Dantess paused. "What?"

"Didn't I raise you to see this opportunity for what it is? This is the faithless' only chance to escape the temples. To rise up and determine their own future, instead of being crushed by the endless tithes and enslavement the gods provide."

Dantess' jaw dropped open. "You want *anarchy?* People will die."

"Priests will die, mostly. Like Morghaust. Listen to me, son. It's worth the price."

Abruptly, Dantess realized this choice is what Warren was trying to prepare him for. Dantess had been trying to please his father, championing his cause and protecting the faithless. But he was also a priest, driven by his faith and the rules of his religion— the way of his grandfather.

Each man had blinded himself to the perspective of the other.

But Dantess saw the world through both lenses.

"Da, I am your son, but I'm *also* a priest."

Tolliver started to say something, but stopped, a look of anguish and frustration on his face.

Dantess continued, "I know now that Grandpa was a horrible person, but you can't judge all priests by his example. You never understood his relationship with his god, but I do. It's not what made him into the person he became.

"You were right when you told me men make the laws." He pointed at the table. "*Those* men. High priests. Morghaust's death gives a chance for someone else to do better, but they can't if the world is burning!"

"Dantess, listen to me," Tolliver clutched at Dantess' shoulder again, but Dantess gently removed his hand.

"I won't let that happen. I can't betray my faith." He grabbed Wayfurl's arm and walked into the room, leaving his father dumbstruck behind him.

307

During their conversation, a few priests of War closest to the Sea King had moved to block the intruders, only to be targeted by Quin's artifact and put down by the Sea King's men. Others held back, unsure what to do. None of them had confronted the power of Chaos before.

"Stop, Twyla!" Dantess called out. His words echoed in the large chamber.

"Is that Dantess?" answered the Sea King. "You're tenacious, my boy! Did you paddle all the way here in a barrel?"

Ignoring the Sea King, Dantess tried again. "Twyla. Quin. Don't do this. You're about to cause the deaths of countless people, faithless and priests."

"Leave, Dantess," said Twyla. "I don't want to hurt you again."

"You're rebelling against the priests, and I understand that—but now you're just serving a different master. The Sea King doesn't care about you. He's using you as a weapon. Please. You don't have to do this."

"It's too late," said Twyla, crying. "What will the priests do to Quin now that they know about her and her stone? They can't allow someone like her to live. They'll never rest until she's dead. There's only one way out of this for her."

Twyla walked Quin to a space in front of the suspended Gifts. "Quin, the Gifts are just above you. Do you feel them?"

Quin nodded.

All the Gifts pulsed with intensity, firing shocks of color across the ceiling, as if in panic.

Dantess' heart dropped. Quin was the perfect example of how his father described a faithless: someone with all her choices stripped from her. She didn't deserve this, but he couldn't let her destroy the foundation of his own faith.

Like her, Dantess had no options left.

"Wayfurl," said Dantess. "Quin is a slave of Evil. She has the collar. Stop her."

Wayfurl's eyes opened wide. "Why didn't you say so?"

Wayfurl and Quin lifted their hands at the same time, Chaos' rock in Quin's grip. But before Quin could launch the motes, Wayfurl's rings glowed red and the indentations in Quin's slave collar—despite being hidden by her cloak—clicked open.

Blood poured from the holes. Quin choked and brought her hand to her neck, which quickly became covered in red. Twyla screamed and caught the slave girl as she dropped. The rock tipped from Quin's hand onto the floor, useless.

The room erupted in confusion.

The Sea King cried out in alarm. "To the boats! Quickly!" He bolted toward the exit, leaving Twyla and Quin behind.

Priests of every faith surged forward. Some of the pirates in front acted as shields as the Sea King slipped out. The priests pursued, but the archway acted as a bottleneck.

Dantess ran to Twyla, who was still kneeling and sobbing at Quin's side. Without giving her an option, he grabbed and lifted her up. She reached desperately for Quin and then tried to beat on Dantess' shoulder and face, but he ignored it.

He knew what would happen to Twyla if he left her—and he was certain these priests would not let him walk out of here with her—so instead, Dantess leapt into the hole at the center of the table.

With his token, he absorbed most of the water's impact and shielded Twyla from any harm. Powerful kicks brought both of them to the surface.

"Let me go!" coughed Twyla.

"I can't."

She screamed, "You killed Quin!"

"I'll have to live with her death the rest of my days—but so will you. By ordering her to destroy the Gifts, you sealed her fate."

"No. It was the Sea King—"

"Quin didn't answer to him. You were her friend. She would have done anything you asked."

Twyla stopped struggling. "I didn't have a choice."

"We always have choices. Like right now, I'm choosing to ignore what my next high priest might intend for you in order to save your life." With Twyla still locked in his arm, he began to swim towards the Glory. "You were right. The temple leadership would never allow Quin to live. Even though you're not the threat Quin was, I'm reasonably sure they'll feel the same way about you. But—despite everything—I owe you for what happened to your father, and I don't want anyone else to die."

Dantess reached the Glory about the same time as his squad, and the others emerged from the tunnel onto the landing. He handed Twyla up to Navar, then hauled himself aboard with Navar's help.

Warren, Motti, and the others—gathered at the landing—climbed aboard as well. His father glowered, looking betrayed. He would not meet Dantess' gaze.

But when Wayfurl tried to climb aboard, Dantess stopped her. "Your ship is close. The Glory doesn't have room for unnecessary passengers."

Wayfurl crossed her arms and stood back. "As you wish. I'll see you soon, priest of War."

"I'm sure." Dantess nodded. "Captain, please get us out of here."

"Navar," announced Captain Sacquidge. "Your choice of exit."

Navar sailed the boat toward the exit nearest to Good's landing, far from both Evil's ship and the last known location of the Leviathan.

As they bumped their way through the stony passage, no one said a word.

CHAPTER TWENTY-EIGHT

"SHOULDN'T WE TOSS him overboard?" asked Warren, staring at Kevik's body.

"No," answered Dantess. "Whatever he did, he is still a priest of War and deserves to be taken back to the temple for his death rites."

Twyla sat in a corner of the hold and sobbed. "What about Quin? They'll probably dump *her* in the ocean. She doesn't get rites. No one will say anything about her. Just a meaningless slave girl."

"Do you want to say something now?" asked Dantess. "We don't know much about her."

Twyla wiped her eyes, but continued to sniff. "She was my best friend for years. She couldn't tell me about her life before I met her because those horrid priests of Evil took her voice as well as her sight. But ever since that day, she was loyal and true. I looked after her, and she looked after me. We were going to change the world together."

"You almost did," said Motti. "Into *this*." He waved his hands at the collection of carvings on the walls. When the others looked at him with disapproval, he said, "What? It's true."

Siriana studied the carvings. "What are all of these pictures? They're terrifying."

"Wait," said Tolliver, examining one. "That's me. Or it's my head on a serpent's body. Over here, my mother is on fire. And this?" He waved at the avian carving on the floor. "We had a bird like that as a pet, although he only had two eyes. What's going on here?"

"They're not from your life, Da," said Dantess. "They're from Varyon's. Poison drove him insane, and the carvings he left prompted my token to make me see what he did. I guess he conflated memories with nightmares. He was convinced all of these," he gestured around the hold, "were coming to destroy him."

"Guilt?" asked Warren.

"Who knows? Through the token, I could only feel his terror and madness and need to end it all. Evil's magic had eaten so much of his brain away at that point. This is what was left."

Tolliver shook his head. "It doesn't surprise me that Varyon's head was packed with terrors, even before that day. Something drove him to be the demon he was. Now, those memories are part of you, too, right? And every other priest of War?"

"I guess that's true," said Dantess.

"And you want me to trust priests of War with our future?" Tolliver pointed at Kevik's body. "You're all on the brink of breaking down—lashing out or killing yourselves. Look what Kevik did when faced with it."

Dantess stood in front of his father until the man looked him in the eyes. "Do you trust me, Da?"

Tolliver did not respond, but he stared pointedly at the deep scratches on Dantess' neck.

The uncomfortable silence was broken by Captain Sacquidge stumbling down the ladder. "Dantess, the Scorpion is almost on us. They're going to board."

"Evil's ship? What do we do?" Warren asked. "If they find my mother, Tolliver, and Twyla on board, they'll throw them into a cell—or worse."

"No time to worry about that," said the captain. "Dantess, you need to go up to greet them. Otherwise, they might not treat this as a friendly visit."

Dantess nodded and began to climb out. "Warren and Motti, with me. Everyone else, stay down here. I'll try to keep them out."

The Scorpion cruised alongside the Mourning Glory. It slowed while the crew threw ropes down to secure the smaller ship to the larger one. Even before they were done, Kaurridon, Wayfurl, and two additional priests of War jumped down to the deck to meet Dantess standing ready.

"You left pretty quickly," said Kaurridon. "I would have liked to talk after everything that happened. Luckily, this helpful priestess of Evil pointed us in the right direction to search for you."

"I'm sorry," said Dantess. "I was worried about Captain Sacquidge and her crew. I didn't know how long the route would be safe to travel for a boat this size, but I thought the Sea King's forces would be distracted, at least for a while. And I owed the captain enough to at least escort her back. What happened to the Sea King, can you say?"

"He escaped. The Leviathan was destroyed by the Tranquility, but only after his flagship sank both the Righteous Fury and the Seven Stars. He must have made it onto the Coming Storm, so you're lucky we found you and not him."

"Thank War," said Dantess.

"But the Sea King wasn't the only one who went missing after everything that happened. The girl leading the one holding the artifact of Chaos? And also your father and Warren's mother. Wayfurl here says you freed them from her ship, and she thought they came aboard this boat."

"Wayfurl was kind enough to release them, when we thought the boat was in danger from the Coming Storm. But you think they're here? There's barely room enough for us."

Kaurridon's eyes narrowed. "You have a weak spot when it comes to those prisoners, as we both know. We'll need to search the ship." He gestured to the two priests with him. "You, search on the main deck. You, come with me into the hold."

Dantess stepped in his way. "You don't want to go into the hold."

"Why is that?"

"Because..." Dantess' thoughts raced. "It's covered with carvings, images pulled from my grandfather's last moments of madness. What happened at Shattered Peak isn't what everyone's been told. Bottom line: using a token around those carvings can drive *any* priest of War insane. You don't have the stone from your office here to help you." He wiped his forehead of the sweat beading there. "It's too dangerous. Kevik learned that the hard way."

"What happened to Kevik?"

"Dead. By his own hand. I assure you, you don't want to risk your life down there."

Kaurridon pushed by him. "Not that I don't believe you, but I have to see this for myself." With that, he began to climb down the ladder.

Dantess' mind raced. What would Kaurridon say when he found their parents and Twyla? What would his punishment be this time? Dantess hadn't actually lied about them, but that wouldn't save him.

He followed Kaurridon down the ladder, into the hold. Captain Sacquidge was there, lying in the hammock. "Welcome aboard, priests of War."

Still on the ladder, Dantess looked around the room, but could not find a single soul except the relaxing captain.

Sacquidge puffed on her pipe. "I must apologize for the state of things. I tried to tidy up, but there's only so much I can do to cover Dantess' idea of decorating. I admit, I find it to be a bit of an eyesore."

Kaurridon stepped from the ladder onto the floor. To Dantess, he asked, "*You* did this?"

"Yes," he answered, landing next to him. "Ever since my visit to Shattered Peak, I can't get these images out of my head. Under stress, I carve them."

"And if I channeled my Longing right now?" Kaurridon ran his hand over one of the nearest images.

Dantess didn't answer. Instead, he pointed to Kevik's body. While he showed injuries from battle, it was clear that the wound that killed him was a slit throat. The bloody dagger was still in his hand.

Kaurridon's eyes softened. "How do you live with this in your head?"

"I don't know yet. I'll tell you when I figure that out."

Kaurridon nodded. "Captain, with your leave, we need to search your hold. We mustn't leave any stone unturned."

"As you wish," said the captain.

While Kaurridon and the other priest of War opened crates and moved cages, Wayfurl climbed down to join them. Given the relatively small size of the hold, it didn't take long to search the entire area.

"There's no one here," said Kaurridon, almost as an accusation to Wayfurl.

"But I saw them come aboard," she said.

"Hand," began Dantess, "I can honestly tell you I do not know where those people are. Perhaps Wayfurl was mistaken. Of course, I'd love to know where my father is, and naturally, we'd all like to find that girl. Imagine the questions she could answer, like where they obtained that artifact of Chaos. If we could just find her, I'm sure everything would come to light!"

Wayfurl's face blanched, catching on. "You're right. It was dark and people were running everywhere. Maybe the Sea King took them?"

Kaurridon frowned. "You sent us on this mission, and you weren't sure of your information? I will have words with your high priest about this." He walked to Dantess and slapped his hand on his shoulder. "We're done here, but I'd like you to bring your squad and join me on the Scorpion. I'll debrief you there. There are a lot of holes in my understanding of this story."

"Of course." Dantess didn't want to leave, but he couldn't refuse Kaurridon.

Kaurridon eyed his priests. "Take Kevik. We will return him to the temple."

After the two priests had removed the body and Kaurridon followed, Dantess began to climb the ladder. Just before he hauled himself onto the upper deck, he looked back.

Captain Sacquidge, taking a leisurely draw of her pipe, winked at him.

"I don't know whether to congratulate you, feel sorry for you, or clap you in irons and throw away the key," said Kaurridon.

Dantess sat in the somber-toned captain's quarters of the Scorpion. Sar Kooris, also on board, reluctantly allowed Kaurridon to borrow it for this conversation. From the grumbling he heard among the crew on the way, it was clear that Evil did not enjoy sharing their ship with anyone—even allies who lost their own ship defending them.

"It's been a busy day," said Dantess. "Maybe we could just do the first two and save the last for another time?"

"You not only skirted the rules, but the *law*. Repeatedly. How am I supposed to respond?"

Dantess told Kaurridon almost everything, with the exception of taking the missing passengers aboard the Glory, but what he revealed could brand him a criminal if the Hand chose to see it that way. Morghaust would have.

"I never disobeyed an order or broke the law—at least, not as I understood it—but certain priorities led me in questionable directions, that's true. I wholeheartedly regret putting the Gifts at risk from the Sea King. I had no idea that would happen."

"Leading faithless to Convergence Island wasn't a crime, because it never occurred to a priest to do it. It is now, though. Law recorded it just before we left." Kaurridon smiled. "And tell me how you freed your father from this ship?"

"I blackmailed Wayfurl," Dantess admitted. "Evil lied about what happened at Shattered Peak. The artifact they claimed was destroyed showed up at the Convergence. I threatened them with losing the responsibility of protecting the temples against Chaos if this came out."

"And the tithe that goes along with it?"

"Especially that." Dantess rubbed his forehead, nervously. "I said that if they didn't release Tolliver and Siriana, I'd tell the high priests."

"Too late," said Kaurridon. Dantess raised an eyebrow as Kaurridon pulled the red crown carved from a single crystal from behind the desk. He placed it gently in front of him.

"You hold War's Gift!" exclaimed Dantess. "In your hands! But that would mean—"

"Yes. I am War's new high priest."

"How? Doesn't the Gift usually take months to select a successor?" Dantess sat back, shocked. "And then there's the ceremony and festival. I don't understand."

"Who can second guess the mind of War? I was selected at the Convergence, perhaps so War could close the event still represented by a high priest. Or, maybe so someone could deal with *you*." Kaurridon removed the crown and replaced it behind the desk. "Regardless, I agree with you about keeping this secret. Good and Law don't need to know, and it might not hurt to have leverage on our ally moving forward."

"You're the new high priest." Dantess couldn't help but repeat the obvious. It was hard to wrap his mind around it.

"I am," Kaurridon agreed. "But let's talk about you, now." A half-smile played on his lips. "Dantess, from the moment you joined the temple, I watched you. It became clear you were cut from a different cloth than most priests, different even than your grandfather. Notably him, knowing more about Varyon now.

"When sponsoring players for the Game, Morghaust found a kindred spirit in Kevik, but I saw something disruptive in you. You were ambitious, but you had a moral center, were open to new ideas, and risked everything if the cause was important enough. I thought, given enough opportunity, you might shake things up in the temple.

"You did. Quite a lot *more* than I expected. I guess I should share some of the blame for that, then."

Dantess began to let his hopes rise. "Does that mean..."

"You stopped Quin from using the artifact of Chaos on the Gifts. You even managed to flush out and deliver that artifact to the council—something Evil failed to do for decades. It's all about how we choose to see these events. Do you agree?"

Dantess nodded vigorously.

"Kevik's death was unfortunate, but clearly a suicide. Morghaust's death was a tragedy, but I've decided to place blame where it deserves to go: on the Sea King. You might consider a mission to bring him to justice as part of your journey to reclaim your rank."

"Of course. With pleasure. But, if I may, what about my father?"

"That's trickier, but I've thought about it." Kaurridon frowned. "I don't consider him or the others threats, so I'm willing to forget about your missing fugitives. If they keep their heads down, wherever they are, I'll let them be. I won't look for them."

"That's more than generous. Thank you, Hand... I mean, High Priest."

Kaurridon chuckled. "I'm doing that for you, not for them. I know your potential. You have a lot of work to do to get others in the temple to believe in you again, but one day, maybe you could even surpass your marks. You're not one who stays down long. *That,* I've learned.

"Go," said Kaurridon. "Tell your squad. I'm sure they're crowded outside the door waiting to hear the news that you won't be dragged away in chains."

Dantess rose from his chair, saluted with his hand over his heart, and walked out of the captain's quarters. For the first time in years, he felt like the temple could actually change.

For the better.

For everyone.

He wished he could tell his father about it.

Captain Sacquidge stood at one end of her empty hold. The Glory rocked just a bit, secured by the lines to her assigned dock at Victor's Folly. They'd reached their destination, they'd made it through inspection, and it was time to release her passengers.

She leaned against the aft wall, placed her hand in one of the knotholes, and pulled it downward. The wood beneath slid and clicked into place. Then she felt for another board and did the same, only pulling it to the right. On and on she repeated the process with different boards, as if she were unlocking a complex puzzle box—which she was.

The final slide uncovered a handle as the board settled into place with a satisfying clunk. Sacquidge pulled on the handle. A panel in the wall levered outward, revealing a cramped but surprisingly large compartment.

One by one, her passengers stepped out, using the open panel as a walkway: Twyla, Siriana, and Tolliver.

"We've arrived at Victor's Folly," said the captain. "Inspections are done. It's safe to disembark."

"Our thanks, captain," said Siriana, taking her hand. "We owe you our lives."

Sacquidge blushed. "You're welcome. Happy to be of service. Couldn't have you falling back into temple hands, now could we? Besides, I know Dantess will pick up your tab."

At the name, Tolliver frowned. "Temple hands, indeed."

"You should give your son some credit. I've never seen a lad so dedicated to saving you lot. He loves you, he does. He showed as much."

Siriana nodded, but Tolliver said nothing.

After a moment of uncomfortable silence, the captain asked, "So, where are you all off to?"

"I'm..." Siriana began before pursing her lips. "I'm not sure."

"Me neither. Where can I go?" asked Twyla. "Should I go back to Seaborn Notch? I lost the only person in my life I cared about. Without her there…"

"No," said Siriana, firmly. "From what you told me, that's a place of horrors, especially for you. Living there would keep you locked in the past, a time of misery and hatred. You need a fresh start." She took Twyla by the shoulders. "You know, I had a daughter about your age."

"What happened to her?"

"She died. While I was stuck in a cell." She sniffed. "A mother shouldn't outlive her children."

Twyla nodded. "I'm sorry."

"I missed her growing up into a woman. I missed being a mother to her." She brushed the hair from Twyla's eyes. "I might be able to show you a place you can go. There are lots of children there."

"A sanctuary of Charity?" Twyla took a step back.

"No. Never. This is a place of laughter and life and… it stays out of sight of the temples."

"Really?"

Siriana nodded, smiling. "Maybe we can both be happier there."

Tolliver slammed the panel back against the door, drawing everyone's gaze. "What are you talking about? There's no peace for faithless, no happiness. Haven't you learned anything from all of this?"

Sternly, Siriana responded, "Tolliver, I know how long we spent in those horrid cells. I'm happy to be out, and I'm *not* going back. You shouldn't want to either. Pick a fight with the temples and you'll lose."

Tolliver shook his head. "I don't care. I can't be here. I can't be this near to the cell that caged me for so long. We're just down the road from a temple full of priests on the verge of going mad." He waved his hand at the carvings that still adorned the walls of the hold.

"Even if you leave Dantess?"

"He made his choice. The future of the faithless was in his hands, and he chose the gods." To Twyla, he said, "You came so close to freeing us all. You shouldn't give up now. You're a strong girl. You can still change the world. Come with me." He held out his hand.

319

Twyla looked at Tolliver's outstretched hand, but turned back to Siriana's smiling face. "I'm tired. I'm especially tired of hating. Dantess gave me a second chance. Maybe I should use it to try something else."

"It's your choice," said Tolliver. "I hope you don't regret it."

○

"This room is *so* much smaller," Warren said disapprovingly of Dantess' new living chamber in War's temple. "Why would you give up your old quarters?"

Still unpacking his belongings, Dantess pulled a couple of shirts from a bag and placed them atop his bed. "I couldn't sleep there anymore. It just didn't feel right. Besides, I don't want anything from Varyon in my life."

"But it was so spacious! Even your new bed is smaller." Warren bounced on it, but it didn't bounce back much. Even so, he did manage to send the shirts there sliding onto the floor. "And harder. Is there any padding in it at all?"

"I don't need much. I'm getting used to it already." Rolling his eyes, Dantess grabbed the shirts from the floor and sat down on a hard, wooden stool—the only chair in the room. "Did you find out anything about our parents? Or Twyla?"

"Oh, yes!" exclaimed Warren. "Wait. Do you want to know, or will your priest-ness make you tell Kaurridon?"

"Kaurridon made it clear he's not interested in finding them as long as they don't flout that. He won't ask, and I won't pass it on. Now, tell me!"

"All right. My mother took Twyla to Mother Nettle's camp. They both help take care of the children there now. According to her note, she's very happy. Twyla is making some new friends— and maybe picking up some new skills."

"Another light-fingered thief roaming the streets of Freethorn Creek? Maybe if we slip Mother Nettle some more gold, she'll keep those urchins in line." Dantess looked down and smiled. "That's great news. And my da?"

"Nothing. I've asked everywhere. I'm starting to think he never got off the boat at Victor's Folly."

There was so much left unsaid between Dantess and his father. With the realization that his silver ring was an artifact,

Dantess understood the lengths Tolliver went to in order to keep Dantess from the temple—to prevent him, in his da's eyes, from becoming his grandfather.

To his father, Dantess' actions at the Convergence only proved that he lost that battle.

Of course, how could that not have crushed him? Driven him away? Every day that passed without speaking, he felt more certain that Tolliver had given up on his son entirely.

After all he'd done to save him, Dantess worried that he'd never see his father again.

"Ready to go to the testing?" asked Warren, perhaps trying to change the subject.

"Almost." Dantess held out the two shirts. "Help me unpack a bit more and we can both go."

Warren grimaced but snatched the shirts. "Fine. Where do you want these?"

"In the closet." Dantess reached into the sack and his fingers touched something cold and metal. He pulled out a music box, loosely wrapped in socks.

A sad smile on his face, Dantess unwrapped it, wound the key, and placed the box gently on the table. Its sweet music filled the room with more warmth than the fireplace.

"Jyn's music box?" asked Warren, turning back from the closet.

Dantess nodded and closed his eyes.

For as long as the song played, they both listened without saying a word. Eventually, the box wound down. As soon as the music stopped, Warren began to cry.

"Warren?" asked Dantess.

Warren shook his head, covered his face, and sobbed. In between breaths, he said, "I'm... sorry. I... don't know why..."

"I do." Dantess reached out and embraced his friend. "You never grieved for her. The moment she died, you became obsessed with vengeance against Kevik. Now he's gone, so it's time."

Warren buried his face in Dantess' shoulder.

After a while, Warren pulled out of the hug and wiped his eyes. "I miss her."

"I do, too. I always will."

Warren picked up the music box. "You know, if you chose her instead of me at the testing, she'd still be here."

Dantess paused a moment—he remembered having that exact thought after her death—but he had long since put that regret away. "Jyn insisted I choose you, Warren. She made that sacrifice to save you. Knowing her, she'd have done it even if she somehow foresaw the final outcome. That's who she was." He grabbed Warren's shoulder. "Maybe she knew how much I would need you. I wouldn't be the person I am without you. I wouldn't even *be* here without you."

Warren chuckled. "I guess I did save your butt a time or two, but who's keeping track?" He turned the music box in his hands. "Where are you going to put this?"

"You decide." Dantess waved about the room. "There aren't too many places to choose from."

Warren walked to the fireplace and set the music box on the mantle.

Dantess smiled and nodded. "You know, unpacking can wait. We should go." He put his arm around Warren's shoulders and began to lead him to the door. "I know you hate to miss the early rounds."

On the way out, Dantess glanced back one last time at the music box.

You'd be proud of him, Jyn.
I hope you'd be proud of me, too.

Dantess and Warren found the rest of their squad seated in the stands inside War's courtyard. The testing was already underway.

"How are the new candidates?" asked Dantess. "See anyone you like?"

"You're not looking to replace me, are you?" asked Motti. "For not taking the squad back to the temple like you asked in Seaborn Notch?"

Khalista punched him in the shoulder. "No, he's not going to replace you. We *saved* him, you idiot."

"Oh, that's right. I guess I did." He buffed his breastplate. "I saved my priest."

She rolled her eyes. "As if you haven't been telling anyone who will listen."

Dantess chuckled and glanced at Warren. "That wasn't the first time my squad saved me, and I doubt it will be the last. Of course, no one's getting replaced. I like to keep an eye on good prospects anyway. Especially ones who may become new priests. You never know who might become an ally later on."

The crowd applauded for a well-delivered blow in the ring below.

"Speaking of prospects, that red-haired kid is on fire!" yelled Motti. "He's got some natural skill. Really handy with those fighting sticks. Wait until he gets to the actual test. He's going to jump rings around those other losers."

"You better hope so," said Khalista. "You bet two gold on him. Do you even *have* any gold?"

Motti joined in the applause. "I will when I win that bet!"

"Your man has a good eye," Withyr said as she sat down next to Dantess. "I'm looking to add to my squad, and that child may be what I need."

"Better hold judgment," said Dantess. "Motti has a history of losing bets. It won't be the first time I've covered him."

Withyr laughed. "You misunderstand. I've sat through enough of these matches to see the Longing in action, and the child doesn't have it. He'll do well enough in the combat portion, but fail the test. That's when I'll recruit him *and* collect my two gold."

"Motti bet *you?*"

"You should train your squad better. Everyone else knows never to bet against me. Just like I wouldn't bet against you."

"What do you mean?"

Withyr rolled her eyes. "Don't you find it curious that the seat next to the high priest is empty?"

Indeed, Kaurridon presided over the testing in the ornate chair reserved for the high priest, but no one sat in the chair next to him.

"That's where the Hand sits. He hasn't appointed one yet."

"That's right, because he's waiting for *you* to get out of the hole you're in." She tugged at his chainmail shirt covering the marks on his arms.

Dantess' jaw dropped. "You think he wants me as his Hand? *Me?* Even after everything that happened?"

"Of course. He chose you for the Game. You may not be the most popular priest at the temple now, but you have a way of climbing the ladder quickly. As I said, I wouldn't bet against you."

"Not just me." Dantess looked over his squad, cheering for the spectacle below. Each member showed heart, courage, and more loyalty than he deserved. But more important, they never quit—even on Dantess. If he achieved this new goal, it would be because of them. Especially *one* of them.

Dantess put his hand on Warren's shoulder. "Withyr thinks I'm destined for that chair. What do you think?" He pointed down to the seat beside Kaurridon.

"Hand, huh? I like it," said Warren. "Let's come up with a plan."

ONE LAST THING...

"THREE MUGS, ROSE," said Captain Sacquidge to the lady behind the counter.

Rose looked over at the table where Navar sat with someone hidden in a travel cloak. "Another strange guest? I don't much like your surprises anymore."

"Just someone who's looking to get away from it all. The Primrose Boarding House is as good a place to do that as any."

She pulled out three mugs and began to fill them. "You're not hiding another priest under that cloak, are you? Word got out that we had one here, and now people are saying we serve priests here. I can't afford to lose business because of that."

"Nope," the captain said. "Don't worry, Rose. This man is about the furthest thing from a priest as you can get."

Skeptical, Rose grabbed the mugs, walked over to the table with the captain, and set them down. "The house's finest."

The man in the cloak grabbed the mug and drained it. When Rose raised her eyebrow, he said, "I haven't had ale this good in years. My compliments."

Rose chuckled. "I was joking. It's not *that* good. But I like your reaction." She stared at the man, hidden under his hood. "So, you just passing through?"

"I don't know." The man sipped the last drop from his mug and placed it on the table. "I'm here to see the place where my father died: Shattered Peak. After that, I'm not sure."

Rose's heart softened a bit. "Your father died there? I'm so sorry. A lot of locals lost friends and family. Even though it was a long time ago, people still feel the hurt. They avoid the place, mostly."

"That's not what I feel. My father got what he deserved."

"Why?"

The man stared into his empty mug. "My father was Varyon, priest of War. He killed everyone in that village and then himself."

"Oh, my," said Rose. She sat down in an empty chair and whispered. "You shouldn't spread that around. People here don't like priests in general, and *him* in particular. They may not take kindly to the son of the one responsible for the massacre at Shattered Peak."

"Good advice." The man noticed that Navar was distracted by a serving girl. He took the opportunity to swap his empty mug with Navar's full one and then drain it, too. "Is it true you have no priests here?"

"That's right. For years."

"Years." He whistled low. "A long time. Seaborn Notch must have gotten away without priests for all this time because it's so remote. No one knew. The temples know about it now, though. I wouldn't be surprised if they sent priests here to fix the situation soon."

That idea lit a fire in Rose. "Let 'em try, I say. Seaborn Notch isn't just our home, it's the Sea King's home, too. He protects us."

"Rose?" said Captain Sacquidge. "You're raising your voice. Maybe we should—"

Ignoring the captain, the man in the cloak leaned forward. "But the Sea King's might is in his fleet. What about on land?"

"Didn't you know? Seaborn Notch is the birthplace of," she cupped her mouth and leaned in so that only the man could hear, "the Harbingers of Chaos."

"Oh. That's interesting. You think they could defend Seaborn Notch against War's soldiers?"

Rose leaned back. "Well... there are some good fighters in the bunch, no question. Maybe they could hold their own. But I admit that they have more enthusiasm than training."

"I'm so glad we met, Rose. It just so happens that I know a lot about War's training. I grew up in their temple. I might be able to help." He pulled back the hood to reveal a gaunt and bearded face. He offered his hand to shake. "Forgive me, I haven't introduced myself yet. My name's Tolliver. Tolliver Tiernocke."

Rose took his hand. "Welcome to Seaborn Notch, Tolliver Tiernocke."

Tolliver smiled. "I think I'm going to like it here."

AUTHOR'S NOTE

IF YOU'RE HERE, I congratulate you not only on making it to the end of the book, but also reading an *author's note!* I hope you enjoyed Dantess' tale, and if you did, I would sincerely appreciate if you could leave a review on Amazon, Goodreads, and/or Bookbub. Independent books live and die by their reviews, and your words can help this book reach more people.

Did you know that it took *twenty years* to complete my first book, the Child of Chaos (the Chronicles of Chaos, Book One)? That journey, carrying the spark of an idea to the top of the publishing mountain, was one of hard work, epiphanies, quite a few pitfalls and disasters, and ultimately success. When I released the manuscript in 2020, it felt amazing to stop changing and finally launch my debut novel. It felt even better when readers responded well to it.

Afterward, when CoVID locked the world down, I decided to see if I could leverage the forced isolation to create something in a little less time than twenty years. I did. Nine months later (the traditional gestation period), I wrote 'The End' on a manuscript called the Game of War, but it wasn't the sequel to Child. Instead, I wrote a prequel featuring Dantess, priest of War.

Why, you may ask? One reason is that Dantess has fans. He was one of the most popular supporting characters in the Child of Chaos. That's understandable. Dantess is pretty much a superhero, after all.

But his fans weren't the only ones demanding that I tell his story. Dantess *himself* let me know that there were secrets in his past that I needed to understand. Why would a priest of War be so open to helping agents of Chaos? Who was he really? What happened to him? What drives him?

With the Game of War behind us, now we *all* know him a little better. And while the Game of War is a stand-alone prequel, the answers to those questions will directly shape the Chronicles of Chaos going forward.

Dantess needed to tell me these things to prepare me for what was coming, and now, you're prepared, too. That's a good thing. Book Two, the Curse of Chaos, uses this foundation to launch something no one could have foreseen.

Please visit me at Mysterium.blog to sign up for my newsletter, read behind-the scenes articles from my game design work, purchase signed books directly from the author, or to contact me directly. I love to stay connected with my readers.

—Glen Dahlgren

ACKNOWLEDGEMENTS

AUTHORING A BOOK is a lonely task, but making the product that actually ended up in your hands requires many, many people. I'm supported by some incredible editors, artists, and readers—most of them dear friends—that make something like this possible.

Early help from alpha/beta readers Christine Brownell, Jim Montanus, John Gavaler, and Teresa Paglino set the stage for my editor Samantha Cook to dig in, and then Lily Luchesi tightened up the result.

From there, I relied on my dedicated team of ARC readers to catch any errors that slipped through and provide some wonderful early reviews to help promote the book.

I'm so lucky and grateful to have these people accompanying me on my author's journey. There's no way I could have made it here (and hopefully beyond) without them.

330

ABOUT THE AUTHOR

GLEN DAHLGREN IS an award-winning game designer and the author of the book series The Chronicles of Chaos, which fantasy legend Piers Anthony called "what fantasy fiction should be."

Glen has written, designed, directed, and produced critically-acclaimed, narrative-driven computer games for the last three decades. What's more, he had the honor of creating original fantasy and science-fiction storylines that took established, world-class literary properties into interactive experiences. He collaborated with celebrated authors Margaret Weis and Tracy Hickman (The Death Gate Cycle), Robert Jordan (The Wheel of Time - now a TV series from Amazon), Frederik Pohl (Heechee saga), Terry Brooks (Shannara), and Piers Anthony (Xanth) to bring their creations to the small screens. In addition, he crafted licensor-approved fiction for the Star Trek franchise as well as Stan Sakai's epic graphic novel series, Usagi Yojimbo.

CONTINUE YOUR JOURNEY

The Child of Chaos, Book One of the Chronicles of Chaos

Nothing can break the stranglehold the gods of Order have on the world . . . except a roll of the dice.

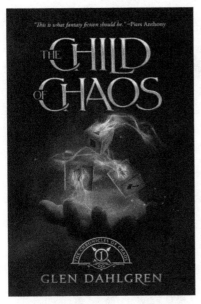

An irresistible longing drags young Galen to an ancient vault where, long ago, the gods of Order locked Chaos away. Chaos promises power to the one destined to liberate it, but Galen's dreams warn of dark consequences.

He isn't the only one racing to the vault, however. Horace, the bully who lives to torment Galen, is determined to unleash Chaos--and he might know how to do it.

Galen's imagination always got him into trouble, but now it may be the only thing that can prevent Horace from unraveling the world.

"This is no ordinary sword and sorcery story. This is what fantasy fiction should be. [Glen Dahlgren is a] novelist who I think will become more widely known as his skill is appreciated." --Piers Anthony. New York Times best-selling author of Xanth

Available in ebook, paperback, hardcover, and audiobook. Or buy signed copies directly from the author at: www.Mysterium.blog

COMING IN 2022

The Curse of Chaos

The Chronicles of Chaos, Book Two

The gods are gone, but that hasn't stopped the temples from ruling over the faithless. The priests may pretend to wield the gods' power still, but there are those that know better.

The Harbingers of Chaos cult has been waiting for the opportunity to reshape society with the faithless at the top. All they need to move forward is their messiah: the Child of Chaos.

But during the months since the choice, Lorre still hasn't woken up. All this time, Galen tried to extract her from the Dreaming, but she refused—and her body can't last much longer without her spirit. Time is running out, and he is getting desperate.

Galen needs a miracle. He learns that people are praying to a new god they claim is Chaos risen. It sounds dubious—but sometimes, those prayers are actually answered.

Wishes aren't free, though, and no one really understands the rules of this new magic. By the time Galen and his friends figure them out, it may be too late. For everyone.

CPSIA information can be obtained
at www.ICGtesting.com
Printed in the USA
LVHW042240100122
708203LV00019B/966/J